LP
LARGE
PRINT

THE ART OF DETECTION

**Center Point
Large Print**

**This Large Print Book carries the
Seal of Approval of N.A.V.H.**

THE ART OF DETECTION

LAURIE R. KING

CENTER POINT PUBLISHING
THORNDIKE, MAINE

This Center Point Large Print edition
is published in the year 2006 by arrangement with
The Bantam Dell Publishing Group,
a division of Random House, Inc.

The text of this Large Print edition is unabridged. In other
aspects, this book may vary from the original edition.
Printed in the United States of America.
Set in 16-point Times New Roman type.

ISBN: 1-58547-816-4
ISBN 13: 978-1-58547-816-3

Library of Congress Cataloging-in-Publication Data

King, Laurie R.
    The art of detection / Laurie R. King.--Center Point large print ed.
        p. cm.
    ISBN 1-58547-816-4 (lib. bdg. : alk. paper)
        1. Martinelli, Kate (Fictitious character)--Fiction. 2. San Francisco (Calif.)--Fiction.
3. Policewomen--California--San Francisco--Fiction. 4. Large type books. I. Title.

PS3561.I4813A89 2006b
813'.54--dc22

2006007556

This book, as all others, I put at the feet of Kate Miciak, editor and friend, without whom my words would just lie on the floor, kicking feebly.

PROLOGUE

Kate Martinelli had been in any number of weird places during her years as a cop. She'd seen the dens of paranoid schizophrenics and the bare, polished surfaces attended by obsessive compulsives; she'd seen homeless shelters under a bridge and one-room apartments inhabited by families of twelve, crack houses that stank of bodily excretions and designer kitchens with blood spatter up the walls, suburban bedrooms full of sex toys, libraries filled with books on death, and once an actual, velvet-lined bordello.

She'd never seen anything quite like this.

The outside had looked normal enough, a San Francisco Victorian not far from Kate's old Russian Hill neighborhood, tall and ornately traced with gingerbread decorations. Actually, in its subdued colors it was considerably more sedate than several of its neighbors—the days of fuchsia and viridian Painted Ladies had passed, mercifully, but brightness and contrast were still too great a temptation for many owners.

The first indication of the house's true nature stood just outside the door, a small brass knob below a neat enamel plaque that said *Pull.*

Kate, feeling a bit like Alice faced with the vial reading *Drink me,* obediently reached out and pulled. When she let go, the little knob jerked back into place and a bell began to clang inside the house—not ring: clang.

The sound died away, with no indication of life within. She rang a second time, with the same lack of result, then she turned around and shrugged at the occupants of the departmental van and the green Porsche, who had hung back until the notification was finished. Since it appeared that the notification was finished before it began, it was just a matter of getting a film record of the house before they went through it, and to have Crime Scene do a quick once-over to be sure the crime had not taken place here. The chances against it were minuscule—why would any murderer remove a body from its own home to dump it?—but the walls had to be checked, the car gone over.

Kate and the Park detective, Chris Williams, split up to hunt down a neighbor with a key.

They did not find such a thing, but a neighbor across the street, a man in his thirties with thinning hair and a boyish face, pruning his roses in a button-down shirt and white pullover, told them that as far as he knew, a single man lived in the house. However, he did know the name of the occupant's security company. A phone call and twenty minutes' wait brought a company truck, from which hopped a brisk young woman with fifteen earrings and bleached-blond hair a quarter of an inch long. She looked at their IDs carefully, made a phone call to confirm that they were who they said they were, then cheerfully unlocked the door for them—or rather she first locked the door, then unlocked it: The dead bolt had not been set, only the automatic lock in the knob itself. Shaking her head at the carelessness of

8

clients, she removed the key from the dead bolt and handed it to Williams, along with the code for the alarm box that her paper said was behind a picture just inside the door. Williams gave Kate the key and wrestled the door open against the heap of accumulated mail inside, moving rapidly along the walls and pulling aside half a dozen pictures before he located the alarm panel, behind a framed pen-and-ink drawing of two men in old-fashioned dress, walking on a street. He hurriedly tapped out the sequence of numbers, using the end of a pen so as not to obscure any possible fingerprints. The official housebreakers held their breath, and when the alarm did not begin screaming, the woman from the department's photo lab stepped inside and started the video camera running. Kate said to the security woman, "Thanks, we'll hang onto the key."

"My notes say there's a pad upstairs, too, on the door to the third-floor study. Do you want me to open that as well?"

"Sure."

The young woman ducked inside and headed for the stairs, with Kate's companion on her heels to make sure she touched nothing. Kate stepped into the victim's house, and with the first breath of pipe tobacco, lavender, and furniture wax, the Wonderland imagery returned, more strongly: She was in another world.

She was also in a remarkably ill-lit world, as the late-January evening was coming on fast and the light switches proved even more thoroughly hidden than the alarm panel had been. Tamsin the photographer wandered off through the gloom, playing the camera through the rooms and up and down the walls, but Kate thought her colleague was working faster than usual, as if afraid that soon she would be recording the inside of a cow's stomach. Kate trotted after Williams to get his car keys, went out to get her flashlight from the briefcase she'd left in his car, then knelt inside the door to pile the mail to one side: The earliest postmark was from the twenty-second of January, nine days before. When the mail was in order, she stood and wandered from the entrance foyer with its dangling bell and framed etchings into the shadowy rooms beyond, open-mouthed with disbelief.

The fireplace, for example. It was a cramped, iron-lined box that would have spilled any self-respecting log onto the carpet, which she thought explained the shiny brass bucket of black lumps. Except that, this being San Francisco in 2004 and not London in nineteen-whenever, the regulations against burning even the cleanest of anthracite coal were stringent. And so the fireplace was in fact a fake, with black and red pseudo-coals that glowed and pulsed and gave out no more heat than a lightbulb. Still, the coal in the brass bucket—wasn't it called a scuttle?—was real.

Her companion came back downstairs, thanking the security company representative as he ushered her out the door, standing back to allow Crime Scene in, then stepping outside himself to make a phone call. Lo-Tec glanced around and, without a word, got out the equipment to search for organic trace evidence, blood spatter and the like: The darkness just meant he didn't have to switch off lights.

There was not much to see in the lower floor, no sign of blood or disturbance, only the one ashtray to collect, no unwashed cups or glasses. The sound of Williams's voice outside stopped, and he came into the sitting room saying, "The upstairs study wasn't locked, but there's a safe—Jesus . . ." He stood staring at the walls.

Kate lifted the powerful beam of her flashlight off the laden bookshelves and asked, "You think we can get some lights on in here?"

"There don't seem to be any."

"Don't be ridiculous, there have to be lights. There's one on over the stairs."

"Well, there's things on the wall that look like light fixtures, but I don't see any switches."

Kate played her flashlight beam at the walls, and there, indeed, were fluted glass shapes that could only be light-covers. She walked over to the nearest and peered up at it, frowning, then stretched up an arm to jiggle what looked like a key. A faint hissing noise emerged from the fixture, and she hastily turned the key back until it stopped.

"Hey Chris, do you see a box of matches anywhere?" she asked. Williams shone his own light around, bringing it to rest on the mantelpiece. He picked up an ornate little box, shook it, and at the familiar noise, handed it to Kate. "Thanks. Hold your light on this thing for a minute," she told him, sliding the butt of her flashlight into a trouser pocket. Gingerly, she opened the stopcock a partial turn and lit a match, holding it to the place where the hissing noise seemed to originate. With a small pop, the flame ignited, and the gloom in the room retreated a bit. Both cops watched the glowing white bowl of the light warily, but when it neither exploded nor sent flames crawling up the wall, Kate went to two other lights and set them aglow.

"Are those things legal?" her temporary partner asked.

"I've never seen anything like them before," she replied, adding, "outside of *Masterpiece Theatre*."

"It reminds me of something," Williams said, looking around the space.

"Yeah. A movie set."

Dark red flocked wallpaper, thick velvet drapes that seemed to suck out the weak dusk light from the windows before it could reach the room—and apparently the air as well, for the atmosphere, though cold, was stuffy. The furniture was of a kind that would have been out of date in her grandmother's time, everything heavy and upholstered except one badly sprung wickerwork chair angled in front of the fake fire. Beside this chair stood a fragile-looking table with an inlaid top all but invisible under a jumble of objects, including two pipes and a laden ashtray that went far to explain the stuffiness of the room. Through the gloom she could see a desk, on one corner of which stood a tall sticklike telephone with the earpiece on a cord, straight out of the dawn of the telephone era. Even the drinks tray looked as if it had been brought here in a time machine, cutglass decanters clustered around one of those tall bottles wrapped in silver mesh that swooshed fizzy water into glasses in period movies.

"I know what this is meant to be!" Williams exclaimed.

"A museum?"

"Just about. Look at this," he said, and Kate turned to see him studying a heavily gouged patch of the flocked wallpaper—and not random vandalism, she realized, but in lines. "You ever read the Sherlock Holmes stories?"

"No. Well, not since I was a kid." She'd seen plenty of dramatizations on the television, her partner Lee being a serious addict of public television—come to think of it, that was probably where the gaslight wisdom had come from.

"But you know who Sherlock Holmes is." Not waiting for a response, he went on. "There's one story where Doctor Watson mentions that the detective had shot up the wallpaper with the initials of the queen—V. R. Wouldn't you say that's a V and an R?"

Kate stepped back, and indeed, the pockmarks could be interpreted as those letters, although lopsidedly so. "You mean the vic shot a bunch of holes in the wall? And the neighbors on the other side didn't end up in the emergency room?"

With his face nearly brushing the flocking, Williams touched one of the holes, then shook his head. "I don't think he really used a gun. These look too clean, and they're not very deep. More like he punched them into the Sheetrock."

"Plaster," Kate corrected absently. After renovating

two houses, there was not much she didn't know about old walls. "So the vic was a Sherlock Holmes nut?"

"Looks like."

"Down to the gas lights. And there's the violin on the table over there."

"Wonder how far he took it?"

"Why don't we go see?"

The answer was, he took it very far indeed. A subject of Victoria Regina would have felt instantly at home with the furniture, the dusty houseplants (aspidistra? Kate's mind provided), and the fountains of pampas-grass and peacock feathers. The kitchen refrigerator was an actual icebox, complete with near-melted stub of ice, and the single tap over the stone sink looked a hundred years old. By some chain of thought connected to the plumbing, Kate was struck by an awful idea.

"God, don't tell me this maniac used an outdoor privy." But upstairs was a vintage water closet, with a flowered porcelain pull-chain to flush its multiple gallons of water. Next to it was the bathroom with a cast-iron claw-foot tub, a peculiar copper device at one end that Kate thought might be an archaic in-line water heater, and a flowered sink with matching porcelain mug, toothbrush holder, and shaving brush with foam-encrusted mug. Looped beneath the nearby cabinet was a wide strap with hooks at the ends, an object that stirred faint childhood memories of her grandfather's morning ritual. Sure enough, when Kate opened the cabinet, there lay the deadly artistry of a straight razor with an ivory handle.

She opened her mouth to call to Lo-Tec, then stopped: Philip Gilbert hadn't died of a cut throat.

The other second-floor rooms included a spacious sitting room with a bow window, considerably brighter than the downstairs sitting room, a guest bedroom that looked as if it had never been used, and across the hallway from it, the owner's bedroom. The ornate iron bedstead was painted white, its mattress so puffy it could only have been filled with feathers. The bedside table held an actual candlestick, the lamp over the bed was again gas, and the man's down-at-heel leather slippers rested on a tufted rug with pink roses in the design. The floorboards were otherwise bare, but scrupulously clean, and two free-standing armoires held clothes that went with the house below: a couple of ornate robes, one silk, though slightly more subdued than the one the house's owner had been wearing when he was found; the other of quilted velvet, such as Kate thought was called a smoking jacket. Half a dozen somber suits; a number of shirts with buttons instead of collars at the necks and holes on the cuffs for links; dignified silk objects that were more like cravats than neckties; wool trousers with cuffs and buttoned flies; and finally, six pieces of headgear, including two tweed caps, two fedoras, a hard bowler, and an actual, gleaming, honest-to-God black silk top hat.

The shoes to go with this sartorial splendor were arranged on shelves inside one of the cupboards, four examples of the cobbler's art: one pair of brown heeled boots, worn but well maintained; a pair of polished black leather shoes, not particularly old-fashioned-looking (then again, Kate reflected, men's classic shoes didn't change a whole lot over the years); a pair of ornate Moroccan-style house slippers, far less run-down than those under the man's bed; and last, glossy patent leather shoes suitable for evening wear.

It wasn't until they approached the third floor that the twentieth, and even the twenty-first, centuries made their appearance: The light burning over the landing was an electric fixture, so bright it spilled down onto the stairs coming up from the first floor as well.

Underfoot, too, there came a marked change of era. In the lower portion of the house, the carpets had been either strips laid down the middle of the hallways and stairs or dark-colored Persian or Turkish rugs atop the polished boards. Here, as soon as one's feet left the halfway landing and started up the last bend, they knew they were in a different place, one that was soft with foam underlay and covered wall to wall with an expensive and modern Berber-style carpet. It extended into some of the rooms, as well, such as the bedroom that lay immediately to the left of the stairs.

This third-floor bedroom was as modern as its carpeting, with box springs and a sophisticated brown-and-tan bedcovering that went nicely with the floor covering. It was a large room, at the back of which was a separate, walk-in closet, holding clothes that could have come from Macy's yesterday: The trousers had zippers, the shirts possessed the normal collars and cuffs, half a dozen pairs of shoes covered the gamut of needs (except for athletic shoes—the Sherlock wannabe apparently hadn't gone in for jogging), the neckties were unremarkable, and there was only one hat, a brown fedora. There were no gaps in the row of shoes, and all the bare wooden hangers were neatly clustered nearest the door.

Next on from the bedroom was a bathroom, tiled on the floor and halfway up the walls. No claw-foot tub here, but instead a glassed-in shower cubicle with chrome fittings. An electric razor stood on the counter next to the sink; the cupboard below held a hair dryer.

At the end of the hallway, the carpeting extended into a sitting room that overlooked the street. Unlike its two brothers below, this one was fitted with electric lights, a matching mocha-colored leather sofa and armchair, two walls of modern books with bright covers, and, behind a discreet cabinet, a combination tape and CD player with an extensive collection of music, most of it classical, with heavy emphasis on pieces for the violin.

Next back from the front, across the hallway from the tiled bathroom, Gilbert had inserted a closet-sized kitchen, considerably more user-friendly than the one on the ground floor. Here was his electric kettle, humming refrigerator, microwave oven, and small gas range. A built-in table would seat two, or four at a pinch.

The final room on the third floor was where the new millennium reigned supreme: Across from the bedroom, Gilbert's study filled the rest of the space on the floor, its lock pad glowing green to show it was open.

Kate turned the handle, and despite the contemporary fittings of this level of the house, it still came as something of a shock to see the blatant display of modernity. True, books covered one wall from floor to ceiling, most of them reference books or antique novels, but apart from the clothbound spines, the room was as modern as an electronics showroom: high-tech telephone with answering machine, desktop computer with scanner and printer tucked underneath, postage meter machine and combination fax/photocopier to one side. Modern halogen lights hung overhead, and a solid-looking safe was built into the wall over the computer. There was even a television set with cable and DVD player, in front of which was arranged a miniature island that might have been transported from the house below: A richly glowing Oriental rug sat on the light-colored hardwood floors; on top of it stood a deep maroon tufted leather chair, a matching sofa, and a low table with lion's claw legs, old but beautifully polished. The glossy wood held a small stack of magazines and catalogues, a coaster of inlaid marble from India, a glass with a glaze of dried brown in the bottom, a heavy marble ashtray with ashes in it and a pipe, lighter, and tobacco pouch to one side, and a bare pad of paper with a silver retracting pencil resting on top; the red leather of the chair was worn along the arms and at the tufts of the headrest.

Only later, and then only because Kate told them to look for it, did Crime Scene find the blood among the leather folds.

ONE

Earlier that morning, the call had come while Inspector Kate Martinelli of the San Francisco Police Department was in the middle of a highly volatile negotiation.

"I'll hurt myself," the person on the other side of the room threatened.

"Now, that's no good." Kate's response employed the voice of patient reason that she had clung to for the last few minutes, as she desperately wished that the official negotiator would return and take command.

"Yes it is good." Her opponent saw with crystal clarity that self-destruction was a powerful weapon against Kate.

"Now, think about it, sweetie. If you hurt yourself, it's going to hurt."

The mop of curly yellow hair went still as the green eyes narrowed in thought, and Kate's soul contracted with the weird mixture of stifled laughter and heart-wrenching submission that had welled up inside ten thousand times over the past three years and ten months: The child was so like her mother—her looks, her intelligence, her innate sensitivity—she might have been a clone. Kate pushed the sensation away from her throat and said, still reasonable, "We'd all be *sad* if you were hurt, but you would be the one that was hurting. Now, if you let me lift you down from there, we'll talk about whether you're old enough and careful enough to play with those things."

"I'm careful," the child insisted.

"You come down, and then we'll talk about it," Kate repeated. A good negotiator only retreated so far, then stood firm.

It worked. Nora's chubby little arms went out and Kate moved quickly forward before her daughter tumbled off the high shelf. The arms clung to her fiercely, giving lie to the small person's declaration of fearlessness; Kate's arms clung just as hard.

Then she set the child firmly down and bent to look directly into those large, bright eyes, arranging her face so she would look very serious. "Nora, you must never do that again. It really would make me very, very sad if you hurt yourself falling down."

"And Mamalee."

"Yes, and Mama Lee, too." In fact, Kate was wondering if it might even be possible to negotiate her way into an agreement with Nora that Lee not be told about this little episode, but voices in the hallway and the sounds of the front door, followed by the approach of Lee's uneven footsteps, told her that it wasn't going to happen.

And indeed, the moment Lee cleared the doorway Nora popped out from behind Kate and informed her mother, "I climbed up high and Mamakay said that if I comed down we'd talk about if I could play with the dollies."

"I had to pee," Kate explained guiltily. "Thirty seconds, and when I came out the little monkey was up on the sideboard."

20

There ensued a protracted discussion as to the nature of trust, which was Lee's current teaching concept, and Kate had to admit, the child seemed to follow most of what her PhD, psychotherapist mother had to say on the matter. After she'd put her two cents' worth in, telling Lee about Nora's willingness to harm herself if it got her the delicate Russian nesting dolls, the discussion turned to the evils of blackmail. That, however, seemed to exhaust the child's patience, and she interrupted to demand that she be given the dolls.

"Not today," Lee said firmly. And over the protest, she explained, "If you hadn't climbed up high after them, if you'd just asked us about it, we might have said yes. But because you didn't, you're going to have to wait until tomorrow."

It was scary, Kate reflected not for the first time, how reasonable the child was: She pouted for a count of five, then allowed Lee to take her hand and lead her to the kitchen for a discussion of the weekend itinerary. Kate watched the two blond heads, the two slim bodies, the two sets of unreliable legs—one pair made so by youth, the other by a bullet—as her partner and their daughter settled in to discuss the relative lunchtime merits of turkey versus peanut butter.

Only then did she remember the phone call that she'd been on her way to answer when she'd glanced up to see the little body clambering high above the hardwood floor. She went over and punched the playback on the machine, and heard the dispatcher ask for her to call back, then add that she was going to call Al Hawkin as well. Kate didn't bother calling Ops, just hit Al's number on the speed dial. From the sound of the background noise when he picked up, he was in the car.

"Hawkin."

"Hey, Al," she said. "What did the Ops center want?"

"There's a body in the park—but it's the other side of the bridge."

"In Marin? So why call us?"

"Jurisdiction over there's an absolute bitch, but the vic lives over here and it looks like the park's just the dump site. So until we find the murder site, the Park Police investigator, and his supervisor, thought we should be brought in early, in case it ends up in our hands. They've already called our Crime Scene out for the site."

"Marin's going to have a fit."

"Our side's going to have the fit. I'd say, if you're doing anything, don't break up your Saturday."

"No, I should come if you're going, and I think Lee's finished with her clients for the day. Let me just check with her."

"Why don't you call me if you *don't* want me to come by? I'm about twenty minutes out." Which meant he'd not been home when he got the call—he lived about an hour south of the city, but knowing Al, he had his full kit with him wherever he'd been, briefcase, forms, gun.

"Will do. Do you want anything to eat?"

"Jani and I had a big breakfast, so no thanks."

"Twenty minutes."

"Oh, and Kate? The guy said to wear sturdy shoes and a warm coat."

"Thanks for the warning."

Lee scowled at the news that Kate would be leaving, but she'd known that Kate was on call, and she'd been with Kate long enough to know that sometimes life came first, and sometimes death did.

"Can you call if you're not going to be home for dinner? I told Nora we'd make pizza."

Nora was neatly distracted from the disappointment of Kate's departure by the reminder. "Yay, pizza!" she cried with a jubilant dance.

"It should be fine, it may not even be our case, depending on how the lines are drawn on jurisdiction, but the d.b. lived here, so they offered us a look-in."

"Oh, what a treat," Lee said dryly.

"What's a deebee?" Nora piped up.

Kate gave her partner an apologetic glance and opened her mouth to try for an explanation about dead bodies that would satisfy the child without planting macabre images in her impressionable mind, but Lee had already begun with, "Well, you see, sweetheart . . ." Kate slipped away, letting Lee deal with that particular matter.

Seventeen minutes later, Kate was out in front of the house, waiting for Al Hawkin's car to round the corner. A neighbor came along the sidewalk at a snail's pace, a dog leash in one hand and a toddler's hand in the other. She greeted Kate, reminding Kate of the planning meeting the following week at the preschool, inquiring about the acupuncturist Lee had mentioned a while ago, and tossing out ideas for the upcoming street fair. The entire conversation was held with the woman moving slowly past, never quite coming to a halt while dog and toddler explored the street; the trio continued at the same pace until the corner, when they turned toward the park.

Kate smiled, and raised a hand to wave to another neighbor. She and Lee had lived in the Noe Valley neighborhood for nearly eight years, and never had a place felt more like home. Kate rarely thought anymore about the magnificent house on tony Russian Hill where they had once lived, cop and therapist rubbing shoulders with the city's cream of socialites and politicos. That place had been Lee's, an inheritance from her overbearing and disapproving mother, and had looked out on two incomparable bridges, San Francisco Bay, Alcatraz Island, and Mount Tamalpais in the background. When Lee finally decided to put the house on the market, it had sold before the print was dry on the advertisement, for more money than Kate could envision.

They had traded the gorgeous, intricately constructed Arts and Crafts–style house with the million-dollar view for a tumbledown Victorian whose chief virtue in their eyes was also, as far as the listing agent was concerned, its chief drawback: The elderly couple who had lived in the house all the five decades of their married life, unwilling to abandon the upper levels but increasingly unable to negotiate the stairs, had hacked up the back rooms and put in a tiny elevator.

Kate turned to gaze affectionately at the house. Most buyers would have been daunted by the enormous expense of ripping out the mechanism and restoring the rooms to their previous condition, but for Kate, the one-person elevator had been her personal deciding factor in its favor: Lee would never have agreed to its installation, but if it was here anyway, well, why not make use of it? The personal lift, just large enough for the wheelchair during Lee's bad times, was an unvoiced recognition that the effects of the bullet through Lee's spine, twelve years before, would never completely leave them; it had made their lives infinitely simpler.

The enormous price brought by the Russian Hill house had enabled them to make other renovations, from new carpeting and fresh paint to a complete rebuilding of the kitchen. Lee had also set up her therapy rooms in the front and was seeing clients again.

Most of all, however, what they had gained with the move was a thing that neither had known they needed: a community. They had traded socialites for Socialists, politicos for legal-aid lawyers, middle-aged white faces for a rainbow coalition of young families. Of the seven people Kate saw as she passed down the front walk that morning, she knew five of them by name, and had eaten dinner with three of those. Two doors down lived Nora's best friend, an eight-year-old girl from China, the oldest of three multiracial children adopted by a bank manager and his aromatherapist wife. Lee's long-time caregiver lived with his new family three blocks away. The woman in the big corner house had recently opened up a Montessori-style child-care facility, which meant that Nora could spend two afternoons a week with her friends. Typically, last summer the neighbor-hood association had voted to close the street one Sunday so everyone could hold a block party.

Small-town life in the big city.

Al's car appeared around the corner. Kate waved one last time, to the woman she sometimes went jogging with (who this morning was out running with her black Lab instead), tossed her coat and briefcase into the backseat, and hopped in beside him.

"How's the kid?" he asked before her buckle had latched.

"Perfect, as always. And yours?"

"They're all fine. Jules has a major crush, I quote, on her lab partner, Maya is thinking about a summer camp run entirely in Latin, and Daniel has discovered guns."

"Oh, Jani must be pleased about that."

"The genetic inclination of boys, I suppose, to make weapons out of anything. Sticks, Legos, organic vege-tarian hot dogs."

"I know, I see it all the time at Nora's preschool."

"Still, he's also into sports—he's wants to try out for Little League next year. That's where I was, throwing balls for the second-graders."

Al was enjoying his second trip through parenting, at the same time his grandchildren were coming along. He sounded more than happy about the whole thing.

"So, speaking of boys and their guns, what's with this one up at Point Bonita?"

"Philip Gilbert, white male, fifty-three. And no guns there, not at first sight."

26

"But Mr. Gilbert didn't just walk up there and die?"

"There's a scalp wound, but the coroner says it doesn't look massive enough to kill him."

"Coroner? Not ME?"

"Marin caught it and declared death, the Park people didn't think they needed to call in our ME as well. Seemed to think Marin wouldn't mind transporting the body to us."

Kate looked at the side of his face, but neither needed to say it: The San Francisco ME wasn't going to be pleased with the arrangement. "So," she said, "the vic was shooting up out in the woods? Or maybe a little sex play that got rougher than he'd intended?"

"If so, he drove in wearing his pajamas, and barefoot. In January," Al added unnecessarily. "The rangers say he wasn't a park resident and he wasn't at either of the last two conferences held there. Once they have a picture they'll take it around and ask if anyone knew him, but in the meantime, like I told you, they're pretty sure he was dumped. No sign of the car DMV has registered to him, so I sent a uniform to drive past his home address, see if it's there."

"But who's got the case? And why isn't it just Marin's?"

"Interesting question. From the little I could get out of the Park investigator I talked to, they need to look at a satellite GPS to decide just what slice of the park the body's in—if it's a federal area, that's one thing; if it's found in a place that used to be owned by the state before the park was glued together, that's another. I'd say most likely it's up to the loudest voice. Which sounds like the Park Police supervisor. Who wants to give it to us."

Kate had been peripherally involved with the issue before, when it came to prosecuting in a park murder in the late Nineties. The Golden Gate National Recreation Area—Ocean Beach, the Presidio, various forts, Crissy Field, and the lump of headland across the Golden Gate Bridge—was an anomaly on the face of the National Parks Service, the only national park located within the boundaries of a city. Some crimes were handled by the Park's own Criminal Investigations Branch, located in the Presidio. Others, particularly the major crimes, were given over to other law enforcement entities.

Who got jurisdiction often depended on historical definitions: A major crime taking place in areas that had been under local control before the GGNRA would be handed to the local force; if that same crime took place in a part that had been an Army base, it might well go directly to the FBI. It was a constant headache, and although cooperative statements such as the recent Interagency Agreement went far to smooth things out, in practice the work just went ahead and got done by whoever got there first. Or, as Al said, who had the loudest voice.

As with most policing, it was all in personal contacts.

"You know Chris Williams?" Hawkin asked her.

"I don't think so."

"He's an Investigator with the Park's CIB, I met him a couple years ago on a case. Nice guy. Anyway, he agreed with his supervisor that we should be brought in. They'll stay involved, of course, since there's a question of illegal disposal, but unless they find something there to show the vic was killed in the park, they'll probably want us to have it. Since, like I say, he lived in the City."

"If he was wearing pajamas, how did they ID him so fast? Did he have his wallet in the pocket?"

"He's got a medical necklace, one of those that holds pills and tells the EMTs you have diabetes or whatever. He'd engraved his name and that of his doctor on it. The doctor happened to be on call, he confirmed that the patient matched the d.b.'s description, gave Williams his address."

"Did he have diabetes?"

"Heart condition."

"So it could have been an argument and somebody hit him with a frying pan, or he could've dropped dead in what they used to call a 'compromising situation' and hit his head on the way down. And whoever was with him panicked and drove him to the nearest convenient open space?"

"Could be."

Kate's proposed scenario became less likely the farther into the park they ventured: As drop spots went, this one was hardly convenient. They crossed the Golden Gate Bridge, thick with traffic on this first sunny Saturday after a week of rain. Pedestrians, bicyclists, and parents pushing strollers washed in both directions, dodging the occasional stationary photographer—few people just stood and looked at the view, not with the fog lying just offshore to make the breeze cool and damp. Dodging the usual tangle of cars waiting to get into the viewing spot, Hawkin pulled off immediately after that and circled under the freeway to climb into the headlands.

Al's eyes were on the curving road and the parking areas busy with cars, motorcycles, bicyclists, and human beings of all sizes, shapes, and geographic origin, but Kate swiveled around to admire the view. The bridge rose magnificent and orange, the city beyond it looking so cinematically perfect as to seem artificial. Traffic slowed, then crawled; they were going uphill, but bicyclists passed them. After a while, they saw why: Two Park rangers with a portable barrier were directing cars to the right, away from the road along the cliffs.

When they eventually reached the two uniforms, Hawkin waved his badge and told the nearest that they were heading for the crime scene. The man nodded and said, "If you wait to get through the tunnel, you'll be all day. You better go this way." He signaled to his partner to shift the barricade and let them pass.

Not that they could move a lot faster once they were past the traffic stop: Bicyclists had been permitted to continue and, given the unexpected luxury of a road unimpeded by cars, were meandering across both lanes, their heads angled toward the view of San Francisco and the Golden Gate Bridge. Hawkin narrowly missed colliding with three oblivious cyclists, and honked at a fourth (who promptly fell over at their front bumper). Both detectives were relieved when they reached the final barricade, at the place where the road narrowed and larger vehicles were banned. The ranger there was turning even the bikers back, but for the SFPD, he pulled back the gate to the one-way section of road. Al drove forward, and the bottom of Kate's stomach dropped out.

The paving appeared to launch its traffic directly out into the gray-green water far, far below. Kate gulped, but before their tires actually took to the air, the track shifted to the right, maintaining its tenuous hold on solid ground, although the thin metal guardrail seemed more suggestion than protection. The roadway was a trickle of asphalt laid along the edge of the world, set with long, wavering striations of close-growing weeds, green lines horribly suggestive of the inevitability of the earth's surrender to the sea; in some of the bends, the green cracks resembled the tracings on a topo-graphical map, accompanied by an alarming dip on the ocean side of the road. Kate would have clung to the landward side, but Hawkin blithely followed the shortest route, aiming directly for the gathering of cracks. A gust of wind scrambled up the cliffs and shook the car, testing its hold on the asphalt. Kate shut her eyes.

"Hope to God you had your brakes serviced recently," she said, her voice tight.

"Been meaning to have them looked at," Hawkin mused, pumping his foot a little to imitate brake failure.

"Funny man," she said grimly, and fixed her eyes with determination on the hills to her right.

The earth here was red where exposed, the plants gray nearest the cliffs, greener now that they were retreating a little from the hungry bays and inlets. Bushes grew low along the cliffs, stunted by the constant blow from the sea, but here and there sprang odd clumps of trees, as if small, random patches of woodland had been preserved from the saw. Ancient metal doors surrounded by equally worn concrete were set into the hillsides, remnants of a race of particularly warlike hobbits. Traces of fog played with the shoreline, filling the westernmost trees for a moment, then dissipating. They could hear a foghorn not far away.

Finally nearing a few buildings, what passed on the headlands for civilization (Kate tried to silence her shuddering breath of relief), they saw a very cold-looking Park ranger huddled into a folding chair. At their appearance, she uncrossed her arms and rose stiffly.

Hawkin left his window up, pressing his badge against the glass. The pinched face looked disappointed and nodded for them to continue, then she pulled a hand out of her pocket to make a rolling gesture at the window. Hawkin lowered it a few inches; a wave of frigid air poured in.

"I wonder, would you mind reminding them that I'm still up here? I haven't had a break in three hours. I could really use a cup of coffee and a toilet."

"I'll let them know."

"Thanks. Have a good day," she added with an automatic professional good cheer, and went back to her chair.

In a minute they were looking at a collection of nondescript buildings that would need considerably more funds to make them resemble anything other than the old Army barracks they were. The sign announced it as a YMCA conference center: Kate could only hope the place was less dismal in the spring and summer.

Hawkin steered to the left, up the hill past a couple of mysterious semicircular concrete artifacts and a sign directing walkers to the Point Bonita lighthouse, and at last they came to the center of activity. Another Park ranger, this one looking not quite as cold as the woman before him, bent to look at Hawkin's badge, then pointed them to a spot at the end of an untidy line of cars, some official, some civilian. He had been standing and talking with a dozen or so men, women, and children, all of them dressed for the weather, but he left the residents behind and walked after the car, and was waiting when their doors opened.

"Morning," he said with the same chronic cheerfulness the woman ranger had shown. "You're here to look at our body?"

He might have been offering sightseers a glimpse of a rare visiting bird or excavated whale skeleton. Kate half expected to be handed an explanatory flyer.

"Inspectors Hawkin and Martinelli, SFPD," Hawkin supplied, retrieving his heavy coat from the car's back-seat and fighting the wind for possession of its flying

33

sleeves. Kate, in the lee of the car, had an easier time of it, but once hers was buttoned, she immediately wished she'd brought a second to go over it. And maybe worn ski pants instead of khaki trousers—the sun was out for the moment in this slice of the headlands, but the fog was a stone's throw out to sea and the clammy air sliced right through garment and flesh, going for the bone. She pulled her knit hat down over her ears and raised her voice to Hawkin.

"That looks like Lo-Tec's car." The incongruous cheery green classic Porsche parked between a Marin County coroner's van and the SFPD crime lab van could only belong to the SFPD's crime-scene inspector, Lawrence Freeman, known with affectionate irony as Lo-Tec, for his addiction to cutting-edge technology. Lo-Tec was small, neat, gay, hyperefficient, and prone to singing softly as he worked, usually Fifties tunes to which he invented his own words. "Traces of Love, On the Sheets," was a classic, published on his website.

"The Park crime lab consists mostly of a drying room," Al commented. "They'd have called either us or Marin in for this."

"And speaking of which, are you taking your binder?"

The leather binder, containing notepad and various forms, was a statement of authority at a crime scene. Taking it would be tantamount to saying they were going to need it.

"Maybe we should leave them here for the time being, until we're sure." Kate nodded, and slammed the door: It didn't do to appear grabby.

It felt odd to be approaching a murder scene with nothing in her hand, but Kate buried her gloved hands in her pockets, feeling the small spiral notebook she'd stuck there, and trudged after Hawkin.

The path wound up the grass toward the top of the hill; halfway up they were intercepted by yet another ranger, older than the others they'd seen. He strode along the hillside from an angle, putting out his hand as he came up to them.

"Dan Culpepper," he said, pumping Al's hand with vigor. "Park Police Patrol—I was the responding officer this morning, though the investigator's here now. He asked me to bring you up."

"Al Hawkin, Kate Martinelli," Al supplied. "SFPD." Dan transferred his powerful grip to Kate's hand.

"Crime Scene's here?" Kate asked when she had retrieved her squashed fingers.

"They've been here for hours. In fact, I think they're nearly finished."

"When was the body found?"

"First thing this morning, a little after eight. Two guys here for the Bunkers tour at ten were poking around the emplacement and noticed that the padlock was broken. They opened the door, saw the body, one of them stayed here to make sure nobody disturbed it while the other came down to the visitor's center to phone it in. I got the call, checked it out, and kept control of the scene until the supervisor got here—that's Diana Sandstrom. Inspector Williams arrived about twenty minutes later, and your Crime Scene people just after that. The Marin coroner came, and half the people with scanners in the county—everyone from the sheriff to the local dog-walker—wanted a look. Your photographer's been and gone, and the supervisor."

"How much has the site been disturbed?" asked Al apprehensively.

"Very little—I put up tape first thing, called in backup, didn't let anyone in at all, and none of my people did, either, so it was clean when Diana got here. Ranger Sandstrom, I mean. She sure didn't let anyone through except for Williams and the coroner. And I don't think the guys who found it did anything other than look in and see the body. They said they could tell from the smell that the guy was beyond help. They just went in far enough to make sure it was a human being and not a sea lion or something, then left."

"A surprisingly sensible reaction," Hawkin commented.

"I know. Second World War vets, you know—we get a lot of them, particularly for the Nike missile site tours. I guess once you smell a dead body, there isn't much doubt about it the next time it happens."

That was very true. Still, both cops made silent mental notes to look at the vets, since people who "discovered" bodies in odd places were often the people who had put them there in the first place.

"If they could smell the body in this weather, it's been here a while," Kate noted. "Any idea why he wasn't found earlier?"

"It's been miserable and cold since Sunday, and this time of year we don't get a lot of traffic through here anyway, except if there's a nice weekend. The people at the conference tend to stick close to the buildings when it's wet. Even the people with dogs keep closer to the parking lot when it's stormy. Off the cuff, I'd say that if the body was here last Saturday, someone would have noticed it. For sure they'd have seen if the door was standing open. People just can't resist a half-open door."

They had been climbing steadily for a quarter mile or so, and were now not only out of breath (two of them, at least) but also high enough to see past the nearby hills. The obliging ranger, aware of their breathing but too polite to mention it even obliquely, paused as if doing so was a regular part of the tour. It might even have been, considering what met their eyes when they obediently turned around to look: magnificent orange bridge, its cables rising and swooping to meet the incongruously forested landscape of the Presidio on the south side of the Golden Gate. Behind the dark vegetation rose the bright white sprawl of the city—low residences along the many hills of the city, high-rises jostling for air in the downtown area to the left. A cloud of sailboats dotted the water inside the bridge, while a ship piled with shipping containers pushed its way out to sea. A multicolored parade of minuscule cars scurried across the bridge; the hillside where they stood felt very far from the world.

A person tended to forget, Kate reflected, living

among San Francisco's high-rise valleys and natural hills, that the city was a major port on the edge of a vast continent. Most commercial shipping had shifted across the Bay to the container-cargo derricks of Oakland and Alameda, but the port, along with the Sacramento River that led up toward the gold fields, was the reason the city existed. Standing here, with the panorama of Bay and city spread out at their feet, the reminder was powerful.

"You have got one gorgeous place to work," Kate told Dan.

"Yeah, this is a real hardship post," the ranger agreed with a grin.

"A miracle the developers didn't grab it when the Army stepped out," Al said. "Can't you imagine what a view like that would bring?"

"It was a very close thing, like with the Presidio," Dan told them. "Although that's going to have to pay for itself. With any luck, this'll be kept natural."

"It's almost enough to restore your faith in the world," Al said, not even sounding very sarcastic.

"You might say that the view is what attracted the Army in the first place—a strategic attraction, of course, not an aesthetic one: Between these guns and the Presidio, the entrance to the Bay was pretty thoroughly covered."

"This is a gun, what do you call it, emplacement, then?" Kate asked.

"Right. DuMaurier was more or less contemporary with Battery Wallace and, other than being smaller, is similar in layout. That's Wallace on the hill over there—those two openings in the hillside? The battery fills the entire hillside between them. There aren't any guns there now, of course, just their settings. You can see Battery Alexander just north of Wallace— Alexander had mortars—and Smith-Guthrie and O'Rourke with four guns each beyond that. Closer in is Mendell, just along the cliffs."

Kate studied the decrepit sprawl of concrete that was Battery Mendell, stretched out along the cliffs and exposed to the elements, then glanced at the gray faces of the double guns of Battery Wallace on the next hill inland from where they stood. Wallace resembled an enormous frog, two elongated concrete eyes set into a wide, green face, its mouth shaped by one long building of the conference center at their feet. She did not bring up her fanciful image, merely said, "Wallace seems to have stood up to the sea air a lot better."

"What you see dates only to the Thirties, when Wallace was casemated and covered. Again like DuMaurier, in fact, although DuMaurier only had a single gun, a twelve-inch breech-loading rifle. The only single gun in Fort Barry, in fact."

"What is that mushroomy thing on the other side of Mendell?"

"That's a base-end station, used for triangulating fire. They're located all up and down the coast. And those concrete half circles you passed where you parked? Cisterns, for the lighthouse. There's also a number of submerged structures used to keep an eye on the minefields laid out in the shipping lanes. To say nothing of the miles of tunnels and storage facilities, most of them falling apart and a real hazard—those doors we check all the time. All of this, as you can well see from here, is harbor defense. Around the time of the gold rush, the powers that be back in Washington noticed that San Francisco was the key port of the entire West Coast, and the cannon they had at Fort Point and Fort Mason wouldn't go far to repel a determined enemy. So they started putting in bigger and bigger guns, on both sides of the Golden Gate and on Alcatraz, cutting edge all the way, until eventually the distances covered became so enormous that it was actually counterproductive, since nobody wants to keep a warhead right on top of the city limits. After Nike missiles became obsolete, harbor defense moved back a bit, like to Nevada. But for the better part of a hundred years, nothing could get into the Bay without being watched by a lot of men with their fingers on some very big triggers. Metaphorically speaking," he added. "Cannon don't have that kind of triggers."

"There's nothing up here but the gun emplacement, then?" Hawkin, having caught his breath, was less interested in history than in the case at hand.

"Right, just Battery DuMaurier," Dan said. And because he seemed incapable of bypassing an opportunity for educating his public, he added, "All the guns have names, usually given to commemorate a soldier—base commander, Great War hero, that sort of thing. DuMaurier is usually understood to have been a Civil

40

War general, but in fact, the name was that of the first base commander's beloved horse."

The two detectives eyed the ranger for a moment, but he was looking over the view, and continued, unaware of their skepticism.

"We've got emplacements on the headlands from the Endicott era, beginning in 1891, to the 1940s. The Nike missiles went in during the Fifties. The early structures are like Mendell, mostly open-air, but by the end of the First World War it became obvious that airplanes were the way of the future, and nobody wanted to sit out in a gun emplacement that might as well have had a giant flashing arrow pointing to it. So they brought in a lot of dirt to cover them with—which, as you can tell, various tree seeds were happy to find—and those emplacements built afterwards were harder to spot from the air."

Kate tried to think if the West Coast had ever been directly attacked, other than the rumors of Japanese submarines. In the end, she asked.

"There was one gun fired at a British ship," Dan told her, "back at the end of the nineteenth century. Missed, of course, since the guns weren't movcable, so the crews had to more or less hope a ship would drift in front of the flight path. But the ship moved on, so they claimed success."

With that note of martial absurdity, the ranger seemed to think he had delivered enough of a lecture for this point on the tour, and turned to resume the trek uphill.

"Oh," Al said in the direction of the ranger's broad back, "I nearly forgot. Your woman back there along the road? She said she needed a coffee break and a toilet. Looked pretty cold."

"Damn, I forgot all about her—normal routine is shot pretty much to hell today. Thanks for telling me, I'd better go spell her. Here, you see where everyone's been walking?" He pointed at the continuation of their route, well to the side of the worn soil of the official path. The damp grasses lay thoroughly beaten down by the passage of many feet. "Just follow that path, okay?"

"Sure, we'll be fine," Al told him. The ranger trotted easily down the hill, quick and surefooted despite the slick grass. The two detectives watched him go, then turned their backs on the view and continued up the hill toward the stand of misshapen trees growing in the disturbed soil around a gun.

Yet another ranger waited at the top of the hill, making Kate wonder if there was anyone left to lead a tour. She stood near a solitary wooden picnic table, on which sat two men with Marin County logos on their jackets. The two Coroner's men were trying hard not to shiver in front of the pretty young ranger, who was wearing a jacket adequate for Arctic service.

"You the San Francisco detectives?" she greeted them cheerfully as they signed the logbook.

"That's right," Al told her.

"Inspector Williams is waiting for you, just in there."

She gestured toward an opening in the hillside, a dark concrete maw whose square opening was set with the foot-high words BATTERY DUMAURIER. The gray concrete echoed with the roar of a generator, set at the

42

far end of the tunnel into the hillside. Halfway down, the generator's cord led through a door that was standing open a crack, bright light spilling from around its edges. Al shone his flashlight along the doorframe, where a mighty padlock dangled uselessly, connecting a hasp to one end but not the other. The frame had been dusted, but from the evenness of the powder, it did not look as if Crime Scene had lifted any prints. Al pushed gently at the door, and they stepped into the gathering of death professionals.

At the increase in sound from the door, the four people inside looked around. The nearest, the only one in uniform, moved briskly to intercept them, slowing when Al flipped open his badge. The two kneeling on the floor turned back to their tasks, but the fourth, a man in jeans and a nice warm-looking fur-lined bomber jacket, rose from his squat against the wall and came to the door.

"Hey, Al," he said, shaking Al's hand, "I was glad it was you on call. Chris Williams," he said to Kate.

Kate shook the man's hand and offered her name in exchange.

"Come on in and let's shut this door so we can hear ourselves think. We won't be long, Crime Scene's just finishing, but I wanted to keep the body here so you could see it."

"Was that the Marin Coroner's van outside?" Al asked, although the question was more *Why is Marin here?* than it was *Was that Marin?* Williams had no problem picking up the real question.

"They'd already answered the call when my supervisor said she wanted to bring San Francisco in. Marin was here, too, of course. I think they were a little pissed. But Sandstrom got out a map and said the body was within five hundred feet of the county line or something, so it could as easily be yours as theirs."

"How on earth does she figure that measurement?" Kate asked in amazement. They were a couple of miles from the shoreline of San Francisco.

"Seems the San Francisco limits run up to the Marin shore, not halfway across the Gate. Personally, I think we're more than five hundred feet from the water here, but I'm not about to argue with my boss."

"So why is Marin's coroner here instead of our ME?"

"The coroner got here before they'd called you in, didn't seem necessary to have two officials dragged out on a Saturday to pronounce death. And these guys agreed to transport the body over to you rather than dragging your guys over. Overtime, you know? So how's it been?"

Williams and Hawkin spent a minute in small talk, which Kate listened to with half an ear—Williams was apparently married, his wife expecting their second in the summer, and there was a mutual friend named Pat they needed to catch up on—while she watched Crime Scene go about their business.

The man, who was indeed Lo-Tec Freeman, glanced up at Kate and nodded his recognition, but did not interrupt his work. He wasn't singing today, not even humming, and Kate wondered if his companion acted as a damper. The woman was new, to Kate anyway, a Hispanic woman in her thirties.

They were both dressed in white jumpsuits, working over a pair of bare feet. It looked as if they had finished the initial photographs and sketching, and were looking for any evidence on the body itself before it was moved. Their equipment was stacked along the wall in two neat piles, one for tools and supplies they might need but had not yet used, the other made up of tools they had finished with and the packaged evidence they had gathered. From the distribution of tools, they had all but finished with the room for a while, and were focused in on the body.

The room was a windowless cement box that had once been whitewashed, although time and damp had peeled off most of the finish; stalactites were beginning to form in one corner. The graffiti on the walls was all old, several messages dated before Kate was born; in the wall opposite the entrance was an opening to a small room or corridor. The air smelled of damp concrete, mildew, gasoline exhaust, and spoiling meat. Kate could only hope Crime Scene didn't keep them standing around for too long.

Williams and Al had come to a pause in their conversation, so Kate asked, "What's through there?"

In answer, Williams called to the two Crime Scenes, "You mind if we go take a look?"

"We're finished in there," Lo-Tec said.

Williams pulled his four-cell Maglight from his deep jacket pocket and led them around the perimeter of the room, keeping near the walls. He switched on his light as they came to the opening, and led them into the darkness.

He stopped when they were free of the glow from the room, and played his flashlight beam down what proved to be a corridor with openings on either side. "I love this place, the headlands. I've talked my way into every one of the batteries, volunteered some time with the cataloguing and repairs, so even though I'm not one of the interpreters, I can give you a decent tour.

"Even a single gun like DuMaurier requires a fair amount of support space," the amateur guide began. "For the personnel you need latrines, a mess, even bunks for when the men and officers are here for an extended period. You need a dry magazine for the powder—that's always well covered with reinforced concrete and earth, in case the enemy shoots back—and rooms for storing the shells. You need a plotting room, a tool room, a guard room, a connection to the roads for deliveries. The two small rooms directly ahead of you are the latrines—one for the men, the smaller one for the officers. Those rusty bits of metal in the walls are where bunks were hung, for long shifts when the barracks were too far away. Those tracks in the ceiling are for moving the shells to the guns, and there would have been other rails in the floor, for the trolleys that carried the powder canisters out to the gun. That door in the front wall is where they kept the generator. A couple of the rooms I have no idea what they were used for, and there's a puzzling piece of tunnel under the floor that seems to come out somewhere on the hillside—where, I don't know. It may have been an emergency exit, in case of fire between the men and the exit, but there's no knowing now because it's half collapsed and I haven't been able to find anyone suicidal enough to go down it and find out where it comes out."

"But these areas are completely unused now?"

"Battery Wallace is used for dry storage, mostly machines and equipment someone might need someday if the park ever gets funding for a complete restoration job. An old telephone exchange, a Nike guidance system, vacuum tubes by the score. They'll never get funding, of course, but it doesn't cost much to keep the things dry, just in case. However, as you can see, Battery DuMaurier is too run-down to store anything in— the road's overgrown, the last time the electricity failed they just disconnected it from the mains, and it hasn't even been fitted with one of the unbreakable padlock housings the doors on the other batteries have. One of these days, there'll be an earthquake or a big storm and the first visitor the next morning will find it gone. It's a matter of priorities," he said apologetically. "As you might imagine, the headlands runs on two dimes and a lot of volunteers."

Kate didn't think he needed to explain the trials of budget constraints to a pair of cops. She said, "What was the first room used for?"

"The room where the vic was found? That I'm not exactly sure about, since there aren't any identifying fixtures in it. Most likely it was used as the staging area, to unload stuff going in or out, a place for the men to wait out of the rain during exercises—the gun itself was out in the open until the late Thirties. Carts or trucks would unload material just outside."

"But it hasn't been used since World War Two?"

"Before that. Seems that when they looked at it with an eye to casemating it like Wallace, they decided that the extra weight would just push it off into the sea. Since it was only a single gun anyway, in the end they just pulled it out and concentrated on Wallace and the others. You seen enough here?"

Hawkin asked, "Did Crime Scene find anything back here?"

"Nothing. No fresh prints, no blood spatter, no blunt objects thrown into corners. They even looked down that tunnel I told you about, but they could see old spiderwebs and so they stopped."

With a last play of the beam along the surrounding walls, he switched it off and they headed back to the glare of the lights.

The two Crime Scenes were still about their labors, and mere detectives had to stand and wait.

"He's not as ripe as I expected," Kate said to Williams. "The guys who found him must have good noses if they could tell he was dead by the smell."

"It was stronger when I first got here. I think having the door open has cleared it out, and of course there's the stink of the generator."

"How'd they see him, do you think?" Hawkin asked. The room had no lights, and even if it was fully open, the door was fifty feet from both ends of the tunnel and would only have let in a dim illumination.

"One of them had a flashlight. He thought they might get the chance to look into dark places on the tour they were going with later that morning."

At last, Lo-Tec, who had been working with his back to them, turned on his heels and said, "Okay, you can approach, just keep clear of the flags," and made a notation in his notebook. Kate and Al followed Williams to the bundle of cloth and flesh.

The body was curled up on its side in the middle of the room, bare feet nearest the entrance, wearing an incongruously bright silk dressing gown over dignified cotton pajamas. The garments had been tucked into place, although one half of the silken belt trailed along the ground. There was something awkward about the man's arms: Instead of being drawn up to his chest, as they would if he had simply laid down here and died, the left one, underneath him, was wrenched up at an angle that would have been uncomfortable for a living man, and the right one had flopped away, its palm tilted.

The man appeared to be in his fifties, six feet or more in height and, beneath the bloat of death, thin enough to give a doctor cause for alarm. His mousy brown-gray hair was thin but worn long, covering the dressing gown's collar. His mouth was open slightly, revealing a glimpse of teeth that appeared good, if stained. His nose was large, his fingernails clean and neatly trimmed, and he'd died needing a shave. They couldn't see the color of his eyes, but his skin, despite the tints of putrefaction, was clearly that of a Caucasian.

Kate squatted down, careful to keep her hands close to her chest—all CSIs were touchy about evidence transfer, but Lo-Tec made it a religion. She squinted at the exposed skin of the ankles, seeing on their undersides the dark tints of livor mortis, which meant that he had laid in this position since the blood became fixed there, eight or so hours after death. If he'd been moved here, it had been early on. The man's bare feet showed no signs of dirt, grass stains, or even dust: If he'd walked here, someone had taken his shoes. She stood and let her eyes travel upward. An inch-long silver cylinder on a chain lay on top of his chest, the engraving visible but from this distance illegible. She could also see the sign of violence: a clot of blood darkening the hair above his right temple.

"Was the medical necklace arranged like that?" Hawkin asked.

"No," Williams told him. "The Coroner spotted it and pulled it out of his clothes. You know both of these people?" he asked.

Lo-Tec answered, although the question had been directed at Al and Kate. "We know each other. I don't think you'll have met Maria, though. Alonzo Hawkin, Kate Martinelli, SFPD; Maria Warbeck." He had not taken his eyes off the invisible mark he was trying to lift from the floor. Maria, however, finished depositing an insect into an evidence container and looked up, saying, "Hey."

"Find anything interesting?" Kate asked.

"All kinds of stuff in here, but nothing that looks promising." To Kate's surprise, the woman then stood up, although from the way her spine cracked when she stretched, it was less a desire to be friendly than the need to get out of her cramped position. Still, it indicated not only that she was unintimidated by her boss, but that she was willing to talk.

"They got in by prying off the padlock?"

"Looks like," she said. "Big padlock, but the screws holding the hook down had disintegrated. Sea air, you know?"

"So whoever brought him here knew what he'd find. He was brought here already dead, I understand?"

The new CSI nodded. "Coroner thought he'd been here about a week, but going by the bloodstains on his clothes, he's been moved a couple times. I'd say he didn't land here until maybe twenty-four hours after death."

"Really?" Kate asked, trying not to sound dubious.

"The left arm of his bathrobe has blood on it, as if his arm was under his head while it was bleeding, which it isn't now. And hypostasis may suggest that he's been in this position all the time, but if you look closely, you can see faint traces of an earlier angle, as if he lay on his back for two or three hours before finally being put on his side like you see him now. But whoever brought him here had a struggle to move him; lots of bumps and postmortem contusions. I'd say he'd gone pretty thoroughly stiff before he was brought here, probably in the trunk of a car. You may be looking for someone with a recent back strain," she added with a grin.

"A perp strong enough to manhandle a stiff body up from the road."

"Which would narrow the field considerably, except that we found some marks outside that might be wheel-barrow tracks. However, they're nearly invisible, and could be from anything."

"They're probably from a bike," said Lo-Tec Freeman. It sounded as if they'd already had an argument about this.

"Probably," Maria agreed cheerfully.

"Even then," Hawkin commented, "shoving a wheel-barrow up all that way would be a job and a half."

"Probably pulled it behind him," Maria said. "But as you say, still work. And he got the body out of the car somehow, although this guy must weigh one sixty, sixty-five."

"And there's no sign of dragging?" Kate asked, hoping it didn't sound like a suggestion that Crime Scene might have overlooked anything.

"In the hallway, we didn't find anything detailed enough to lift, other than the possible wheelbarrow or bicycle. Outside in the open, there's been too much rain to leave us anything. Inside here, the floor looks like it was wiped, probably with a towel. We haven't found much to lift. Don't worry," she said. "We've taken soil samples, in case it comes to matching the ground to a wheel somewhere. And of course once we unwrap him in the lab we'll see what he has to tell us. Maybe the perp left hairs across the middle by a fireman's carry."

"Any idea why someone would want to stash a dead body here?"

"None whatsoever," the woman replied with a grin that said, *Not my job, thank God,* and bent down again to her work.

Chris Williams waited while the two San Francisco detectives looked the scene over, then led them back outside the battery, where the noise of the generator dropped enough to carry on a conversation. He waved at the men of the Marin Coroner's office. The two disentangled themselves from the picnic table and grabbed their equipment, pushing past the detectives impatiently. Kate noticed Hawkin glance surreptitiously at his watch, and realized that this was the second time he'd done so.

"You need to be somewhere, Al?"

"Not really. Maya has a thing, I told her I might not be able to make it."

"I don't know that there's a lot more we can do here. Is there, Chris?"

"Your CSI will be here for another hour or so, and since my supervisor made me Incident Commander, I've got to hang on here. After we're finished, though, I'd like to go with you to do the notification, if you don't mind. I could give you a call and you can meet me there, if you like?"

Kate turned to her partner. "Al, why don't you go on back and I'll hang out here until Chris is ready to go—let me just come with you and fetch my bag."

Williams spoke up. "If you want to leave anything

here, you can have the ranger on duty down there stick it in my car. I gave him the keys."

"Nah," said Al, "I'll just call and tell Jani I'm going to be late. It's only a meeting about a school trip in the spring."

"Al, look, Chris and I can do the notification, and he can take me home afterwards."

"You sure?"

"Why not? I may even be back in time for Nora's homemade pizza."

"I'll be thinking of you as I grind my way through the raw vegetables."

"Jani still have you on the low-fat diet, huh?"

Her partner's look was eloquent, although as she watched him set off down the hillside, she had to admit that the minor heart scare he'd had the previous year had done him a lot of good. He was in better shape than when she'd first met him, what was it, a dozen years ago?

The younger, fitter, more conventionally good-looking man at her side was also watching Hawkin's steady progress down the hill, and he now said, "Must be great to work with a man like him."

"He's been a good partner," she agreed; sometimes she and Al acted like an old married couple, finishing each other's sentences.

"You know, he's one of the reasons I'm a cop. My first year in the criminal justice program down in LA, when I was thinking that this whole cop thing wasn't for me, he came to speak to one of the classes. This would have been maybe fifteen, sixteen years ago. He was just such a . . . solid person, I decided to stick with it. I think maybe I wanted to be like him when I grew up." Williams was grinning when he said it, but Kate thought it was not altogether a joke. Once she'd made it past the initial intimidation factor, she'd wanted to grow up to be like Hawkin, too.

"Anything I can do to lend a hand?" she asked.

"Nah. I'm just here to oversee, when they quit we can go."

"Okay. You mind if I go down and talk to the Park rangers? Not taking statements, just to get a feel for the place."

"Help yourself."

"I'll watch for you in the parking area. Which car is yours?"

"Dark blue Jeep."

"Honk if you don't see me," she said, then launched herself down the hill in Hawkin's footsteps. To her chagrin, her progress was no more nimble than her partner's had been.

SHE found her pet ranger, Dan Culpepper, down in the parking area, patiently explaining to a hiking couple that no, they could not let their three large dogs race around unleashed, tormenting the wildlife. He nodded in sympathy with their plaints, agreeing that it was a pity that modern life did not allow for all the traditional freedoms, and gently mentioned that the fines were considerable, although if they agreed to keep the animals leashed, he would not write up a ticket this time. Grumbling but fatalistic, the pair tugged on the nylon that attached them to a couple hundred pounds of dog, and staggered off in their wake.

"Squirrels have rights, too," Kate commented.

Dan grinned at her, looking like a schoolboy, and said, "I didn't think that was quite the argument to use with them. Talking about the fines is usually more effective."

"Still, interesting job you have. From homicide to leash laws in one morning."

"And by this afternoon it'll be drunks falling in the lagoon; never a dull moment. Something I can help you with?"

"I just thought I'd take a look at the place. Living in San Francisco, I know all about the Presidio, but this is mostly a patch of hillside I see from the other side of the bridge. You have a YMCA conference center here, and year-round housing?"

"We have what are called park partnerships—the Y conference center, the Headlands Center for the Arts, the Marine Mammal Center, the Discovery Museum—nonprofit organizations with interests that overlap those of the headlands. And that need cheap housing."

"Now that coastal defense takes place in Nevada and the Army doesn't need the barracks."

"That's right."

"How many people live here, full-time?"

"In the whole park? Gee, let's see. Maybe eighty or ninety. Most of those work for one of the nonprofits."

"And the conference center, how often is that used?"

"Constantly. There'll be some group or another in there more than three hundred days a year."

"And the park hours?"

"It's an open park. The visitor center's only open during the day, of course, but we never shut."

"And there's no guard shack, to check people in and out."

"No."

Kate began to see the problem.

"No gates."

"No. Well, there's a gate at the top of the one-way section along the cliffs, but anyone can come in through the tunnel, around the clock."

"And you probably don't have any closed-circuit cameras on the roads."

"Nope."

"And this close to"—Kate thought maybe she shouldn't use the word *civilization*—"the Bay Area, you don't have problems with vandals?"

"Oh, some, sure. But we do have night patrols, and if anyone hears something they call us. That's the advantage of live-ins. I admit, we have had a few problems with full-moon skateboarders, down the cliff road."

Kate felt herself go pale. "Kids ride skateboards down that road? At *night*?"

"Sometimes they use bicycle headlights strapped to their helmet. They'll have a buddy drop them at the top and drive around to pick them up at the bottom. Or sometimes they'll break the lock, that doesn't happen often, it's too much work. They only get one or two runs in before someone calls us."

She suppressed a shudder, and pulled her mind back from the sensation of flying out over a cliff in the moonlight.

"Tell me about Battery DuMaurier."

"Actually, DuMaurier was the only single gun to be established in Fort Barry, a part of the expansion in—"

Kate interrupted. "What I'm wondering is, why was the body left in that particular spot? I'd have said it's hardly the first place that springs to mind."

"That's for sure. If you want to leave a body here, Wallace is closer to the road, Alexander is more private, Mendell doesn't even have padlocks to break. Maybe it was just the challenge?"

Great, thought Kate. A killer with a quirk. "As far as you know, there haven't been other bodies found there?"

"We've had deaths in the park, sure. Heart attacks mostly. But specifically DuMaurier? Not that I know of."

Still, Kate told herself, you never know: They might do a five-minute search through the records and find that the tall, skinny man in the pajamas had been chief suspect in an assault at Battery DuMaurier two years before or something, and this would turn out to be the assault victim's revenge and statement. Stranger things had happened.

Kate thanked her informant and wandered off to look over the remains of Fort Barry. Forty minutes later the faint echo of a car horn reached her where she stood on the windy bluff overlooking the ocean. She looked back at the parking area, saw the figure standing beside the blue Jeep, and waved a wide response before starting back along the crumbling concrete of Mendell.

When she reached the car, she found Lo-Tec Freeman and his new partner packing up their kits and Williams leaning against the Jeep, talking to Dan. As she came up, the Park CIB detective stood away from the car and shook hands with the ranger, saying, "I'll be back Monday to look over the records. Thanks a lot."

"Happy to help. Have a good weekend, you two."

"Ready?" Chris asked Kate.

"Sure. You got everything?"

"Such as it was. We put another padlock on and sealed the door, but I don't think there's much there. However, I had a call from Hawkin to say that he had someone dig into the records, and it looks like maybe Gilbert lived alone."

"You want to go anyway?"

"Oh yeah, just wanted you to know that we might not have to break the news to anyone. Al also asked me to tell you that he'd talked to your lieutenant, but you're to phone him, too, when you're finished at the house."

It did cheer the drive back across the bridge, thinking that they might not have to face the whole shock-and-grief process, and that it would only be a matter of finding what the house could tell them.

And when they had eventually followed the young woman from the security company through the front door, what the house had to tell them was that, from gas lamps to icebox, its master had been a bizarrely committed devotee of a character of detective fiction.

TWO

L ee, you know anything about Sherlock Holmes?"
Kate was sitting in the room with the flocked wallpaper, talking on her cell phone, a scrap of technology that felt like some intrusion from another universe. Still, Gilbert's wicker chair was surprisingly comfortable, and the usual sounds made by Crime Scene—voices, footsteps—were oddly soothing in the otherwise empty house.

"Sherlock Holmes? A self-medicating bipolar with obsessive-compulsive tendencies," said the psychotherapist. "Why?"

"Oh, nothing, just that our victim seems to've had a serious thing for the man."

"My sweet, you do know that Sherlock Holmes is a fictional character?"

"Not too sure this guy did. You should see his place." Kate stood up to look at another drawing like that concealing the door alarm, but this one showed a single man holding a flower in one hand, and behind it was nothing but a patch of wall. She sat down again.

"That's where you are?"

"Yeah. I just wanted to let you know that I may be late for pizza. We're waiting for the vic's lawyer to come, he says he has the combination to the safe, but he wouldn't give it to us over the phone."

"That's okay, we'll save you some. Will you be back for bedtime?"

"Absolutely." Even if it meant she had to borrow Williams's car to drive across town and back just to tuck Nora in; she'd only missed a handful of bedtimes in the last three years.

"I'll let her know. Say hi to Al for me."

"He went back already—there was a school event he needed to be at."

"Okay, well, have fun with the pipe and violin."

"And you with the pizza."

As she flipped the phone shut, a voice said, "Sorry about your dinner."

She turned around in the chair, to see the Park detective running his gaze methodically along the shelves. He had gloves on, as she did. Lo-Tec had found no particular reason to think this was a crime scene, but still.

"It's nothing. But if we're still here at eight, I'm going to need to leave you alone for a little while. I like to say goodnight to my daughter."

"Her name's Nora?" he asked. "I heard you say something to Hawkin about Nora's pizza."

"Right."

"It's a nice, old-fashioned name."

"A variation on her mother's name—Leonora."

Chris turned around with a puzzled look on his face. "She's adopted, then?"

"Oh, no. Lee—my partner—is her biological mother."

61

"Ah," he said, understanding at last. "Sorry."

Sorry for the misunderstanding, Kate translated, not sorry that she was a lesbian. It was somewhat surprising that he hadn't already known who (and what) she was, and encouraging to think that the name Kate Martinelli no longer produced instant flags of alarm in people's minds. Her last bout with infamy had been several years earlier; with any luck, the next would be a long time coming. She stood and dropped her phone into her pocket.

"Finding anything of interest?"

"The whole place is weirdly fascinating—you know that antique telephone actually has a dial tone? But not a lot of paperwork—it must all be in the safe."

They had found the safe in the third-floor office, but the woman from the security service did not have its code. When the photographer finished with the desk, Kate went back upstairs to make a methodical search through it for any record of Philip Gilbert's family. She found no trace of them, but she did spot a letter from a law firm across the Bay in Oakland, something to do with establishing a nonprofit foundation. She called the number on the stationery, listened to the recording, then dialed the number it referred her to in case of emergency. It took her some time to convince the answering service to hunt the lawyer down, but when she had done so, her cell phone rang in barely two minutes.

"This is Tom Rutland," said the voice, which bristled with a lawyer's inborn suspicion. "My service said you were trying urgently to get in touch with me."

Kate thanked him for calling her back, and explained that she had found his name on a letter addressed to a person whose death was under investigation.

"Who is that?" he said, as if she might be trying to put one over on him.

But when she said the name Philip Gilbert, Rutland went silent.

"Mr. Rutland? Is Philip Gilbert your client?"

"God. *Philip?* What happened?"

"All I can tell you is the death is under investigation. At the moment, I'm in his home trying to find the name and location of his next of kin."

"He doesn't really have family. I can't believe it. Are you sure it's him?"

"He had a medical necklace and his doctor confirmed his general appearance. We'll need someone to identify him, when we can find the family."

"He doesn't . . . You say you're in his house? How did you get in?"

"A neighbor gave us the name of his security company. Mr. Rutland—"

"I think I better come over there. I'm his executor, I'll bring you what information I have. I'm at home in Berkeley, I'll be there in forty-five minutes."

"That won't be necessary, Mr.—"

But Rutland's mind was made up, and if he really wanted to spend his Saturday afternoon driving across the Bay, Kate wasn't going to bar the door against him. She asked him if he had the code to the safe, and he said he'd bring it with him.

She closed the phone, looking distractedly at a framed photograph of Philip Gilbert with a television actor who had played Sherlock Holmes: Gilbert was a head taller, thinner of nose and sparser of hair, and looked more the character than the professional did.

She was looking at the photograph, but she was thinking about lawyers. Helpful lawyers were a rare breed, in her experience, and she'd never come across one willing to drop everything for a dead client—foot-dragging was an entire section in the bar exam. Too, Tom Rutland's reaction to the news had been more personal than professional, with his voice going tight, his thoughts distracted.

She called to Williams that they were going to have a visitor, and returned to her search.

The desk itself contained a minimum of paper, mostly paid bills and catalogues from auction houses all over the world. The answering machine held eleven messages, most of which sounded like business, since the callers left their full name and numbers and had invariably phoned during weekday work hours. The only exceptions were the second and seventh calls, both left by the same English voice, identifying himself merely as "Ian." Ian's first message had come at 8:21 the previous Monday morning:

"Philip, this is Ian. God, man, this is really something, but honestly, you can't be serious. Can you? Anyway, give me a ring on my mobile."

Then at 7:49 Thursday evening he had called again:

"Philip, I don't know if you got the message I left the

other day, but do ring me when you get a chance. I'll be back the first of the week, but call me any time. I need to talk to you about this before it goes any further."

Williams made note of the names, numbers, and times they had been left. The earliest one was the previous Sunday, January the twenty-fifth, the latest yesterday, Friday the thirtieth.

They also found Gilbert's keys, to the house and to the Lexus parked up the block. They were in a small bowl on the back of the desk, a bowl that, going by the scratches and nicks in its surface, was where they usually lived. Kate picked them up curiously. "Don't you think it's odd to keep your house keys up on the third floor?"

"Maybe he has another set downstairs."

But if he did, they couldn't find them. Maybe he had left in a hurry, and couldn't be bothered climbing upstairs to get the keys; hence the unturned dead bolt on the door.

Kate happened to be looking out of the window when a brand-new, glossy black BMW purred past the house, searching for a parking space. It found one up the block, and a vigorous, thickset man in his forties got out, dressed in expensive designer jeans, leather loafers worn without socks, and a gleaming black leather bomber jacket over a shirt printed with a sort of Balinese design, carrying a slightly less pristine leather briefcase in his hand. The entire package read: lawyer called in on his day off. His hair was carefully styled to hide the fact that it was going thin on top, and the tan of his face in winter testified to either a Mexican holiday or hours on the slopes. One hand jabbed his controls at the car, which responded with a flash of lights. Kate heard him call a greeting to the rose pruner across the street as she opened the door to let him in.

"Inspector Martinelli? Tom Rutland. Sorry to make you wait for me." He didn't sound in the least sorry; still, in spite of her instant antagonism it was all Kate could do not to reach out and caress the sumptuous leather of his jacket. His casual day-off shirt was either silk or heavy rayon, and just under the fold of the collar was a small pin that read "221B." He had no goggle marks around his eyes: Mexico, not ski slopes.

"No problem," she replied easily, standing back to let him in. "This is Inspector Williams, from the Park Police."

Hands were shaken, then the lawyer arranged his face into a suitably mournful set, lowered his voice, and said, "I was shocked to hear of Philip's death. He was a friend, as well as a client. What happened? Not an automobile accident—I saw his car outside." He directed his question to Williams, and Kate allowed the Park Service man to answer.

"No," Williams said. "Mr. Rutland, there appears to be a possibility that Mr. Gilbert was murdered."

"*Murdered?* Philip? A break-in, oh God, I told him he should upgrade that alarm system of his—"

"We've found no signs of a break-in, Mr. Rutland, and his body was found elsewhere."

"Then, what?"

66

"As I said, it's under investigation. Were you friends?"

"Murdered?" Rutland repeated, working to get his mind around the idea. Clearly, the lawyer's practice did not embrace a lot of criminal law.

"You say you were friends?" Williams prompted. This time, to effect.

"Yes. Not close friends, but I suppose about as close as Philip had. The kind of friendship that, when he needed to consult me about something, he'd schedule it for late morning and when we finished we'd go for lunch. Mostly I saw him at a dinner group we both belonged to. I'd be seeing him next week. I'll have to tell the others about it. Christ, it's hard to believe."

"Mr. Rutland, do you know of any business Mr. Gilbert might have had in the parkland just north of the Golden Gate Bridge?"

"What, on Point Bonita? Not that I know of. He isn't—wasn't—much of an outdoorsman."

To say nothing of the fact that he was in his pajamas, thought Kate.

"Why?" the lawyer asked. "Is that where he . . . where you found him?"

"Yes," Williams answered, "although it would appear that he died elsewhere."

"Murdered. Jesus."

"It is only a possibility," Williams reminded him. "Is there at least some family?"

"He has a cousin somewhere in the Midwest, two nieces in Texas, an ex-wife in Boston. I don't think he was close to any of them. If it's someone to identify the body you need, I could do it."

"Thank you. In the meantime, if you could let us have the family's names and phone numbers, we'll at least need to talk to them."

"I didn't bring that information with me. I'll put it together for you when I get back, and e-mail or fax it to you. But I did bring a copy of the will, I figured you'd need me to go over it with you."

"That was very thoughtful."

Rutland looked around, as if realizing for the first time that they'd been standing in the gloomy entranceway all this time. "You want to go up to the study, where there's light?"

"Um, let me just check if the room's clear." Kate left Williams and the lawyer downstairs and trotted up to stick her head inside the door to the study. "The lawyer's here, has some papers he wants to go over. How long until we won't be in your way?"

"We're pretty much finished in here. Lots of prints, a drinking glass and an ashtray, nothing else obvious. You want me to collect all the stuff in the desk?"

"Let's go over it first, see if there's anything there." Anything like a threatening letter or evidence of a crime, but she didn't think Philip Gilbert had been a white-collar crime lord. "Mostly I'd just like Tamsin to record the safe when we get it open, then as far as I'm concerned, you guys can go."

Kate went back downstairs and said to the lawyer, "We can go up now." She held out her arm to indicate that he could lead the way, and he did.

"You seem to know the house fairly well, Mr. Rutland," Williams commented as they trooped upstairs.

"Sure. I've been here a lot, for business and the occasional dinner."

"This is with the dinner group you mentioned, or just as Mr. Gilbert's guest?"

"Usually with them. Once or twice we ate here after I'd brought him some papers to sign—nothing formal then."

"Your dinner group meets regularly?" Kate asked.

"Once a month. We call ourselves the Strand Diners. We're, well, devotees of the Sherlock Holmes stories. Not a BSI scion, although some of us belong to one or another; we're just an informal group."

"BSI?" Williams asked.

"Oh, sorry. Baker Street Irregulars. That's the biggest worldwide organization of Sherlockians, or Holmesians as they call themselves in England."

"Mr. Gilbert seems to have been a real fan."

"The place is really something, isn't it? Sherlockians don't usually go quite so far, but it was Philip's livelihood as well as his passion, so it made sense, in a way."

"How do you mean, livelihood?"

"Philip was one of the world's leading experts on Sherlock Holmes and Arthur Conan Doyle. He had universities drooling to get their hands on some of the things in his collection, and private collectors would kill—" He stopped suddenly on the stairs, looking back over his shoulder. "I don't mean that literally, of course

69

not. But some of the things Philip has—had, were without parallel."

"So who inherits?"

Instead of answering, the lawyer continued up the last flight of stairs and headed for the study. He glanced curiously at the closed door of the bedroom as he went past, where Lo-Tec and Maria were checking out the walls and furniture, then went ahead into the study, pulling the desk chair over to the low lion's claw table and leaving the chair and sofa to Kate and Williams. He laid his leather case on the table and took out two stapled sheaves of paper, handing one to each of them.

"This is Philip's will. Normally I'd need to wait until you had notified his family, but really, as you'll see there's little point in delaying. Basically, Philip wanted his collection to remain intact and attached to his name. You'll find that I am executor of his estate, and that I am to offer the house and its contents to a number of institutions for bidding. Not to sell outright, but to go to the institution that offers the best support to the collection, in archiving, preserving, and making it available to the public. That last will be the biggest problem, because this house is in a residential area, and the neighbors aren't going to permit a lot of traffic going in and out. Philip had enough headaches just holding the occasional meeting here."

"So his relatives get nothing?" Williams asked, flicking the pages but clearly not intending to settle in and read the entire document there and then.

"Small bequests, but they were not close, and his two

nieces are neither interested in the collection nor are they exactly poor. Their mother, Philip's sister, married into oil."

"What about the ex-wife?"

"They were married for barely two years, more than twenty years ago. I shouldn't think she has expectations of much."

"When did you last see Mr. Gilbert?"

"On the fourteenth, a Wednesday. He had some papers he wanted me to go over, and I happened to be coming over to the city, so we met downtown for lunch."

"And you haven't spoken to him since then?"

"He called me a couple days later to let me know that the papers had arrived and all was well—it had to do with the sale of a little carving, the buyer was being prickly—but that was it."

"So you last spoke to him on the sixteenth?"

"Yes. No—he called briefly about a week later, on Friday, I think it was. He wanted to know if I was free later that afternoon, but I wasn't. I was leaving town by three. So he said he'd call back on Monday or Tuesday to make an appointment. He never called."

"He didn't say what the appointment was for?"

"No."

Kate let her own copy of the will fall shut, and asked, "Could you tell us something about Mr. Gilbert?"

"Like what?"

Start at the beginning, Kate thought. "How did you meet him? What was he like? What did he do?"

Rutland glanced at her, his mouth twisting in a crooked imitation of a smile. "Hard to think of Philip in the past tense. He was, I don't know, a little bigger than life. A little smarter, a little more self-assured. Philip could be a pain, but he was . . . it sounds odd, surrounded by this place, but he was *real*.

"We met through the Diners, six, seven years ago. I'd just moved down from Davis, going through a divorce, trying to set up a practice. That first dinner—it was here, in fact, a friend brought me—it was exactly what I needed. Intelligent, friendly people with a sense of humor about the source of their common interest. I wasn't in period dress, I'd been told it wasn't absolutely required, and I felt a little uncomfortable because everyone else was. But Philip made some friendly joke about my being undercover and it was fine. The following week he phoned and asked me to set up a will for him, and that's how it's been since then."

"He was the head of your dinner group, would you say?"

"Philip has always been the most committed to the Diners. He was one of the founding members, fifteen, twenty years ago. I doubt he's missed more than one or two meetings in all the years I've known him."

"How many in the group?"

"The numbers vary, but at the moment we're ten. Well, nine without him."

"Were any of the others particularly friendly with him?"

Rutland thought for a moment. "I'd say most of us

have met with him occasionally outside the dinners, but I don't know if that would count as particularly friendly. Philip seems, seemed, to have an amazingly . . . democratic relationship to people. I mean to say, a couple of times we've had members who thought they were becoming close to him personally because they worked with him on some project or another, and both had their noses badly bruised when they came up against his self-protective shield. It just never seemed to have occurred to Philip that some people might think they had a greater claim on his time and energy than others."

"Self-centered," Kate commented.

"Very. He was a lovely man until you expected him to open up with you, and then you'd find him looking at you with a puzzled expression on his face before going on to whatever bit of business concerned him."

"Sounds frustrating."

"It could be. But once you got to know him, it was just Philip. Sort of taking British coolness to an extreme."

"Was he British?"

"No, actually he was born in Wisconsin, but he went to the University of London for a couple of years, and kept something of the accent. It was more that he culti-vated the Englishness of Holmes in his own life. The eccentricities, the tight focus, the distaste for emotional excess."

"Do you know if he had any friends, or regular acquaintances, outside the dinner group?"

"He never mentioned any to me, but then he wouldn't have had reason to."

"What about professional contacts? I take it from his papers that he made his living as a dealer in Sherlock Holmes . . ." What was it called? Junk? Paraphernalia? ". . . collectibles."

"In the English system, Philip would be classified as 'gentleman,' meaning he did not have to earn his living. He wasn't wealthy, but there was an inheritance that cushioned life, from early on. I think he worked for a while, a long time ago, but certainly in the time I've known him he has been a collector and dealer. As for his contacts in that world, I'd probably know a fraction of them. But that information should be in his things, either in the safe or his computer. Philip was good at keeping records."

"What about a PDA?"

"No, I don't think so. He didn't like modern machinery a whole lot. He did have a cell phone, but he usually left it sitting on the charger."

They'd found the charger, but not the phone, not in his desk, beside his bed, in a coat pocket, or in his sock drawer: They had looked. Kate asked Rutland, "Do you have the number for the phone?"

He took out his own and, after much scrolling, gave it to Kate. She wrote it down, and asked, "He didn't like cell phones or PDAs, but he's got a nice computer setup here."

"He had to—a lot of his work was done over the Internet—but I think he'd have been just as happy to go back to snail mail and ads in the monthly journals. Basically, Philip disliked the accoutrements of modern life. I've actually seen him sit down to that monstrosity of a typewriter downstairs and pound out a letter. With a carbon copy, if you can believe that—I didn't even know you could still buy carbon paper."

"Maybe we should have a look in the safe," Williams suggested.

Rutland opened his briefcase again and took out an envelope, laying it facedown on the table between the two detectives. The back flap was sealed, and across it ran the ornate signature of Philip William Gilbert. "I told him it wasn't necessary for me to know the combination of the safe, and said that he should leave the number in his bank deposit box, but he said he trusted me and that he might need me to gain access, if, for example, he was traveling and wanted something. This was our compromise."

"So you never opened it?"

"I never needed to use it, no."

Williams looked at Kate over the envelope, one of those delicate moments of territoriality. He had been first in the house, stepping in to work the door alarm, but there, the security woman had handed him the paper and he'd gone ahead without considering any overtones. Here, the next step lay between them. After a moment, Kate reached out and picked up the envelope, and the Park Police investigator did not object.

Kate called Tamsin in and waited until the camera was running before she opened the safe. It was built into the wall, eighteen inches square and looking both new and formidable, but it opened without a protest under her fingers. She stepped back so the camera would record the contents.

Half a dozen file folders stood against the left wall, held upright by an assortment of small boxes, mailing envelopes, and books with shiny clear wrappers. One folder was about an inch thick, some sort of document printed on heavy buff paper. Two were nearly flat. The last one was less than half the thickness of the buff paper, its cover light blue.

"Last time I saw it, Philip's ongoing business file was in a sort of bluish folder," the lawyer told them.

Kate pulled out the blue file, glanced inside, and carried it over to the low table. The tab had been labeled LEDGER, although it held not a bound book, but perhaps thirty sheets of legal-sized paper fastened together at one corner by an oversized clip; each page had lines running the long direction, cross-divided with the resulting columns labeled: item, source, price paid, appraised value, comments, and price received, all in pinched but immaculate handwriting. In earlier pages, many of the items had every box filled, showing when he had bought a thing, how much he'd paid, and how much he'd sold it for or, occasionally, the laconic note "retained." In others, the columns were blank when it came to "sold" or "appraised value." Each step along the way was dated; the earliest transaction was from August, five months before.

When she ran a finger down the second column, the

appraised value of each item, Kate's shoulders went back in surprise; Williams frankly whistled; Rutland was nodding when they both looked up at him.

"Like I said, he was a serious collector and dealer."

"This stuff's not all in the house, is it?"

"Some of it, although he wouldn't have displayed anything of great value downstairs. Even in the safe, I'd imagine there was nothing worth more than five or ten thousand. You might think he'd want his best things close at hand, but in fact, the real prizes he kept mostly in the bank. He was there regularly."

Kate tore her eyes off the open door of the safe and looked back at the printout. "You mean to tell me someone would spend a hundred forty thousand dollars on a *magazine?*" Moreover, one whose note said "retained."

"Oh, man, October was a hell of a great month for Philip—apparently he'd been working that old man for years to get his hands on the *Beeton's Annual*—nobody else even knew the fellow had it, Philip tracked it down, God only knows how. That magazine is the first appearance of Sherlock Holmes in the world, one of maybe thirty still in existence. And of those, only two or three were signed by Conan Doyle. Plus, to top it off, it was in excellent and original condition—almost all of the survivors have been bound into hard covers at some time, to preserve them. Oh, it was worth every cent of what he paid. And prices are shooting up—you could get twice that today, easy. Hang on to it for a couple years, that magazine could hit a million dollars."

"Jesus H. Christ," Chris Williams breathed. "Makes me wish I'd kept some of those comics I used to collect when I was a kid."

Kate studied the number of zeros on the list of Philip Gilbert's possessions—and this showed only those transactions of the past five months. She shook her head: a whole lot of motive here for murder, had the beneficiary been an individual rather than an institution. "What about that list of associates?"

"Their names are under the column 'sources,'" Rutland pointed out.

"Didn't he have an address book or Rolodex, something like that?"

"There were so many, he'd probably have them all in his files, either in the cabinet or on the computer. Oh, and you'll want his password for that as well. It's Sigerson." He spelled it for them, explaining, "That's one of the false identities Sherlock Holmes constructs. A Norwegian explorer."

"Right. And these sources will all be business partners of some kind?"

"Philip didn't have what you'd call partners, just contacts—antiquarian book dealers, other collectors, auction houses."

"And no real friends, you'd say?"

"A wide number of acquaintances, certainly, he knew by first name most of the prominent Sherlockians here and abroad, but as far as I know, when it came to actual friendships, those of us in the dinner club were pretty much it. If he even knew anyone outside the Sherlockian world, I never heard him speak of them."

"No romantic relationships?"

"Like I said, he was married once, in his late twenties, but she left him after two or three years, and I don't believe he's even heard from her in, oh, ten years. Maybe longer. I only know about her because I wrote his will. And they didn't have any children. As to any current relationships, I wasn't privy to his personal life. All I can say is, there weren't any permanent enough to earn a place in his will."

"Was he gay?"

Rutland shrugged, a gesture that as often covered discomfort as it expressed uncertainty. "He could have been, or he might have been asexual, as Holmes himself appears to have been. I just couldn't say."

"Well, maybe we could just get the names of the dinner club members, then."

"Sure, I'll send them along with the names of his family. Although he may have a file for them on his computer. Want me to look?"

"We'll do that, Mr. Rutland. I may phone you to confirm that we've got them all."

"Sure. I'd start with Ian Nicholson, if I were you. He's probably the member Philip was closest to—although, come to think of it, Ian's out of town for a few days. He's sure to be back by Wednesday, that's our monthly dinner night. Unless we cancel it because of . . . Well, I'll have to consult the others about that."

"Now, just to check, Mr. Rutland: You live and work in Berkeley, is that right?"

"My office is actually just inside the border of Oakland, but yes."

"But you come to San Francisco regularly." Kate waited until he had said yes, then asked, "And you know the Marin headlands."

"Only to walk around. It's a great place to take out-of-town visitors, to get a perspective on San Francisco. Blows them away."

He answered without hesitation, and with no apparent awareness of having made an admission. However, people who left bodies invariably chose a place within their comfort zone, generally fifteen or twenty miles from where they felt at home. The problem here was, the Marin headlands were fifteen or twenty miles from half the population of northern California.

There was not much more they could ask the lawyer just then, and little point in detailed inquiries as to his alibi without a closer idea of when Gilbert had died. They did ask, and he told them, that he had last spoken to his client on the morning of Friday, January 23, before leaving at 3:30 for a weekend with golfing friends in Palm Springs. (Palm Springs, Kate noted; not Mexico.) They thanked him for his assistance, gave him their cards with e-mail addresses for the information he'd promised, and Kate saw him to the door.

They finished a cursory search of Gilbert's desk, noting his various numbers—phone, credit card, bank account—for the warrants they would need and to request that the banks be on the lookout for any uses, then packed up the records for Lo-Tec to take away with him.

In another room, a little tune played, a tune Kate had heard before. She was not surprised when Lo-Tec appeared in the doorway.

"I checked out the car, no signs of disturbance, I don't think we need to take it in. Are we about finished here?"

"Yeah, I think so. That was your phone I heard—you got another call?"

"Break-in, practically around the corner. It can wait if you need us."

"No, I'm just boxing these files for you."

"What about the hard drive? You want me to take that?"

"We found the guy in his pajamas, it's far more likely to be sex than his business records. Let's leave it for the time being."

"Okay."

They carried their collection of evidence out to the van. Kate closed up the safe, logged everyone out, set the door alarm, turned the deadbolt lock on the front door, and posted seals across the front and back doors. Williams drove her home, turned down her offer of something to drink, and said he'd phone her the next day.

Kate left a text message for the lieutenant, to follow up on his conversation with Hawkin that afternoon.

Even so, she was still in good time to read Nora to sleep.

But at five minutes past ten o'clock, as Kate was

81

thinking of heading for an early bed herself, her cell phone rang. It was Thomas Rutland.

"I'm sorry to call you so late," the lawyer said, "but I just realized, I think there was something missing from Philip's study. Did you happen to notice a statue of the Maltese Falcon—like in the movie, shiny black thing about ten inches tall—on the shelf beside the door?"

Kate admitted that she hadn't noticed a Maltese Falcon on Gilbert's shelf.

"I'm so used to seeing it that I don't see it anymore, if you know what I mean. It just came to me that there was a hole in his study where it stands."

"A Maltese Falcon? What is it made out of?" Kate asked, thinking all the while, *Damn, damn.*

"Pottery or porcelain, something glazed. It's an award he got from the Crime Club of Canada for a book he wrote about collecting, five years ago. He was very proud of it."

"And it's usually in his study?"

"With the other awards, yes. It would be anachronistic downstairs, so he kept it up there. I'm sure it was there the last time I was in the study, after the dinner party, on January seventh. I remember him saying something about a book he was thinking about writing, that maybe he'd get the falcon a mate. I suppose he could have moved it," he said, sounding unconvinced.

"We'll keep an eye out for it," she told him, and hung up. Blunt object: head injury. *Shit.*

She eyed the phone. If she called Lo-Tec and asked if he'd seen a black bird statue, he would insist on going out to the Gilbert house then and there, no matter how long his day had been. Or hers.

Instead, she phoned Chris Williams.

He answered on the fourth ring; a child was wailing in the background.

"Sorry, Chris, this is Kate. I hope I didn't wake your"—was it a son? a daughter? Kate couldn't remember the overheard conversation well enough—"kid?"

"Oh no, he's working on a tooth, decided to give up sleep until he starts school. In three years. What's up?"

Kate explained about the bird statue, asked if he remembered seeing it. "No, nothing of that sort. You going out to look for it tonight?" He tried to sound willing, but the lack of enthusiasm came through loud and clear.

"No, that's why I'm calling you rather than Crime Scene. I just wanted to check if it rang a bell with you, but I'll go out in the morning, and if necessary, call CSI out again."

"Want me to meet you there?"

"That's up to you."

"What time?"

"Ten-thirty?"

"I'll be there."

Tight money was a harsh reality of policing, and it cost too much to have a microscopic search done on every site faintly related to a homicide—and in this case, it was only a possible homicide. If the body had been found inside the house, or if they had seen any indication that Gilbert had died there, a thorough search would have been justified, but neither had led them in that direction. However, a missing blunt object? That was another matter entirely.

THREE

S unday morning dawned, the first sun of February spilling through the kitchen windows. Lee made waffles, the Sunday paper drifted in all directions, and Kate dared a leisurely third cup of coffee.

At 9:37, her phone rang.

"Martinelli, have you heard anything from Williams?"

Al's voice was taut, and Kate felt her body go tight in response. "No, I was going to meet him at Gilbert's house later this—"

"They've had an incident in Marin," he interrupted.

"What kind?"

"Sounds like a church shooting in Tiburon, unknown number of people down, the shooter drove west, reports are into Muir Woods."

"Is that part of the park?"

"Who knows? It's near, everybody'll be called in."

"Shit." Kate suddenly became aware that both Lee and Nora were staring at her. She gave Lee an apologetic smile and tipped her head at Nora; Lee instantly stood up and began urging the child toward the sink and its soap bubbles.

Kate turned away and carried the phone into the next

room. Al was describing a brief report heard by Jani on the radio twenty minutes before and the difficulties in getting information. He ended, "But I thought I should give you the heads-up, in case you hadn't heard."

"I'll phone Williams."

"You want me to come up? I've got an interview with the ADA in the Broadlands case, Sunday was the only day he could fit it in, but I can cut it short."

"No, it's just a matter of looking for a blunt object the lawyer thought might be missing, and if it's not there, letting Crime Scene in to do a more thorough search. I'll call Williams, tell him not to worry, I'll be there."

"Fine. I'll have my cell on, if you want me."

"Let me know if you hear anything."

"Will do. Hi to Lee."

Kate hung up, envisioning the heartbreaking chaos up above the headlands at that moment. It was less likely for a Tiburon shooting to be gang-related than a similar incident in the city, but that didn't mean the residents lacked guns.

She walked back out to the kitchen, where Lee and Nora were elbow-deep in suds. Nora stared up at her, emerald eyes dancing in glee. "Mamakay, you used a naughty word!"

"I did, love, I'm sorry. What's my punishment?"

The gamine face screwed in thought, hands dripping suds on the towels spread across the chair she stood on. "You have to read me *two* stories tonight."

Kate picked her up, suds and all, and hugged her into a squeal. "That's no punishment, little monkey."

"Was that Al?" Lee asked.

"Yep, he said hi to you, just wanted me to know that something's come up in Marin, the guy from there might be tied up. Is there any local news, do you know?"

Kate found a channel eventually, showing the aftermath of disaster. Al had been right, there were bodies, three covered figures on the ground outside the church and God knew what within. The live feed was interrupted by loops showing ambulances driving away, weeping churchgoers, and men with blood on their white shirts.

Kate opened her phone, punched in the number Williams had given her, and said to the prompt of his recording, "Hey Chris, that looks like a hell of a mess you've got up there. Don't worry about coming down today, I'll take care of everything. Give me a ring on my cell phone when you get a chance."

Territoriality was a touchy part of policing, and when the boundaries were not distinct, such as in this case, it was best to recognize that early and often. She would need to get statements from the Park residents, with or without the Park investigator, but it was best to make him feel like he remained in the loop.

She got dressed and drove to the Gilbert house, breaking the seal and walking through the deserted rooms, ending up in the upstairs study. The shelf to the immediate left of the door held a nest of awards, including a clear Lucite globe with an inscription so ornate it was illegible, a miniature bronze bust of some heavily jowled man, and a plaque marking Ten Years Service to the Strand Diners. Among them was a dust-less oval, about five inches across. Just the size of a ten-inch statue's base.

She got down on her knees and shone her flashlight under the desk, then into the narrow gap between wall and filing cabinet. There, at the farthest reaches, the beam caught on some small, shiny black object perhaps an inch across. It looked very like a piece of broken porcelain.

She took out her phone and called the Operations Center, finding that, as she had thought, Lo-Tec was still on call.

He and Maria arrived within half an hour. Lo-Tec looked deeply affronted, as if Kate had accused him of missing something vital.

"Yesterday, we had no reason to believe we were looking at a crime scene," she told him. "But the lawyer had time to think about it, and he phoned to ask if we'd found this thing. That makes it a different matter."

She made it sound as if the lawyer had called her that morning, rather than the night before, and took them upstairs to show them what she had found. Then, because she would only be in their way, she left them to it.

Normally she would have waited until Al was there to interview the neighbors—either that or left it to the local beat cops to do a door-to-door. But she had to wait around while Crime Scene worked, and she might as well be of use. And as it turned out, Sunday proved to be a pretty good day to meet the neighbors, with about two-thirds of them answering their doorbells (none of which had knobs saying *Pull*). Although only two of them knew the resident of 927 by name, every one of them knew him by sight. Moreover, they knew both Philip Gilberts.

The woman next door to Gilbert, on the right as Kate came down the Gilbert steps, was a whip-slim, black-haired woman whose every gesture shouted *dancer,* although when she came to the door she was dressed in baggy sweats with grass stains and bore the powerful aroma of new-cut lawn. Kate displayed her badge, gave the woman her name, received that of Naomi de la Veaga in return, and asked her about the man who lived next door.

"You mean Raffles?"

"Did he tell you that was his name?" What kind of a nickname was *Raffles?* Did Gilbert go around the neighborhood selling tickets for prizes?

"Oh no, his name's Gilbert. His last name, his first is Peter, I think? Or maybe Philip? Anyway, my husband and I call him Raffles, just to ourselves, of course. You know the books about the gentleman thief, dressed to the nines one day and in disguise the next? Raffles the Cracksman, by what's-his-name, Arthur Conan Doyle's brother-in-law or something? Anyway, that's Mr. Gilbert. Nice guy, but a little odd even for San Francisco."

Kate had never heard of Raffles, but she had no intention of pausing for a literature lesson. "You're not saying he's a thief?"

"Oh, God no, nothing of the sort. Just that he looks like, oh, never mind, it's really a stupid name. Forget I said anything." Her face had gone pink, making her look as adorable as Nora.

"How long have you known him?"

"I wouldn't say I know him, but I first met him a couple weeks after we'd moved in, when UPS changed drivers and left us a package meant for him. This was about, oh, eighteen months ago. When I got home and found the box on my doorstep, I took it over and asked if it was his, and it was. I gave it to him, we introduced ourselves, did one of those 'We must have you over for coffee one day' things, although somehow we haven't done it yet, probably never will. But I wave at him when I see him, say hi when he goes by, both of him."

"I'm sorry?" Did she mean that Gilbert had a twin?

"The man has, like, two personalities. Not that he's bonkers or talks to the lampposts or anything, it's just that most of the time he looks like anyone else, comes out of his door in clothes that could have come from the Gap, says hi, gets into his car, drives away. But other times he looks like something out of a Fred Astaire movie, black suit, top hat, cane—I even saw him in spats once. When he's dressed like that, he even talks formally—'Good afternoon' instead of 'Hi'—and he always walks instead of driving. I'm not sure where he goes, but my husband spotted him once waiting for the cable car down on Hyde. The tourists must have thought he was part of the show. Nice guy, I'll really have to ask him for coffee. Maybe I should ask you first, though, what's he done?"

"He's died," Kate said bluntly, then softened it to, "He was found dead over the weekend. Can you tell me if he had any regular visitors?"

"Dead? Oh, the poor man! How did he die?"

"We're still investigating the cause of death. His visitors?"

"Right. Well, he had costume parties from time to time—every three or four months. Small groups, in the evening, and they were always quiet and left by eleven. Other than that, I think he may have run some kind of business out of his home. People would drop in during the day, usually in the mornings, but they never stayed for long." She gave Kate a sharp look, and explained, "It isn't that I sit and spy on the neighbors, but I'm working on my master's and my desk is in the upstairs window, so I spend more time staring out at the street than I might otherwise. A lot of the houses are only occupied during the evenings, but like I said, Raff—I mean, Mr. Gilbert tended to have people during the day. I figured out early that it was to do with business because he'd usually shake their hands as they left, and they were often carrying things. Then a few weeks ago one of the other neighbors went around with a petition complaining that the street wasn't zoned for a business. I didn't sign it, his parties never bothered me, actually I thought they were kind of fun. And unlike some of the people around here, he never sat out in the backyard drinking beer and playing loud music. I hope he wasn't lonely. I suppose it was thoughtless of me not to invite him over."

"Which of your neighbors circulated the petition?" Kate asked, alert for conflict.

"Oh, I don't really remember," the dancer said vaguely, her face going bright pink again. Embarrassment at ratting on a neighbor, Kate decided, not fear of reprisal. She let it go, retrieving her original question.

"What about Gilbert's other visitors, outside the parties—were any of them regular?"

"Not really. There's a guy with a really nice black BMW, he shows up every couple of weeks, and the people who come to his dinner parties show up sometimes. Other than them, the only regular is Nika, the cleaning woman."

"Would you by any chance know her full name?"

"It's something Russian, I think. But I have her phone number; you want that?"

"Thank you, that would be helpful."

"Sure, come on in, I'll get it for you. Shut the door, would you?"

Kate followed the woman's nice muscular backside through the house into a bright, modern kitchen overlooking the back garden. Naomi picked up a well-used address book from a shelf near the wall phone, copied down a phone number on a bright orange Post-it, and peeled it off to give to Kate. "Like I said, I can't remember her last name, it starts with a K, but her first name is Nika. She cleans for me once a month—I saw her going in and out from next door and asked Raffles—sorry, Mr. Gilbert—if he'd recommend her, he did and gave me her number. She's been really great."

Kate pressed the number into her notebook. "When did you last see Mr. Gilbert?"

"Oh gee, I don't know. It's been a few days anyway."

"Did you see him last weekend, do you remember? Saturday maybe? It was clear, though Sunday it was raining pretty hard. You might have noticed him Saturday, in the garden or washing the car or something?"

"Saturday. Yeah, you're right, I was outside for a while then, but I can't say I remember seeing him."

"What about hearing him moving around, playing music, on the phone? The windows might have been open, did you get the impression that he was home?"

The woman shook her head slowly. "I just don't remember, sorry. His car was here, down the block a ways—in fact," she said, suddenly animated, "his car hasn't moved in a long time. God, isn't that awful? Like those people that die in their homes and nobody finds them for weeks."

Kate moved to rein in the dancer's imagination. "Was it unusual for his car to remain in one place for days on end?"

"Well, not really. I mean, it would stay put for two or three days, but usually not more than that. Parking on the streets like he and I both do, you kind of notice how far the neighbors—those who don't rent a garage—have to park from their houses. It sort of makes you feel better when you find yourself hiking two blocks with a load of groceries."

"What about last weekend, or the end of the week?"

"You know, there was one day he was in and out a lot,

I remember noticing that. What day would that have been?" She struck an unconscious one-legged pose as she thought about it, then abruptly stood on both feet and looked at Kate. "It was Friday—a week ago Friday. I had to go pick up my printer at the shop, and when I got back, there was a place right out in front. He'd been parked there earlier, I'm sure of it."

"What time of day was that?"

"Late morning. And after I'd taken it upstairs and got it plugged in again, after a while I looked out and noticed his Lexus parked across the street, and I was glad he hadn't lost out too much by my getting his spot."

"Late morning, Friday the twenty-third of January," Kate repeated.

Naomi turned automatically to check the calendar, then said, "That's right."

"And the car stayed there the rest of the day?"

"It was there for a while, but I don't think the whole time. Like I said, as far I remember, he was in and out a lot that day."

"What about the evening? Did you hear him come in?"

But she was already shaking her head. "No, I'm in bed early, and we sleep at the back of the house."

"How about Saturday morning?"

Her thin face screwed up, unwilling to commit to that. "I really don't know when I noticed it next. It could have been Saturday morning, or afternoon. It could even have been Sunday. I just know that it was down the block the next time I saw it, and that was where it stayed."

Kate couldn't see that the woman had much more to tell her. She handed her a card and said, "Thank you for all your help, Ms. de la Veaga. If you think of anything else, please give me a call."

She continued working her way through the neighbors, visiting all the houses for two blocks down, then crossing over and working her way back up the other side. Some of the neighbors knew Gilbert's name, one of them even had heard of his death on the news, all of them knew him as the man in the funny clothes. Three residents knew the name of the security company Gilbert used, including the balding, boy-faced neighbor across the street who had interrupted his rose pruning to give Kate the information the previous day; he also knew that the lawyer's BMW was a regular visitor, and that Gilbert held the occasional costume-dress party. This neighbor's name was Simon Wallace, and he seemed the equivalent of the curtain-tugging village grandmother, so eager to share his knowledge of his cross-the-street neighbor that he ended up wagging his tail like his fluffy little dog.

Unfortunately for both sides, he didn't have any knowledge of the previous weekend, since he'd been in bed with a cold.

With another person his age, Kate would have raised a disbelieving eyebrow, but he was still coughing and blowing his nose, and Simon Wallace seemed just the type to take to his bed with hot tea and a steamer for days on end, thermometer and doctor's phone number in easy reach.

As it turned out, most of the houses for a block in either direction were aware of Philip Gilbert, if only through his eccentric dress and his occasional parking-space-disrupting dinner parties. Two of the neighbors were aware that the inside of Gilbert's house was something unusual: The man three down on the right had provided the name of a contractor for some of Gilbert's renovations, six years earlier, and the builder, being his brother-in-law, had told him about some of the peculiar work Gilbert had wanted done, the gaslights and the wholesale covering-over of electrical outlets. He in turn had told his running partner across the street and two doors down.

The only other oddity was Gilbert's neighbor to the immediate left. When Kate rang the bell (electronic chimes, playing a tune) she heard movement inside, but no one came to the door. She rang again, then knocked, half expecting to hear a dog's bark, but instead the door crept open and a thin, nervous-looking woman in her mid-fifties looked out from the crack.

The hesitation before opening and the nervousness woke Kate's cop instincts, and she eyed the woman closely as she identified herself, confirmed that she was Mrs. Nadine Murray, and told Mrs. Murray that she would like to ask some questions about her neighbor.

The woman frowned and opened the door a fraction more, as if she hadn't heard correctly. "Which neighbor is that?"

"Philip Gilbert," Kate said, and instead of giving the number, stepped back slightly and pointed in the direction of the house. "Over there."

The door came open a little more and now Kate could see both hands and half her body, which was dressed in a faded garment that in the Eisenhower era would have been called a housecoat. The woman's hair showed half an inch of gray roots under the mousy brown, although her nails had been manicured in the not-too-distant past, and she had put on lipstick that morning. She looked in the direction Kate had indicated, and a degree of her nervousness faded, to be replaced by scorn.

"You mean the weirdo?"

"Is that what he was?"

"Sure. Dressed like something from a TV show, snooty as hell, wanted to turn his place into a museum and thought nobody should mind. That's all we need, more parking problems."

"Did Mr. Gilbert tell you he was turning his house into a museum?" The interrogation technique of repeating the person's last statement always made Kate feel like a cliché therapist, but it often gave results.

"Not him. One of his fancy friends, I stopped him when they were having one of those parties they had to ask what they thought they were doing in there, the guy said the house was a showplace and I should be honored to have it next door. Showplace. Ha!"

"Did he actually say Mr. Gilbert was wanting to make it into a museum?"

"Not in so many words, but that's what a showplace

96

is, isn't it? I like living here because it's quiet, and that would be the end of the quiet."

"Is that why you circulated the petition?"

"It wasn't my—" She caught herself. Her eyes shifted away from Kate and she said, "Yeah, that's why."

Kate studied her curiously. The instantaneous denial would have made sense, except that the admission that followed sounded like the lie. *It wasn't my*—what? My idea? Then whose was it? And was the minor puzzle worth digging for here and now?

No, Gilbert hadn't been murdered over some parking petition, and there was no point in alienating this witness just yet. Still, she would keep Mrs. Murray in mind, and return to the question later if need be.

It also demonstrated the limits to the neighborhood's knowledge of itself: Had this neighbor known that the renovations on Gilbert's house included those gaslights, she would surely have turned him in for a code violation rather than bothering with a petition.

"Mrs. Murray, we're interested in Mr. Gilbert's activities the end of the week before last—the twenty-first to twenty-fifth, say. Did you notice any particular activity around those days?"

"I work twelve-hour shifts at the nursing home, noon to midnight, Tuesday through Friday. I don't see much of anything those days, and the others, I'm catching up on my sleep. No, I didn't see anything."

"Are you the only person who lives here, Mrs. Murray?"

The remnants of pink lipstick puckered up in reaction. "You think a woman can't live alone in a house?"

"I think many woman do, Mrs. Murray," Kate replied, hanging on to politeness with an effort. "Are you one of them?"

"My sister lives here," the woman admitted grudgingly. "She moved in after my husband died two years ago. He bought this house in the days when the hippies were dying off, before it got popular with the yuppies and then the dot-commers, and we never saw reason to sell it just because the neighborhood changed."

"Could I speak with her?"

"She's out of town. Helping our brother get settled in Houston."

"Will she be back soon?"

"Should be home on the weekend."

"That's fine, then, I won't ask you for her phone number there. I just wanted to see if anyone else might have noticed anything at the Gilbert house."

"What kind of thing?"

"Visitors, perhaps?"

"I can tell you he hasn't had one of his fancy-dress parties in a while."

"How can you tell, if you work evenings?"

"Because when he has one, his friends all drive here and they take up all the parking places until late, so everyone who lives here has to look elsewhere."

"And some of you resent this?"

"Some of them do. Tell you the truth, I was never here for his parties, and when I did come home, all those people leaving late meant I always found a place right close. The only good thing about Mr. Gilbert, you ask me."

Tell you the truth generally flagged an oncoming lie, but in this case, Kate suspected that the woman did in fact appreciate the convenience. Which meant that her previous cut-off statement, *It wasn't my idea,* was also true.

"Who gave you the petition to circulate, Mrs. Murray?"

But that was one step too far for the night nurse. She drew herself up, fixed Kate with a glare, and replied, "It was my petition, I already told you that, and I won't have you harassing me. If you want to talk to me further, you'll have to arrange it with my lawyer."

And with that, she shut the door.

That wasn't how it worked, and the woman probably didn't have a lawyer, but Kate was well used to indignant witnesses, and she retreated without a second thought.

The chronic parking problem of areas like this, with single-family homes built at a time when a car was a luxury and now divided into three or four apartments, each with its car, meant that people came to blows over a patch of curb. Maybe Gilbert had been shifting his car in his pajamas when an irate neighbor came out to object and things got out of hand. . . . But Kate rejected the scenario as soon as it appeared in her mind: Somebody would have noticed a violent shouting match on the street.

She silently thanked Mrs. Murray and, having completed the circuit of their victim's neighbors, went to sit on the steps of the Gilbert house. Sure enough, the lace curtains on the house across the way twitched slightly, and she smiled to herself as she took out her phone and the Post-it the dancer had given her for Gilbert's possibly Russian housecleaner.

Nika's last name proved to be Kilanovitch, emphasis on the *o,* and her English was somewhat better than Kate had feared. Kilanovitch was saddened to hear of her employer's death, and it sounded to Kate as if the concern over lost income might actually be the secondary concern.

"I afraid something happen, when he not there and I come to clean. I not have key—I only have key when he there, he give me one if he going out, so if door shut on me I not lock out. Is clear, what I say?"

"When you were there and Mr. Gilbert had to go out, he lent you a key in case the door swung shut and locked you out. What day was it that you came to clean and he wasn't there?"

"Thursday. Three day ago. I wait in car, half hour, forty minute, but he not come, I go. I say to husband, maybe should I call police? But he say no, say I should go again maybe Monday and then call. Should have called. He not lying there, when I knock?"

Her voice was so apprehensive that Kate hastened to reassure her.

"Oh, no, don't worry, he died somewhere else."

Kilanovitch had worked for Gilbert for seven years, coming once a week all year except for the period

100

between Christmas and New Year's. Certain tasks were weekly, others—wiping down woodwork, cleaning the windows—were done on rotation throughout the month.

"He was nice man, spend too much time on silly games, but he laugh when I say he need wife, ask me if I want to divorce and marry him. Only joke, you know? Never rude to me, never . . ." Her English deserted her, and she put in a Russian word. Kate figured she was trying to say that Gilbert had never hit on her, and made understanding noises. "I clean, part of silly games. Want me not use vacuum, not if he home, I say okay, you boss. And also want me use, how say?" Again she used a Russian phrase, then tried in English, "Put on furniture, yes?"

"Polish?" Kate offered. "Wax?"

The front door of the house across the way opened, and Simon Wallace came out with his dog on a bright yellow leash. She watched him as Kilanovitch was talking, and was not in the least surprised when, coming out of his gate onto the sidewalk, he made a show of perusing the street, saw Kate, and did a double take worthy of vaudeville. She waved her free hand, he waved back happily with his free arm, and walked on, slowly, down the street.

"Furniture polish, yes. Old kind, come from Europe, cost—phew! Part of game, you know? For the smell?"

"He wanted you to use special cleaning materials in order to make the house smell authentic? Like an old house?"

"Yes! He say, sorry if this a problem, I say no problem for me, *I* not have to pay all that for little bit of wax, but sorry back, because it hard to clean good using just old kind things, mop and broom and rags, you know? So, some days when I finish he say, 'Next week I going to be on walk.' And next week he let me in, he go for walk, I use vacuum not just on top floor but through whole house, rugs and furniture and curtains, then put away vacuum, he come home from walk, everybody happy."

Kate laughed, inexplicably relieved at this indication of Gilbert's mental flexibility and perhaps even humor. A stickler for detail, but willing to turn a blind eye for the sake of practicality, and for the sake of his cleaner's pride.

However, the cleaning woman could tell Kate little about Gilbert's visitors. "He have party there three, four times year. One last month, a Wednesday. He clean before, I clean day after."

"Did he ever have houseguests?"

"One, maybe two times a year."

"What room did the guests stay in?"

"Guest bedroom second floor," she said without hesitation. "Room used twice in year, silly. Waste, you know?"

"I know," Kate agreed. She explained that Kilanovitch would need to sign a statement and provide some fingerprints so they could eliminate her from the household, added her standard request to be called if the woman thought of anything else, and closed the phone, raising her face to the winter sun.

No sign of enemies yet, no greedy relatives, no love life, even.

So why had Philip Gilbert ended up in a deserted gun emplacement on the Marin headlands?

The sun did not tell her, so she dusted herself off and went inside to see how Crime Scene was getting on.

This time, they had turned the study inside out, scrutinizing not just the walls, but the floor, the underside of the desk, and all the room's furniture. Almost immediately, they had discovered the remnants of a bloodstain along the headrest of the tufted leather chair. The chair had been thoroughly wiped (with, it later turned out, an old sponge from the bucket of cleaning supplies kept under the bathroom sink across the hall) but Luminol showed an outline of where the blood had been, a rough smear approximately four inches by two. They found no fingerprints at all along the top of the chair, and only those of Gilbert and one other (who turned out to be the cleaning woman) on the bucket. In fact, there were a limited number of prints from the rest of the top floor as a whole, most of those Gilbert's with an assortment of others in the study itself. The ground-floor rooms gave forth a daunting number, but that would be expected, if he used the rooms as his meeting room and showplace. The basement held an impressive collection of wine, but little else, and most of the surfaces were so dusty that they could not concern the events of the past two weeks.

The sheets on most of the beds had been clean and

unused, the exception being Gilbert's bed on the third floor. Those sheets had shown no indication of sexual activity, and there had been nothing of interest in the laundry basket.

However, on an upper shelf in the closet attached to that same room, the team had found a box of bullets and a can of gun oil. The box was half empty, both it and the can were covered with dust, and the rag draped across the can of oil had not been used in months, possibly years. The bullets were .38s, but they had found no sign of a gun.

"Maybe he just bought them to pound into the wall," Kate suggested, holding the evidence envelope up to the light.

"What?" Crime Scene Maria asked.

"Nothing."

The most promising piece of evidence was the object Kate had spotted between the filing cabinet and the wall: an irregular slip of black porcelain an inch long and a quarter of an inch wide.

"There were also some tiny splinters of the same material in the carpet under the chair," Lo-Tec told her. "We've got those in the vacuum. Although it looks like they cleaned it up pretty thoroughly—nothing in the trash and the vacuum bag has been emptied."

Kate held this evidence bag, too, up to the light and studied the tiny, sharp-sided remnant, seeing the trace of fingerprint powder. "No print?"

"That would've been too lucky."

"We can always wish for some blood and hair?"

"It looks pretty clean, but we'll see."

"Where did you find it?"

He handed her his characteristically neat sketch of the room: rectangular space, door on the left, chair in front of it facing the television on the right-hand wall, desk and computer wrapping around the upper wall, narrow shelf running the squared U shape at the top of the room, a complete wall of bookshelves along the bottom wall. The hidden scrap of black-glazed porcelain had been lodged behind the filing cabinet immediately to the left of a person coming in the door, directly below the shelf holding the awards. If Gilbert had been watching the television, an assailant could have snatched the statue off the shelf, taken one step forward, and swung it right-handed at the seated man's head, which in Gilbert's case would have protruded five or six inches above the top of the chair. His injury had been just behind his temple, indicating that he turned his head as the blow was falling. If the statue had been particularly fragile, pieces of it would have flown in all directions, lodging in Gilbert's garments and hair, the carpets, and the chair. Most of the bits would have fallen down or continued their trajectory to the left, but the killer might well have kicked one chunk out of sight, in back of the filing cabinet, away from the rest and outside the easy reach of a broom. Even if the statue had been too sturdy to shatter into a thousand pieces, clearly it had broken. They would find traces on Gilbert, and they would find it in the clothing of his assailant.

And if they found half-healed cuts along the right hand of a suspect, they would know that the assailant had not worn gloves.

"One last thing," Lo-Tec told Kate. "We're taking the hard drive, but there's one hookup I can't immediately tell what it goes to. The way it's set up, it's like he intended to put a viewer onto the front door that he could check from upstairs, but I can't see any camera there. The wire runs inside the wall, so it's tough to trace. I don't want to bother taking the place apart now, since we'll find where it goes anyway as soon as we get into the hard drive, but I just thought I'd mention it."

"A security camera of some kind?"

"Nanny-cam, front door viewer, webcam, no telling. I'd normally leave the hard drive for our computer guys, but if you think it's important I'll open it up myself and see what I can find. Might take a while."

"How long have you been on?"

"Nine hours. Twelve yesterday."

"It's Sunday afternoon, man. Go home, it'll wait."

"Okay, but if you see a camera lens poking out of somewhere, let us know."

"And if you find a video of someone bashing our guy, don't hesitate to call."

There were no other chunks of black-glazed porcelain, but the team had collected bags of vacuumed evidence from each room, and would see what they found. They collected their evidence bags, packed up the Gilbert computer, carted all the material and equipment out to the van, and Kate locked the Gilbert house behind them not long after five o'clock. The winter sun was still above the horizon.

KATE arrived home to discover Lee and Nora in the kitchen and half the neighborhood in the backyard: Lee had organized a potluck barbecue, including all the usual suspects.

"I hope you don't mind," she said to Kate. "I just couldn't bear to waste the sunlight."

Kate kissed her partner, who tasted of some exotic marinade, and then kitchen assistant Nora, who tasted of cinnamon. "Of course not. I just have to check my e-mail and phone Al, I'll be down in ten minutes."

"Any longer and you get to do the dishes."

Since Kate generally did the dishes anyway, this was not much of a threat. She trotted upstairs and locked her gun away, changed into jeans and a long-sleeved T-shirt, and plopped down in front of the desktop.

Tom Rutland had e-mailed her the promised list of Gilbert's relatives and the members of the Sherlockian dinner club. She had not checked her e-mail that morning, but found that this had been sent off less than two hours after he had left the Gilbert house the night before.

Kate printed the document, and mused over the names of the dining club:

Philip Gilbert
Wendell Bauer
Jeannine Cartfield

Alex Climpson
Soong Li
Ian Nicholson
Geraldine O'Malley
Rajindra Pandi
Thomas Rutland
Johnny Venkatarama

Alphabetical, but for Philip Gilbert, and unlike Gilbert's, which stood unadorned at the top, all the other names were followed by two or three phone numbers, home addresses, places of business, a few fax numbers, and, for six of them, e-mail addresses.

An extraordinarily cooperative lawyer, indeed.

The other e-mails did not seem to be of any importance, so she closed the computer down and punched Al's number on the phone.

"Hey," she said when he answered. "Lee's organizing a barbecue, if you guys aren't doing anything for dinner."

"Yeah, she called and invited us, but we're entertaining some of Jules's friends. Mostly a boy. How'd it go?"

"Crime Scene found blood on the back of Gilbert's armchair—just a little, but they said they'd hurry that one through the lab for us. And I managed to reach most of the neighbors, nothing that jumps out at me from what they had to say—I'll write it up and give it to you tomorrow. And I have the names of the next of kin. Should I call them tonight? The ex-wife's on the East Coast."

"Kind of late. Tomorrow's fine, since the lawyer seemed to think none of them were very close to the man."

"I've got to say, that lawyer of Gilbert's bothers me. He's too helpful by far."

"A helpful lawyer? Definitely suspicious," Al growled. "Let's go arrest him now."

"I don't mean—"

"Yeah, I know. We'll do a search on him tomorrow. Still set for the bank in the morning?"

"I thought I'd go in early and make these calls. Meet me at the office?"

"Will do."

"See you then," Kate said. "Hi to Jules and the others."

"And to Lee."

But before going back downstairs, Kate did a quick search on Thomas Rutland.

He moved along the edges of the Bay Area social elite. He had established himself among the corporate executives of the dot-com boom, which had gone bust but was beginning to show signs of recovery. A cursory glance at the appearances of his name showed that he was a regular at San Francisco social events—one *Chronicle* photograph showed him at a table before the annual Black and White Ball, laughing with five other formally clad power brokers. The only indication that he was not truly one of the blessed was the eagerness of his laugh, and a slight yearning in the arm that stretched along his companion's seat back.

Or perhaps that was Kate's imagination.

As she'd thought, Rutland's legal life dealt with dollars, not with the everyday crimes of drugs, prostitution, and violence. The only sign of conflict she came across in her brief read was the statement that he had divorced three wives, which seemed a bit excessive for a man not yet forty-five.

The doorbell rang, and she made haste to shut the machine down and join the others.

Jon Sampson was just coming in the front door when Kate got downstairs, followed by his partner Sione, who cradled their sleepy two-year-old daughter, Lalu, to his chest. Once upon a time, Jon had been Lee's client, then later her caregiver, in the months after the shooting when she had needed help just to get around. Now he was simply her friend—and Kate's, which still rather surprised her, considering how grating she had once found his personality. The child in Sione's arms stirred, spotted Nora, and flung herself in the direction of the older girl, to spend the next two hours glued to Nora's hip, blond Nora's little Polynesian shadow. Kate handed Jon a beer and his partner a Pellegrino—Sione was a dancer, in constant battle against his own hearty Polynesian genes.

Roz Hall arrived, ordained minister and powerbroker, followed by gorgeous sixteen-year-old Mina, who carried a promising-looking bowl; nine-year-old Satch, whose arms were full of baguettes; and an elderly Mutton, whose graying muzzle was stretched around a soggy tennis ball, and who immediately attached himself to the Nora-Lalu duo. Roz swept through the house and out the kitchen door into the yard, calling out instructions to her children and dog, catching up a glass of wine as she passed, greeting every person with a hug or a kiss or both, then taking over a chair that immediately became the center of the party. She greeted those she knew, shook the hands of the two adults she did not, then launched with her usual panache into her own inimitable brand of News of the Day. However, instead of some juicy tidbit concerning the mayor or City Hall, her first announcement was that Mina had driven them over.

"Well done, Mina," Jon said. "How many bicyclists did you kill on the way?"

"Not one," the girl shot back, "and I missed most of the joggers I was aiming at."

"Better luck on the way home," he commiserated.

"No Maj?" Lee asked Roz, when Roz's partner failed to bring up her customary quiet place behind the rest. Maj—pronounced "My," although her looks were far from Scandanavian—was Mina and Satch's birth mother, an expert on the human brain, and a woman with a history of devotion to shadowy radical causes.

"She's helping out a friend who was in that church in Marin this morning. She's all right, but shaken, as you can imagine. Maj's spending the night with her."

Talk veered in the direction of the catastrophe, but Lee eyed the kids running around at their feet and interposed firmly, "I'm sure there'll be more about it in the papers tomorrow." Obediently, they turned to other things.

"How's the new hizzoner, Roz?" Jon asked.

"Surprising us all," she admitted. San Francisco's new mayor had looked so clean-cut and talked so correctly, everyone had assumed that, Democrat or not, he would tug the city back toward the right. Instead, even the most fearful of pundits were admitting to a cautious optimism, Roz among them. Maj had told Lee, who had told Kate, that Roz was spending a considerable amount of time with the man, a task she appeared to find more energizing than frustrating, rare with politicians. The mayor seemed honestly interested in what his city had to tell him, and in Roz, he found a voice both articulate and experienced.

Before the last election, rumors had made their way around the city that Reverend Roz Hall would cast her hat into the ring. Everyone who was anyone in the city considered themselves a friend of Roz's; a few of them even were. Kate, too, had considered herself a friend until Roz, and especially Maj, had skirted far too close to felonious acts for a cop's taste. But that was nine years ago, when Maj was pregnant with Satch. With Roz's burn scars as a visible reminder of consequences, and the sobering effects of motherhood, Maj had stepped back from the borderlands of activism. Over the last year or two, Kate had begun to relax and see them socially again, brought together by Lee, the children (Mina sometimes babysat Nora), Maj's apparent reformation, and most of all by Maj's cancer scare the year before.

Kate wondered how Roz had kept the scandal out of

the newspapers. To this day, few people even suspected that public office would blow up in Roz's face and peel her family wide open: Kate had never heard so much as a whisper linking Maj with the group of feminist vigilantes that had set the entire city on its ears. But the tie was there, if more philosophical than purely criminal, and since that episode, Roz had seemed content to play the role of backroom powerhouse in the city's politics. However, it was beginning to sound as if the new mayor might be Roz's conduit back into the center of things.

The fish and vegetable kebabs came off the grill just before six o'clock; two minutes later, the phone in Kate's pocket began to chirp. She checked the display, and abandoned her place in line. "Sorry," she murmured, and took the phone into the house to talk to Chris Williams.

They'd caught the shooter, who in the end turned his gun on himself, but now all available personnel had been brought in to work the two crime scenes. Marin had the church scene, but the scene where the suicide occurred was on park land, and Williams was needed.

"Look, Chris, don't worry about Gilbert, I've got it."

"Gilbert, right, I couldn't remember his name—I was thinking of him as Pajama Man." Williams's voice was hoarse with prolonged tension and fatigue, a state Kate knew all too well. "What do you think?"

"There's a good chance he died in his own house, certainly better than the chance he was killed on your turf." She told him about the missing statue that had prompted the summons for Crime Scene, and went over their preliminary findings with him—hard results would be days, even weeks in coming, but one thing was certain: There had been blood on the back of the chair.

"Okay," he said. "My illegal disposal case can wait. Keep me informed, and let me know when you're going to be in the park; if I'm free I'll join you."

In the meantime, Pajama Man was all theirs.

FOUR

First thing Monday morning, Kate and Al were facing their lieutenant across his desk in the fourth-floor Homicide Detail, presenting their review of the case thus far. It was not one of their more satisfactory briefings, since they had no answer to his insistent question of why the Park had given it to San Francisco in the first place. However, the Park CIB had done so, and considering the events of Sunday morning, the option of the SFPD passing it back to Marin did not seem a great idea. He subsided, with grumbles about his own briefing to the captain later that morning, and let them get on with their jobs.

Back at her cubicle in the cluttered Detail, Kate phoned the numbers Rutland had given her for Gilbert's known family members. The immediate reaction of the Boston ex-wife, whose name was Corina Ferguson, was "Who?" Her second question, despite Rutland's assurances that the woman would expect nothing, concerned the inheritance. Kate suggested she contact Gilbert's lawyer, asked who would be claiming the body, and was not in the least surprised when the woman reacted with distaste.

"Why would I want to claim Philip's body?" she asked. "I haven't even heard from him in years. Let his friends bury him out there."

Hawkin, who had been doing his own hunt into the lawyer's past, spoke up from the adjacent desk. "Only thing I see on Rutland is three divorces and a couple of complaints from families of old people who died and left him generous thank-yous in their wills."

"Any indication of the grounds for divorce?"

"Looks to me like he was marrying up. Not necessarily money, but each woman had a bigger circle of important friends."

"Neither of those things is illegal," Kate commented, although both indicated that Rutland was none too rigid in his personal, or professional, code of ethics. She went back to her calls.

The Midwestern cousin sounded more sympathetic at first, but it did not take long for Kate to realize that it was feeblemindedness, not sympathy, and that the elderly woman had little or no concept of who Philip Gilbert was. Kate thanked her and gave the woman her number—a process that took nearly ten minutes, between the search for a pencil, a second search for a piece of paper, and the sounds of the woman wandering vaguely through the kitchen opening the refrigerator and filling a glass before she either remembered her caller or noticed the phone off the hook.

The two Texas nieces were more vigorous than the cousin and more concerned than the ex-wife, but neither volunteered to fly out to San Francisco to claim the body, and both found it difficult to remember when they had last heard from Gilbert apart from his annual Christmas card—no message, just signed. She gave them both her number, then Rutland's, and finally called the lawyer himself, to tell him that it looked like he'd be in charge of choosing cremation or burial, funeral or memorial service. He didn't sound very surprised.

Her next call was to the Medical Examiner's office, to inform them that there wouldn't be a family member coming to identify the body, and they should either use Gilbert's lawyer or send for Gilbert's dental records. The ME's assistant she talked to was a little vague about the body, although in the end she was definite that the autopsy wouldn't be that morning.

With that out of the way, they could begin to organize their case. Two things were basic here: a time frame and a list of Gilbert's known associates. While Hawkin was putting together everything they knew about the former, Kate compiled a list from Rutland's e-mail and started on the names in the ledger they'd found in the safe. Many of those appeared regularly, sometimes in the "bought from" column, other times in the "sold to." An incestuous little world, that of collectors. Which helped when one of them was killed.

If one of them was killed: Kate shot a brief glare at the

telephone, knowing full well that she and Al might be devoting days of work to lay the ground for a mere illegal body disposal case. If they'd been more pressed, they might be justified in moving a little slowly on the Gilbert case, at least until the Medical Examiner got around to giving them a pronouncement on cause. However, though at times she and Al juggled as many as thirty or forty open homicides, things had been slack recently in the homicide business, and Gilbert's was the only call they'd caught during the week's cycle. Pajama Man was in the center of their plate.

"The neighbor de la Veaga didn't have any definite times for the afternoon when it came to Gilbert's car?" Hawkin asked.

"Just the one in the late morning."

"Why don't people look at their watches?" complained the man who didn't even wear one.

According to the ledger, Gilbert had bought the pricey magazine in the first week of October for $139,500. Two columns over, the appraised value notation was:

$300,000 (est.)

"Can you imagine paying a hundred forty thousand dollars for an old magazine?" she asked Hawkin.

He raised an eyebrow at that, but only for a moment. "Bad as stamp collecting," he noted, and went back to his papers.

Kate's list of Gilbert's close associates ended up with a little over fifty names on it. She turned to the computer and printed off whatever she could find about the people. A few of them had criminal records, mostly small stuff. Twenty-three of them had websites, which made sense as most of those bought and sold online, and most of those home pages gave some degree of personal information. One of the dinner club members, Jeannine Cartfield, wrote mystery novels, although she hadn't published in three and a half years. Two of the antiquarian dealers had criminal records more serious than traffic violations or teenage pot possession, although both of those crimes were white-collar: one had sold a forgery, the other had run a scam to sell a painting several times over. She set aside for the moment those over the age of sixty, who might have had a problem carrying Gilbert's inert body. With them she put most of those living overseas or on the other side of the country. Finally she added the people her gut told her would be a waste of time: Surely a woman named Amanda Blessing who sold limited-production bone china teasets painted with the images of classical mystery characters was an unlikely suspect, even if she was only thirty-two and lived two hours away in Modesto.

That left her with the nine living members of the dinner club, ten West Coast dealers, six of Gilbert's closest neighbors, and four others.

Hawkin saw her sit back to survey her work, and dragged his chair over to her desk.

"Looks like Friday the twenty-third to Sunday the twenty-fifth are the days we need to look at," he told her. "The neighbor sees his car come and go on the

Friday, although the last time she's sure about is late morning. He makes various phone calls that afternoon, but only one on Saturday morning, from his cell phone. That follows his general phoning pattern, which is mostly during business hours, with very few calls on the weekends. But on Monday morning, when he tends to make a lot of calls—see, Monday the nineteenth there are fifteen, Monday the twelfth, eighteen—this Monday there are none at all, and four messages left on his machine. And looking at the dates on the mail, I'd guess he wasn't there to see Saturday's delivery, although you can never be sure with the Post Office."

"Friday and Saturday," Kate repeated. "That gives us a starting place. Nothing on your list ring any bells?"

"Nope. Even Rutland came up squeaky clean."

"Highly suspicious," Kate said darkly.

"You want to get started on these interviews, or take off for the headlands?"

"Neither—let's go to the bank first. I've got to see what a magazine worth one hundred forty thousand looks like."

Philip Gilbert's bank was a five-minute walk from his front door. Kate and Al presented themselves to the manager, explained the situation, handed him their warrant, and followed him to the vault.

Inside a protective box, underneath a careful cellophane wrapping, the prized *Beeton's Annual* looked like, well, like an old magazine. It was a little smaller than a *National Geographic*, with a once-garish cover in red and yellow picturing a man at a desk, stretching toward the light hanging over his head. If Kate had seen the thing lying on a hearth, she would not have hesitated to rip it up as a convenient fire starter. She looked at the ledger, which they had brought along for comparison, and it did indeed say under the appraised value column: $300,000 (est).

She laid the magazine back into its box, put a tick next to its description in the ledger, and pulled away the bubble wrap from the next item, a photograph of Queen Victoria in a worn wooden frame. They saw several more magazines, half a dozen old books, some pieces of jewelry, an old-looking typescript short story or novella in a clear plastic envelope, three pipes, and a sheaf of signed photographs, one of which showed a stocky, middle-aged man with a large mustache, dressed in outdoor tweeds.

"I think this is Conan Doyle," she said, turning it toward Hawkin. He studied the figure—who looked, she realized, like a distant relation of his—then went back to the loose photographs of opera singers and writers, most of them signed, each of them separated from its neighbor by a sheet of tissue.

The arcane contents of the deposit box gave no insight into their owner's death, however, other than the staggering sum of their appraised value. The bank had no doubt been chosen for its proximity to home, for visits to the vault were a regular part of Gilbert's business week. He had come here twice during the week he had died, on Monday the nineteenth in the afternoon, and the morning of Friday the twenty-third. On

Monday he had left behind slips of paper recording the dispatch of items to Sotheby's auction house for appraisal and to a gentleman in London for approval; on the Friday he had made a notation on the outside of the manila envelope containing the typescript short story, "to Mr. Ian Nicholson for analysis."

Kate showed the envelope to Hawkin. "Does this mean that on Friday the twenty-third, Gilbert sent a copy of this to Ian Nicholson? Or does it mean that he meant to give this envelope to him, and didn't get around to it?"

But Al could only shake his head. "Nicholson is the friend who the lawyer thinks is out of town."

"And who left two messages on Gilbert's machine during the week."

Kate stripped off her gloves and took out her phone, saw by its display that reception was shrouded by the bank, and closed it again.

"Do you want to take any of this in as evidence?" she asked Hawkin.

"I really don't," he said with feeling. Stashing evidence with the property clerk was one thing; leaving solid gold there was another. "Let's just seal the box and make sure the bank knows they're not to let anyone into it."

When they had finished and were back on the street, she took out her phone again, got Nicholson's number from the list she'd compiled, and listened to a polite English accent suggesting that she be so kind as to leave a message. She did, and closed the phone. Al was also talking on his, speaking to the Medical Examiner's office about the autopsy of Philip Gilbert. She looked around, saw a coffee shop, and tapped on Hawkin's elbow to gesture that she would meet him there.

She had her latte and his café Americana (plain black coffee given a fancy name and price) on the table in the corner when he entered, looking disgusted.

"Not good?" she asked him.

"Turns out the reason the ME's assistant was a little uncertain about the autopsy is that Marin hasn't even brought the body over yet—he's in their storage locker, and now they're too busy to bring him over to us. And because he didn't land here, the ME doesn't even have paperwork on him."

"In other words, Marin's pissed at us. You want to hire a U-Haul and go get him?"

"I talked to one of the drivers, told him he could have my sister in marriage if he managed to get us the body today."

"You don't have a sister."

"So I lied."

"Okay, you want to tackle the headlands interviews today, or the friends-of-Gilbert?"

"I'd say we start with Gilbert's life, rather than how his body was dumped."

"Fine with me." Kate laid a copy of her list of known associates on the table. "Here's a beginning on Gilbert's circle of nonfriends. The family's a little out of reach, and I don't know that we can question his business contacts until we know more about what he had going.

Which leaves us the Sherlockian dinner club—nine members: Rutland we've talked to, Nicholson's out of town. How do you want to approach these?"

He looked at the addresses: two at the western side of the South Bay, three to the north of the East Bay. It was going to take them all day just to cover the ground.

"You want to split up?" she asked.

"Somehow I can't picture a member of a Sherlock Holmes dinner club coming to the door with a shotgun in his hand," Hawkin said. "You want to go it alone on the out-of-town names? We can get them out of the way today, meet up and do the San Francisco names after."

"Fine with me. You want the peninsula or the East Bay?"

"I'll take Berkeley and Napa, you can have Palo Alto and Sunnyvale. We'll meet up for the two in the city."

Kate circled the names Geraldine O'Malley and Rajindra Pandi, then noticed a link she hadn't caught before. "Venkatarama lives in Berkeley, but he works at the same address as Pandi. They'll probably both be there now."

"Fine, I'll just do Alex Climpson in Napa, circle over to Berkeley for Wendell Bauer, and come back for Jeannine Cartfield and Soong Li. Call me when you get back in town," Al said, and left her to pay for the coffee.

GERALDINE O'Malley might have been given a name straight out of Blarney, but the woman Kate tracked down in her real estate office on the outskirts of Palo Alto looked about as Irish as Jon's Samoan partner

Sione Kalefu. Kate assumed that it was her mother who had been the African-American in the mix, with her father providing the O'Malley, but California was too full of ethnic blends for it to be a sure bet, or even to matter much. She merely introduced herself and asked O'Malley if there was somewhere they could talk.

Wordlessly, the sturdy woman with the tidy dreads and pantsuit led Kate into a sort of boardroom office with an oval table and a dozen chairs. She shut the door and stood, braced for Kate's explanation.

"I'm with the San Francisco Police Department, assigned to look into the death of Philip Gilbert."

O'Malley blinked: She hadn't expected the name, looked almost relieved at it. "Philip. Yes, certainly. Look, why don't we sit down?" She pulled the nearest chair away from the gleaming table and went around to sit on one facing it. Kate took the seat.

"You looked surprised when I said why I was here," she told the woman.

"Did I? Yes, I suppose I did. I just, well, it's my nephew. He's a problem kid and he hasn't been seen in a couple of days, I was afraid . . . But Philip. Yes, God, what a tragedy."

"You heard about his death, then?"

"Of course. Tom Rutland—you know Tom?" Kate nodded. "Of course you do. Tom called me about it on Saturday night, and said someone might be by to talk with me. I guess I'd expected you before this, so it had sort of left my mind. Anyway, what can I tell you?"

"When did you last see Mr. Gilbert?"

"I went to the dinner at his house, the first Wednesday in January. I haven't seen him since then."

"What about talking with him, communicating by e-mail?"

"No. Oh, wait a minute, there was a thing. Maybe a week later, there was something in the paper, a rumor about a lost Sherlock Holmes story. It came without comment, but I'm pretty sure it was from Philip. You want me to check?"

"In a minute. But first, tell me something about Philip Gilbert," Kate suggested. "Help me get a sense of him. Did you like him?"

"Did I like him? I suppose so, although he could be pretty abrasive at times. It helped if you didn't take him too seriously."

"He seems to have taken this Sherlock Holmes business quite seriously, himself."

"He wasn't all light and fun, that's for sure. But Jeannie—Jeannie Cartfield? She and I had a good time, tweaking the boys. A lot of BSI scions—branches of the main Sherlockian group—are men-only, in other parts of the country, and she and I belong to a couple of the women-only ones. But here, they integrated a long time ago."

"Tell me about the dinner club."

"It's mostly just that. We eat dinner, usually at some restaurant that we think Holmes might have enjoyed— you know, hearty English fare, beef and potatoes and cream poured onto the desserts. Every so often we pick an ethnic one, on the argument that Holmes would have eaten curry, say, on the London docks. You do get tired of beef and boiled vegetables."

"But sometimes you meet at the home of one of the members?"

"Three of the men like to host dinners, Philip was one of those. They'd choose a menu, one or two of us would go early and help, but it's a lot of work, and ten people takes a sizeable dining room. Those of us who live in apartments have trouble with that, so we scrub carrots and set the tables. Personally, I rather enjoy having the men wait on me."

"The dinner last month was at Philip's house."

"Yep, with the full English fare: standing rib roast, Yorkshire pudding, Brussels sprouts, roast potatoes, candied carrots. Trifle for dessert, and a couple of very nice wines."

"Sounds great," Kate commented, reflecting that breakfast had been a long time ago. "Philip cooked?"

"He and Jeannie."

Kate eyed the woman, her attention caught by the noncommittal flatness of the response. "Did Philip and Jeannine Cartfield have a relationship?"

"We all had a relationship. We were the Strand Diners."

"I meant—"

"Yes, Detective, I know what you meant. The two of them were closer in some ways than the rest of us. But that may have been because they'd known each other for so many years. They went to college together, what, thirty years ago? If you're asking me if they were sleeping together, I'm sorry, you'll have to ask Jeannie that. They are both private people. Were, in Philip's case."

"Remarkably private," Kate agreed. "So much so, it's difficult to get a clear image of him. What would you say he was like?"

O'Malley sat for a minute, twisting the ring she wore on the index finger of her right hand. "He was sad, in a way. Oh, I know that a lot of people would say that about most of us Holmes fans, but really, we just have fun with it. But with Philip, it was something else. It was his job, sure, but more than that, he took it all extremely seriously. He took it personally if someone made a mistake about one of the stories during one of the dinners, as if our lack of seriousness was a failure on his part."

"Sounds a bit hard to live with."

"I guess it does. But it wasn't like he was scolding us or anything, he was always good at making a game out of it. It was more like you could feel his pain, if you'll pardon the cliché. Making a goof was like, I don't know, stepping on your partner's toe when you're dancing, maybe. Any teacher expects to get stepped on a lot, but that doesn't make the toes any happier. Philip was a mile better than any of us at the game, but I think he honestly took great pleasure in turning us all into better players."

"What do you mean by 'the game'?"

"Immersing yourself in the world of Sherlock Holmes. Treating Holmes and his fellows as more real than Conan Doyle was, conversing about the stories as if they were historical fact. Some Holmes groups insist on scrupulously accurate costumes and Victorian speech, but we only don costume some of the time. Dinner at Philip's was always in costume. Which is fun, but damned uncomfortable. You have any idea what those dresses weigh? And the hats—to say nothing of what the corsets do to your ribs! God. The men have it easy."

"Would you have said that Philip had any enemies?"

The left hand fiddling with the ring went still, and O'Malley looked at Kate. "So it's true, that he was murdered?"

"We really don't know at this point, but we're proceeding under the assumption that he was."

"Philip handled some extremely valuable items. Some of which were things that people had strong feelings about, completely apart from their monetary value—there was a very private and personal note from Conan Doyle to his second wife that Philip sold a while back, with a lot of controversy, because people thought he shouldn't have made it public. Certainly Philip had rivals. Whether some of those turned into enemies, I wouldn't know. His sort of collection was way too rich for my blood."

"Did he show you his copy of that magazine?"

"The *Beeton's Annual*? Yes, he showed it to us at the dinner after he'd bought it, in October I think it was. I wouldn't even touch it, knowing what it was worth. He's got something else, too. I don't know what it is, but he said something in passing during the January dinner, that he might not have to sell the *Annual* after all."

"Was he thinking of selling it?"

"Even for Philip, I gather that was a lot of working capital to have tied up in one object. I know he'd been eyeing a couple of things that came onto the market, but after buying the *Annual*, he couldn't quite swing the price. He was torn, because the *Beeton's Annual* made his collection authoritative in a way it would not have been without it."

"How is it 'authoritative'?"

"An already rare piece, in pristine condition, and signed by Doyle: Nobody has that. Nobody in the world. If this is genuine, and if the signature is not a forgery, it would be absolutely unique. Yes, it's price-less—by which I mean enormously valuable, but beyond that, the magazine puts its owner on the map. As collections go, Philip's was very, very good—he even had two original manuscript stories by Doyle; with this copy of *Beeton's Annual*, his collection shoots to the top of the heap. If, that is, he could afford to hang on to it."

"And this other thing he'd found, that would have made it possible to keep the magazine?"

"That was the impression I got. No details, just one of his raised eyebrows and a knowing look. But for Philip, that was excitement."

"Would he have told anyone what it was?"

"If he had, it would have been Tom, Ian, or Jeannie."

"He was closest to them, then?"

"He worked most closely with them, certainly."

"The way people talk about Gilbert makes him sound inaccessible. Aloof."

"He was. But like I said, there was a sadness there. I don't know where it came from, but something in his past was painful. He never talked about his past at all. I only know what university he went to because Jeannie told me."

"I see. So you never, oh, I don't know, went with him to Marin on a wine tour?"

"With Philip? No, I'd have a hard time imagining that."

"But he was into wine, he had a lot of expensive-looking bottles in his basement."

"Yes, but I can't imagine him hanging out in wineries talking about nose and overtones."

"Do you go up to Marin often? Not necessarily to the wineries?"

"I have family in Santa Rosa, a cousin I see a couple times a year. Why?"

"I just wondered if you knew the headlands at all."

"That's where he was found, wasn't it? No, it's one of those places I keep meaning to explore, and never have."

"Well, thank you for seeing me. If you think of any-thing else, please call me." She asked O'Malley for her fingerprints, to eliminate her from the prints in Gilbert's house, and got them without objection. She handed O'Malley one of her cards, and the woman walked her to the door.

"You'd be welcome to join the Strand Diners this Wednesday, Detective. As my guest if nothing else."

"You've decided to go ahead with it, then? Tom Rutland didn't know what the others would want to do."

"We thought we might. As a wake, if nothing else."

"Thank you, but I've got some family commitments Wednesday night," Kate lied easily.

O'Malley looked at her sideways, her face suddenly transformed by an unexpected sparkle. "Probably for the best. Rajindra and Johnny want us to solve the case among ourselves."

"Thank you for the warning," Kate told her, returning the grin. Which faded as soon as she had left the office. All she needed was a collection of earnest Sherlockian amateur sleuths running around in their deerstalkers and magnifying glasses. And here she'd thought the press might pass on this case.

RAJINDRA Pandi and Johnny Venkatarama were business partners and, apparently, some sort of distant or honorary cousins on their mothers' sides. She found them at their office in Sunnyvale, in one of those sprawling and featureless office parks that could conceal the next earthshaking discovery or a stash of terrorist weaponry. In this case, she was not exactly sure what the office held, other than a receptionist who answered the phone with the phrase "Diagram Research."

Whatever Diagram Research entailed, it did not require a large staff. Its blank front was broken by a door, which to Kate's surprise was not locked. Inside was an entrance foyer with a glass back wall, through which could be seen a second room with an angular leather-and-steel sofa, two paintings, and a receptionist with a desk. The woman was wearing a thick sweater and reading a book, and she looked up, startled, at the movement in her outer room. Kate tried that door's knob, found it locked, searched for a speaker, failed to see one, and held her badge up to the glass. The woman took one hand from her book and reached below the surface of the desk. A buzzer sounded, and Kate leaned against the door. She had to put some effort into it, and the air sucked and swirled as the door popped open.

"Good afternoon," she said. "I'm looking for Rajindra Pandi and Johnny Venkatarama."

"They're busy," the woman said.

"This is an official matter."

"You'll have to make an appointment."

"I'm not going to make an appointment, I just need a few minutes."

The woman was so nonplussed she laid her book down on the desk and stared at the intruder. Kate just stood before her and returned her gaze, until the woman finally picked up the phone.

"Mr. Pandi? I have a policewoman here who wants to see you and Mr. V.—I don't know."

"Tell him it's about the death of Philip Gilbert," Kate said.

"She says it's about the death of Philip Gilbert," the receptionist parroted. After a moment, her eyebrows rose and she hung up the phone. "You can go in," she said, sounding astonished; her job, clearly, was less to receive visitors than to repel them.

The third room contained the remaining staff of Diagram Research, two young men with black hair and brown skin, whose desks faced each other across a remarkably bare room. On each desk was a mirror arrangement of computer, printer, and telephone; on the wall to the left of the entrance was a clean whiteboard laid with four colors of pen; but on the wall opposite were two doors, one of them steel, from behind which came the low hum of machinery. Combined with the temperature of the suite and the air-filtering foyer, Kate suspected serious amounts of mainframe in close proximity. Hawkin's stepdaughter Jules might be able to figure out what Diagram Research did; Kate wasn't even going to ask.

"Mr. Pandi?" she asked. The slightly more solid young man on the far side lifted his finger, and she walked across to shake his hand and introduce herself. "And you must be Mr. Venkatarama?" she said, going to the other. Both men seemed rather taken aback, at her presence or at her handshake she did not know. She looked around: no spare chairs. Pandi saw her gaze, and stood up, walking over to the nonsteel door on the back wall and coming out with a plastic chair. He stood indecisively, then put it down halfway between the two desks, and went back to his own chair.

Neither man had said a word.

"I am investigating the death of Mr. Philip Gilbert,

whose body was found on Saturday up in Marin. I believe you were friends of his?"

Finally, Venkatarama stirred. "We had shared interests, we enjoyed his company, so yes, I suppose we were friends." Other than the precision of his words, his accent was straight California.

"How did you meet him?"

Pandi answered. "There was reference to the Strand Diners in one of the chat rooms fifteen months ago. Sherlock Holmes chat rooms," he clarified for her; unlike his cousin's, Pandi's voice was accented, melodious and Indian. "We researched its members, arranged to be invited as guests, and found the company pleasing. We are regular attendees, even though the actual menus are rarely to our taste. We do not eat meat," he explained.

"When was the last time you saw Mr. Gilbert?" she asked him, but it seemed to be Venkatarama's turn, so her head swiveled back in his direction.

"We saw him at the January dinner, on the seventh. It was at his home."

"Dead cow, yet again," his cousin noted sadly.

"And you haven't been in communication since then?"

"No," said Venkatarama.

"Yes," said Pandi.

The cousins looked at each other, and Pandi explained, "We had an e-mail, a group mailing to the dinner group, perhaps two weeks ago, concerning an article in the newspaper. Philip forwarded it on to us all."

134

"Ah," said his cousin. "That must have been your day for the e-mail, so I did not see it."

Satisfied, the two sets of dark eyes turned back to Kate expectantly.

"An article in the paper?" she queried.

"Not even an article, a mere mention of three or four lines, a rumor some woman picked up at a party concerning yet another 'lost Sherlock Holmes manuscript.' Sometimes such things are mildly amusing; this was not even that."

"But he thought it worth telling you about."

"Philip often did so. We all do. But in this case, there was nothing personal from him, merely the mention."

"When you saw him, on the seventh, did he seem at all different? Upset, preoccupied, excited?"

"The meeting was at his house, which always exaggerates a person's normal behavior. Philip was as he generally is."

"Perhaps a smidgen more pedantic, a touch more authoritative," Venkatarama suggested.

Pandi considered this, then nodded. "Perhaps a little. I might even say condescending."

Kate broke in before the cousins could get involved in a thesaurus duel. "Have you any idea why?"

The cousins locked eyes, as if in telepathic discussion. After a minute, Pandi suggested, "He was that way in October, when he finally got his hands on the *Beeton's Annual*."

"You are right," said the other. "Lofty and set apart from mere mortals."

"Sounds annoying," Kate said: conflict among the Sherlockians?

"Perhaps," Pandi admitted. "He would invariably prove generous with his good fortune, and permit everyone to take pleasure in his trophy, but Philip was in the end goal-oriented. He was, to his mind, the keeper of a shrine, and had little outside his possessions. For those of us who have family, interests, lives, his attitude could be a touch . . . claustrophobic."

Kate was taken aback, and realized that she'd fallen into the trap of seeing this sterile place and the fantasy world of the dinner club as the entirety of the two men's existence.

Looking at the even brown gaze across the desk, she wondered if Pandi had seen this, and chosen his words deliberately. Seeing the tiny smile on his face, she knew he had.

"Do either of you know of any friends Mr. Gilbert might have had outside the dinner club?"

The dark eyes consulted, to a count of five, then Pandi said to his cousin, "There was that woman."

"I still think it was Jeannine."

Pandi did not answer, but instead said to Kate, "Perhaps three months ago, we saw Philip driving with a woman in the car. However, it was only a glimpse, and the passenger side was away from us. She appeared to be wearing a hat of some kind as well, so it could have been anyone."

"But you thought it was a woman?"

"We did. Looking back, I do not know why."

"The hat," Venkatarama said. "And the gesture." To Kate he explained, "The colors the passenger wore would have been unlikely on a man, and in addition, she was making a hand gesture as they passed, a rather feminine motion."

"When was this, do you remember?"

"The weekend before Christmas," Pandi spoke up. "Either Saturday the twentieth or Sunday the twenty-first. We took our families to the city to see the *Nutcracker*, staying the night."

"I think it was the Sunday, when we were in Union Square," Venkatarama said.

"Sunday, December twenty-first," Kate repeated, dutifully writing it down, although she doubted it had anything to do with the case.

"And she was in his house," Pandi added.

Venkatarama shook his head, disagreeing. "We cannot know that for certain," but Kate was staring at Pandi.

"Why do you say that?" she asked him.

"She—or someone in a woman's shoes—passed by the HolmesCam that afternoon." His accent gave the name three syllables, so it took Kate a minute.

"The Holmes . . . ?"

"HolmesCam. That's what Philip called it, although others had rude names for it. Johnny and I call it the Spying Eye of Sherlock. Do you not know of it?"

"Perhaps you'd better explain."

"A webcam link, to Philip's sitting room."

Lo-Tec had thought it would be a nanny-cam, or

security monitor—*if you see a camera lens poking out of somewhere, let us know.* "We found the hookup, but we hadn't got around to the site itself yet. It's a camera operating in the living room?"

By way of answer, Pandi hit some buttons on his desktop and swiveled the screen around to Kate.

The comfortable chair, the fireplace, the littered tables, the drinks tray, in living color, a clock at the bottom frozen at 14:43.

"This is not live?"

"Not now, the feed went down on Sunday afternoon. Philip generally set it up to replay one event or another, such as one of the dinner parties. Many people use the website for their desktop."

"The camera sees everything?"

"Only in this room, and not if Philip tripped the off switch near the door, at which time it would loop back, as I said, into a recording. Generally one where something interesting was happening."

"The January dinner was on, last I saw," said Venkatarama.

"The camera saw you, last weekend," Pandi told Kate.

"Me?"

"Oh yes." He turned the screen back to his side, typing as he continued, "You and a man. Your presence created quite a buzz on the comments. Nobody could figure out who these anachronisms were." Kate went around behind him. Up came a website home page with an etching of what could only be Sherlock Holmes, superimposed by the name of her victim. Pandi chose one of the site's pages, and the sitting room came on, stills of the room with dates going back over the past year down the left side. He chose the previous Saturday's date, and asked, "Do you remember what time you were there?"

"From four-thirty to about eight," she said weakly.

He chose 18:30, then went rapidly forward through the unchanging display of furniture and cold fireplace until a sudden flash of motion broke onto the screen. He slowed, and sat to one side so she could see.

A rather puzzled-looking woman with hair in need of a cut stood in the doorway, surveying the room. After a minute, she walked over to the chair, her movement jerky in the camera, and sat, taking out her cell phone. She slumped into the chair, legs crossed and one foot bouncing as she talked, her eyes moving up and down all the while. At one point, the eyes seemed to lock onto the camera, then passed on. The lens was concealed up near the ceiling in the corner near the dining room.

"No sound?" Kate asked.

"No, just the camera."

Thank God for small favors, she thought. "Okay," she told him, not wanting to watch the rest of her conversation with Lee, or Chris Williams's entrance.

"Do you want to see some of the dinner party?"

"Sure," she told him. She was only half aware of Venkatarama bringing her chair around for her.

The camera was arranged so the fireplace was center screen, a person sitting in the frayed chair dead in the middle of the picture, the bullet holes of "V. R." clear on the wall overhead. The very right edge of the screen was defined by the velvet curtains which, even pulled back, allowed no glimpse of the outside world onscreen. On the left was the doorway to the hall, with the front door invisible beyond it. If someone came in the door and went directly upstairs, the camera would only catch passing feet. Kate opened her mouth to request to see the person they had seen that weekend in December, but then the screen filled and she forgot what she was going to ask.

It might have been a scene out of Victorian England. Half a dozen people in old-fashioned dress chatted and laughed, glasses of sparkling wine in their hands. The men wore formal evening wear, and Kate would have bet money that their bow ties had been hand-knotted. There was only one woman, a regal figure in her early fifties, graying blond hair swept into an elaborate hairdo, dressed in a black-and-white gown as severe as the men's evening wear.

Some noise came from offscreen, causing two or three of the heads to turn. A back passed through the crowd, heading toward the front door. "That is Philip," Pandi said. The man disappeared, and a minute later came back with Geraldine O'Malley, dressed in an enormous bustled gown made of what looked like upholstery material. She walked into the room, clearly knowing everyone there, and accepted the glass one of the men took from a silver tray and held out to her.

The tall man came back into the room, and Kate

asked, "Can you pause it?"

Pandi obediently stopped the motion, and she leaned forward to look at the animate version of the man she had first seen crumpled on a dirty concrete floor.

Philip Gilbert was indeed tall and slim, but whereas she'd always sort of pictured Sherlock Holmes as skinny, pale, and nerdy, the Gilbert version of the man was simply elegant. Gilbert was not handsome, his features too sharp for conventional good looks, but he was so self-assured that a person couldn't help finding him attractive. He moved into the room the epitome of the host—calm, solicitous, interested, and clearly wanting nothing but for his guests to enjoy themselves. The video had paused just as Gilbert reached the group in front of the fire, and his face wore an expression of intelligence and humor, as if he was about to hear the punch line of a joke he'd heard once before, but liked well enough to listen to again.

"Can you give me the URL for that?" she asked. Pandi touched keys, and an invisible motor started to whine. He pulled open the lower drawer in his desk and lifted out a piece of paper printed with the picture of Philip Gilbert and, at the top, the address of the site.

"Thank you. Tell me, do you know Marin well?"

The two men wordlessly consulted, then Pandi answered, "Not well, I think. Our wives like to go to a spa in St. Helena, one of those with mud baths and massages, and once talked us into going. I think we spent the day playing golf, wasn't it?"

His cousin nodded.

"I just wondered if you might have any idea why Philip was over at the Marin headlands," she said, but they could suggest no reason.

"Okay, that's about it— Oh, just one last thing. Can I ask where you were Friday and Saturday a week ago— the twenty-third and twenty-fourth?"

"A conference in Anaheim," Pandi answered. "We went down with our families on the Wednesday and came back on Sunday. Do you want the name of the hotel?"

She collected the relevant information that would allow her to check alibis if she wanted, although she had a feeling she needn't bother, asked for and received their fingerprints, and laid a couple of business cards on the pristine desk. "Thank you, gentlemen, I won't take up any more of your time. Please let me know if anything else comes to mind."

Outside the offices, the world seemed a remarkably warm and soft-edged place. She looked over her notes, to make sure she hadn't missed anything. None of the three witnesses had set any of her bells off: Their eyes had not suddenly shifted when she mentioned Marin, they had not started to sweat when she asked about Philip Gilbert's irritating habits, none of them had slipped by revealing they knew more about the circumstances of his discovery than they should. Of course, they were all very bright people, as bright as Tom Rutland was, and in addition they had spent years thinking about criminal behavior, even if it was in the realm of fiction.

She took out her phone, driven as much by the wish to talk to a familiar voice as by mere necessity. However, she just got Hawkin's voice mail, and had to be satisfied with leaving a message.

"Al, I'm finished here, I'm going to start back now. Give me a ring when you're free."

Al's return call caught her on the freeway, and he suggested they meet for a late lunch. She knew a place not far from the one address still on the list, and found him at a table when she walked in.

They ordered and Kate told him about her two interviews. Al in turn described a completely uninformative conversation with Alex Climpson, a winery supervisor, who had also last seen Gilbert at the dinner party and last heard from him on the sixteenth about the piece in the newspaper, and seemed to have no particular feelings about Gilbert one way or the other. Wendell Bauer, a grad student in history at Cal, was the newest member of the Diners, having joined it in November and missed the December meeting due to the flu. Bauer, too, had little light to shed on the matter of Gilbert's death.

Because traffic had been light and the conversations even lighter, Al had managed to fit one of the San Francisco residents into his schedule. Soong Li had been in touch with Gilbert later than the circular e-mail of the sixteenth, conducting a brisk correspondence over the nineteenth and twentieth, concerning a Sherlock Holmes teapot for sale in Hong Kong that he wanted Gilbert's opinion about.

"He was peeved when Gilbert told him he wouldn't

judge it without looking at it, and that he wasn't about to fly to Hong Kong unless Li paid for the trip. Li seemed to think Gilbert should do the thing out of sheer goodwill."

"A Sherlock Holmes teapot?" Kate asked.

"With the pipe as its handle and the lid a deerstalker cap."

"Please don't spoil my appetite," she protested.

"You want to go together and see Jeannine Cartfield when we're done?"

"Sure. She and the other woman, Geraldine O'Malley, are friends outside the dinner club. She thinks that Cartfield—she calls her Jeannie—and Gilbert might have known each other in college."

"Anything beyond friendship?"

"Not so far as O'Malley knew. Actually, I found it reassuring to hear that the man had that much of a tie. He seems to have cut himself off from anything smacking of emotion."

"A man with one passion."

"Yeah, and that directed at a dead, made-up character."

"Wrong there."

"What do you mean? You're not trying to tell me that Sherlock Holmes wasn't made up?"

"The people I saw today might take those as fighting words, but I meant the dead part. I was informed by Soong Li, quite seriously, that since no Holmes obituary has yet to appear in the *Times* of London, clearly he has not yet died."

Kate stared at Al, who looked back at her over the top of his glass, one eyebrow lifted. She began to laugh, and he joined her, which was about the high point of this, their case's third day. Particularly as Jeannine Cartfield, onetime mystery writer who worked for the Ferry Building, was in Sacramento until at least the following afternoon.

So they both went home, to write up their notes in the comforting midst of their respective families and meet again for a trip to the Marin headlands in the morning. At her car, Kate glanced at her watch, saw that Lee would just have finished with Monday's final, late-afternoon client, and phoned to see if she needed anything on the way.

"I was going to start dinner," Lee said, "but if you want to grab something, I'll go get Nora and then put my feet up."

"Let me get Nora. She can help me pick up groceries." Anything that let Lee put her feet up was good, and besides, for some reason Nora counted a trip to the grocery store as a great treat.

"Okay, if you want. Let her choose the salad makings. Maybe that will encourage her to eat some greens."

Not if she chooses Jell-O and canned fruit, Kate thought but did not say aloud. Lee's approach to parenting was inevitably colored by her life as a therapist; still, Nora appeared to have been born with skills of resistance that could meet the challenge of a too-clever mother.

However, the moment Kate saw Nora, standing in the

145

hallway of the nursery school getting her coat put on, she was seized by the cowardly wish that she had let that other, more clever mother come pick the child up today: Nora was moping.

A moping Nora was Eeyore with a thundercloud overhead: glum, listless, unable to summon enough energy to meet another's eye. She allowed her young teacher, Rowena, to thread her limp arms into the jacket, deaf to the young woman's cheery chatter. When the buttons were done up and the day's art masterpieces pressed into the small hand, she still just stood, until the teacher's hand gently urged her in Kate's direction. Kate had to stretch down for Nora's hand, and as she straightened, she looked a question at Rowena.

The teacher shrugged, and told Kate, "Nora was great all day, but something seems to have happened during recess. She won't tell me what it was, but she seems very sad."

Nora's response was to allow her head and shoulders to droop even farther, the very image of despondency. It was all Kate could do not to laugh, seeing her curly-headed three-year-old acting out depression. She winked at Rowena, who appeared relieved that Kate wasn't taking it too seriously, and took Nora's hand more firmly, leading her to the car and buckling her into her car seat.

All the way to the grocery store, Kate carried on a running conversation about nothing. Nora said not a word, but Kate didn't press her. And she didn't make the mistake of offering her an ice cream to cheer her up, merely lifted her into the cart and debated aloud the merits of red tomatoes versus yellow, frizzy lettuce versus crunchy.

"Don't like frizzy," said a small gloomy voice.

"You don't feel like spring mix today, huh? Well, shall we get some for Mamalee, and you and I can have iceberg?"

"With glop."

Kate laughed at the word. "That's right, with blue cheese glop on top." She repeated the inadvertent rhyme a few times, making a song out of the last three words, but Nora wasn't quite ready to respond, so they continued with their shopping.

Finally, standing in front of the deli section waiting for their sliced turkey, Nora broke. She leaned forward in the cart until she was resting against Kate's chest, and Kate wrapped her arms around the child, bending her head over, a still island in the middle of the busy store. When Nora spoke, it was in a voice too low to hear.

"I'm sorry, love, I can't hear you. Could you say that again?"

"Am I illemut?"

"Are you what?"

"Illemut!"

"I'm really sorry, sweetheart," Kate said, hating herself as a failure, "but I don't know what that word means. Can you tell me where you heard it?"

"Dierdre Carter, I really hate her, she said I was illemut, and that you were going to go away and

Mamalee won't love me."

Shocked, Kate stood back and tipped Nora's head up so she could see. The child's eyes trembled with unshed tears. "Who the hell is this Dierdre Carter and why would she say such stupid things?"

"She's Alda's big sister and she had to come today 'cause her school's out and she bossed us all and took all the toys and then she was teasing Steven because his parents are getting a 'vorce and she said they were never really married and that he's illemut and, and, she said I was, too."

Illegitimate. *Fuck.* Kate wanted to hunt down Dierdre Carter and throttle the child. But more immediately, she leaned down until her face was inches from Nora's. "This Dierdre sounds like a very stupid little girl, and a bully." Bully was a concept much in play in modern schools, a thing nobody wanted to be. "Illegitimate is a really old-fashioned idea that means two people had a baby by accident, before they were really ready for it. But I guarantee you, there was nothing even a little bit accidental about you. We had to work really hard to get you, and we wanted you and we loved you before you were even a lump in Mamalee's belly. Do you understand me?"

Nora nodded, already looking relieved.

"As for the other, just because some people get a divorce, not everybody does. Steven's parents have a lot of problems we don't, and sometimes everyone is happier if the parents don't live together and fight all the time. Do Mamalee and I fight all the time?"

"Not *all* the time," Nora agreed, unwilling to let go of her worry.

"You rat," Kate said, her indignation exaggerated in an attempt at comic relief. "We don't fight at all, we just argue a little."

"Okay."

She bent back again, holding Nora's gaze. "I will not leave you. And Mamalee will never, ever stop loving you. You got that?"

Nora nodded, the black cloud dispersing from above her curls.

"Okay, now I'm finished with Dierdre the bully. Do you want cheddar or jack cheese in your sandwich tomorrow?"

"Gorgonzola," said Nora with a wicked twinkle in her eye, and succeeded in cracking her mother up.

FIVE

Nora went to bed early that night, exhausted by her emotional excess, and only when she was safely asleep did Kate tell Lee about the incident. Lee's first impulse was also to strangle the other girl, although she quickly recovered and speculated about the security of Dierdre's own family structure. Kate frankly didn't care, and knew that Lee would have it out with the nursery school director the following day.

She waited for the kettle to come to a boil, making her responses in the right places, her mind moving away from their daughter's distress. She dropped a tea bag into one mug, reflecting that not long ago, she would have been making coffee. Probably the first sign of middle age, giving up coffee at night. No, the second sign—the first was gray hair Down There. At least she could still manage real tea, not the caffeine-free twigs mixture that Lee seemed actually to like.

She scooped twigs into the hinged teaspoon and put it in the other mug, poured boiling water over both, and moved toward the refrigerator, only to come up hard against Lee, standing and looking at her, the milk in one hand.

"Thanks," she said, taking the carton, then looked more closely at Lee's face. "Sorry, did I miss something?"

"I said, do you want to watch a movie?" Lee asked.

"Um," Kate said.

"You have work."

"I do, I'm sorry. You go ahead, I'll come down when I'm finished."

"By the distracted look on your face, I'll be waiting until tomorrow. Is this the Case of the Murdered Sherlockian? How's it coming along?"

"The man's a puzzle. As far as I can see, he didn't have a single soul in the world that he just hung out and had a beer with. However, he seems to have had a live camera operating in his sitting room. That's what I need to look at tonight."

"A webcam?"

"Looks like. Pointing right at the chair in his Sherlock Holmes sitting room, where people could tune in and see him sitting and waiting for Dr. Watson."

"The man's entire life was a construct," Lee commented sadly.

Not, Kate reflected as she walked upstairs to the computer, a very desirable epitaph.

THE screen came up, showing the same image she had seen in the offices of Diagram Research, the clock frozen at 14:43 Sunday. She moved the cursor to the archives and clicked on January 23, the Friday around which he had died. The room appeared, looking much as she had seen it on Rajindra Pandi's monitor that afternoon. The clock in the lower corner said 7:24; the "fire" was glowing and the gas lamps were burning bright to supplement the winter sun. She explored the site for a while, found a means of speeding things up, and watched nothing move at a faster rate, the clock spinning quickly forward.

Suddenly a figure flashed past, and she slowed, reversed, and saw a tall man in an old-fashioned suit walk across to the bookshelf, stand there for a couple of minutes, then come over to the chair with a slim book in his hand. Philip Gilbert laid the book on the littered table, trading it for a pipe, which he dug around in for a while before reaching forward to remove the tobacco pouch from the decorative slipper tacked onto the fireplace. He loaded the pipe and tamped it down, returned the tobacco pouch to its resting place, and lit a match, holding it to the bowl of the pipe. A cloud of smoke obscured his face briefly, then dispersed. He propped his feet up on the leather hassock that sat in front of his chair, took the book from the table and opened it, and sat, reading and smoking.

"You sure got an exciting life for yourself there, Phil," she told the man on the monitor.

He turned a page.

The nose that had looked so sharp in death fit his living face more comfortably. It was actually not a bad-looking face. A little extreme in its features, between the big nose, the deep-set eyes, and the high cheek-bones, but an interesting face, which looked younger than his fifty-three years. His hair was not as thick as she'd thought it; either that or the pomade he used was freshly applied. His body was long, his hands thin and sensitive—surgeon's hands, they were called, or perhaps a pianist's. No rings. No watch, although a shiny chain was visible across his vest, under the suit's jacket.

She made a note on her pad: No such timepiece had come to light in the house.

"Where's your damn watch, Sherlock?" she asked him. He did not look up from his page. She advanced the record in fits and starts, until at 8:40 he closed his book and took a final puff on his pipe, leaving it propped against some unidentifiable rubbish on the table.

He then reached into his inner pocket and took out a small notebook with a dark cover. He opened it, pulled a miniature silver writing instrument from within— pencil? pen?—and bent over the notebook. Of course, what he was writing could not be seen from the camera's angle.

Kate sat back in disgust and told the man, "Phil, you're going to be dead soon, and if you don't help me out here, I'm not going to figure out what happened to you."

She reached for her cup, but her hand froze as the man on the screen seemed to respond to her complaint. He slipped away the pen, snapped the book shut, and dropped it into his pocket. He placed his hands on the arms of the chair, and as he prepared to rise, he looked directly into Kate's eyes and winked at her.

The frisson of reaction passed before the man was even on his feet: He'd been winking at the camera, not at her, and the coincidence in timing was just that. Still, she thought as her fingers finished closing on the mug, it had been an eerie sensation, that instant of communication with the dead. When he had left the room, she played the moment back, and decided that yes, it was a faint but deliberate movement of his right eyelid. A wink.

She drank her tea and watched the empty room for a while. Friday morning, the last Friday morning of Philip Gilbert's life.

After a while, she stopped the clock, made note of the time, and went back into the archives for the day of the dinner party, January 7.

Geraldine O'Malley had said that Jeannine Cartfield, one of the dinner club members they hadn't spoken to that day, had helped Gilbert make dinner that night.

Probably that meant she had come by after work, so Kate scrolled to five o'clock and set the speed high. At 17:21 a brief blip registered on the left side of the screen. She rewound, and saw through the doorway a man's feet passing left to right, then after a moment, the same feet, accompanied by a woman's legs and heeled pumps, going from right to left: Gilbert letting someone in the front door. The woman was carrying something, but Kate could only catch the corner of a dark shape at about knee level. Neither came into the sitting room, which meant that they had either gone upstairs, or walked directly back into the kitchen.

Or, she decided ten minutes later, they had split up. Philip Gilbert passed through the room to set a tray with glasses on one of the fireside tables—which, Kate only now noticed, had been cleared off for the purpose. He left, and seconds later, from the hallway, came the woman, whom Kate assumed was Cartfield. Her feet were now brushed by a long skirt, which appeared in full as she came through the doorway: long skirt, trim white blouse (did they call those shirtwaists?), a black and silver broach pinned at the hollow of her throat. She was Philip's age, if they had gone to university together, but she looked years younger. Her hair was gathered in a large Edwardian pouf on top of her head, a style that surely must have taken her longer to achieve than the quarter of an hour she'd been gone. A wig, or had she arrived with it like that? The woman stood in the doorway, surveying the room, then whisked offstage left, her skirts snapping around her ankles.

Only twice over the next two hours were the two together in the room in front of the camera, and both times were brief and businesslike, involving a flower arrangement and a discussion about a tray of canapés. No indication of any relationship beyond that of friendship; indeed, the woman might have been playing a young Mrs. Hudson, the housekeeper.

The two Indian cousins were the first to arrive, at thirty seconds past seven o'clock, dressed in Indian garb: Venkatarama even had a turban on, a decorative spray of feathers at the front. Gilbert let them in, although twice in the next quarter hour the woman went to answer the door in his place. By half past seven, all ten members of the Sherlock Holmes dinner club were in front of the camera, glasses in their hands. Gilbert must have said something, because they began to turn toward him, listening. His back was to the camera, and he talked for a few minutes. They responded with smiles at one point, raised eyebrows and nods of appreciation at another. At the end, his arm with the glass in it came up, and the other nine mimicked the gesture: a toast, accompanied by an exclamation of approval and then a lifting of glasses to mouths. Kate went back in time to freeze the image, and hit the print button. The printer spat out an ink version of the picture on the monitor.

Eight men, two women, meeting to celebrate the life of a man who had never lived. Ten grown and responsible individuals, comfortable in their heavy and constricting costumes, none of them in the least self-conscious about the arcane setting. The nine individuals facing the camera looked relaxed and at home. They looked like a group of native Victorians, in fact.

Kate printed two more copies of the frozen shot, and went on.

The dinner itself took place out of sight, but after an hour and a bit, the guests began reappearing before the fire. Chairs were pulled up, Jeannine Cartfield settled onto the leather hassock, Gilbert handed around cups of coffee and small glasses of liqueurs, and the party wound on. With sound, or to a lip-reader, it might have been mildly interesting, but limited as she was to peering through a window at the festivities, it was not the most enthralling party Kate had ever attended. When Gilbert brought out his violin and began sawing away, it bordered on the farce of a silent film. Fortunately, he limited himself to a single six-minute performance, after which he struck up a couple of songs, in which all joined in with gusto, their mouths opening and shutting like a tank full of goldfish.

Still, the ten people on the screen seemed to be having a fine old time. After their coffee, they played some kind of game that involved one member reading something short from a piece of paper and one of the others shooting up a hand, to answer a question or maybe identify a passage. Most of the answers seemed to be correct, but when one of them got it wrong—the chubby fellow who was either Alex Climpson, winery employee; Ian Nicholson, job unknown; or Wendell Bauer, grad student, had the worst track record—the others would rise up in good-natured ragging until one of them had provided the correct response. There seemed to be no punishment for being wrong, merely the teasing, although judging by the sheepish glances at the master of ceremonies, the withholding of approval from Gilbert seemed punishment enough.

Kate printed half a dozen other stills showing various group members, then speeded through the rest of the party. The clock read 22:08 when all of a sudden everyone stood up and left the room. Not, however, in the direction of the front door, but turning left, either upstairs or to the kitchen. Kate itched to tilt the camera off the wall in their wake, and found herself wishing Gilbert had installed a series of these damn webcams, for her sake if no other.

Twenty minutes went by before the party reappeared, at which time they did start to leave. A few of them paused for a last chat in front of the fireplace, Rutland and the Indian cousins, the two women, and the redheaded man; then they too began to put on their coats and go. To her surprise, Jeannine Cartfield departed with the others, giving Gilbert a brief kiss on the cheek, exactly as Geraldine O'Malley had done thirty seconds earlier. The last to leave was the lawyer Rutland, who shook hands, tipped his silk hat onto his head, and left.

Gilbert came back from the door, gathered a few glasses onto the tray and carried them out. Kate's finger prepared to hit the fast-forward button, but he came back in, dropping wearily into the frayed chair. He took a cigarette from a fancy little box on the hearth, lit it with a match, shook the match out and dropped it into the ashtray, and then he sat back in the chair, head resting on its high back, all his muscles going limp. The cigarette between his fingers trailed a dancing line of smoke into the air, and Gilbert sat, eyes shut, before his artificial fire. He looked tired beyond the results of a dinner party, as if only the press of people had kept at bay a deeper exhaustion. Or depression.

The untended ash grew, but before it became too long to resist gravity, Gilbert lifted it to the ashtray, flicked it off, took a puff, and then crushed the remains out. He scrubbed his hands over his face, stood up, and went around the room, winding down the gas lamps. When he left, the monitor was dark, but for the low-burning fire in the center of the screen.

Did Gilbert occasionally forget the camera was there? Or had that momentary demonstration of deep tiredness been part of the act, too?

The dinner party was over, and Kate glanced at the actual clock on her wall, then looked again. After eleven; she'd been watching the HolmesCam for over three hours. Lee was sure to be in bed.

Might as well check out one other day.

The computer cousins had seen Gilbert with a woman on the weekend before Christmas, probably Sunday, the twenty-first. She found the day and started the recording, expecting hours of nothing. But instead, the monitor went right into Gilbert settling into the chair. This time he had a tea service with him, and he poured a cup out of the flowered pot, added milk and sugar, and

158

picked up his book. According to the clock, it was four in the afternoon, and instead of a suit jacket, he was wearing the velvety smoking jacket she'd noticed in the second-floor cupboards.

He sipped his tea, read his book, and Kate told herself to shut the thing off, but then the figure in the chair looked up, his attention caught by the doorbell, it would seem. He put down his volume and walked out, turning right. His feet disappeared, and Kate waited to see if one set of feet or two came back down the hallway. Suddenly the scene jumped. The sunlight that had been coming through the window was gone, the lights were on, and Gilbert was walking through the doorway wearing his suit jacket instead of the velvet one. The clock said it was the next morning.

Kate backtracked and examined the archives for the missing hours, but they were gone, with no sign of the women's shoes that Pandi claimed to have seen. And when she went on with the recording, she found almost none of the staring-at-the-empty-room times. Instead, the scene jumped ahead, hours at a time, and nearly always had something happening onstage.

Gilbert edited the recordings. It made sense, she figured; few viewers would be interested in accessing huge files of nothingness, and storing them would burden a server's mainframe, so perhaps every so often he would go through and dump the long hours of live-action scenery, leaving only the times when people were moving about. Going forward, she found a chess game with Thomas Rutland made up most of the recording for December twenty-second, and nothing at all on the twenty-third. She was going ahead to the following day, but suddenly dreaded seeing what the man had resorted to for the Christmas festivities, and shut the link down.

The house was silent, the street outside empty, the only sound a faint click of the hard drive going cool. She stood up, stretched hard, then paused to look at the printouts she had made.

During the toast, there were ten faces, Gilbert with his side to the camera and the others with expressions ranging from serious to distracted. On the far left, Thomas Rutland, attentive to the toast and with his glass already half raised. Beside him a Chinese man, no doubt Soong Li, frowning with concentration: Kate wondered if he had some problems following English conversation. Geraldine O'Malley came next, looking not at Gilbert but at Jeannine Cartfield, at the far right. She was wrapped up, not in Gilbert's toast, but in her own thoughts; her glass tilted, half forgotten in her hand.

Looking over O'Malley's shoulder was a man with gray-blue eyes and reddish hair, slicked down like most of the other men wore theirs. Only part of his face was visible, as he was not much taller than the woman in front of him, but his eyes seemed to be fixed on Gilbert, his mouth half-open in preparation for the "Hear, hear!" Next to him stood the two Indians, seriously attentive, and to their right two young men, one of them the pudgy boy who was not very good at the quizzes, the other a quiet, even younger man who had spent the entire evening in the background, looking a little lost. Finally, Jeannine Cartfield brought up the right.

Now, there was an interesting woman. Dressed like a schoolmarm, her face and posture might have suited a crown. She looked strong yet moved with an easy grace, at home in her body as in her clothes. The outlandish hairdo (it had to be a wig) disturbed her not in the least, and when she stood, she did not fidget as the others did, merely took up a position and held it.

Cartfield listened to Gilbert calmly, neither fixed on his words nor distracted. Was that the attitude of possession? Or simply knowingness? Kate was not sure. But she wanted to know more about this woman, who she was, what she did.

If she had the muscles to carry a dead man up a hill.

She leafed through the other prints she had made, seeing a handsome group of well-off individuals having a good time.

Except, she saw, for Philip Gilbert himself. Three of the six shots she had made included the host, and in each one, he was standing slightly apart, looking on. In one, Jeannine Cartfield, Geraldine O'Malley, and the redheaded man were laughing together over something one of them held—a picture of some kind. Behind Cartfield's back, Gilbert watched them, one corner of his thin mouth turned up in a wistful smile.

Kate laid the pictures down on the desk and turned out the lights, feeling oddly self-conscious, as if she had Gilbert's audience looking over her shoulder. She climbed the stairs, unable to shake the sensation, and went about the rituals of tooth brushing and face washing with more vigor than usual. She tossed her clothes into the hamper, pulled on the T-shirt and shorts she wore to bed, and climbed in between the cold cotton sheets.

Lee's side of the bed radiated warmth; gently, Kate eased herself in that direction, but despite her care, Lee abruptly raised her head to glare at the clock and murmured something unintelligible but disapproving.

"Sorry," Kate said.

Lee dropped her head back onto the pillow, but then reached around and pulled Kate's free hand around her. Needing no further invitation, Kate scooted into the warmth and wrapped her arm around her lover, feeling Lee slide again into sleep.

Kate couldn't, quite.

As a homicide detective, Kate rarely had any real contact with the victim before his or her death. Her perception of the living person was secondary to that of the dead one, and her interest in the victim's life confined to how that life might have led to that death. The victim was largely two-dimensional, a thing pieced together out of static images and pieces of information: letters, photographs, the memories of family and friends, memories that became increasingly detached from reality with each passing day. Occasionally, the victim's family would have a video they wanted to play for the investigators; almost always, Kate avoided looking too closely at it. Far better to work with a dead victim, who did not intrude into the emotional world of those charged with solving the murder. Far better to remain aloof—committed, determined, passionate, but aloof.

With this victim, too, the protective distance had held, until that evening. She'd been quite content to know that her victim was comfortably well-off, that he was a nut about the Sherlock Holmes stuff, and that he was friendly enough on the surface, although it rarely went any further. She would work no less determinedly just because his friendship had been tepid, his life verging on, well, silly.

The wink had changed that. With one infinitesimal droop of the eyelid, Philip Gilbert had transformed himself from a nut to an actor. From someone with a decidedly peculiar fixation, to a man inviting his audience to play along with him. A man who sat in his chair after his only friends had left him, and looked desperately tired.

She liked him, damn it.

And she didn't want him to have died.

FIRST thing Tuesday morning, sitting at her desk while Hawkin battled the morning traffic, Kate made two phone calls. The first confirmed that the San Francisco Medical Examiner had finally received the body of Philip Gilbert, and their victim was now in the system. The second was to Lawrence Freeman at the crime lab.

"Hey Lo," she said. "I found out what that connection was on the Gilbert computer—it's a webcam."

"Yes, I was just about to call you about that. When did *you* find it?"

"Last night," she told him, fudging a little. "Late. By the time I got the details, it was too late to call you. I hope you hadn't spent a lot of time on it."

"Not a lot. Thanks for letting me know." Freeman hung up, clearly miffed, not that she had wasted his time, but that she had figured out his puzzle first. Lo was a man who loved his work.

She switched on her computer and started working on the reports she hadn't finished the night before. Twenty minutes into it, Kate Martinelli's phone rang. As she was short on sleep, needed another cup of coffee, and paperwork wasn't exactly her favorite part of the job, she probably sounded a bit terse as she answered with a "Yes?"

"Um, I beg your pardon," said a pleasant English voice. "I'm trying to reach an Inspector Martinelli?"

"This is she."

"Ian Nicholson here." When she failed to respond, he prompted, "You left a message on my machine yesterday morning, asking urgently that I call you back?"

Ian Nicholson: missing friend of Pajama Man Philip Gilbert. She shoved away the papers and leaned back in her chair, gazing at the cloudy window. "Yes, thanks for returning my call. Mr. Nicholson, I'm with the San Francisco Police Department, and we're working on a case in which your name came up as a possible witness. I wonder if we might meet and talk about it?"

"Witness to what?" the Englishman asked warily.

"Perhaps if we could meet?"

"What kind of a case is this?" His voice took on an edge; Kate gave way.

"It's a homicide, Mr. Nicholson. When would be a good time for you?"

"A hom— Someone was killed? Who?"

"Mr. Nicholson, if we could just—"

"Inspector Martinelli, the machine is telling me that I have twenty-three unplayed messages following yours, and only three came in all of last week. I phoned you immediately I heard your message, as it sounded important. If the victim is someone I know, I should think that information will be the subject of most of those waiting on the machine."

She sighed; an intelligent witness could be a real pain in the ass. "The body of Mr. Philip Gilbert was discovered over the weekend in—"

"Philip?" The man's voice rose in disbelief until it sounded halfway to laughter. "You've got to be mistaken."

"Sir, we need to speak."

There was a moment of silence as Nicholson confronted the possibility; when he spoke, any trace of amusement had vanished. "Yes, certainly. Do you need me to come downtown?"

"I'll come to you, if that's convenient."

He gave her the address and said he'd be there the rest of the morning. She told him she'd be there shortly, and called Al. He was in his car.

"Do you know what a bad idea it is to talk on the

phone while you're driving?" she asked him.

"Is that what you called to ask me?"

"No, I called because Ian Nicholson's surfaced. You want me to say we'll see him this afternoon, when we finish on the headlands?"

"Those headlands interviews are probably going to take most of the day. Why don't I go start on them, you talk to Nicholson and join me over there when you're through?"

"You sure?" she asked, although she'd anticipated his proposal. One of the great things about Al was his comfort with working solo.

"Why not? See you later."

Nicholson lived in a freshly converted warehouse-turned-apartment-building in what had once been San Francisco's industrial underbelly, an area now being mined for its square footage. This appeared to be an area whose zoning had only recently changed: For-sale signs stood on several of the warehouses she had seen, and the cross streets were quiet. The two-story building across the street from Nicholson's freshly painted address was windowless and blank on its upper half, although the lower had been set with a symmetrical row of single-car-width garage doors. With the price of garage rental in the city, the owners of that warehouse probably didn't need to convert to housing.

She left her car on the street and walked down the sidewalk to the expanse of glass that marked the entranceway. Inside was an impressive foyer, a thousand square feet of intricately patterned marble, mailboxes set into one wall, a lively mural depicting an Italian landscape with hill town on the other, and one large potted tree in a corner between them. All of it was brightly lit, readily visible from the street, and protected by the unbreakable glass. Kate stood beneath a security camera and located the name Nicholson set into the still-shiny brass plate, one of only seven labels among the twenty slots; she identified herself to the English voice. The speaker buzzed, and she pushed open the door.

The entrance foyer led into a bare and sunless courtyard clearly intended to host large parties, but as yet lacking so much as a plastic lawn chair. The surrounding walls had been painted various warm earth tones, and a fountain played in its center, the water splashing down its angular sides, but in that stark setting, in the absence of furniture, people, or even birds, the fountain looked like a sculpture that had been temporarily abandoned on its way into an actual living space. With all that concrete emptiness, appealing though the colors were, the walls seemed very high and far away.

A door across the courtyard was standing open, framing the redheaded man who had been standing behind Geraldine O'Malley during the toast, a man in his late forties dressed today in jeans, a much-washed green linen shirt, and dark socks but no shoes. He was not much taller than Kate, perhaps five feet eight inches, but sturdy as a rugby player. His was an interesting face, with a crooked nose, gray-blue eyes, and the texture of freckles beneath the weathered skin. It was an appealing whole, not just from the boyish features, but from the glint of humor that lay in face and shoulders, as if to say there wasn't much he could do about the youth there except grin at it, and invite others to do the same.

Kate was not grinning, exactly, but she did feel her mood lightening as she approached. "Mr. Nicholson?" she asked; the surrounding walls bounced back echoes.

"Thanks for coming down here," said the English voice she'd heard on the phone. "I've been living in the car for the past week, hated the thought of having to climb back inside." They shook hands, his hard and cool, and he stood back to let her enter.

"Nice place," she remarked.

"The flats themselves are great, although that courtyard I find depressing as hell."

"It does look a bit raw."

"I think the designer had a sort of Tuscan village flavor in mind, but he overlooked the fact that the effect depends on a full complement of residents, preferably people who are home for more than a few hours a day, and a judicious sprinkling of aged grandmothers in black, small barefoot children, and dogs. To say nothing of bedding draped out of the windows and the occasional chicken. Of course, pets are forbidden here, half the apartments are vacant, what neighbors there are seem to be all between the ages of twenty-five and forty, and building regulations prohibit anything as offensively prosaic as hanging laundry. Perhaps it will be better when it fills up. Coffee? It's fresh."

During this monologue, which could have been a sign of nerves at the presence of the police or merely the genetic effusiveness of a redhead, Nicholson had led her into the apartment and up a set of polished wooden stairs; by pleasing contrast, the brick wall at her right hand was soft with wear—clearly the bricks were an original feature of the onetime warehouse. At the top of the stairs lay a light-washed space, one end a wall of glass, the other a sleek and modern kitchen filled with expensive equipment. On the wall beside the telephone was a small screen showing the apartment house's entranceway. Nicholson turned toward the kitchen; Kate drifted into an open room with tan leather sofas and a fireplace.

"Yes, thanks," she told him. "I'd like some coffee."

She heard a cupboard door open and cups rattle as they were being placed on a tray—real cups, with saucers—followed by the suck of a refrigerator door and the gurgle of milk into a pitcher. The living room was a remarkably comfortable space for a modern apartment building, the expanse of glass warmed by the brick and the rich colors of an ethnic rug on the floor. The windows were bare of curtains, and high enough to overlook an expanse of urban life that stretched east nearly to the waterfront; it felt as if the apartment occupied the peak of a cliff above—well, a Tuscan village. A bright splash of paint on a large canvas, meaningless but cheerful, woke up the area above the fireplace; on the other wall was hung a long, precise row of color photographs in identical black frames: a Mexican village market day; an expanse of snowy hillside with two leafless trees, nearly monochromatic; a young woman with blond hair, a beautifully even tan, and enormous gold hoops in her ears, grinning at the camera from her seat atop a stone wall, the sea in the background the precise startling blue as her eyes. A second picture of the woman—girl, really—in a more formal portrait gazed out from a standing frame on the left side of Nicholson's desk, tucked under the stairs leading to the third-floor loft. On the right side was the fading snapshot of a redheaded teenager wearing mud and a rugby outfit: she'd guessed right about Nicholson's sport.

Kate spoke over her shoulder. "Do you live here by yourself?"

"At the moment, yes."

"Is this a friend of yours?"

Nicholson was coming through from the kitchen, accompanied by a tinkle of bone china, and he stopped beside her to look at the photograph of the grinning blond woman. "Something more than a friend, you might say."

"That's Baja, isn't it? Cabo San Lucas?"

"It is, yes. Taken a couple of months ago. Have you been there?"

"Years ago. I hear it's getting pretty commercial and touristy."

"Some parts of it are, others are not too bad." He resumed his path into the living room, and Kate followed, taking one of the chairs while he set the tray on the low table that stood between sofa and fireplace. Watching his masculine hands arrange the delicate cups and pick up the glass carafe, Kate smiled at the contrast, but when she looked at his face, she saw the man's tiredness slipping through. His clothes were fresh and his short hair slightly damp, but he hadn't shaved, and his eyes were bloodshot—he'd either driven through the night, or else fallen into bed late and slept badly.

"I was terribly sorry to hear about Philip," Nicholson said. "As I guessed, most of the messages on the machine were about him. Not that anyone seemed to know anything, other than that he had been found in Marin over the weekend. His name must have been released after you phoned here."

"Late on Monday, yes, after his family had been notified. Mr. Gilbert's lawyer said that you and Philip were friends?"

"Ah, you talked with Tom—I wondered how my name had come up. We were friends. As much as Philip actually had friends."

Rutland had made a similar remark, Kate reflected, although the lawyer had been matter-of-fact about it, whereas in Nicholson she sensed a well of regret. "Mr. Gilbert seems to have led a rich fantasy life."

At that, Nicholson's face shifted into a crooked smile, and he reached forward to spoon sugar into his cup. "You're talking about his house? He did carry it all a good way beyond the necessary."

"You know him through the Sherlock Holmes thing?" Kate asked.

He finished stirring his drink, set the spoon on the tray, and eased himself back into the embrace of the sofa. "We met about five or six years ago, when I was living in New York. I was at one of the big auction houses, and they'd put me in charge of organizing a Holmes collection for sale. Philip came out for the auction. He has—" Nicholson caught himself, and repeated the crooked smile. "He *had* a good working knowledge of antiquities and collectibles, but my own area of expertise is manuscripts, and there were a couple of letters from Conan Doyle in the lot. They were genuine, although not particularly valuable, and Philip ended up buying them. Then a few weeks later he wrote to me about another set of letters he'd come across, asking if I would authenticate them for him—for a fee, of course. I looked, found that three of the seven were fakes, and he said he'd thought something was wrong but couldn't figure out what. Anyway, to save you the tiresome details, perhaps two or three times a year he'd either show up for an auction or bring me something to look at—he found some fascinating stuff, had a real nose for it, so to speak. Sorry, bad joke. Anyway, when I moved out here, about five years ago, I started seeing him socially as well. He was a real character, was Philip. He could be difficult, or utterly charming, even at the same time. Not unlike Holmes himself, I have to say. We're all going to miss him terribly."

Kate sipped her coffee and listened to the echoes of that last statement. The sentiment was honest, she thought, but there was also a kind of formulaic meaninglessness that concealed the opposite, as if one might also speak of missing a toothache. Certainly it would seem that in general, people's reactions to Philip Gilbert were complex.

"When did you last see Philip?"

"Just before I left. Which was Saturday. Saturday before last, that is, the twenty, what is it? Twenty-fourth, I guess. I've been up in Seattle for a friend's funeral, and making various duty visits to family in Oregon on the way back down."

"And you drove? That's a lot of miles."

"I don't like flying." From the flat tone of his voice, Nicholson meant that he *really* didn't like flying.

"I see. What time was that, on the Saturday?"

"He called around, oh, eight, eight-fifteen, just as I was loading the car, to ask if I would look at something for him. I told him I'd be gone for a while, he said that in that case he'd give me a photocopy to look at while I was away. He sounded terribly excited, which was unlike him—he invariably cultivated a phlegmatic air. I tried to put him off, but he wouldn't take no for an answer, said I'd regret passing on it, that he'd be here in an hour with the thing. I didn't much want to wait around, but he was insistent, so I said I would.

"He was a lot more than an hour, but I waited, and when he came I could see why he'd given me a copy—there were over a hundred pages of typescript. He wanted me to read it, get a preliminary feel for its content, and then when I returned, he'd let me see the original. I won't render judgment on a document I haven't

173

actually handled, of course, but I'd done these preliminary reports before, and they come with no guarantee.

"So I took the folder—rather churlishly I'm afraid, since it was by then nearly noon—and told him I'd try to look at it but I couldn't promise, I'd be busy. But he was so, I don't know, cock-a-hoop over the thing that he practically rubbed his hands and said he didn't think I'd want to wait too long, that he was going to be showing it to others very soon.

"I finally managed to leave, and since I clearly wasn't going to make it to my friends in Salem before dark I figured I might as well take my time. When I drove through the Lake Shasta area, it looked worth stopping at, so I found a motel and wandered around for a while, which was actually quite restful. Silver linings and all that. Then when I was going through my bag before dinner, I came across the typescript and took it along for a look. At first glance, my heart sank, because as far as I could see it was just another pastiche. Er, are you familiar with the word?"

"I know what a pastiche is." More or less.

"The world of the Sherlockian is littered with pastiches, most of them either bad or just plain silly. Even while Conan Doyle was still active, people were writing 'missing Holmes adventures,' often under the pretense that Conan Doyle had written it but for one reason or another not published it. Perhaps I should make clear that, with the possible exception of one story written by his son, these aren't forgeries, they're just, as it were, homages. It's a game, played openly.

For one thing, it's patently absurd to assume that Sir Arthur left much of anything unpublished. In the early days, he had a family to support and a sick wife, but even after he became famous he didn't tend to write something and then leave it in his desk. Particularly not something the length of what Philip gave me."

Kate nodded her head, as she'd done at regular intervals ever since his tale began, although she had to wonder where this was leading, and what it could possibly have to do with murder.

As if he had heard her doubt, Nicholson was shaking his head and looking distressed. "By the time I finished it, I already wished I could say that the thing was a joke. But I couldn't, not anywhere near, and that meant Philip was going to land in it with both feet. You probably have no concept of the size of the controversy that was going to blow up over this, but I've seen the whole machinery of claim and counterclaim, and it's an ugly thing to have descend on a friend.

"In any case, within the first few pages, the thing pricked my interest. As a pastiche, it's not half bad, and on the surface it has something of Conan Doyle's style—although I would wish to subject it to a detailed linguistic analysis before I put that into a report. Thematically, the story, if one lays aside the considerable problem of content and the lesser problems of setting— it takes place here in San Francisco—and an unusual length, is nonetheless sufficiently complex and atmospheric to pass for an original. The writer even managed to avoid the more common markers of a fake—giving

Holmes a calabash pipe, for example, which Conan Doyle never did, or trundling out the hackneyed old phrase 'Elementary, my dear Watson.' Also not used by Sir Arthur.

"So although I started out assuming Philip had bought a pig in a poke, if not fallen victim to an outright hoax, once I'd read the thing, I was forced to treat it like a serious project. I got out my laptop and did some research, and found that as I had vaguely remembered, Conan Doyle did indeed spend some time here in San Francisco, on one of his Spiritualist tours—were you aware that Doyle was a believer in the spirit world?"

"Er, no," Kate replied.

"A real nutter, Doyle was—mediums, ectoplasm, automatic writing, the lot. Believed that Houdini actually dematerialized to get out of his chains, for example. He kept trying to get in touch with his dead son and his beloved mother, refused to believe that they were absolutely gone. He went on worldwide speaking tours for the cause, including San Francisco in 1923, and as the story Philip gave me appears to be set at about that time, it's not out of all possibility."

Kate finished her coffee and put her cup into its saucer, firmly; clearly the tale was not leading anywhere, and she'd merely stumbled into another nutter's passion. "Sir," she started, but he wasn't finished with his thought, and spoke as he reached for the coffee to refill their cups.

"Actually, there's a funny coincidence there, or not funny, just sad, I suppose. Unless of course Philip's body was found in a gun emplacement." The offhand final remark was accompanied by a smile, but when Kate didn't immediately answer, Nicholson's eyes rose, and at the expression on her face he sat up sharply, the carafe in his hand forgotten. "You don't mean to tell me . . . ?"

"Why did you ask about the location of the body, Mr. Nicholson?"

"In the gun emplacement, you mean? I meant it as a joke—you don't mean to say that's where he was found?"

"Why?" she repeated.

"Because in the story, that's where the body is found. In a gun emplacement on the Marin headlands."

"Mr. Nicholson," Kate said grimly, "maybe I'd better have a look at this story of yours."

WHEN Kate walked back through the bare courtyard, some forty minutes after she had arrived, she startled a solitary sparrow from its bath in the fountain. The tiny bird circled around and around the high enclosing walls, gradually gaining height with cach pass of the spiral until it came to a gap between apartments and ducked away into the sunlight.

Back at the car, Kate tossed the photocopy Nicholson had made for her onto the passenger seat, a sheaf of plain white paper held together with a big clip. His had been printed on a substantial buff-colored paper and tucked into a clear cover; she had been inclined to demand his original, but when he seemed loath to let it go, she relented, and allowed him to make her a copy on his home printer. When he'd taken it off the machine and handed it to her, she realized she'd probably seen the original in Gilbert's bank vault, a hundred-odd pages of old typescript in a plastic envelope. But she said nothing to Nicholson, and took the copy of his copy.

She paused with the car door open, running her eyes across the row of garages, wondering how many of them were occupied. She then turned to look back at the apartment building's empty foyer. She hadn't seen another soul in the place, no sign of life besides Nicholson and the small brown bird. Once upon a time, that might have seemed normal to her, even desirable. Now it just seemed sad.

She checked her cell phone for messages, finding nothing of any importance, then started the car and set off for the Hall of Justice. As she waited to cross Market Street, she glanced down at the passenger seat, flipping the document over so the print side was up. As she read the opening lines, she felt her face twist, either in irritation or amusement, she could not have said which:

```
The mind is a machine ill suited to
desuetude. The occasional holiday is
all very well, but without the oil of
challenge and the heat generated by
effort, the mind rusts and seizes and
is unavailable when needed.
```

I found myself in San Francisco one spring evening, my travelling companion temporarily about other business and my mind at a loss for a load to carry. Recent days had seen the successful conclusion of a case not without interest, but after forty-eight hours of solitary leisure, a dangerous restlessness had begun to set in, so I cast

An impatient horn sounded; Kate slapped the car into gear and drove off, lifting an apologetic hand to the man behind her.

She'd worked homicide for going on a dozen years now. She'd come across bodies dead from gang disputes and domestic madness, drug-fueled rage and cold-blooded greed, sexual perversion and criminal neglect. Never in all that time had she even heard hint of a person killed over an eighty-year-old short story.

Lee was going to love this.

And what the hell was *desuetude,* anyway?

SIX

Kate worked the phone for a while from her desk, first checking on Ian Nicholson's alibi—and indeed, all was as he told her, from his Saturday motel to his Sunday arrival in Seattle—then trying to get a handle on the history of this document with the odd coincidence. She started with the bigger dealers in town who handled manuscripts and old maps, but after three of those suave individuals went from polite to hungry in seconds flat, she turned to Tom Rutland. He had indeed heard the rumors of a Sherlock Holmes story— the Sherlockian world had been aflutter for weeks with talk of such a thing, even before the brief *Chronicle* article that Philip had sent the Diners in the middle of January, but no one, including Philip Gilbert, had admitted to knowing anything concrete about it.

"Would it surprise you to know that your client had a copy of the story?"

"Did he? What a rat bas— I mean, what a rat. He sat there at the last dinner and said not a thing, even though that rumor was the main topic of conversation."

"That would have been the dinner at his house?"

"That's right. We keep talking about having the January meeting set on the sixth, which is generally accepted as Holmes's birthday, but since some of us go back to New York for the BSI dinner, which is always that first weekend in the year, we've decided to keep ours on the Wednesday. That way we can have a report, if anyone goes back."

"Right. The seventh of January. Which is funny, because according to his ledger, he received the manuscript in the first part of December."

"He actually had it, then? We're talking about an unpublished Sherlock Holmes story, by Arthur Conan Doyle?" He sounded torn between frank disbelief and yearning.

"That I don't know, Mr. Rutland. I haven't read it yet."

"But you've seen it? I can't believe it. My God. Why on earth did Philip not tell anyone about it, I wonder? Christ, he must have been just exploding with the news. I wonder where he got it? Can you tell me that?"

"I'm sorry, I can't."

"Where is it now?"

That she could divulge, since he would guess anyway; best to leave Nicholson out of it until he chose to step in. "I have a photocopy. The original is in the bank vault, safe and sound."

"My God," he repeated. "Look, I'd be happy to look it over for you—as an expert in things Sherlockian, you know. If it would do you any good. Would you say it's got any chance at all of being genuine?"

"Mr. Rutland—"

"No, of course you wouldn't know. And probably someone like Ian would do a better job of judging it, anyway. I wonder how Philip planned on letting us know?" No little resentment there, Kate could hear it ringing loud. The lawyer kept her on the phone, practically pleading for more information; when she hung up, she was thoughtful.

She regretted phoning him; should have gone to see him instead, so she could have watched his face. Something about the conversation had sounded a faint wrong note, as if he had been staging a piece of courtroom drama. Nothing she could pin down, and admittedly, most of the time when she felt that, it turned out to be either some unrelated matter the witness was concealing, or else Kate's personal dislike for the individual. Both of which could easily be the case here.

Still, she wished she could have seen his face.

Of one thing, however, there was no doubt: If the mere possibility of such a manuscript so thrilled not only Thomas Rutland, but experienced antiquarians, its existence had to be a remarkable thing. For a dyed-in-the-wool collector like Philip Gilbert, it must have taken his weak heart to the edge of failure.

Although maybe it had actually taken his heart past the edge of failure, she thought sourly, and phoned the ME's office, yet again.

Hawkin called a while later, the reception thin and crackly.

"Martinelli? Can you hear me?"

"Barely. Where are you?"

"I was calling to ask you the same thing. I'm out on the Marin headlands."

"Sounds like the moon. I had an interesting talk with Mr. Nicholson." She told him about the manuscript, its apparent worth and importance. "I've been trying to find the guy Gilbert bought it from, according to the ledger. You ever hear of someone named Paul Kobata?"

"Never came across him."

"Me neither. Anyway, I've been calling around to see if any of the dealers know where he is, and every time I say anything about a Sherlock Holmes story, they practically crawl down the phone line at me. What the hell is it with these people? Anyway, I can do that later, where do you want me to meet you?"

"Sounds to me like your time's better spent working that angle. I looked through the park records for crimes and found a lot of nothing, and I'm now working my way through the people who live here. Nice bunch, completely clueless, reminds me of Tyler's Road." Their first case together, a dozen years before.

"You don't think I'm wasting my time on the story, then?"

"We've known stranger reasons for killing."

"True, and from what Nicholson said, it might be worth some money. This could be a botched robbery, someone heard about it and thought Gilbert had it at home."

"If nothing else, it sounds like it may explain why his body was found where it was."

"True. And hey, the autopsy's scheduled for tomorrow."

"Finally," he said. "Anything else?"

"Just the story. I thought I'd look at it this afternoon."

"One of us ought to. 'Work the weird,' as Jules tells me."

"What the hell does that mean?"

"In her case, I'm not absolutely sure, although when she was explaining it to me she started out talking about a 'software glitch,' on one of her programs. Seems that when you have software problems, you have to figure out all the spots where it's not doing what you expect, and that leads you to the flaw. She says she has to collect all the strange incidents of behavior, find how they are connected, and trace them backwards to their source. What she calls 'working the weird.' "

"And the story and the body's location are the weird here."

"Work it, baby," Hawkin told her.

The entry in Gilbert's loose-leaf ledger read:

6 December, typed manuscript, 117 pages, unbound, clean condition, foxed corners; from Paul Kobata; a Sherlock Holmes pastiche, poss. Early 20th century. $30.

The appraised value was left blank, and although he'd made a note on his vault copy, here he had not recorded giving the photocopy to Ian Nicholson.

She found Kobata late that morning at his current place of business, the basement depths of a shop selling what they claimed were antiques, but looked to her like used furniture. The woman working the desk, whose heavy makeup put a good five years on top of her honest sixty, answered Kate's inquiry with a jab of the thumb toward the back of the store. Kate picked her way cautiously between the beaten-up iron bedsteads and the chipped paint of various objects with ill-fitting drawers, finally coming across a hole in the floor from which, on closer examination, a set of ill-lit stairs descended. She glanced at the woman for confirmation, and took the lack of response for a yes. Gingerly grasping the rough wood handrail, Kate descended.

Thumps and a ragged cough led her to a back corner of the dim cellar. When she was near enough to feel that she could catch him if he turned and ran, she called out, "Mr. Kobata?"

A larger thump followed, a gargling noise that might have been the clearing of a throat, and a hat rose from a heap of unidentifiable objects, with a head attached to it. "Yeah?"

When she got close enough for her badge to be visible, she held it out, introduced herself, and said, "I'm interested in a typed document you sold to Mr. Philip Gilbert a few weeks ago."

"Yeah?" he said again, not appearing too impressed with her badge.

"Do you know the manuscript I mean?"

"Sure. Some detective story from the Twenties, a body in the Presidio or something. Never much of one for that kinda shit, myself. Mysteries, you know."

Not to get waylaid in literary criticism, Kate pressed on. "I'm interested in where it came from."

"Dunno. I picked it up at a book fair in the East Bay, back in, oh, maybe October?"

"Can you give me a few more details?"

"San Leandro, I think. A fund-raiser for the library, put on in the high school gym. No, it musta been November, it was tit-freezing cold."

"Who did you buy it from?"

"Who *did* I buy it from?" Kobata mused. He emerged more fully from the cartons, and walked around to a sturdy wooden box, sitting down on it and taking an old-fashioned tobacco pouch from the pocket of his plaid shirt. He tugged a paper from the packet and began to dribble tobacco down the middle, frowning all the while. "The kid I'm s'posed to be training spotted it, in a loose box with a whole lot of other dreck, magazines mostly, a few prints, the odd newspaper from some event or other—Pearl Harbor headlines, that was one of them." The leaves on the paper and the memories in his mind arranged themselves slowly, and Kate waited. "The box was marked 'Curiosities, $5,' I remember that. A woman selling them. Didn't know her." He ran his tongue thoughtfully along the edge of the cigarette paper, then nodded decisively. "Last booth but one along the back. Number fifty-two."

Kate had worked with too many witnesses to feel any surprise at the twists of memory that produced a number when the person attached to it was forgotten. "I take it these are reserved spaces, and someone is in charge of assigning them?" she asked.

"How the hell would I know? I just go and sort through the crap."

"Tell me, Mr. Kobata, how did you come to sell it to Mr. Gilbert?"

"I'd brought him one or two things over the years, I knew he was interested in that Sherlock Holmes crap, thought maybe he'd like this, too."

"Was it a Sherlock Holmes story?"

"Wasn't a story at all, in the sense of it being published, just a bunch of typing. But it was old, and it never ceases to amaze me what absolute tripe your average collector will hand over cash for because they're afraid they might miss something. Anyway, it only cost me a phone call to ask, and as it turned out, when he stopped by a couple days later, he bought it."

"But you didn't actually read it?"

"Like I said, I'm not much for detective stories. I just thought maybe it was something that'd been published in one of the pulps, maybe even by a writer that made something of himself—like Dashiell Hammett or someone, although it wasn't anything like his stuff, that much I could tell. Hammett lived in San Francisco for a while, you know? But because the story didn't have a name on it, you'd have to know absolutely everything that was published back then to know when it appeared, and I don't. Anyway, Gilbert came out, glanced through it, peeled off a twenty and two fives, and had me sign and date his receipt. Four minutes, start to finish."

"Did he say anything in particular about it?"

"Not much. Just asked me where I'd got it, and said that it would be an amusing addition to his collection, something like that. I'd been hoping to make maybe ten bucks, but in the end, I asked thirty and kicked myself when he paid it so fast." He shook his head, and stood up. "Shoulda asked fifty."

IT took half a dozen phone calls, beginning with the San Leandro library and working through several of its book fair volunteers, before Kate could identify the date of the book fair as November 15, and the seller of "curiosities" in space 52 as Magnolia Brook. She drove across the Bay Bridge to speak with her.

Magnolia's Antiquities was a traveling business run out of its owner's home, a dark-shingled 1930s building on the north side of College Avenue in Berkeley. A teenage girl wearing zebra-striped pajamas and holding a wad of tissues to her red nose answered the bell, and in a gravelly voice directed Kate to the garage around the side of the house.

She found the garage set back from the street along a narrow drive, a tidy structure with shingles that matched the house. It had to be a rarity, Kate thought, to find a freestanding garage that hadn't been converted into living quarters and rented to students. Still, it looked as if the woman was making good use of the space.

"Ms. Brook?"

Magnolia Brook was oddly suited to her name, being large, blowsy, colorful, and given to the habit of wide, loose gestures. The only thing that wasn't magnolia-like was her complexion, which had seen far too much sunshine ever again to be luminously pallid.

"Yes, you're the Inspector?"

"Kate Martinelli," Kate agreed, showing her badge.

"What can I do for you, Inspector Martinelli? I hope you don't mind talking while I work, I've got a ton of stuff to do this afternoon."

If the other option was going inside to breathe the teenager's germs, Kate was happy to be in the open air. "This is fine," she replied. "I'm interested in an item you sold during the San Leandro book fair last November."

Ms. Brook looked up sharply from a box of tattered books. "That again? Why is everyone so interested in that manuscript? Is there something illegal about it? Is it stolen merchandise or something?"

It was Kate's turn to look startled. "Was someone else here asking about it?"

"Yes, two or three weeks after the book fair, a fellow came asking about it. Tall, thin man with longish hair and a big nose." Philip Gilbert. "He asked me to write out how I got it, its condition when I first saw it, what I did with it, all that. Then I had to sign and date it. He gave me twenty-five dollars for the statement, which was more than I'd sold the thing for in the first place, so I was happy to do it. Honest, I don't deal in stolen merchandise."

"No, of course not, no one thinks you do. Look, just to make sure we're talking about the same thing, this is a sort of short story, typed, about a hundred pages?"

"That's right, a detective story. It wasn't signed or even dated, so I figured it wasn't worth much."

"You had it in a box marked 'Curiosities' and sold it to a San Francisco dealer named Kobata for five dollars?"

"That's right," she said, and asked again, "Why are you all so interested?"

"I can't speak for your other visitor, but as for me, the thing has come up in an investigation, and we need to clear up where it came from."

"It was just a story. Mildly amusing, but nothing special—still, I thought maybe someone would buy it, so I stuck it in the box. And they did. When you say it came up, in what way? Don't tell me it was actually worth something?"

"I wouldn't know," Kate replied honestly.

"It's every dealer's nightmare, that some absolute gem passes through their hands unnoticed. What was it you wanted to know about it?"

"Did you read it?"

"I did, mostly to make sure all the pages were there and that it wasn't pornographic. In the end, I enjoyed the thing."

"I was told it was a Sherlock Holmes story."

"Was it? No, I don't think so. I'd have remembered that. About an English detective, yes, probably patterned on Sherlock Holmes."

"Where did it come from?"

"One of my customers, as much a friend as a customer I suppose, was hired to do some work on a house in San Francisco, a really lovely old, pre-Earthquake place in Pacific Heights. He came across a whole pile of stuff that at some point had been closed up inside the attic—you know how it is, someone slaps wallpaper over a door and forgets it's there. But to the owner's disappointment, there weren't any particular treasures, and after she'd gone through and taken out the things she liked, she had him haul the rest of it away. He offered the stuff to me, and I gave him a hundred dollars for the lot. Some of it really was junk, I even ended up throwing a couple bags of stuff out, but a few things were worth troubling over. I made twice what I'd paid him off two old dolls that I cleaned up and sold to a collector I know, sent an old typewriter and an embroidered footstool to an antiques dealer friend in Carmel—it's all in who you know, this business. The rest I put in my own stock. Most of the books went at the San Leandro sale."

"This was the only manuscript?"

"The only one. There were some old garden journals, handwritten, that followed the development of the house's landscaping. And a few magazines from the 1920s, one of those had an F. Scott Fitzgerald story in it, as I remember. That brought a few dollars. But as I say, the rest of it was junk. Typical attic debris—it's one of life's mysteries, why people save the stuff they do."

"I'd like the name of the person you got the things from," Kate asked.

"Sure, I've got his number in the house. Come on in."

Kate followed Brook to the back door, and hovered in the clear air while she pawed through a drawer near the telephone, found an address book, and copied down a name and number on a card that she handed to Kate. "He's a nice guy, not the brightest bulb in the box, but honest down to his toes. Was there anything else?"

"Not right now, thank you. Give me a call if you think of anything else," Kate said, handing over her own card.

"You don't want the name of my friend in Carmel, too?"

"Why would I want that?"

"I don't know, but everything else you've asked I

already told the man. I thought you might want Tessie's number, as well."

"Okay, maybe you should give it to me," Kate said, and watched her write down the phone number, this time from memory.

She thanked the woman, and walked thoughtfully back up the driveway to the street. What had Gilbert been after, and why had he wanted to speak with the Carmel dealer? Just complete thoroughness?

She opened her cell phone and called both numbers; the Carmel shop was closed but invited her to leave a message, the other number answered, barely audible over a cacophony of hammers.

The nice, dim, honest-to-his-toes handyman that Kate tracked down to the building site told essentially the same story that Magnolia had given. And back across the Bay Bridge just in front of the rush-hour traffic, the owner of the Pacific Heights house came to the door with a laden paint roller in one hand and a cell phone in the other. Once she had gotten rid of the caller and the paint roller, she invited Kate inside the plastic-draped rooms and affirmed the details of what Kate had already learned: She and her handyman had been stripping wallpaper early last fall when they'd come across an unexpected access door to the attic. He had retrieved his longer ladder and they had gone up, with flashlights, hoping to find, if not treasure, then at least some usable space under the eaves. The head space had proved too low and the floor joists too small to make it economic, but as storage space it was useful, once the odds and ends left by former owners had been cleared away.

Kate asked about those odds and ends. The woman's eyes went up in thought. "Two nice old metal bed frames, simple but attractive, that we sent down to be stripped and repainted. Half a dozen watercolors, none of them worth anything but they were nice period pieces, once they were cleaned and rematted. There were some old photographs that were too badly faded by the heat and damp to bother restoring, but they were mounted in really lovely silver frames, which polished up beautifully. The rest of it was just junk—old books and magazines, a massive old typewriter, three empty hatboxes."

She didn't remember the manuscript, except in general terms, and mostly because she, as Magnolia Brook before her, had received a visit from a gentleman with thin hair and a long nose, in the first part of December.

He had left here, too, with a signed statement concerning the discovery of the typescript.

Finally, just as Kate was sliding the key into the car's ignition, her cell phone rang. The Carmel antiques dealer knew exactly the man Kate was talking about, he'd been to her shop about two months earlier. What did he want? Why, the typewriter, of course. And no she didn't still have it, not exactly.

"What do you mean, 'not exactly'?" Kate asked.

"You see, your man called just after he'd talked to Maggie Brook, to see if I still had the machine and if I'd cleaned it up yet, which I had, and I hadn't—I mean, I had it, but I hadn't gotten around to cleaning it, I'd only had it two or three weeks. Maybe a little longer, but still, fall's a busy time, and I figured I'd get around to it after Christmas when the tourists were gone."

Kate interrupted the flow with a question. "Can you remember just when this was?"

"It was a Tuesday, and I'm sure it was December. I know it was a Tuesday because I'm closed Monday and Tuesday, and he'd left a message on my day off. But which Tuesday? Oh yes, I know. I was putting up my Christmas decorations, which I always do the first week after Thanksgiving, but I'd had that terrible flu that was going around over Thanksgiving, just knocked me out for two weeks, so it wasn't until the first part of December that I could manage it. Many of the shops put up their Christmas things before Thanksgiving, so as to encourage the shoppers on the day after, but it just seems to me that Thanksgiving decorations get short shrift, and they're beautiful on their own, the cornucopias and the gourds and all, that I hate to hurry them out the door just to jolly customers along into thinking about gift giving. Don't you agree?"

"Er, yes. So the first Tuesday in December. That would have been, let's see, the second of December?"

"No, that's too early, I was sick for a good two weeks. It must have been the following week. The ninth, would that be? Anyway, I went in that Tuesday to get a start on the Christmas tree and found the message from him, and when I called him back he asked me if I had the machine that Maggie had sold me, and I said yes, and he said he wanted it in its current condition—didn't ask first how much I wanted for it, which is always a good sign, you know? Just that he wanted it as it was, and then he sort of remembered and asked how much I wanted. So I told him a hundred dollars, although I probably would have taken forty, and he said he'd give me a hundred fifty dollars for it if it was in its original condition, and he'd come down then and there. But I knew he was in Berkeley because he told me he'd just left Maggie's house and it was four-thirty and he'd hit all that traffic and I was still tired because of the flu and I wasn't about to wait around for him at the shop when my cats were used to eating at six, so I told him to come in the morning. And at first he didn't want to, but then he sort of seemed to think of something and he changed his mind and he asked me what time I opened and I told him and then he asked if there was a secure storage place nearby. Which there is, I use it sometimes when I have something big or the shop is getting crowded.

"But anyway, long story short, there he was waiting on the sidewalk when I came to open the next morning, nice fellow, good clothes, tall and kind of old-fashioned for his age, you know, actually tipped his hat at me—actually wore a hat, come to that, men don't tend to these days. I took him to the back room and showed him the typewriter, all grubby and a little rusty but not too bad, just a couple of the keys were sticking, and anyway, who uses the things these days, they're just for decoration and it would clean up nice enough for show. But he takes off his hat and coat and sets his briefcase on this nice étagère I picked up in Lodi last fall and pops it open, and whips out a pair of white cotton gloves and a package of typing paper. He puts on the gloves and feeds a sheet of paper into the machine and starts to type, although of course the thing is practically frozen solid and the ribbon falls to shreds as soon as the first key hits it.

"But that doesn't seem to bother him a bit. He's actually humming under his breath as he goes back into the briefcase and pulls out a typing ribbon—the real thing, an actual ribbon. The spools don't fit, of course, so he very carefully snips the old ribbon with a pair of scissors he's brought and winds a length of the new stuff directly over it on the spools, and pulls the keys back and forth for a while with his fingers to loosen them up and then rattles off half a page of 'quick brown dog jumps over the lazy fox,' or anyway he would've rattled it off if the keys didn't stick so much, but he gets a few lines and pulls it out of the machine and goes back into his briefcase again and pulls out a folder. In it he's got a page of typing, looks like a photocopy, and some blowups of the same page. And he takes this magnifying glass out of the briefcase and bends over the two pages, the one he brought and the one he's just done— looks like some sort of Sherlock Holmes there, you know, without the deerstalker cap—and compares the two. And then he sits back with this giant grin on his face—which you know, seeing his face originally you wouldn't have thought he could look like that, like a kid you'd handed the keys to a candy store—and says that if it wasn't impolite he'd kiss me, for my impeccable preservation of this gorgeous machine. That's exactly what he said, my 'impeccable preservation of this gorgeous machine,' even though his white gloves were nearly black with the dirt and ink and the bits of disintegrating ribbon.

"So I ask him if he wants to buy the machine and he says yes real fast, but, he says, what I really want is for you to safeguard it for me.

" 'You want to leave it here?' I ask him, but he sort of looks around—the back of the store isn't really very tidy, I admit—and he says that it would be better if we could transfer it to the storage facility I mentioned and lock it up. And he'd pay for it all, he says, and pay me for my trouble.

"I said I'd take it down and put it into the storage room I rent, but he said he'd really rather have the typewriter in a room to itself. Which is pretty strange, to rent a place and just have a typewriter in it, but it was his money so I said I guess it was okay, I'd take care of it that evening.

"But he wanted me to do it then and there. I told him I had a shop to run and no help until the afternoon, and with that he pulls out a wallet and starts peeling off fifty-dollar bills. One, two, three, four. We got to six of them, not that I was aiming at three hundred dollars, it just took me that long to realize what was going on, and I told him okay, I'd close the shop and go to the storage place right then.

"Then he brings out this clean white sheet he's got folded up in his case and wraps the machine in it. I stuck a note on the door saying I'd be back and he carried the machine out to the car for me. We stopped at the hardware store so I could buy a padlock—he went in with me, paid for the most expensive lock they had—and went to the place. I filled out the papers, rather than him, and he insisted on putting my name on it, even though it was him who paid for the first six months' rent. We drove around to the number we were given, he took the typewriter inside, and left it, still in its sheet, in the back of the room. He pulled down the door, had me put the lock in the door—even made me get the thing out of its package, which is always such a battle, don't you think? Those awful plastic shrouds they seal everything into these days. I fought with it for a while and tried to hand it to him, but he wouldn't touch it, just gave me his pocketknife and had me saw the package open.

"Then he made me keep both the keys, and when we went back to my shop, he peeled off two more fifty-dollar bills and made me write out everything we'd done since he walked into the shop that morning. Oh, yes, and I signed the page he'd typed on the machine earlier. And then he put the pages into an oversized envelope with some papers in it, and had me drop the keys in, then seal it, and I signed that, too. Across the sealed flap, with the date and even the time.

"Then he paid for the typewriter itself with a credit card, gave me his business card, thanked me, and left. Oh, and he asked me to recommend a good local bank. Then he left, and that's the last I've seen of him. Far as

I know, the typewriter's still sitting there in lonely splendor. I hope he hasn't been running a meth lab in the storage facility or something?"

The casual reference to everyday crime on top of the winding narrative of a Sherlockian's antics came as a bit of a jolt, but Kate told the woman that, as far as she knew, no meth lab was suspected. She asked for the name of the storage facility and the bank, gave her own phone number in return, and hung up.

What Gilbert was doing sounded remarkably like a police chain of evidence record, down to his refusal to touch the package containing the keys, lest someone, somewhere accuse him of tampering with evidence. And Kate was not surprised when the Carmel bank told her that the safe-deposit box in the name of Philip Gilbert had not been visited since it had been rented on Wednesday, the tenth of December. She'd bet that it contained not only the keys, but all the statements he'd collected along the way.

So. Gilbert had bought the typescript from Paul Kobata on December sixth, taken it home and read it, seen its potential value, and set off to establish its provenance. He had followed the same trail that Kate had, nearly two months later, from Kobata to Maggie Brook back to the owner of the remodeled house in Pacific Heights, and then he had gone Kate one better, laying claim to a machine that, she was relatively certain, would prove to have been the machine on which the story had been typed. Certainly, Gilbert had thought the type identical, otherwise he would have walked off and left it to Tessie's Antiques.

He had locked the machine away, and put its keys and the related evidence in a bank. No doubt he had taken care to establish the time of day he had rented the box, to show that he would not have had time, between leaving Tessie's Antiques and entering the bank, to make a copy of the key.

A huge effort, a major expense (peeling off those fifty-dollar bills to buy Tessie's time). For what?

The only answer could be, to establish provenance. Or if not that, at least to prove beyond a shadow of doubt that it could not have been manufactured by Philip Gilbert. Each set of hands the story had passed through had signed a statement bearing witness to its passage; the machine on which it was typed had been similarly nailed down.

Clearly, to Philip Gilbert, the story with the unlikely beginning had been of enormous importance, from the moment he'd laid eyes on it.

Still behind the wheel of the parked car, Kate took out her cell phone and called Al. He answered on the second ring.

"Hey," she said. "You come up with anything?"

"A hell of a lot of fresh air and a whole lot of nothing. One woman was up with her baby and might have heard a car go by in the middle of the night, but she couldn't swear whether it was Friday or Saturday night."

"Where was she?"

"She lives in one of those houses along the road

between the visitor's center and the tunnel."

"Right on the road."

"Yeah, but it was raining and there was a bit of wind, so she couldn't be sure."

"Was it raining both nights?"

"A little bit Friday night, then it cleared most of Saturday, but it started raining seriously Saturday night, then continued Sunday morning and the whole rest of the week."

"Helpful."

"What about you?"

She outlined her day's activities, considerably more productive than his own.

"You've got the story?" he asked at the end of it.

"I let Nicholson make me a copy. I didn't see that we needed the exact one Gilbert made for him, and he was very reluctant to give it up. Looked to me like the same exact thing that's in Gilbert's safe-deposit box. I thought I'd swing by the bank on my way home and check."

"Other than that, you're finished for the day?"

"More or less. I'll take a look at the story tonight."

"Good. The autopsy's first thing tomorrow. I may be working at home if you need me, or call the cell."

Kate switched off the phone and turned the car's key, this time without interruption. The bank was shut to customers, although by tapping on the window with her badge, she summoned a gatekeeper who let her in. It was the work of two minutes to compare the old typescript with the photocopy Nicholson had given her, but when a dozen randomly chosen pages matched the original exactly, she was satisfied.

At last, she pointed the car's nose toward home, and invited her family out to dinner.

Later that night, after sushi, after bath, toothbrushing, and bedtime stories, Kate retrieved the folder Nicholson had given her and settled into one of the living room chairs to look it over. Before she had done more than remove the clip, Lee stuck her head in and asked, "You want a cup of tea?"

"Uh, sure. I'll make it."

"You just sat down. I'll get it."

Some faint edge in Lee's voice advised Kate not to press the matter, so she subsided, with a meek "Thanks, hon."

Kate could tell that Lee had had a long day, because she was using the cane. The doctors said that Lee would always have problems with her balance, but she'd never once fallen while carrying Nora, and hadn't fallen on her own in months.

However, one of the rules was that Kate did not offer to help for everyday things like carrying a single bag of groceries in from the car or fetching a book from the next room. Or bringing cups of tea. Even now, ten years after a bitter and frightening separation that lasted several long and dreary months, when Lee had gone away to test her own strengths and boundaries, Kate regularly found herself biting her tongue, reminding herself that Lee needed to do things for herself.

Allowances were made. The mugs Lee chose from

the shelf were generally those with deep handles, suitable for steady carrying even when held two to a hand. And the tea when it came would be nowhere near the top of the cup, since the two-in-one-hand carry combined with the lurch of the cane tended to dribble liquids across the floor. Such things were classed with sensible precautions such as a baby stroller sturdy enough to take some leaning on, a car with automatic transmission, and a walk-in shower level with the floor: things decided upon, then forgotten.

Lee put the cups onto the low table and lowered herself onto the sofa, stifling a small grunt.

"Hard day?" Kate asked.

"I need to start swimming again."

And not walking two miles round trip to the park, Kate did not say aloud. "Good idea. Maybe we could find a time that worked for both of us—I'd like to swim, too."

"Your schedule being so amenable to regular dates. Would you shove my laptop over here? Thanks."

Lee stretched her legs out on the sofa and settled the machine onto her lap. Kate had a brief picture of the tall, big-nosed Philip Gilbert bent over an ancient typewriter, pounding stiff-fingered at its round black keys—*Sitting down to that monstrosity of a typewriter downstairs and pounding out a letter,* as Rutland had described it. Kate heard the sleek little machine in Lee's lap whine as it woke up, and shook her head in amusement.

Lee took a sip of her twig tea and glanced at Kate's sheaf of papers. "What's that?"

"I am," Kate told her, " 'working the weird.' "

"Sorry?"

"Oh, nothing, just something Jules told Al. You know that case of the dead Sherlockian?"

"It is a great title."

"I'll save it for my memoirs. Anyway, the guy had recently got his hands on what may or may not have been a valuable manuscript, that may or may not be a lost Sherlock Holmes story, which I am told may or may not hold some similarities to how the body was actually found. So I need to look it over."

"One thing I love about your job, you deal with so much hard reality."

"What may or may not be hard reality," Kate said.

While she waited for the machine to find its niche in the household wireless system—another, recent, concession to comfort, freeing her from the upstairs desktop—Lee glanced over at the crisp white paper in Kate's hands. "That paper's not from the Twenties," she stated.

"This is a photocopy of a photocopy. The original's in a bank vault, along with a ton of other ridiculously valuable junk. Collectors," she said with a shrug.

Lee stared absently into the screen. "A lost Sherlock Holmes story."

"That's what I'm told," Kate agreed. She kicked off her shoes and put her stockinged feet up on the table.

"I heard something about that, not too long ago. Where was it?"

But Kate could only shake her head. In a minute, Lee

turned to the keyboard, and Kate settled to her reading, but before she had reached the end of the first page, Lee interrupted. "Got it. It was a little piece in the *Chron*, Leah Garchik's column about three weeks ago."

"Leah Garchik. The gossip columnist?"

"She's a friend of Roz's, often sticks things in there about her or Maj."

"And she had something about this story?"

"Well, about *a* story. Look."

She passed Kate the laptop. The screen showed an archived column of the *San Francisco Chronicle* from, as Lee had said, the middle of the previous month. The third paragraph read:

Fans of Sherlock Holmes are abuzz (sorry!) over a rumor that a previously unknown story about the detective has surfaced right here in San Francisco. I'm told that Arthur Conan Doyle spent a few days in the City back in the Twenties, but came away unimpressed. Seems he preferred LA, where his "message" of Spiritualism was more enthusiastically embraced. Isn't it good to know things haven't changed much? No one I could find knows anything about the rumor, but while I'm on holiday, I'll keep my magnifying glass and deerstalker cap out, just in case.

Kate handed the machine back to Lee. "Thanks, I'll look into it," she said, took a swallow of tea, and opened the manuscript.

SEVEN

The mind is a machine ill suited to desuetude. The occasional holiday is all very well, but without the oil of challenge and the heat generated by effort, the mind rusts and seizes and is unavailable when needed.

I found myself in San Francisco one spring evening, my travelling companion temporarily about other business and my mind at a loss for a load to carry. Recent days had seen the successful conclusion of a case not without interest, but after forty-eight hours of solitary leisure, a dangerous restlessness had begun to set in, so I cast about for other forms of stimulation to see me through the days ahead.

In the brief time I had been in this brash city on the Pacific, I had come to appreciate its idiosyncrasies and, despite its youth, its powerful sense of personality. A remarkably diverse metropolis, with nearly three-quarters of its residents born elsewhere, it seemed less a part of these United States than a country unto itself. It claimed, only half-humorously, its own emperor, a poor madman who had wandered the streets during the previous century; it had faced the worst fire any modern city had ever known and had built anew within a decade; its port linked the disparate parts of the world more than any other I had seen; it even chose which federal mandates it should apply to itself, so that the Volstead Act that was currently shredding the social orders of the rest of the nation went all but unacknowledged in San Francisco, where the prohibition of alcohol was given merely token recognition in restaurants and public houses alike: I had myself seen the chief of police with a glass of wine in his hand. The main effect of Prohibition that I had found was in the reduction of quality, not quantity.

I decided that, in keeping with my long-held belief that matriculation in the university of life ends only with the great final lesson, my education might benefit by an exploration of this remarkable city of the future. Not, however, the sort of exploration available to me by light of day--I had already spent more time than I cared playing the tourist. Thus, as evening fell I took up my overcoat against the night's mists and my stick against any possible assailant, and walked out of the doors of my hotel.

The city had come far from its days of being little more than a polite adjunct to the roaring Barbary Coast. The humorously named Maiden Lane, once the centre of bawdy entertainments, was now a staid enclave of the fashion industry, and these days, few men woke after a night out on the town to find themselves on a ship bound for Shanghai.

Still, though the Barbary Coast might have been shut down and the Chinese district cleansed of its more noxious corners, this remained, I had been assured, a 'wide open town'.

In the interest of research, then, I went to investigate its self-professed openness.

In San Francisco, those wishing the less salubrious quarters keep away from the hills and make for the low-lying ground. I had been in the city long enough to know the general direction, and made my way out of the commercial centre towards Market Street, and beyond. Within ten minutes I had found what I was looking for, paid a twenty-five-cent 'membership fee', ordered an overpriced glass of a beverage that in better times would have been swilled around the floor with a string-mop, and soon had found my evening's guide.

My guide introduced himself by a surreptitious insinuation of his fingers into my pocket. When I had his wrist firmly locked between my own fingers, I said without turning around, 'I see that the New World pickpockets have yet to attain the skill of their London brothers. Or perhaps I have simply come across an incompetent.'

Give the lad credit, he did not attempt to struggle against my grip, feeling no doubt the threat of broken bones in the particular arrangement of my finger-tips. Actually, I should admit that 'incompetent' was something of an exaggeration, a word chosen more for effect than accuracy. The boy was good enough for most purposes, just not good enough to lift the contents of my pocket. Particularly not in a place where I had half expected something of the sort.

I twisted his arm in a manner that forced him to circle around me, and nodded at the chair behind him. 'Do sit down,' I suggested firmly.

He hesitated, and I bent my restraining hand by way of encouragement. When he was seated, I let go.

'May I buy you a drink?' I asked him.

He did not immediately bolt for the door, as nine of ten young men in his position would do. He rubbed at his wrist, then sat back in his chair, eyeing me curiously.

Returning the favour, I saw a slim young man of perhaps nineteen or twenty, dressed in the compensatory fashion of one who has more sense of style than means of paying for it: quiet and slightly threadbare coat over flamboyant collar, waistcoat, and cravat, freshly polished shoes that had been cut for some other man's feet, quality trousers slightly bunched at the waist, with knees on the edge of shiny and cuff-edges that had worn through and been neatly turned up. The whole was put together as if to say that if he couldn't dress well, he would dress with panache. His blond hair (in need of a trim) was sleeked back over his head, and had not known a hat since it was last combed; his cheeks were freshly shaved, albeit by his own hand and with an inadequate looking-glass, or perhaps simply inadequate light; his nails were clean and well trimmed; his teeth had regular acquaintance with a brush and tooth-powder.

It was his gaze that gave him away. As they wandered across my person, seeing a grey-haired man in expensive London clothes to suit the accent, his pale blue eyes took on a knowing cast. I was not surprised to see him lean back a trifle more, tucking one arm behind the back of the chair so his coat fell slightly away from the clean, innocent whiteness of his shirt, of which one button did not quite match the others. He gave me the sort of smile I had seen before, one no doubt intended to be sultry.

I laughed aloud; his carefully composed smile wavered, his eye-brows tipped into a scowl.

'My dear young man,' I said, 'when I offered to buy you a drink, it was merely for the purpose of conversation, nothing more. If you are looking for companionship, I would suggest you approach that male person in the unfortunate cap sitting along the back wall. His collars might not be clean, but he is clearly interested in making your acquaintance.'

My companion hesitated, glanced over his shoulder at the unprepossessing gentleman in question, and settled again with a dismissive shake to his shoulders. 'Sure,' he said. 'I'll have a drink.'

He ordered a cocktail of the sort that had been invented by a bored and sadistic barkeep the week before, and while we waited I ran a small wager with myself as to its colour and the shape of glass it would come inside. I won on colour--a sickly lavender tint--but the glass was an ordinary water-glass rather than one of those broad plates better suited to olives or salted nuts than liquid. He held his drink up to me by way of toast, took a sip without wincing, then by way of thanks thrust his hand out at me and said, 'Martin Ledbetter.'

I gave him a name and my hand, and when we had settled the matter of identities, I sampled my local California claret-type, which to my relief did not actually scour off the membranes of my palate. I then bent to examine the small bowl of assorted oddments that had arrived with the drinks.

'Are these intended to be eaten?' I asked my companion.

'If you've got a hard stomach and good teeth, they probably won't kill you,' he replied. I nudged the bowl across the table for him, and he happily scooped up a handful and began snapping off the shells of what I decided were either large pistachios or wizened peanuts, depositing them onto the floor to mix with the sawdust, shells, and assorted waste. 'So, what brings you to our fair city, Mr Sigerson?'

'My wife's family live here,' I replied, which statement had as much truth in it as the names we had given each other. 'She's off for a few days on business, so I thought I'd take a look at the other side of San Francisco.'

'The seamy tour, eh?' he said, wagging his nicely shaped eye-brows in a raffish commentary on the whims of the old and rich.

'More by way of comparison. I have spent a great deal of my life in places such as this, for the most part in London. I was curious to see if this new town had any variations to play on the old themes.'

His eyes again ran down my trousers, paused on the shoes made for me by a man in Piccadilly, went to the immaculate silk of the tie I wore, before he blurted out, 'Why would someone like you spend time in places like this?'

'And what is someone like me?' I wondered aloud.

His gaze went from the ebony cuff-links I had been given in Japan to the heavy gold watch-chain across my waistcoat, and he shook his head in thought. 'You're not beat-up enough to be a lifelong drunk or an addict, and you walked right past the girls near the door, so you're not looking for them. Or for me. Are you some kind of do-gooder? A church reformer or something?'

'I have absolutely no desire to reform any of these good people,' I assured him.

'Then why come here?'

I held up my wine to the dim light leaking from the bar, noting the evidence of sugar added to the fermentation, then told him, 'You might say I come here in a professional capacity.'

I could see him pick over my statement, saw his eyes narrow for a brief instant as he considered the possibility that my profession might be within the bounds of law enforcement, then go on to more likely roles. Eventually he cocked his head at me, appraisingly, no doubt recalling the ease with which I had intercepted his intrusive fingers. 'Con-man? Dance-hall owner? No, I've got it--you're a professional gambler--a card-sharp!'

'I have been known to play the Great Game, but lesser forms such as baccarat and poker have never interested me. As to the other possibilities, well, shall we say merely that I try not to limit myself?'

I nearly laughed out loud at the sudden bloom of respect in his pale eyes. Young men are ever gullible to the siren call of romance, and the romance of crime has the sweetest voice of all. 'Tell me, Mr Ledbetter, have you any pressing engagements for the rest of the evening? I find myself in need of a guide to the city's underworld, and you seem well placed for the position. A paid position,' I added.

'How much?' he responded.

'Not as much as you'd have got had you managed to lift my note-case, but more than you would get were you to depend on the generosity of the man in the cloth cap.'

We negotiated for a time, agreed on a sum, and after I had paid him half, he rose and led me out onto the street.

It was a curious evening, the first I had spent among the demimonde in some years, and although I found it much as I had left it, decades before and half a world away, it was every bit as sad, as tawdry, and as entrancing as it had ever been, from the ladies tapping at the upstairs windows to attract custom to the curiously appealing foodstuffs each establishment presented to keep its patrons on the premises--although in this town, the free food tended to be spiced meats wrapped in Mexican flat-breads or diminutive ham sandwiches rather than the Scotch eggs and kidney pies of my native land.

Ledbetter, understandably enough, began with the higher end of the spectrum, those establishments where the gin came in a distillery's bottles and the singers could hit a reasonable percentage of the notes. However, once he had figured out that I was not easily shocked, he rose to the challenge, and led me to half a dozen holes that I would never have discovered on my own. As his piece de résistance, in the wee hours of the morning he pulled me into a narrow doorway in a part of town north of Market Street. A window slid open, an eye gazed out, the window slid shut, and the door opened: one breath, and I was transported to the days of my youth.

'An opium den, by Jove,' I exclaimed, and laughed aloud at his expression. Looking back, I suspect that the accumulation of odd spirits I had consumed had begun to affect me, but it had been in truth a far more entertaining evening than I could have anticipated.

When we were back out on the street some time later, I said something of the sort as I paid my guide the remainder of his evening's hire. 'I have to thank you, young man, for a most enlightening tour. It has assured me that the human imagination, while somewhat stuck in its old grooves, is not completely moribund.'

He accepted his money with an owlish blink, watched me slip the note-case back into my pocket, and said, 'I can't let you walk back to your hotel by yourself. What if you're robbed?'

'That is very kind of you,' I told him, politely not deigning to point out that attempted robbery was precisely what had brought us together. Too, considering his condition, I thought it not unlikely that he would be the one to wake in some dark alley with a bleeding head and empty pockets. 'But I shall be fine.'

Still, nothing would do but that he walk me out of the dark areas where the taxis do not ply, by which time we were nearly at my hotel. He accompanied me to the steps, looking considerably more sober for the effort, and shook my hand.

'Mr Sigerson, any time you want a tour, just say the word.'

'What about tonight?' I asked. Midnight had gone, long before.

'Again?'

'Something slightly different, perhaps. Shall we say nine o'clock, here at the hotel? At the same rates, of course. Yes? Very well, see you tonight.'

I do not know which man watched me pass through the doors of the hotel with more amazement on his face, the night doorman, or young Mr Ledbetter.

The following evening I took an early dinner and dressed in a manner even more formal than I had the previous evening. My silk hat gleamed, my immaculate suit (not evening wear, which I deemed would create too much of a distraction) did not; I gave my ebony stick a polish with a face-flannel and tucked my prized emerald stickpin into the folds of my silk tie. Thus besplendoured, I waited in the park across the street from the hotel. When the young man came striding up the western side of Powell Street, I gave a sharp whistle, and he crossed over to join me.

He stopped in front of me and eyed the gold chain across my front. 'Don't you want to dress down just a little?'

'So that I look less like a toff, you mean?'

'I don't know what a toff is, but you look like a man just asking to be robbed.'

'As good a definition as any. I find contrast offers a <u>soupçon</u> of spice to one's social encounters. And besides, had I not looked like a man asking to be robbed, you and I might never have met.'

I was amused to see the lad blush, amused and encouraged: A pickpocket who could feel shame was by no means lost. I set my top-hat at an angle and declared, 'Mr Ledbetter, I am in your hands.'

The previous evening, I had visited half a dozen establishments in his company, and only the opium den had qualified for the term 'dive'. This evening, my guide appeared determined to complete my experience of the city's night-life.

At the third such place of business --dark, dismal, and so dispirited, the owners had not even bothered to maintain the electric bells behind the bar to warn of a raid, I poured my glass of so-called whisky onto the matted sawdust underfoot and said, 'These sorts of places are, I agree, worthy of note, but I fear my liver will not survive too many more of them. What about the Blue Tiger?'

'You know about the Blue Tiger?' he enquired in surprise.

'It came up in a conversation the other day.' In fact, I had sat surveillance across the street from its door for several hours; however, it was also true that the place did later enter into the conversation with the subject of that surveillance.

'Okay, it's your nickel.'

We took a taxi, and joined a brief

queue of private cars and taxis dis-
gorging their brightly dressed Young
Things at the door. There we received
our first hitch: The doorman knew my
companion, and blocked our entrance
with a mighty scowl and an impressive
set of shoulders.

'Marty, I told you not to come back
here,' he growled.

'Oh, Henry, don't be wet. I'm on my
best behaviour tonight--this is my
friend, Mr Sigerson. He'll keep an
eye on me.'

'We had complaints, last time.'

'Unsubstantiated,' the lad
retorted, although he gave me an
apologetic smile.

The retired pugilist looked me over
dubiously, no doubt caught on the
possible meanings of 'friend'. Obediently, I told him in my plummiest of
voices, 'I assure you, Mr Ledbetter
will behave himself.'

The man nodded reluctantly, but
leant forward to shake one massive
finger in my guide's face. 'We have
one lady say her handbag's gone
missing, you're out--and with a set
of bruises you won't forget easy.'

'Ooh, Mr Toughie,' Ledbetter

purred, and slipped past the doorman into the club beyond.

The Blue Tiger was a dance hall, but it had a balcony that circled three-quarters of the floor. It was there we took our seats, with--such was the 'membership fee' I had paid on entering--a clear view of the stage. At the moment, the raised space was as bare of players as the dance floor was of couples, but the disarray of chairs and instruments indicated a mere break in the music.

A waiter appeared at my elbow, and I glanced at the surrounding tables. The customary drink here, unless one wished a named cocktail, appeared to be champagne; I ordered a bottle. It was priced at only five or six times what I would have paid for the same beverage in Europe, and it arrived in a not too badly tarnished silver bucket with a pair of admirably clean glasses.

My young companion waved the waiter away and set to removing the cork. He did so expertly, directing the upwelling foam into a glass before it could be lost. He raised his glass to me in a wordless toast, a habit that was either his own or that of his American generation. Before I could enquire, the band spilt back onto the stage, six comely Negro ladies, and resumed their instruments.

Their music was not at all bad--not to my taste, of course, but the notes were accurate and the syncopation precise. A hundred gaily dressed young people bobbed and spun out on the floor, and the temperature and humidity climbed. It was as well, I reflected, that the female dancers were as lightly clad as they were, all open backs and exposed arms. The young men, on the other hand, succumbing to the dictates of wool and linen, had faces as shiny as their hair. Ledbetter's foot tapped under the table, but when I assured him that I would not feel abandoned were he to go out onto the dance floor, he merely shook his head and refilled our glasses.

Perhaps he feared that, once among the crowd, he might find it difficult to keep his promise to the doorman. This hesitation could have been another vestige of ethics, or merely the knowledge that I could too easily abandon him unpaid.

A likeable young rogue, Mr Martin Ledbetter.

When the band broke for another brief intermission, I signalled for a second bottle of the wine and then said to the lad, 'Tell me about yourself, Mr Ledbetter.'

'Why?' he replied, his voice short.

'I suppose I could point out that conversation is what I am employing you for, in my search for understanding of the American way of life. Or I could say that I am interested in how a personable and clearly intelligent young man comes to find picking pockets more lucrative than, say, working in an office. However, let us merely say that a break in the music is intended to provide an interlude for conversation, and it would be churlish of us to pass the opportunity by.'

He stood up abruptly, and said, 'A break is also intended to provide the chance to whiz. Which I am going to do.'

He made his deliberate way between the tables, hands slightly outstretched as counterbalance to the wine in his blood. The music started again and he was not back, but by the second dance, he reappeared up the stairway.

He sat down, fortified himself with half the contents of the glass, and said abruptly, 'I was born here in 1901, never knew my father, my mother was killed in the Earthquake, and the aunt who raised me died when I was sixteen. I make a living how I can, and nobody gets hurt but me.' He made the toast gesture again, polished off the contents of his glass, and reached for the bottle, defiantly allowing it to slosh over the side.

Looking only at the hard-working jazz band, I told him, 'You were born in 1903 or four, and spent your early years in Minnesota. Your father may well be dead, but someone put you through school, some male friend or relative who was two inches taller and forty pounds heavier than you, who had a certain amount of money about ten years ago, and who died within perhaps the last two years.'

I did not need to look at his face to see the look of confusion and alarm there: I had seen that expression often enough, and as I usually did, I relented with an explanation.

'You can't be more than twenty now. To a trained ear, your voice provides clear evidence of where you were when you first learnt to speak. You have been to school, although not university. And the clothing you wear was expensive ten years ago, but tailored to a larger man, who died and left his wardrobe to you.' I finally looked at him, to explain, 'You are wearing a complete change of clothing from what you had on last night, yet both sets of suit, shirt, and shoes have the same ill fit. And the amount of wear evidenced by the shirt collars would take about two years to accumulate, given an original two-week supply. If you stole the clothes rather than inherited them, you would surely have replenished your supply of shirts over the years.'

The young man's jaw worked, his pale eyes went icy; for an instant, I expected him to dash the contents of his glass in my face and storm out, never to cross my path again.

Instead, he controlled himself. He set his glass carefully on the table and leant forward until his face was inches from mine. 'I'll show you around; I'll play your games; I won't talk about who I am.'

'Very well,' I answered equably. 'Then tell me about these gentlemen on the stage.'

The boy's face remained taut for a minute, then slowly relaxed into a grin. 'You caught that, did you?'

'That all the ladies are men wearing frocks and make-up? Certainly.'

'You must've heard about them before. That's why you wanted to come here.'

'I will admit, I heard something of the sort. But I would have known in any case. It's hardly a new act, you know. London had trans-vestites of both varieties long before Victoria was on the throne. The Romans in Londinium probably watched a similar performance.'

He had no answer for that, although as he sat watching the stage, I knew that a part of his mind was taken up with the idea that former generations had flavours of sin that were not so very different. Such an idea invariably takes the young by surprise.

The song ended, the overhead light changed subtly, and Ledbetter sat forward in his chair. I watched curiously as the entire cabaret held its drinks and came to attention. The lights dipped to nothing, there was a sound of machinery and motion, and a minute later the lights rose again, glittering off the polished bars of a golden bird-cage a good ten feet tall. It swung gently a few feet from the boards, then descended, and as it lowered the lights gradually revealed a person seated on the cage's swinging perch. The moment she became visible, the audience erupted with applause, hooting and whistling their appreciation. The woman's pretty head remained inclined in modest recognition; when the cage touched ground, its door fell open, and she stepped out into the fanfare, head still looking at the ground.

She was small and exotically handsome, her theatrical make-up emphasising the large eyes and full lips Nature had given. A gold-and-pearl head-piece wrapped her head like a bandeau, but with cross-pieces that connected over the crown of her sleek ebony hair and continued down on either side to make ear-pieces. Her dress was long and golden, the slippers peeping from beneath its hem were gold, her finger-nails were painted gold, even her warm coppery skin seemed to glitter; the white explosion of a lengthy feather boa around her throat only emphasised the overall colour.

When the tribute had begun to fade, she took a step forward and threw back her arms and her head, showing for the first time a pair of blazing green eyes. She opened her mouth, and the band came in precisely on the first beat.

Her signature song was, of course, 'The Bird in the Golden Cage', a tune that I had first heard when I was not much older than Martin Ledbetter, in those gay _fin de siècle_ days that the Twenties already seemed determined to emulate, if not surpass. The notes emerged from the singer's throat completely unhindered by any trace of masculinity; if one closed one's eyes, one would hear only a saucy and self-assured woman at the height of her powers; when the song had ended, I applauded as freely as the rest.

Ledbetter leant over to speak in my ear. 'That's Billy Birdsong. Just returned from half a year in Europe.'

'Ah yes, Miss Birdsong. I have heard of her.'

'Originally William,' he said, pouncing on the words as if he had caught me out. I suppose he still expected me to be shocked at the daring sins of his generation, sins previously unseen upon the earth.

I concealed my smile, and said merely, 'Of course. However, good manners require that one accept at face value whichever identity a person presents. Wouldn't you agree, "Mr Ledbetter"?'

He gave me a sharp glance, then turned back to the stage.

The chanteuse was no operatic voice, but her contralto range was true, and had clearly been trained. She was pleasing on the eyes, her jokes were clever if on the racy side, her costumes remarkable, and I could easily understand if this home-grown talent had made a successful conquest among the sophisticates of Europe.

At the end of her set of songs, she retired from the stage amidst whistles and hoots, and the dancers settled in for the more mundane talents of other singers.

It was here that Ledbetter justified his salary.

He stood up and said, 'Be back in a minute.'

As the young man did not appear to be using his disappearances to ingest any substances more illicit than the alcohol on the table, I wondered if he had a medical condition that should be seen to. When he had not returned in a reasonable time, I further began to wonder if perhaps I had been abandoned--I will admit that I even felt at my inner pocket to reassure myself that my note-case was still with me.

However, I had neither been robbed nor abandoned; indeed, it turned out that I was being served well by my hireling, who had gone to fetch the evening's entertainment.

I rose at the approach of Ledbetter's companion, taking the delicate hand and bowing deeply over it as my guide made the introductions.

The singer's green eyes danced with pleasure.

'Marty here told me I had an admirer from a far-off land. I just had to come see.'

Billy Birdsong was a fine womanly figure of a man, five feet four inches of smooth racially mixed skin over a dancer's muscles and pleasingly languid bones. Modern dictates of fashion made re-forming the male form less of an engineering feat than it had a generation before--these days, even women were required to appear boyish. The casual drape of a sheer scarf around the singer's neck concealed the masculinity of the throat, and she navigated with assurance on heels higher than many women dared.

I invited her to sit while Ledbetter summoned up a new bottle of champagne and another glass. Miss Birdsong fluttered her eye-lashes with only the slightest exaggeration of femininity, and said, 'You are from England, Mr Sigerson?'

'London, yes.'

'I was there for most of February.'

'Pity, the spring can be quite

lovely. Alas, I was in India then, or I would surely have seen you. Where did you perform?'

She told me, acted gratified that I had heard of the place, and set about the sort of conversation that is required of professional ladies. She was, however, distracted. Before a minute had passed, her avid attention to my description of the Suez Canal slid sideways--only momentarily, and only those green eyes shifted--but clearly she was searching her surroundings for something, or someone. And not finding them.

This intrigued me in a way her professional demeanour had not. Billy Birdsong was the most prominent person in the place; why should she give the most surreptitious of glances at her surroundings? She could easily rise up and gaze imperiously about, and no one would be taken aback.

Either she did not wish to offend me, or she did not wish to be seen looking about. And although I could indeed have represented a potential source of patronage, her lack of interest made that seem unlikely.

No; she was scouring the room for someone, a face she did not want to be seen searching out, and she was not finding that person. Furthermore, that absence made her increasingly anxious: While her eyes probed the corners of the balconies, her fingers sought out the large, beautifully mounted pink pearl she wore on a silver chain, tugging at it and rolling it between finger and thumb.

When her hand rose to her mouth and her sharp little teeth began to work at the cuticles of the finger holding the pearl, I knew something was amiss.

'Miss Birdsong,' I began.

'Call me Billy,' she broke in. 'Everybody does.'

'Yes. Miss Birdsong, you appear to be agitated. May I be of any help?'

At that, her gaze snapped back to me, her spine went straight, and her gnawed finger dropped away. 'Agitated? Don't be ridiculous,' she protested, and laughed. 'Why should I be agitated while I'm sitting with admirers and drinking their bubbly? Silly man.'

One thing I am not is silly, and I

believe she saw that, despite the setting and my proximity to the pick-pocketing ne'er-do-well at the other side of the table. She laughed again, a well-trained noise, finished her champagne, and rose to make a wide and easy circuit of the balcony before retreating down the stairs.

But <u>la donna è mobile</u>, even when <u>la donna</u> is an artifice, and thus I was not in the least surprised when a note arrived, on scented paper and in an elaborately calligraphed script:

> If you would like to buy a girl some dinner after her second show, come to the dressing rooms at twelve-thirty.
>
> --BB

Ledbetter was, I believe, rather taken aback.

EIGHT

W hat on earth are you chuckling at?" said a foam-clotted voice.

Kate looked up from the photocopied typescript to see her partner looking around the doorway from the hall, a toothbrush jutting from her lips at a jaunty angle.

"You better not let Nora see you doing that," she warned. "Granny Martinelli will rise up from her grave in horror if her great-granddaughter starts running around the house with a stick in her mouth."

Lee went back into the bathroom and came out a minute later sans brush. She moved with deliberation around the foot of the bed, hands out to balance herself, her cane left leaning against the dressing table.

"I take it that story's entertaining?" she asked as she lowered herself onto the bed. "You're giggling like a schoolgirl."

"It's a hoot. Can you picture Sherlock Holmes in earnest conversation with a drag queen?"

That startled a laugh out of Lee. "Oh, come on now. Is this one of those porn stories that have Holmes and Watson in bed together?"

"Are there such things? The mind boggles. No, so far it's all very decorous, although reading between the lines you begin to suspect a fair amount of leg-pulling is going on. And actually, so far there doesn't seem to be any evidence that the main character even *is* Sherlock Holmes, although he's every bit as pompous as the original. Far as I can see, the main reason for interest would be if it was actually written by Conan Doyle, which I wouldn't know, although it sounds like it's set in the early Twenties."

"Early soft-core gay porn. Sure, I'd kill someone for that. In fact," she said, rolling languorously over until she was taking up a large portion of Kate's side of the bed, "I'd kill for some of the later kind."

"Murder is not necessary," Kate replied. She dropped the sheaf of papers to the floor, turned off the reading light, and before long had her partner giggling, like a schoolgirl.

KATE never failed to step back and wonder at the morning ritual. Even on those days when Nora was in a temper, when Lee was snappish with aches, when Kate herself was rushed out the door, there would be a moment when she would pause and savor the precious fact of the day. This Wednesday morning it came while she stood in the door of the sun-filled kitchen and bit into a cold, leathery, half-burned English muffin, Nora's latest culinary venture. Lee, still in the thigh-length T-shirt she used as a nightie and hair awry, was holding the glass carafe of the coffeemaker up to the window to see if what it held was still drinkable. Nora, in her school clothes and hair brushed but nonetheless nearly as awry as her mother's, was scowling with concentration at the complexities of spreading jam on muffin.

"Strawberry jam's harder to get even than other kinds," the child complained.

"That's because they leave the strawberries whole instead of grinding them up," Lee explained.

"Why don't they grind them up?"

"I guess they want to give you the surprise of biting into a berry here and just jam there." Lee had decided the coffee passed muster, poured it, and slid into the built-in table across from Nora. Her T-shirt rode up on the vinyl seating, and without thinking she tugged it down, disappointing Kate.

"Maybe I should just put more on and make it even," Nora said.

"That might be too much jam even for me," Kate told her. "Next time we'll buy cheaper jam and it'll go on even."

"Okay."

And that was the moment she held with her for the day: solemn child, sleepy partner, and a bubble of laughter rising in her chest. She kissed one sticky face and one coffee-flavored mouth, and let herself out of the house.

With one foot in the car, Kate heard someone call her name, and looked up to see the next-door neighbor coming up the block. Hadassah Levitson was one of the few people Kate had ever met who made her feel tall: She couldn't have been more than five two. She also reminded Kate of a Jack Russell terrier, her nose in everything and absolutely fearless.

"Kate, glad to catch you."

"How are you, Hadassah?"

Typically, the woman didn't bother with an answer but went straight to business. "You know old Mrs. Kirchbaum in the next block?"

"Er."

"Nice lady, no grandchildren, works at the children's center?"

"Poppy seed rolls?" Kate remembered.

"You got her. Anyway, I hadn't seen her in a couple

days so I went around, and she's hurt her leg, finding it hard to get around. I'm organizing people to drop in with dinners, but I know she has a son down in LA or something and I want to talk to him without her knowing. You have any idea how to get in touch with him?"

"I could probably hunt him down," Kate told her, figuring she was being asked because cops can do anything. "But it would be faster to ask Lee. I think she's got a list of emergency contact numbers for everyone at the center."

"Great, I'll see if she's got it."

"She's home now," Kate told her neighbor, but she was already talking to Hadassah's back.

She finished getting into the car, a smile on her face. Small-town life.

I should not by choice have sat through the second arrangement of Miss Birdsong's music, as the increasing intoxication of the audience and its dancers did nothing to make their feverish gaiety any more appealing. But I held myself in patience, observing the behaviour of this self-avowedly barbaric race of moderns and making notes on the stylistic oddities of American slang, Jazz music, and the parallel between the men/women musicians before me and their reverse equivalents (actresses in breeches) of the eighteenth century London stage. All three being topics with the potential for engrossing monographs (the number of euphemisms for drunkenness alone would fill a small note-book), the evening was not wasted.

Eventually, however, the singer waved her way merrily off the stage for the second time that night (or, by that time, morning). The crowds began to thin as those who had gainful employ the next morning took themselves home for a few hours' rest, and Ledbetter and I made our way down the stairs and to the dressing rooms behind the stage.

One of my first questions regarding the singer was answered when I saw that the costume draped over the screen, clearly for her to don once she had shed her stage finery, was also a frock: Some performers acting the part of women make it a point to assert a strongly masculine identity off of the stage. Miss Birdsong was one of those whose act merged into everyday life.

'Sit down, dear boys, I'll just be

a jiffy. Have a bonbon.' We pushed
aside the chocolates and orchids and
sat on the stools beside the gifts
while the singer swabbed the heavy
pancake make-up from her face,
revealing delicate features that, had
the eye-brows preserved their natural
thickness and the side-burns been
permitted to grow, would have read as
that of a boy. As it was, she looked
like a somewhat boyish girl--as
indeed had half the audience, to my
eyes. When her face was clean, however, she did not leave it bare, but
replaced the heavy theatrical mask
with lighter but equally effective
powder and paint, chatting gaily all
the time, mostly about Paris and
London.

When she had finished to her satisfaction, she rose, loosing the belt of
her mauve silk dressing-gown as she
walked towards the three-panelled
screen. When she had stepped into
hiding, the dressing-gown shot art-
fully up to drape itself over the top
of the screen, the frock waiting there
vanished a moment later, and soon she
came back, adjusting the seams of her
embroidered stockings coquettishly.

A most entertaining performance; I could already see that this excursion into the night-life of the city of St Francis was bound to add to my education.

She caught up my silk hat and tipped it onto my head, permitted young Ledbetter to help her into her brilliant white sealskin coat, picked up her tiny gold mesh handbag, and sashayed down the corridor to the stage door, calling farewells to various fellow musicians and staff as she went. Outside of the door, she repeated the performance with the men and a few women waiting there, signing autographs and exchanging banter. The nightclub diva seemed well liked by all.

She hooked her two hands through our arms and steered us up two streets to a small bistro that was doing a brisk business despite the hour. Clearly a regular customer, she was whisked to a table, where she shrugged out of her furs and accepted a cigarette and light from Ledbetter.

When we had ordered, however, her first words were to me. 'Mr Sigerson, how can you possibly imagine that I am in need of your help?'

'You were hoping to see someone back in the balcony, a person whose absence both surprised and troubled you. The person, I venture to say, who gave you that pearl you wear.'

Her fingers dropped away from the object as if it had gone suddenly hot. 'Ridiculous!' she said, her fists clenching in a most unladylike manner.

'You scarcely listened to what Mr Ledbetter and I had to say, you worried that necklace to the breaking point, and you chewed your fingernails into an early manicure. How else to explain that level of anxiety?'

She reared back her head and stared at me. 'What are you, some kind of Sherlock Holmes?'

It was a question I had encountered before. 'I am a gentleman who finds himself with leisure on his hands, willing to assist a lady in distress.'

The series of expressions on the face across the table from me was inimitable, and priceless, as the singer wrestled with the improbable

possibility that this grey-hair
English gent might be far more of a
innocent than was either likely, or
desirable. In the end, the body
inside the frock sat forward, subtly
changing form, as the voice dropped
the better part of an octave to ask,
'You do know I'm not actually a
woman?'

'Mr Birdsong, how you choose to
present yourself matters not in the
least to me. And if you prefer to
keep to yourself whatever troubled
you on the balcony, I shall happily
share a meal with you and take my
leave.'

The man studied my face for a long
moment, then sat back and slowly
resumed the woman's skin. Such a
talent is no common thing, nor an
easy one, and my curiosity about the
person gave another stir.

Birdsong--patently not the singer's
birth name, although I thought the
William might be original--was by
feature and accent from the American
south-west, Arizona or New Mexico.
The thick, straight black hair and
exotically tinted skin revealed a
percentage of blood older to these

lands than that of the European set-
tlers, although the light green eyes
were imports--in northern India one
found this mixture of brown skin and
green eyes, but not in America, and
not with those cheek-bones. Close
quarters revealed that he was older
than the twenty-eight or thirty years
old that he looked, perhaps by as
much as a decade. As an adolescent,
he would have been remarkably beautiful; the complications accompanying great beauty had, no doubt,
contributed to set him on the road to
his choice of profession.

Still, the singer seemed happy
enough. Apart, that is, from those
anxious eyes in the balcony.

'I was looking for a friend,' she
said abruptly. 'He said he'd be there
and he wasn't. It's not like him.'

'And you are unable to make
enquiries?' I suggested. She had,
after all, failed to reach her
dressing room's telephone.

Still she hesitated, before
explaining, 'I think he may be a soldier.' The shrug of shoulders was
eloquent.

'Ah. Yes, that would create difficulties. A person such as myself, however, might gain access where you would be rebuffed.'

'Impossible. If he is, and if his commanding officer got wind of where he spends his free time, he'd be in the brig before you could snap your fingers.'

'My dear Miss Birdsong, kindly give me a modicum of credit. In a long and mis-spent life, I have at least learnt how to ask questions that lead nowhere.'

'I couldn't take the chance.'

'You and your friend were, I take it, seen together in public?'

'Occasionally.'

'That alone is more of a risk than any queries I might make.'

I have been told that my manner with the fairer sex, although far from intimate, can be remarkably comforting. So it proved with this artificial female. Our meal arrived, and as she ate, the singer spoke about other things, keeping up a flirtatious repartee with Ledbetter, but all the time her eyes kept coming back to my face, trying to decipher what lay there.

Finally, when the plates had been cleared and I had settled the cheque, she studied me, then seemed to come to a decision, laying her pretty hand on my sleeve.

'If you do anything to give him away, you will destroy the life of a fine man.'

'Miss Birdsong, you have my word: If his superiors discover his secret, it will not be through me.'

'I don't know why I'm trusting you with this. I shouldn't. But I do. His name is Jack Raynor.

'I met him a little more than a month ago, my second night back at the Tiger. I'd only been home from Europe a few days, but the travel expenses for that trip were monstrous, so I came right along to work. He sent a bottle of bubbly to my dressing room after the second show, along with an enormous armful of pink roses and a note saying how much he'd enjoyed the show. I invited him back, along with about twenty others, and thanked him politely, and by the time the crowd thinned out he was gone.

'But the next night he was there

again, with the champagne and the roses--yellow this time. I had him back, told him to wait until the others had left, and then we went for dinner. He was a very sweet, well-spoken boy. No- a man. Quiet but very self-assured.'

'He did not wear a uniform to the club?'

'Heavens no!'

'Yet you thought <u>soldier</u> rather than <u>sailor</u>.' The San Francisco Bay was home to both Army and Navy personnel.

'Yes. I'm not sure why. Perhaps it was the hair-cut and the straight back. Those generally say <u>soldier</u>, don't they?'

There might be a score of more definitive indicators, I reflected, but a singer in a port city such as this would have encountered enough of both varieties of military personnel to render an immediate impulse relatively trustworthy.

'How old is he?'

'In his early thirties, perhaps. He'd spent time in the tropics, and had that kind of baked look to his skin that makes it hard to tell. And

I think, too, that he'd been sick. Not now, but not so long ago--his skin was a little sallow, and he spoke once about fevers.'

'But you think he was still actively in the services, rather than an ex-soldier?' A man in his early thirties would have been in his middle twenties during the War, and could easily have left the service since then.

'I really don't know. Does it matter?'

'All detail matters.'

'I suppose so,' she said doubt-fully.

'What about his history? Is he from San Francisco? Did you ever meet any of his friends?'

'He wasn't from here, no. I got the impression that he hadn't been in the city very long.'

'Why do you say that?'

'He had that kind of new-kid interest in the place, kept coming up with items of local interest that tickled him. He especially liked our sizeable collection of dotty charac-ters--he got a kick out of Emperor Norton, I remember. Have you heard about him? One of our local eccentrics of the last century, who got involved in some shady deal, lost everything including his mind, and then went around telling everyone he was the Emperor of California and making sweeping commands and pronouncements. Another eccentric he liked was Charley Pankhurst, a stagecoach driver down near Watsonville. "Mountain Charley" owned an inn, voted in elections, had a lot of friends in the area--only when Charley died, they discovered he was a woman. Yes, the San Francisco area has its fair share of characters.'

'I see,' I told her, taking care to keep my voice even, lest she think I might be so bold as to include her among the eccentrics. 'What about Raynor's friends?'

'I never met any, and I don't even know--well now, wait just a tick. He did one time let slip that he had a friend who talked about music and books. Oh dear, I'm so bad with names. Joe? Gary? I'm sorry, it was just in passing. And there was a night, we were leaving the club to walk back to my apartment, and he spotted someone he knew. That fellow was even more of a soldier than Jack --he might as well have been marching on the parade ground. You know, heels down, shoulders back?'

'Did you speak with this man?'

'Oh no, Jack steered me away from him right quick.'

'Pity.' It sounded more and more as if the man Raynor was indeed on active duty, if he was so chary of meeting a fellow soldier while in the company of Billy Birdsong.

'To return to his presence at the Blue Tiger--You saw him there with some regularity?'

'After that first time, he would show up three, four, sometimes five times a week. After the third night I invited him home, and . . . well, he turned out to be a real sweet-heart.'

'Quite. And when was the last time you saw him?'

'Five nights ago. When he left, Friday just before dawn, he said, "See you tomorrow", meaning Saturday. But he didn't show up, and I haven't seen him since.'

'Could he not simply have been

taken away by unexpected responsibil-
ities?'

'Well, he had something to do
Friday night, but once before when
we'd had a date and he couldn't make
it, he sent me a note--a post-card,
sent to my home, an innocent message
but just something to let me know he
wouldn't be there. Something like,
"Tell your Aunt Tillie she'll have to
see the sights without me, hope to
get there tomorrow." That's when he
told me about the fevers--he'd been
too sick to come.'

'But this time you've had no post-
card.'

'Not a word.'

'Very well, I shall see what I can
find out about your friend. Is there
anything else he said that would
indicate his employment, interests,
habits?'

'Well, he didn't like to talk about
his work at all. We talked mostly
about music, and art, and Europe. Not
about what he did during the days. He
liked to chat about imaginary things,
and what he'd like to do with his
life. He'd pose a question, and we'd
both talk about that. Things like, if

you were a painter, who would you be? Or, where would you live if you didn't have to work? And, what one thing would make you give up every-thing else?'

'What did he say to that last?'

'Love, of course. We both agreed that love was better than anything.'

I shook off this claptrap of a side-track. 'If he was a soldier, you would say that he was an officer?'

'I assumed he was. He was educated and well-spoken--and he had no shortage of spending money. I don't know for certain. Stranger things have happened.'

'They have indeed,' I agreed. Just the previous year I had worked on a case involving a baronet who changed his name in order to enlist as a common soldier, with harsh conse-quences. 'Can you give me a descrip-tion of Mr Raynor?'

'I have a photograph, if you'd like to see it.'

That gave me pause: If he had granted her a photograph, it indi-cated more than a casual fling.

'Yes, I would like to see it.'

She opened the clasp of her bag and

took out a small cabinet photograph some four inches tall and three wide, popping open the lock and holding the resulting silver clamshell out on her palm. I took it from her, and saw a fit young man in his early thirties, pale of hair and eye. He was clean shaven, easy to look upon, and faced the camera with a tilt of the head that could have been confidence, or a trace of defiance. Still, the lines gathering at the corners of his eyes suggested an easy good humour; at the same time, the inward set of his lips told of secrets unspoken.

'His eyes are blue?' I asked.

'Blue as lapis lazuli,' the singer answered. 'He's more tan than he appears in the photograph, although in certain lights he appears a little sallow-looking. And you can't tell from the portrait, but he's about as tall as you, though heavier around the shoulders. He has a scar about an inch and a half long just above his left jaw-bone, which you can't see there. And I don't know if it matters, but he has a little mole the shape of a kite on his back just above the belt-line.'

I handed her back the portrait; she tucked it away with care. 'And can you give me a more specific idea of the days and times he came to the club?'

'To be absolutely certain I'd have to look at my diary. But I do know that in the early days he would only be at my first set, then half-way through the second he'd stand up, give me a wave, and race away like Cinderella from the ball.'

'You mean he left at midnight?'

'Not as early as that, but pretty much like clockwork at, oh, say one o'clock.'

'Those were the early days. And later on?'

'After the first week or so, when I got to know him better, we'd meet in the afternoon before I had to come here, and have a little early supper. And later still, Jack began to stay for both sets, have some dinner afterwards, and take me home. Sometimes he even sleeps for a little while before waking up at around four-thirty to leave.'

'But there have been some days he didn't have to leave early,' I said, and when she nodded in agreement, I asked which nights those might have been.

Her pretty brow wrinkled in thought, creating lines that confirmed my suspicion of her true age: a good seven or eight years older than her missing friend.

'Mostly he's free weekends, so sometimes he's with me from Friday afternoon until Sunday night. It's really lovely to have all day Sunday together. Jack likes to go to church, then maybe out to the beach or take the ferry across the Bay. Once we took the trolley out to see how that new museum is coming along, the one out near the ocean, and afterwards we went down to ride the Ferris wheel, then had dinner at the Cliff House. He's very knowledgeable about art, isn't as well versed in music, likes good food but hasn't a clue about wine. He's a confident dancer, he has a lively sense of the ridiculous, lovely manners, and an eye for clothes. He's . . . I'd have to call him a gentleman.'

'I see. Well, when you have your diary to hand, I would appreciate a more exact reckoning of his times in the city.'

'I'll do it as soon as I get home.'

'Tomorrow will suffice. Send it to me at the St Francis, if you would.'

'Certainly.'

'Now, when he leaves you in the mornings, have you happened to see which way he goes?'

'Early on, he'd walk straight down towards Van Ness. You know, east of my place. Now, though, he goes just one block in that direction and then turns left.'

'That would be going north?' She agreed, and I reflected that habitually rising at four-thirty in the morning to watch one's friend depart indicated a high degree of affection.

'One last thing. Your necklace. How long have you had it?'

The singer's hand went to the luminous gem nestled at her throat. 'He gave it to me eight days ago. Our three-week anniversary, he said. He brought the pearl from the South Pacific himself, and had it made up.'

'I should like to borrow it, if I may.'

The singer's fingers tightened pro-
tectively. 'Why?'

'That necklace appears to be the
only piece of evidence Raynor has
left behind.'

'How do I know this isn't some elaborate con, you disappearing with my
pearl as soon as my back is turned?'
She nobly refrained from glancing at
the third party at our table.

'It would be an elaborate con,
indeed,' I remarked, but had to agree
that she deserved some concrete reas-
surance. I started to pull my note-
case from my pocket, by way of
surety, then stopped; there was something more appropriate than mere
money. If, that is, I trusted the
singer with it.

With some reluctance, I removed the
emerald stickpin from my neck-tie and
held it out. 'This was given me by a
lady I held in the highest esteem. I
would have given my life for her, and
this was a token of her thanks for a
service rendered. As ransoms go, this
may be the possession I hold most
dear.'

The thing glittered on the palm of
my hand. In a moment, the pearl on

the chain spilt onto my palm beside it; then the pearl lay there alone, while the stick-pin was fastened onto the bodice of the singer's dress.

I took my leave of guide and chanteuse, and walked through streets that seemed to shimmer with a con-tralto voice, like the fading image of sudden brightness on the eye.

The next morning, I went in search of the silversmith who had made the pearl necklace. I began on Market Street, at the large emporium called Samuel's--not that I thought they had produced it, as a glance showed me that most of what Samuel's carried was manufactured elsewhere, but I hoped that they could recommend a direction for me to set my enquiries. As indeed they did. Mr Samuel himself, once I produced the name of a mutual acquaintance, proved highly knowledgeable about his competitors in the trade, and willingly suggested the sort of silversmiths who might have made the setting for the pearl. I found my man at the third such establishment, a bijou house of treasures situated just two streets from the hotel.

The sleek but friendly young woman who greeted me took one surprised look at the article in my hand, settled me in a chair, and retreated to the back of the store, returning with her employer.

'This is Mr Minovski,' she told me. 'He can answer any questions you have about your necklace.'

'Yes, yes,' said the gentleman in question, a wizened fellow with a full head of pure white hair, the characteristic stoop of the jeweller or watch-maker, and the identifying stains, scars, and calluses of the trade on his fingers. 'What has happened to this little beauty? Surely my chain has not parted?' He poured it from his palm onto a square of black velvet, bending over with his loupe adjusted for examination.

'No, nothing of the sort,' I reassured him. 'I merely borrowed it from its owner, who has asked me to locate the young man who gave it to her.'

The jeweller fixed me with an attentive eye. 'The boy's gone missing?'

'Shall we say, he did not appear where he was expected to be. And it seemed to me that anyone presenting a lady with such a gift as this was not a mere casual acquaintance.'

'Indeed no. He brought me the pearl, asked me to design a setting worthy of it, and offered half again my price if he could have it in half the time.'

'When was this?'

'Annabeth, my dear, could you please look up the date for this kind gentleman? Lovely piece, this, I was quite happy with it. So was he, for that matter. Ah yes, here, it was two weeks ago, on the Thursday. I took a liking to the lad, and set aside one or two other commissions in order to give it to him in the time he asked. He picked it up on the Monday.'

And gave it to Billy that night. 'Did he leave a manner of getting into touch with him?'

'I wouldn't know. Do you have anything there in the order book, Annabeth?'

'No, Mr Minovski, he didn't leave an address or telephone number. You remember, he said he was staying with friends and it would spoil the surprise if they found out? That was why he paid for it entirely when he ordered the work.'

'Did he say anything else, about the pearl perhaps, or what he was doing in San Francisco?'

I had asked the question in general; Minovski answered. 'Oh yes. I specifically asked about the pearl, since it's such a beauty, and he said it came from Manila, or in any case, that's where he bought it. He bought several, thinking to have them made into necklaces for his sisters, but he particularly liked the colour and lustre of this one. I asked him, purely from professional interest, how much he had paid for it, and although it had seemed to him quite a price, I assured him that he could make his cost back several times over if he cared to sell it here and now, it or some of the others hc'd bought.

'He laughed and said that the others were nothing near as special as this one, but that he'd keep it in mind if he found himself in need of cash. Mostly he was interested in a setting that would flatter the pearl, and decided on an old-fashioned, almost Baroque sort of work, heavy and ornate by comparison with modern tastes. You have to admit, it's a splendid piece.'

'It is indeed.' More than that, it was a splendid mystery, who this gentleman was that had paid a year's salary for a soldier for a singer's token. I began to take my leave of the jeweller, when his next words froze my hand with the hat half-way to my head.

'The young man seemed to think so, as well, since he went on to make enquiries concerning a pair of rings.'

'A pair?' I said sharply. 'Wedding rings?'

'He did not use the phrase, but when a man looks at designs for two matching bands, one makes assumptions.'

I lowered the hat and sat for a time in thought. It was, I supposed, on the edge of possible that Raynor would be contemplating a pair of friendship rings to be shared with the singer. However, the stronger, and considerably darker, possibility was that the wedding bands were precisely that. After all, a man in

Raynor's situation--a 'gentleman' in his early thirties, with means, position, and apparently from a good family--might well be considering marriage, a conventional relationship with an unexceptional and appropriate mate. Indeed, the fling with Billy Birdsong might be just that, a final dance of Bohemian youth in San Francisco before the sombre establishment of a marriage elsewhere: That he had failed to tell her anything of his life pointed in that direction. The pearl necklace could well have been intended as a thank-you, and a wordless farewell, four days before he left the city.

I thanked the jeweller, tipped my hat to his assistant, and made my thoughtful way back to the hotel. Once there, a borrowed ferry schedule, the telephone, and a handful of shag tobacco provided me with a modicum of light in the darkness and a plan of action for the afternoon.

The next problem facing me was that of impersonating an officer.

THE telephone on the desk beside her interrupted

Kate's reading. She fumbled for the receiver, her eyes still on the page, until the voice at the other end had her removing her heels from the out-pulled desk drawer and sitting upright.

"Yes, Mr. Nicholson. How are you today?"

"Enjoying the stationary life, thank you. Have you had a chance to look at the story?"

"I'm about halfway through it."

"Then I won't spoil it for you by telling you the end."

"Okay."

"However, it occurred to me this morning that, tired as I was yesterday, I failed to give you any of its background information. Of course, I haven't written the report Philip asked me for, having not seen the actual manuscript yet, but my preliminary judgment would probably have weighed against a Conan Doyle authorship. For one thing, Doyle wrote only two other Holmes stories as narrated by Holmes in the first person—all the others were narrated by Watson, or in one case a third-person narrative. Second, a point which carries considerably more weight, Conan Doyle absolutely did not write about sex. Or if he was required to for the sake of the story, it would be heavily couched in Victorian terms—this particular story may have been written in the Twenties, but Conan Doyle was, birth to death, a Victorian gentleman. The idea of this particular man writing openly about transvestite singers and gay relationships would be, to say the least, startling. And absolutely unique in the canon."

"So someone else wrote it."

"Either that, or the story provides a hitherto unsuspected side of the man. You may or may not be aware that the Victorians were very fond of erotica, but they kept it well hidden, and written anonymously or pseudonymously. I have never come across the faintest breath of a suggestion that Conan Doyle wrote any."

"And if he did?" She couldn't quite see where he was going with his insistence.

"If this were to be verified as a Conan Doyle story, it would change the face of the Holmesian scholarship. And incidentally, it would be worth a fortune."

Now, there was a point she could grasp.

"Well, the original is safe in the bank, in any case."

"Good. Give me a ring when you've finished it."

"I will."

Inspector Martinelli went back to her reading.

NINE

The next problem facing me was that of impersonating an officer.

I had done it in the past, of course, any number of times. However, my present age made appearing as anything short of a high-ranking officer unlikely, and the irritatingly instantaneous communication offered by the telephone made exposing my ruse all too easy.

Instead, I decided that the appearance of a dignified and persistent legal person, formerly of the officer class, might be equally effective. I considered a car and driver, decided that the measure of verisimilitude they might offer was not worth the inconvenience of being tied to them, and turned to my storage trunks to assemble a legal personage: intimidatingly formal if slightly out-of-date suit, golden pince-nez, and much-used leather despatch case. This last necessitated a trawl through the pawn shops in the vicinity of the Flood Building, in the third of which I uncovered the one-time possessions of a failed stock-broker. Adding a tightly furled black umbrella borrowed from the doorman, I inserted myself with dignity through the doors of a taxi and directed the driver to the Ferry Building.

San Francisco, that key portal to the western United States, is guarded by no less than nine forts: North of the Golden Gate, the gap through which the sea ebbs and flows, lie Cronkhite, Barry, and Baker; McDowell stands on an island in the Bay; Mason, Scott, and Miley form the Presidio along the city's northern shore; with Funston down the coast a distance with the longer-range guns. This is in addition to Alcatraz Island, currently a federal prison, and the distant guns at Milagra Ridge even further down the peninsula.

An embarrassment of riches when it came to hunting for one lone soldier who may or may not be a junior officer.

However, this Cinderella soldier had tended to scurry off before his coach turned into a pumpkin--or rather, before he was stranded on the wrong side of his day's duties. The Army launch would serve for ordinary business, but for Raynor's no doubt clandestine activities, the anonymity of the ferry might have better suited him. A printed schedule obtained from the hotel clerk informed me that my last opportunity for a ferry to Sausalito, the town nearest those forts north of the city, departed at 1:30 in the morning, precisely correct for a man having to hurry away from his musical entertainments just before the strike of one. I thought a destination of

Fort McDowell unlikely since, being an island, McDowell would have involved Raynor in further transportation beyond Sausalito; this left the contiguous forts of Baker, Barry, and Cronkhite.

Fort Baker, occupying the sheltered eastern stretch of the south-facing peninsula called Marin, was closest to the ferry's landing. And according to my most reliable local informant, a boot-black who plied his trade around the corner from the hotel, Baker was the most active of the three northern forts. This was only sensible, that those fortifications facing the sea should come into their own in times of war, but be allowed to rest during the peace.

It was nearing three o'clock when a taxi hired from the Sausalito dock delivered me to the gates of Fort Baker. I informed the guard that I needed to speak with the commander, who proved to be a Major Morris. It was not, of course, as easy as all that, but persistence, coupled with my accent, clothing, and grey head, eventually had me in the presence of a large man with jutting iron-grey eyebrows and a body showing the strain of desk work.

'I don't have much time,' the major began by telling me. 'I have an inspection at four, you should have made an appointment.' He transferred some papers from one side of his desk to the other, to illustrate how extremely busy he was.

'Had I telephoned for an appointment, you would have given it me next week. And had you seen me when first I entered your offices, we might have been finished by now. I am looking for a man under your command by the name of Jack Raynor.'

'You and half the post,' he snapped.

The phrase was sufficiently colloquial that I thought it advisable to clarify his meaning. 'Am I to understand that Mr Raynor is absent without leave?'

'You are indeed. <u>Lieutenant</u> Raynor is officially absent without leave, taken off with some floozy no doubt. I tell you, mister, this is a hell of a place to command. Much easier out in the middle of nowhere, the boys have nothing to tempt them away.'

This time, I perceived a trace of actual concern beneath the bluster, and thought it time to ingratiate myself into the major's affections. With a wry smile on my face, I told him, 'I can understand that. My last command was surrounded by nothing but sand and rats, and any discipline problems we had were due to boredom rather than opportunity.'

He perked right up at that, as I had anticipated. 'What command was that?'

The regiment to which I claimed allegiance had in fact served in South Africa, although so far as I know, it had never possessed a young officer by the name of Sigerson. Still, anecdotes about inadequate arms, wretched food, and wily enemy action bring a bond to such men, and Morris was feeling considerably more beneficent towards the one-time English captain before him when I worked our conversation back to his missing lieutenant.

I arranged a look of sympathy on my face and leant forward to reinforce it. 'Has Lieutenant Raynor pulled a disappearing act before this?' Now that I had Jack Raynor's proper rank,

I took care to pronounce it in the American style, so as not to distract my informant.

'Raynor? He hasn't been with us all that long, but I've never had cause to reprimand him. Lately he's looked a little the worse for wear some mornings, but he's never so much as reported late, far less failed to appear entirely.'

'Why do you suppose he has seemed, er, "the worse for wear"?'

'Why do you think?' he answered with a snort. 'Good-looking young officer, a little money behind him, he's a catch. I figured he'd get tired of the hours pretty soon and either drop her or marry her.'

I did not inform the major that the lady in question and the lady to marry might comprise two separate problems.

'You say he hasn't long been under your command?'

The major fixed me with a curious look. 'I thought you were the family lawyer?'

'I represent the family lawyer, who did not feel the matter required his personal presence. I was charged simply with the delivery of certain papers, which did not at the time appear to necessitate a knowledge of Raynor's history.'

'Not enough to bring the big man himself from Minneapolis, eh? Or was it St Paul?'

'The firm has offices in both cities,' I replied equably.

'Right. Well, Raynor's only been here going on three months. He was in Manila, but came down with the malaria and the medics said if he didn't get himself into a cooler climate for a while, he'd be a goner. So they transferred him to the Presidio, and since he wasn't good for much, they sent him to me. Not that I needed another young officer, especially one who's not up to much, but Barry--you know Fort Barry, just to the west along the headlands? Barry's on caretaker status, with just a detail to keep an eye on things-- pretty boring station, so we keep it turned over fairly regularly. There's really just a handful of men, and sometimes there's just a non-com in charge, although at the moment I've got a young lieutenant over there.

When Raynor came, I sent him over there, mostly to get him out from under my feet--last thing I needed was an invalid lieutenant to nurse. And I figured Raynor could keep the other young man company. Once Raynor was back on his feet, I thought I'd bring him back over here and let him do some work. Now that he's getting his health back, Raynor's shown signs of being a good officer. The men like him, he fits in well with the other officers, no problems. Until this.'

'When was he last seen?'

'Friday. Five days ago--another two days and he's going on the books as a desertion, and he's in big trouble. He led a detail to service Battery Wallace, supervised the shooting range in the afternoon, came back here to Baker to lead a night-time manoeuvre, and the next day he was missing.'

'Did he take any possessions with him?'

'His clothes are still in his rooms, but who knows what else he had?'

'There might be one thing to indicate whether he planned to be away

for good,' I suggested. 'I happened
to be shown a letter he wrote some
time ago, from Manila, which referred
to a number of pearls that he'd
bought to have made into jewellery
for various family members. If we
looked in his rooms and found them,
that would be fairly definitive indication of an accidental absence.'

The major thought this over for a
minute, and nodded. He opened his
mouth to summon his adjutant outside
the door, then changed his mind.
Instead, he opened a drawer in the
desk and came out with a formidable
ring of keys, stood and set his cap
on his head, and told me, 'I'll do
this myself. I'll be back in a few
minutes.'

I, however, was standing as well.
'I can come with you, see if anything
catches my eye. I will give you my
promise that I will touch nothing, if
you like. The family will want to
know,' I added. I intended to see the
inside of the young officer's rooms,
even if it meant breaking into an
Army base at midnight.

Such a venture proved unnecessary,
for the major only hesitated a moment

before deciding that a fellow officer could be trusted that far, and shouted for his car.

The major, it seemed, preferred to motor under his own power rather than use the driver that rank might have expected. No sooner were we away from the parade ground than I began to wish him more concerned with appearance than the art of motoring. Major Morris was a terror behind the wheel, one of those men who can scarcely bear to glance at the road ahead, and instead peers to either side, into his passenger's face, and even around to the back window. I clung to the front and attempted to empty my mind of all thought.

The road to the neighbouring fort was steep, but brief, and cut through the intervening hills in a distressingly long and narrow tunnel which was in a condition my younger associates might term 'dodgy'. It couldn't have been more than eight or ten years old, but the massive timbers making up its damp walls and ceiling looked as soft as old bed sheets, and when the major had to shift into a lower gear with the gradient, I expected the sound to shake the walls down onto our heads. I came closer to prayer than I have at any time since I gave up the habit as a schoolboy.

After a small eternity, blessed daylight opened up around us, and I peeled my fingers out from the dents on the dash-board and reminded myself to breathe.

The fort on the other side of the tunnel was a collection of buildings overlooking a long, narrow lagoon. It was an attractive setting, but appeared nearly deserted, as I saw only two men in uniform between the tunnel's mouth and the apparent centre of the fort. We passed the chapel and pulled to a stop--adding a large dent to the smaller ones in the dash-board, as the major's use of the brake was as vigorous as might be expected. I lowered myself to solid ground and followed him up the steps into the officer's housing.

'This is a duplex,' he informed me. 'Raynor's got the west half, Lieutenant Halston the other. The houseboy lives in the back.'

Raynor's quarters had the methodical tidiness of an experienced soldier, with everything in its place and, apart from the furniture, capable of being packed up in an hour. The books on his shelves were the usual--Thackeray, Defoe, Hugo, two poetry collections--although the recordings stacked neatly by the Victrola were more classical than the Jazz I might have expected. Some of them I owned myself.

His most personal effects were a small, intricately worked Chinese carpet on the floor between his armchair and the fireplace, its thick pile depicting a lively and colourful twisting dragon, and three similarly intricate carvings on the table beside his armchair, each a different form of dragon. The smallest was of age-darkened ivory, no bigger than a chestnut, the creature turned back on itself and with features picked out by a knife-blade like the point of a needle. The next was of a lustrous jade the colour of the ocean across the next ridge, grey tinting the green and giving it a depth and mystery. This dragon was simpler, but muscular, if that word can be used to describe a thing that would fit into a fist.

The third dragon was of some tropical wood, a glossy dark substance almost without texture. The seven-inch-high creature was sitting on its haunches like a begging lap-dog, its tail curled around its rear legs and both small fore-legs in the air. It was the sort of thing an amateur critic would instantly dismiss as rough and whimsical, but in fact, the eye kept returning to it, for behind the whimsy the dragon gave off an air of watchful deliberation, and the roughness of the carving was of a kind with the rough surface of a master Japanese potter. A curious object, all the more so to find it in the establishment of a junior Army officer.

I pulled myself away from Raynor's collection of dragons and turned to the man's desk, but before I had done more than open a drawer, Major Morris came upon the small velvet bag of pearls. It was in the first place he looked, the bottom of his lieutenant's sea bag. 'They always hide things in their travelling kit,' he mused, the black bag pulled open on his palm, but his mind was clearly taken up with the implications of the pearls rather than the habits of young soldiers. 'If he left them here . . .'

'Then he did not intend to be gone,' I finished his sentence for him, equally preoccupied with the scrap of paper in my own hand. (I had not actually promised to touch nothing, merely said that I would make such a promise if he had asked. He had not.) 'Do you know a man whose name begins with DuM? The "M" is a capital letter, so perhaps DuMons, DuMont, something of the sort?'

'No,' he said, pulling the strings shut on the bag. Then he added, 'There's DuMaurier, but that's not a man, it's a battery. Was a battery, I should say.'

'It is no longer?' I asked, but he was already set on his historical lecture.

'The emplacements are all named for Army men. DuMaurier was a captain who led a daring raid against Fort Sumter in the Civil War. DuMaurier is one of the older emplacements, although the gun itself was pulled out in 1917 and sent to France. Probably melted down by now and being used to tin peaches. Anyway, turns out there's no point in having a gun you can see from the air, not any more. Airplanes are changing everything.'

'Quite.'

'Why do you ask?'

'Because he's made a note here, "DuM 2:00".'

The major dropped his find back in the duffel bag and came to look at the paper in my hand. He scowled at it, then at me, for the paper I held had nothing written on it, but then, I'd had more practice than most in the art of reading pencil indentations pressed from one sheet to another. I had needed only the light through the window, but for the major, I took a pencil from the desk drawer and gently rubbed at the sheet until the letters appeared.

He raised one of those bushy eyebrows, and without another word walked to Raynor's door. I hesitated, my fingers yearning after the envelopes that lay so tantalising in the drawer behind the pencils, but Morris was standing there waiting. I closed the drawer reluctantly and wondered again about the difficulties of a night-time raid on Army grounds. I was glad to see him turn the key in the door behind us.

As he marched down the steps of Raynor's 'duplex' the major spotted a callow uniform approaching, and raised his voice in that effortless parade-ground bellow of the career soldier.

'Corporal, double-time it over to the stables and have a horse saddled by the time I get there.'

'I say, Major,' I began.

'And another horse for this gentleman here. You do ride?' he demanded of me.

Not by preference in a city suit and shoes, but if the alternative was to be left behind, then ride in a city suit and shoes I would.

Before long I could see why the major had called for four-legged transport over that with four wheels. The road was well enough maintained, but when we turned off it for the cliffs that first climb, then precipitously drop down to the sea, we should have had to proceed on foot. As it was, the way the horses picked their cautious path downhill, it might well have been more comfortable to have walked. Certainly it would have been faster. However, a major requires the dignity of transport, even if it be just for a mile, so transport we had. Morris led the way, his voice reaching me in uneven phrases, snatched away by the perpetual wind from the sea. '. . . not maintained . . . new long-range guns . . . minefields . . . bird-watchers . . .'

Eventually, we reached the gun emplacement, a low, grey, weed-choked concrete structure rooted in the cliffs like the nest of some enormous sea-faring bird. Unlike the other batteries we had passed, this one was, as the major had been trying to tell me, not well maintained. One of the cliffs had slumped across the narrow roadway, and the horses were not happy about picking their way across. We reached the gun and dismounted, tying our reins onto an iron ring clearly set there for the purpose, and walked past the circular clearing where once the gun had thundered. To the south had been built a set of rooms for the storage of powder and such, although as the gun was inactive, and looked to remain that way, the wide doorway was not supplied with so much as a padlock. The major wrestled with the rust-clotted handle, then laid his shoulder against the door. The hinges gave way with a groan that appeared to embarrass him, as evidence of neglect.

Neither of us said anything, however, and in a moment the thought of rusted metal had fled from our minds. For inside the first room, slumped in a heap against the northernmost wall, we found the body of Lieutenant Jack Raynor.

INSPECTOR Kate Martinelli, reading this section of typescript in a busy office crowded with ringing telephones and well-used computers, sitting beneath fluorescent lights and holding a half-forgotten focaccia, turkey, and provolone sandwich in one hand, exclaimed aloud. The two other detectives in the room at the time looked up at her, and one of them asked her a question. She looked up at him blankly, more aware of a hillside eight decades earlier than the room she was in, then lowered her eyes again to the story.

. . . the body of Lieutenant Jack Raynor.

The moment I saw the figure, I was aware of a considerable feeling of satisfaction. Not, I hasten to say, that the man was dead, but rather that Major Morris and I had come here alone. It was rare to be given the opportunity to examine a body before the police arrived with their clumsy ways. I held out no hope that the Army methods would prove any more gentle.

'You must go back and summon assistance,' I told him, wincing at the way his great boots scuffed the floor around Raynor's head.

'I can't leave you alone here,' he declared.

'But the poor fellow, he'll be eaten by the foxes,' I protested, with more sentiment than accuracy. 'I can't very well go for help, your men wouldn't obey my orders—indeed, they'd probably clap me in the brig for trespassing. I'll just remain here and chase away the vermin. You won't be long.'

The man gave a brief and disapproving look at the remains of his lieutenant, mounted up, and rode off. I took up a position just outside the entrance of the emplacement and lit a cigarette, sketching a brisk salute as Morris turned to look back at the top of the rise. And the moment his hat had vanished behind the hill, I tossed the half-smoked cigarette over my shoulder and stepped inside.

The room had clearly gone unused for some months, if not years, which vastly simplified my examination of the floor. From the door, I shone my pocket-torch at an oblique angle, comparing what I saw there with the soles of the shoes worn by the dead man. I could see no sign that Raynor had walked over the accumulated dirt; instead, he had been bodily carried inside by a size- nine boot with a heavily worn right toe, then dropped. I then continued inside to look at the body itself.

Raynor lay on his left side, and had done so for some days, long enough for rigor to come and go, long enough to attract the interest of flies and a few small teeth. He had been described as handsome, but no one would say that now. He possessed the requisite facial structures of nose and lips; his teeth had been good and his hair light; that was about all that could be said of his appearance.

Fortunately, he had come to this place fully dressed, and the thick wool of his uniform had preserved the rest of his skin against encroachment. I searched the pockets, finding a silver cigar-case in one pocket, containing two slim, brown cigarillos, and a matching silver windproof lighter. In another pocket lay his note-case. This held eighteen dollars in assorted denominations, a letter from his mother, and an assortment of scraps and receipts that seemed to have no immediate bearing on the case, although I made note of them, for future reference, before returning them to their respective places. The case also contained two items of interest to a limited number of people; those I transferred into my own pocket, for the sake of the young man's reputation.

I then loosed his clothes, primarily to confirm his identity, and found just above one hip the kite-shaped birth-mark described by Billy Birdsong. I looked over the rest of the man's torso, then scrupulously restored the clothing to its previous arrangement.

I examined the head wounds closely, then tipped Raynor onto his back. The dark stains along the left side of his body showed that he had been placed here while his blood was still liquid enough to pool with gravity. He had not, however, been killed here. I could see no blood on the walls, none but the stains directly under his head--indeed, when I turned on my heels to look back at the floor, there were not even any droplets between the body and the entrance. I became aware that I was softly humming one of the Bach cantatas, a sign that the case had just become interesting.

The wounds to Raynor's head had been done with a smooth, rounded piece of wood as big around as a girl's wrist, which had left a few slim splinters embedded in the wreckage. The first injury described a line a fraction of an inch above the right ear, descending slightly towards the chin. The second injury, the fatal one, had come straight down into Raynor's face, driving everything from brow to jaw back into the brain. A thorough autopsy could prove the sequence, based on the intersecting fracture lines of the skull, but I thought it unlikely that a trained soldier would placidly sit and watch a blow coming at his face. Nor would his assailant have reason then to hit the side of a dead man's head.

No: Raynor was sitting and calmly smoking an evening cigar--a glance into his mouth revealed the chunk of tobacco leaves bitten involuntarily by his front teeth--when someone behind and above had swung a vicious blow at his head. The lieutenant had collapsed to the ground. His assailant had then kicked him onto his back, leaving a sharp semicircle of discolouration on Raynor's belly, before standing over his victim and delivering the <u>coup de grâce</u>, straight down onto the once-handsome face.

Even with the rudimentary tools of pocket-torch and magnifying glass, I could see among the smashed flesh and bone a splinter of wood and some threads of white cotton. The latter, I decided, explained the lack of dripped blood: The murderer had wrapped Raynor's head in a bath-towel as he transported his victim, so as not to leave a trail, or incriminating stains on his own person; the threads I saw now had remained behind on the drying blood when the cloth was ripped free.

I sat back on my heels and considered the figure before me.

The note in Raynor's room indicated a meeting here at two in the morning. It was remotely possible, taking into account the perpetual breezes playing across this exposed spot, that he had failed to notice a man with a bat sneaking up behind him. Still, I thought it more likely that Raynor had known his assailant, and trusted him enough to allow him to pass behind his back.

Raynor's scribbled note, the location of their meeting, clandestine or not, and his acquaintance with the man determined his identity: a fellow soldier.

It shouldn't be difficult to identify him, I knew, not with the evidence at hand and the limited pool of individuals. The main problem would be preserving the evidence, that he might be convicted.

I was conducting a close but fruitless search of the emplacement's forecourt when the sound of voices reached my ears. I met the Army halfway, Morris with four privates, one corporal, and a sergeant.

'They're sending a man over from the Presidio,' Morris said without preamble, and sounding none too pleased at the interloper. 'We're to take the body back to Baker.'

'Major, a word?' I asked. He glanced at his men, and told the sergeant to allow them a smoke while we stepped aside for a little chat.

'Sir,' I began, 'I have had occasion once or twice to work with the police, and have some little experience with their methods of gathering information on criminal cases. I would suggest, therefore, that before you have your men take up Lieutenant

Raynor's body, you make an effort to preserve those things that might lead to his murderer. It is, of course, possible that the man from the Presidio would do the same, but after all, Raynor wasn't his man.'

'I can hardly leave the poor fellow lying here until morning, and it'll be dark by the time the investigator gets across.'

I stifled the impulse to point out that another evening would make no difference to Raynor, and thought instead about the resentful edge to his voice. Morris cared nothing for ordering his soldiers to stand about --that, after all, is what soldiers do best. No, what the major resented was for his men to be forced to wait on an outside authority. And I was very willing to play on his territoriality to maintain personal control of the investigation, before it was taken forcibly from my hands.

'Would you like me to begin one or two actions a professional investigator might take?' I offered. 'For example, there's a foot-print that must have been left by the man who put Raynor here. It needs only some care not to be trod upon, and later a small pot of plaster-of-Paris. And if I might borrow one or two of your men, we could search for the place where Lieutenant Raynor was killed.' Again, I took care to pronounce the man's rank in the American fashion, lest the introduction of a leftenant remind Morris that I, too, was an outsider.

The major readily agreed to this--although less, I believe, in any hope that I might solve his case before the outsider could, than to get me out of his hair while he took control of Raynor's corpse. To him, the discipline of restoring a missing soldier to his post, even if he be an inanimate soldier, was foremost.

At his command, the men resumed with their lamps and the canvas stretcher they had brought. I stood over the foot-print while they worked, to save it from their heavy boots, and when Morris mounted up, I reminded him that a small pot of plaster would be very helpful. He nodded and turned his ceremonial little procession in the direction of Fort Baker, leaving me with the corporal, a diminutive tow-head by the name of Larsen. My miniature platoon and I removed our hats in recognition of the sombre occasion, then got to work.

'We have but a few hours of daylight left,' I told Larsen. 'We need to find where Lieutenant Raynor was killed.'

'Wasn't he killed here?' he asked.

'A blow like that would cause the blood to splash about, and there was no sign of that inside.'

'So we're looking for a lot of blood?' he enquired, casting a dubious glance at the expanse of hillside.

'Yes, although it rained briefly on Sunday night, so there may not be much visible. Let us instead search the ground for one of two things: a stick or bat, broken in pieces, or a half-smoked cigarillo. Brown, about the size of your little finger.'

Three invisible items on some acres of hillside: dried blood, wooden stick, and brown cigar. With the sun already working its way down in the sky.

We began our search in the vicinity

of the emplacement, the most logical place to sit while waiting for a meeting to begin. We found nothing, and I directed my troop to begin a sweep in circles out from the gun.

For myself, however, I find a systematic approach both unsympathetic and ineffective. Much better to step aside and allow the human sense known as intuition to take command. I settled on a grass-covered rock and took out my pipe.

It is two o'clock in the morning, at $37\frac{1}{2}$ degrees north, with a moon that is five nights past full riding in what until Sunday evening would be a clear night sky: enough light that, were I a young man well familiar with the terrain, I would not require a lamp to make out my path. I am a young artillery officer, fully dressed, anticipating a difficult interview--were the conversation to be simple, it could have been held in closer proximity to the base. This was most probably the wee hours of Saturday morning, since Raynor left Birdsong early, expecting to see the singer on Saturday night--'See you tomorrow,' he'd said at dawn Friday.

It is two o'clock in the morning, I am a young man with concerns on my mind, a young man who has also been looking at wedding rings, and I sit to smoke one of the slim cigars from my case. The sky is clear--and the moon . . .

I rose and looked around the daylight hillside, then strode downhill nearly to the cliff face. The waves below crashed and churned, the great Pacific stretched out endlessly, and the number of available protruding boulders grew.

But I would want to watch for the approach of the person I was meeting. I would sit where I could keep the emplacement in view.

I followed the ridge south, scarcely conscious of the precipitous drop to my right, and suddenly there it was, a three-inch-long scrap of brown marginally darker than the red-brown colour of the soil. I bent down and teased it out of the grasses. One end showed the uneven remains of a cigar allowed to burn itself out, but the other, despite the intervening rain, still appeared sharply broken off: cut, by Raynor's teeth when the crashing blow came to the side of his head.

I tucked the cigarillo remnant into an envelope and in my pocket, pulled out my glass, and dropped to my knees for a close examination of the vicinity.

Ten minutes later I spoke.

'That is close enough. You risk treading on the marks.'

'I saw that you'd found something,' my corporal said, somewhat unnecessarily. 'I wondered if you wanted my help over here instead.'

'You found nothing?'

'A wad of chewing gum, a dead seagull, a sheet of week-old newspaper caught on some branches. No blood.'

'The blood and the cigar are here. And two tiny slivers of wood, although the remains of the bat appear to have been carried off. Or perhaps thrown. But the pattern of the blood, although diminished by the rain, presents a clear picture. I don't know if you have noticed, but when a viscous liquid such as blood falls, its manner of striking the ground testifies to the direction of its fall.' The young soldier murmured some response, but I paid him no heed. I do find it useful to have a pair of ears in the vicinity--when no audience is to hand, I will even talk to myself to aid the process of thought. The best assistant is the one who contributes nothing, acting as pure sounding-board to reflect my thoughts. My audience here was, at least, experienced in volunteering nothing.

'Blood dripping straight down produces a circular shape, ragged at the edges but essentially round,' I continued. 'Blood thrown up from a wound that then hits a vertical surface tends to slump, leaving a tear-drop shape that can be traced back to its source. Similarly, when shed from a moving man, it leaves its tail in the direction from which the man is moving. I am writing a monograph on the subject, for the use of crime investigators. I call it "The Science of Blood Splash Analysis." Now, young man, what do you make of this? You may come this way, there's nothing to be damaged along the path.'

I was not actually interested in what he made of the mark on the ground, although what he had to say would tell me what kind of man I had been given to assist me. The corporal picked his way across the ground, following the faint path left by generations of deer, and looked at the soil where I pointed.

'That from a boot?' he offered.

I looked up in surprise. Not only had he seen the gentle depression cut into the turf, he had recognised it.

'Very good,' I told him. 'Anything else?'

'The lieutenant was sitting on that rock, wasn't he?'

For this, I wanted to look my assistant in the eye or, in any event, from a standing position. I braced myself to rise, and the polite lad took my elbow to help me.

An unremarkable face, with pale brown eyes and corn-silk hair, crooked teeth, the upper-body musculature that comes with physical labour from childhood, and the exaggerated muscles of hand and wrist that indicate far too many hours bent over a cow's udders: dairy farmer's younger son, escaped into the Army, I diagnosed. His was a face of boyish innocence, which on closer examination hinted of a vein of well-concealed humour. That combination can only mean intelligence.

'How do you know that's where he was sitting?' I asked Larsen.

'The marks on the stone. The moss is all mussed along the top, and there's a scratch where a metal grommet scraped it.'

'Lichen, not moss,' I corrected absently. He grinned suddenly, so that he looked about eleven years old.

'Me and my pappy did a lot of hunting. They sometimes use me as a tracker here, when one of the horses wanders off or something.'

I sent a vote of thanks in the direction of Major Morris, and said, 'A veritable Natty Bumppo. What see you here, young man?'

'I'm not that good, and there's probably not all that much to see, what with the ground being a little on the dry side beforehand and then the rain afterwards. One man was sitting here smoking, another man came up behind him and knocked him off the rock. Looks like one or both of 'em

sort of rolled around the ground a
little, and although I don't know
about blood splash patterns and all,
you can sure see the blood right
there.'

'Where Lieutenant Raynor lay
dying.'

'He was a good man.' The lad pulled
off his cap in an unconscious
tribute, staring at the hand-sized
smear of red-brown.

'You knew him.'

'He'd only been here for a little
while, but it's not a very large
base, you get to know most of the
officers. And he was one of the good
ones.'

'Any ideas about who would have
wanted to do this?'

'Nope. Most of the fellows felt the
same way about him I did.'

'I see.'

'What was he doing out here, do you
know?'

I turned to look over the great
shining expanse of the Pacific, set
alight by the low-lying sun. 'He was
sitting and looking at the moon,
smoking one of his small cigars, and
waiting to meet a man he regarded as

a friend. And I suspect that the man who did this had his own ambiguous feelings about Raynor. He killed him, but he couldn't quite bear to turn his back and abandon Raynor's dead body out here on the hillside, knowing what the gulls would do to it. Nor could he bring himself to push Raynor off the cliff to the sea.'

'Wouldn't be all that easy, to push him off.'

'Why do you say that?'

'Oh, it looks simple, just roll something over and splash, but in fact the slope's just a little too gentle for that. 'Bout six months ago, we had a horse break its leg along here, had to shoot it, and the major ordered us to shove it off the cliff. Took ten of us the better part of the day to get the cursed thing anywhere near the water. 'Course, a man'd be simpler, but not real easy. Not unless you could pick him up and throw him.'

I studied him for a while, so intently that the young man began to look nervous, as young men do. 'Let us take a closer look at that cliff,'

I said. At that, his nervousness increased.

'Uh, mister, I really wouldn't if I was you. I mean, no offence meant, but you're not a real young man.'

'I shall endeavour to remain on the land side of the water-line, Corporal.'

My youthful helpmeet sheltered my every step as we approached the steeper portion of the cliff, although I could see what he meant, that at this part of the cliffs, there was no convenient spot at which one could absolutely guarantee that a rolled object would continue rolling without fetching up on rock or shrub.

I could also see something else. At the very point at which the slope became impossible, when I had resorted to hunkering onto my heels with one hand on the ground and Corporal Larsen's firm grip on my coat-tails for support--the point, in short, at which farther progress became impossible--I spotted a lump of white half-way to the breaking waves, and even more precipitously, a light shape that could be the raw colour of broken wood.

I looked around into the worried brown eyes of my assistant. 'Which position on a belaying rope do you prefer?' I asked. 'The anchoring end, or the dangling?'

TEN

The lad would not hear of my dangling out over the ocean. In fact, he came perilously near to arguing with me entirely, considering that he was a soldier under orders, and only agreed to assist me when I pointed out that our other, equine companion might also serve to anchor the rope.

Further delay came when he would have set out for the fort, where the nearest rope lay, on foot. It appeared that the nag which had transported me here was an officer's horse, thus rendered off-limits to a mere corporal.

'Don't be ridiculous,' I told Larsen. 'Even if you travel at a jog-trot we'll be working that cliff in the dark. Take the horse and go. If anyone questions you, you're on a personal mission from Major Morris. But, lad? Don't give anyone details.'

In the end, the threat of impending darkness tipped him into obedience. With none of the caution demonstrated by the major and me, Larsen flung himself into the saddle and dug in his heels, not even pausing to adjust the stirrups to his shorter legs. Rider and mount flashed over the top of the hill, and he must have kept up the breakneck racing attitude because he rode the two-mile journey to the barn and back again in far less time than I would have credited to that particular creature. He dropped off the winded animal, led it along the slope to where I stood and, as soon as I had the reins in my hand, began dragging his equipment from the saddle.

Along with the sack, the rope, and three apples, he had brought a lantern, which indicated how long he thought this was going to take us.

I showed him how to fashion a climbing harness out of the rope, then tied the other end of it to the saddle, looping the middle around the saddle-horn. The corporal eyed the process dubiously, but seemed reassured by my knots as much as the attitude of disinterested competence I created for his benefit. He set off down the hill uncertainly, testing the play of rope as he went, but by the time he reached the sharper decline, he was moving easily, trusting my control of the situation.

Before long, he turned around to traverse the slope backwards, braced fully against the rope that was scouring my palms. The horse was tired enough that the peculiarity did not cause it to startle, which was as well. The sun rested a thumb's breadth from the horizon, and Corporal Larsen was invisible to me, nothing but a tension on the hemp running through my hands. I felt him move down, responding to the single tug by holding the rope firm, then at the double tug played out more of the line. There was a single loop remaining at my feet, and I was considering the challenge of persuading the horse to move down the hillside a few yards when another single tug came, and I held fast. Finally there came a series of sharp tugs, and I began to haul the line steadily in against the pommel. In a few minutes the bulk of the rope lay across my boots, then a long shadow wavered across the hillside as the last rays of the sun gave outline to my assistant's form.

His boyish face with flushed with adventure and triumph as he wrestled himself free from the no-doubt painfully constricting harness, then walked over to present me with his treasure. However, he took one glance at the state of my palms and gave an exclamation of dismay.

'Your hands! Oh, that was really stupid of me, not to have brought gloves! Here, let me wrap them.'

'Your California weather is so clement, I neglected to wear my own,' I admitted. 'It's nothing, I shall just need to take care that I do not add my own stains to the marks on the towel. Show me what you've found, lad, and stop fussing over me.'

He insisted on tying off his relatively clean handkerchief, however, before he would give me his sack. While I opened its top, he tidied the rope like a good soldier, but his eyes never left what I was doing, and his actions were somewhat distracted by his attentions.

The wooden object I had spotted was the business end of a base-ball bat, split from the handle by the force of the blows, still clotted despite the rain with the killing residue. Shards of bone had been driven an eighth of an inch into the hard wood.

'I couldn't find the other part,' Larsen said, sounding apologetic.

'It's probably floated half-way to Hawaii by now,' I reassured him, and reached for the other object in the sack.

There is a shroud held in veneration by the Roman Church, displayed in a church in the Italian city of Turin, that appears to show the face of a bearded man around whom it was wrapped at death. Being old and odd, this remarkable object is of course identified as the winding-sheet of the Saviour, although there is no proof of the matter.

The cloth I unwrapped on that darkening hillside was weirdly similar to the Turin shroud. As I unpeeled the sodden object, stains appeared; I spread it flat, and in a peculiar coincidence, the last rays of that day's sunlight travelled across it, then went dim, as Corporal Larsen and I stood staring down at the clear imprint of a man's agonised face, pressed into the cloth.

We made use of the lamp Larsen had brought, darkness catching us up as we passed through the tunnel to Fort Baker. Although he would have had me in the saddle, I could see no reason to perch on high while the corporal laboured at my side, and in the end we walked together in front of the horse, which bore the stained towel and the murder weapon as if bearing Raynor's body home.

Back at Fort Baker, I was disappointed to find the military police from the Presidio in possession. I needed a conversation with the good major, but such would not be provided this evening. Instead, I turned over the items my young friend had recovered from the cliffside, and made an appointment for the following afternoon.

The Army launch El Aquario was busy shuttling back and forth across the passage, and after retrieving my unnecessary brief-case from Morris's office, I went down to the dock to await its next trip. As it happened, Lieutenant Jack Raynor waited there as well, on his final voyage across to the Army mortuary. I stood on the pier, and later on the tossing deck, contemplating the wrapped form of the young officer and addressing him with my silent questions. A promising young officer with secrets to keep: Why had he died?

The lieutenant did not say.

When I returned to the hotel, the desk-man handed me an envelope with the hand-written initials BB at the upper left corner. I opened it as I rode up in the lift, and found inside the dates of Lieutenant Raynor's presence in the city over the last month of his life, both at the club, and when he had been free during the daylight hours. At this juncture, I did not know that it would do me any good, but I folded it into my pocket and walked down the silent hallway to my empty room.

It was long since dark, and truth to tell, I was feeling my age. I should have liked nothing better than a large and leisurely meal, a book, and my currently solitary bed, but my day was far from finished. Instead, I called for a hurried plate of sandwiches and descended to the hotel's Turkish baths, which restored me sufficiently that I might consider the remainder of the night without outright loathing. I resumed my semiformal evening wear, dropped my silk hat onto my freshly trimmed head, pulled a pair of thin leather gloves over my abused hands, and set out for the Blue Tiger cabaret.

The man at the door tipped his hat to me, recognising instantly the generous patron of the night before. I was guided up the stairs again to the balcony, shown to a table overlooking the stage, and provided a bottle of champagne on ice. I was later than I had anticipated, and Martin Ledbetter gave a sour glance at the sweating silver bucket.

'They wouldn't bring the bubbly until you were here to pay for it,' he said, reaching for the glasses.

'Still, they did allow you to sit down,' I pointed out.

He did not deign to answer.

Billy Birdsong was already on the stage, half-way through the second of her two evening's performances. I was interested to hear a different set of songs from the previous evening, an indication that many of the audience were repeat visitors. She also wore a different costume from those she had appeared in; I wondered idly just how extensive her repertoire and her wardrobe were.

Again, we were summoned to her dressing room after the show, and seated amongst the chocolate and flower tributes. She stripped off her stage face, painted on her other face of less exaggerated femininity, and changed into an embroidered frock of light wool.

When she emerged from behind the screen, I stood up, but instead of accompanying her down the street to her bistro, I escorted the remaining staff and hangers-on out of the room, placed Ledbetter outside in the hallway to keep them from returning, and closed the door firmly.

Wordlessly, I held out the pearl necklace; the singer took it, with

hands that were uncertain with apprehension, and returned to me my stickpin.

'Sit down,' I told her, and reached
for the nearest bottle of an
admirer's wine, scrabbling through
the debris atop the table for a cork-
screw.

Hesitantly, frightened, she obeyed.
She took the glass I handed her,
drank its contents as if it held med-
icine, and sat expectantly.

'He's dead,' I told her.

The green eyes closed. 'I knew it,'
she whispered. 'He'd have come back,
otherwise. How?'

'Murdered.'

The singer stared up at me in
horror, and said, 'God. Because of
me?'

'As yet, there is no reason to
believe his death had anything to do
with you. The Army police are looking
into it, but more to the point, I
will continue to investigate the
matter.'

'The police? Oh no.'

'In my cursory search of your Lieutenant Raynor's quarters, I saw
nothing that would bring your name

314

into this at all. The only thing I found was this.' I took from my note-case one of the two items I had removed from Raynor's pocket, and placed it on the table in front of the singer. 'He had it in his wallet. I thought you might want it returned.'

She looked at the studio portrait of herself, which was signed,

With love and kisses from Billy

'No, I don't suppose his family needed to see that.'

She sounded bitter, as would any person required to deny their very existence; my need to move the inves-tigation forward had to be put, tem-porarily, behind reassuring my client. 'His family is of no impor-tance,' I said firmly. 'What matters is that Lieutenant Raynor cared enough to risk carrying your photo-graph in his breast pocket.'

There followed the usual teary self-recrimination of a client, which becomes no less tiresome with the number of times one is forced to witness it. However, eventually the singer's tears receded and she sat

315

staring at herself in the dressing-table mirror; I knew that in a moment, she would see her ravaged face and reach, half-heartedly but inevitably, for the make-up pots.

For a performer, the sentiment 'Life must go on' runs closer to the surface than for other people.

'The first night, you told me that one evening when you were walking with Lieutenant Raynor, he saw someone he knew, and retreated from a confrontation.'

'Yes.'

'I need to know every detail of that incident.'

'What's to tell? We were walking arm-in-arm, he spots two people a couple blocks up, he pulls me into an alley and we take another route to my place.'

'When would this have been?'

'I don't know,' she replied in a despairing little voice. I felt like shaking her, but instead merely leant forward so that I dominated her vision.

'Think, Billy. What you were doing, how you felt, what was going on that night.'

'I really don't--Wait a minute,' she broke off. 'It was the night after he gave me the pearl. And that was on the full moon, I remember because Jack held it up to the window and compared the two, and said I would remember that night whenever the moon was full. He was such a romantic boy,' she said, and began to weep again.

Ruthlessly, I pressed on. 'So he gave you the necklace on the Sunday?'

'Monday,' she said, and blew her nose.

The moon had been at its fullest on the Sunday night, but I did not think the singer would have perceived the difference. 'Monday, then. So you saw these other people on the Tuesday night?'

'That sounds right.'

'What did they look like?'

'I only caught a glimpse.' Her hand sought out a piece of cotton wool, and absently dabbed it into the jar of cold cream.

'Men or women?'

'Well, that's the thing. There was a man and a figure in a dress. It was night and there was a street-light, but it was behind them, so between the fact that I only had a glance before Jack pulled me off the street and the fact that I couldn't see their faces, I can't be sure. But afterwards I thought maybe the woman was a kid who used to work with me, a few years ago when I was just getting started.'

'A boy?'

'Right. Very pretty face but couldn't sing worth a plugged nickel, and two left feet when it came to dancing. As soon as I could afford better, I let him go. But I hadn't seen him in years, and I can't be at all certain it was him.'

'What was his name?'

'He called himself Merry, Merry Whisker was it? No, Winkle. Merry Winkle. I probably have a photo of him in my scrapbook at home, if you like.'

'That would be extraordinarily helpful.'

'I'll send it to the hotel, shall I?'

'Thank you. What about the man? Old or young?'

'I really couldn't see him--'

'I understand, but impressions can be remarkably accurate.'

'Well, young then.'

'Tall or short?'

'Short,' she answered immediately. 'That much I did see, that Merry, if it was Merry, was taller than him.'

'Clothes?'

'Against the light that way, he was just an overcoat and a hat. No uniform, if that's what you're after.'

'And when you call to mind the attitudes of their persons, how they walked and the manner in which they moved, what would you say was their relationship? Brothers? Friends?'

'Frankly, they looked like a pro and her john. A professional. Which is why I even remember it, because once it came to me that it looked like Merry, I thought how sad his life must be.'

'I see. Where precisely did this take place?'

By this time I had been in San Francisco slightly over a month, and bore in my mind a clear map of her primary streets and districts. When Billy Birdsong told me the name of the street on which she and Raynor had been walking, the approximate cross-street, and in what direction the other two had been seen, I knew precisely where the encounter had taken place. I got from her a description of 'Merry Winkle' and questioned her further for some minor detail of dress or person, but she had nothing else, and soon her eyes began to tear up again. I summoned her dresser from the hall-way outside, and asked the woman to accompany Miss Birdsong home.

Outside of the Blue Tiger, young Ledbetter hovered at my elbow, the very picture of impatience. 'What happened?' he demanded. 'Why were you talking to her for so long? And what are we doing now?'

I raised my eyes, then looked past him at the nighttime street. 'I believe,' I said slowly, 'that I need to find a male prostitute.'

His dropped jaw said that I had succeeded in amazing him, yet again.

ELEVEN

Martin Ledbetter was only somewhat reassured when he found that it was a specific prostitute I sought, and not for any carnal purposes.

'Er, you don't know who he is?'

'I know a possible <u>nom de nuit</u>, if that be the proper phrase, and I know more or less where he plies his trade. I am relying on you, Mr Ledbetter, to lead me to him.'

As we made our way in the direction of the sighting, I explained the situation: acquaintance of Jack Raynor seen with a person who might be a failed dancer with trans-vestite proclivities, where seen, accompanying whom.

'And you think I know him?'

'I should doubt it, as your circle is somewhat more exalted than his. However, you may know the sorts of places someone of that sort would ply his trade. A street-corner, do you think, or inside an establishment?'

'Did his, er, client know he was a trans-vestite?' Ledbetter asked.

'That,' I told him, 'is indeed the question.'

It was now close to three o'clock in the morning, and I had my doubts that we would find the person in question still lingering at a street-corner or inside a speakeasy. Ledbetter knew the area as well as I had thought, and one or two of the denizens claimed some degree of recognition to my description of the person we sought, but in the end, the hour was too far advanced, and the hypothesis was not to be proved that night. I should have to return on the morrow, when the working girls, and boys, are fresh.

However, this did not mean that my work was done.

'You perhaps should go home, Ledbetter,' I suggested. 'You look as if you could use some sleep.'

'The night is young,' he protested, although a moment before he had been stifling a yawn.

'Very well, perhaps you could recommend an all-night diner, at which we might while away an hour. Preferably along the water-front.'

He located a small building, little more than a hut with greasy windows, that nonetheless was warm and smelt pleasingly of fresh coffee and bacon. The other patrons were either early labourers on their way to work or revellers endeavouring to sober themselves for the trip home; I reflected with amusement that my companion and I fit with either category.

The coffee and breakfast fare restored us both to a second wind, and provided a layer of insulation against the damp air when we went out of the door at a quarter to five.

My valiant young guide paused in the doorway to get his cigarette alight, then asked, 'Where to now?'

'Fisherman's Wharf,' I told him absently, occupied with studying the figure he cut. 'I say, wait here for a moment.'

I went back inside, and within two minutes had made the necessary arrangements, returning with a hat in my hand. 'Put this on,' I told him. He took it with fastidious fingers, wrinkling his nose at the pomade stains that darkened its interior. Admittedly, it was not a very nice hat, but it was the only one in the diner that was neither a cloth working-man's cap or a tall formal article such as the one I wore. All we required was the silhouette.

He lowered it with distaste onto his slick hair; I studied the effect, and nodded. 'You may take it off if you prefer, and save it until it is needed. Come now, dawn will be here shortly.'

'Why are we going to Fisherman's Wharf?'

'We seek an informal water-taxi service.'

'But the hire-boats are down closer to the Ferry Building.'

'Miss Birdsong lives on the southern slopes of Pacific Heights. When Raynor left her flat in latter weeks, he was in the habit of turning due north. This would lead him directly up the hills; if he were heading for the ferry, he would turn east, as he was wont to do in earlier days, in order to avoid the steep climb. I believe that in the early days he was dependent on the ferry to take him across the Golden Gate. Later, he made other arrangements.'

As dawn approached, this area of the water-front had become a hive of activity. Italian was the language of choice among San Francisco's fishing fleet, and the boats were built and rigged along a more or less Mediterranean pattern. However, as we stood and studied the bustle, I noticed that in the less desirable corners of the mooring areas were one or two boats with a touch of exoticism to their lines and sails. I was not surprised to see that the men moving about on the decks were similarly alien. I turned to Ledbetter, half dozing as he leant against a wall.

'I want you to put on the hat, button up your overcoat, and walk along the wharf to where that blue boat is just putting out. When you get there, take a dollar bill out of your pocket and hold it high in the air. Just stand there with it raised until I tell you otherwise.'

'Er,' he began.

'You haven't a dollar,' I said for him, and reached for my note-case.

I remained in the shadows, watching the reaction to Ledbetter's movements. Most of the fishermen were too busy to pay him any attention; one of two glanced at him curiously, and kept glancing, attracted by the money in his hand. But as I had thought, once the furthest boats noticed his figure, the entire crew of one of the alien boats stood and stared. After a minute, I saw a figure slip from the boat onto the dock and trot in Ledbetter's direction, only to slow, pause, and, after much peering and hesitation, retreat.

I quickly left my post and gathered up my young assistant, hurrying him along lest the boat leave its moorage before we could speak with the captain.

'Can I take off this damned hat now?' Ledbetter panted behind me.

'We are finished with it,' I answered, and heard a faint plop as it landed in the water.

When we were within speaking distance of the boat, which was rapidly casting off to depart, I said loudly, 'We are nothing to do with the police. I will pay you for the answer to a question.'

The crew continued its rapid movements, but one figure stopped to listen. I came to a halt at the edge of the boards and called, 'Please, I will pay. I just need to ask about the man who had you take him across the Bay in the mornings.'

The boat drifted farther away, but

then the man spoke some words over his shoulder and the vessel's outward progress slowed. After a moment, the anchor went down, and the man climbed into the small boat to row himself back within talking distance. He stopped twenty feet away, his oars playing in the water to keep him in his place. I squatted down onto my heels.

'What you want know?' he asked.

'About three weeks ago, a young man with light hair made an arrangement with you to carry him across the Bay several mornings a week.'

The fisherman did not answer, but neither did he deny it. I went on.

'Where did you take him?'

All I needed, in fact, was mere confirmation, but the question would do as well as any other.

He studied me, looked more closely at my companion, then grunted, 'Fo't Barry. He go Barry dock, near lighthouse.'

'Why did he come to you rather than ask one of the Italians?'

The man shrugged. 'He speak some Chinee. Live in Manila, know Chinee there. Mebbee like Chinee. Who know?'

'Who indeed,' I agreed. 'Thank you, I hope I have not unduly delayed your day's work.' I looked around and spotted an empty tin that, according to the label, had once held pineapple. I pushed a five-dollar bill into it, stepped on its open end to secure the money, and tossed it under-hand into the skiff at the man's feet. He nodded, then pulled at the oars, taking himself back to his boat.

With age, a man's bones become weary, and stiffen with a night's fog; I will admit that I regretted the lack of taxi ranks in this part of town, and that I was relieved beyond all proportion when Ledbetter spotted a cab driving in the direction of the Ferry Building, and whistled it to a stop.

I had not paused to reflect how very long my day had been until I was walking down the corridor to my room minutes later. My overcoat felt as if it were lined with lead, and my fingers fumbled with key, then buttons, and finally laces. Then when I sat down on my piled clothing to remove my shoes, I heard the rustle of paper beneath me. I pulled my coat from the pile and felt for its inner pocket, then sat upon the edge of the bed to look yet again at the second item I had removed from the dead man's person.

Ten hours later, I woke half-dressed, inadequately blanketed, and with the letter still in my hand. An hour after that, bathed, shaved, and fed, I took up the envelope, which was addressed to 'Joseph Raynor' at a post office box, and slid out the letter. It bore the imprint of a law office in Los Angeles, dated the week before Raynor was last seen, and read:

Dear Sir:

I received your letter, and the payment, which as you noted, serves to assure me that this is no stunt. You will understand, I think, that working in proximity to the area's growing moving-picture industry, we are well used to stunts.

However, taking your inquiry as a serious one, I would have to agree that, setting aside for the moment the question of criminal charges, the solidity of the contract would appear to depend heavily on sympathetic and closemouthed servants and, in the event of ill health, a doctor of similar characteristics. I cannot tell you what the status is in foreign parts, although I can direct you to colleagues if you wish.

I do not, however, believe it possible to avoid a lawsuit entirely. It is true, as you suggest, that personal possessions can legally be left to whomever one wishes, be it man, woman, or four-legged creature. Family inheritances would be a different matter, and if it came before a court, might well create an enormous string of legal difficulties. Speaking personally, I would relish tackling such a matter, but I can certainly understand that the person or persons involved in such an inevitably drawn-out court battle would do much to avoid it.

Please let me know if you would like my help in making the arrangements you mentioned in your letter. However, I would urge you to come and talk to me first about the potential for prosecution this course of action could conceivably open you up to, with permanent effects on your future.

Yours,
Samuel Kapinsky

I went downstairs to compose a wire to Mr Kapinsky, then deposited the letter in the hotel's safe, and made ready for a third crossing of San Francisco's Golden Gate.

I presented myself to the major's office, as arranged, at three o'clock in the afternoon. As I had feared, his superior had laid ham-fisted claim to the investigation; as I had hoped, Morris was not happy about it.

'Don't know why we have to turn it over to him,' he grumbled when first I appeared. 'I was doing perfectly well.'

'Disruptive, eh?' I asked in sympathy.

'Exactly! Disruptive, that's the very word. Man thinks I should bring the whole day's schedule to a halt so he can talk to everyone on the post. Idiot.'

'I don't suppose I could be of service?' I suggested. 'Just to move him in the right direction and help him solve the case more quickly?'

'You'd do that?' Clearly, Captain Sigerson's long-ago and fictional experiences weighed more with the major than any so-called superior's qualifications. I hastened to agree with him.

'Certainly. I owe it to the family to conclude this sad business as soon as possible.' To say nothing of owing it to myself to finish here before one of the bereaved family could arrive and tell the major that they had not sent any lawyer.

'Very well,' Morris declared. 'See what you can do. I'll give you an officer to help you, what about--'

'What about that young corporal you left with me yesterday?' I suggested smoothly. 'Seems a sensible lad.'

'But Lieutenant Halston is free today while they're clearing up the shooting range. He knew Raynor, might be able to answer some questions.'

The last thing I wanted was a friend of the dead officer. 'All I need is a man in a uniform, so as not to be continually stopped for an explanation,' I assured Morris. 'Corporal Larsen will be fine. If he can be spared.'

He did not bother to respond to the preposterous notion that a corporal might be urgently needed elsewhere, merely raised his voice to call, 'Baxter!' The door opened and the adjutant looked in. 'Get Corporal Larsen. He's to be seconded to this gentleman until further notice, on or off the base.'

Baxter saluted and closed the door. Before the major could move on to the next item on his calendar, I asked him what he'd thought of his dead lieutenant.

'What do you mean, what did I think of him? He was a competent officer, but like I told you, he hadn't been here long enough to get to know him.'

'Do you think he looked upon the Army as a permanent career?' I asked.

At that, he sat back in his chair. 'You know, when he first got here I'd have said yes, even though he was about as sickly as I've seen a man. But later on, I don't know. His heart seemed to go out of it. Maybe just the malaria; fever does wear a man down after a while.'

'You sound as though you would have been disappointed, had he left the services.'

'I thought he had the makings of a first-class officer. Not just an everyday officer, and he'd have been wasted in peace-time, but given another war, Raynor could have made a hell of a name for himself. Had that kind of quirky way of looking at things that all the great commanders of history have had. The ability to rewrite the rules of warfare, if you follow me. 'Course, as I say, in peace-time that could make for terrible problems. Sort of like your own country's Major Lawrence. If he'd spent his career drilling the ranks, he'd have ended up drinking himself to death, or putting a gun in his mouth. Instead, he goes out into the desert and finds the Arabs, and takes off like a rocket. That was Raynor all over. All he needed was a good war.'

It was an unexpected insight, revealing and perceptive. I did not tell the major that the peace-time ranks were precisely where Lawrence had put himself, for indeed, I thought Morris was right about the man. Morris's judgement, nonetheless, added another piece to my understanding of Jack Raynor: Idiosyncratic military minds also have a tendency to make bitter enemies.

I thanked the major and left him to his paperwork, and in a very few minutes, Larsen came pounding up at double-time, red of face and as alarmed as one might expect at a summons to the commanding officer. He looked greatly relieved when he received his orders, but also puzzled, not understanding quite what my position here was.

'Larsen,' I explained, 'the major wants you and me to try and solve Raynor's murder before the police can.'

That, he understood.

The major's key and his relayed command to the soldier standing guard over Raynor's quarters opened the door. Before we could walk through it, a door down the corridor opened and a young officer with black hair and hazel eyes looked out, the slippers on his feet and a slim book in his left hand indicating that we had disturbed his rest. He propped the hand with the book against the door frame as he leant out, the three fingers draped across the volume's cloth cover showing the scars and embedded gravel of an old injury. He looked at the three of us curiously.

'What's up?' he asked, his question directed, I thought, at the guard.

'Orders from Major Morris, sir. This gentleman's the Raynor family lawyer.'

The brown head nodded and his door closed as he went back to his reading. I appreciated this confirmation of the major's efficiency: Clearly, the guard had been a continuous presence here.

Once inside, Corporal Larsen stood with his back to the door, looking around him uneasily.

'Sir, what are we looking for?'

'Anything the Presidio men might have overlooked,' I told him, settling at the desk for a look at those tantalising envelopes: If Jack Raynor had a fiancée for whom he was contemplating the purchase of wedding bands, there would surely be letters.

A less experienced investigator might assume that the two items Raynor had carried on his person, the Birdsong photograph and the enigmatic letter from the Los Angeles lawyer, had been in his breast pocket because he attached a high degree of emotional import to them. I knew, however, that their presence over his heart could as easily be due to any number of factors, from a recent receipt to a general disinclination to leave problematic documents where others might find them; indeed, he may even have had them with him the night he died because he planned to tear them into a thousand tiny pieces and set them free on the wind from the Pacific--such romantic notions were not unheard of, in a man in his situation. But he was, I had no doubt, genuinely fond of the singer, no matter what his plans for marriage might be; clearly, despite the lawyer's cautiously enigmatic wording, Raynor intended to leave Birdsong something in his will in the face of potential family objections.

Still, however problematic the

signed photograph of a trans-vestite singer and a lawyer's letter might be, there would be no reason for Raynor to conceal his love-notes from a fiancée. I expected to find them. I did not.

Instead, the three letters in the drawer were from his mother, his brother, and his sister.

The mother possessed what appeared to me an excessive interest in the game of whist, and furthermore assumed a similar obsession on the part of her son. Only at the very end did she add the lines, 'I would of course adore seeing you this summer, if you decide to come home for a time, and we can talk about your plans for the future at that time. If only California wasn't so very far away!'

The brother's letter addressed Jack Raynor's summer plans with slightly more detail, all of which underscored Major Morris's unvoiced fears about the renewal of his lieutenant's con-tract with the United States Army. The brother, whose name was given as Edward, seemed most concerned with Jack's possible desire for the summer house, which Edward hoped to use for the entire month of August.

It was the sister's brief note that hit the nail square:

Dearest Jack,

As you asked, I haven't said anything to the family, although really I think you're being a little silly about this. If you love this girl, then we surely will, and there's no need to go straight back to California. You know how Mummy adores planning a party, she's going to be so disappointed if you go to a registry office.

But you know best, and I can't argue that Mummy's getting any better as she gets older. The other day she had Eddy's wife in tears because little Iris had dirt on her dress after playing outside! I'd live in California, too, if I could!

> Kisses always,
> your loving sister
> Caroline

'Does it seem to you unusual that Lieutenant Raynor only has three letters in his desk?' I asked the corporal, who had begun picking hesitantly through the officer's cupboard.

'I've only kept two letters in six years,' the lad told me. 'Not a lot of room for keepsakes in this life, even for an officer.'

I had not expected a sensible answer--I never expected a sensible answer from my assistants, with one shining exception--but I had to agree, the lad had it right. The rest of Raynor's quarters gave the same impression, of a tidy man who dealt with things as they came up, then rid himself of encumbrances.

Which left me with the question: Had Billy Birdsong become one of those encumbrances?

My missing-person mystery was now clearly two, possibly separate, mysteries: Who had killed Lieutenant Jack Raynor? And, what was I to tell the singer about her lover's intentions?

TWELVE

I did not go to the Blue Tiger that night, but I was not surprised, when I entered the speakeasy where we had left off the previous night, to find Martin Ledbetter leaning one elbow against the filthy bar, a cautious handkerchief resting between fabric and wood. He made his customary glass-raising gesture; I noted that he not only had sufficient funds to purchase his own drink, he'd had his hair cut and wore a crisp new shirt.

'How long have you been here?' I asked when I had ordered my own drink.

'Just a few minutes,' he replied; the slight difficulty he had with the letter s made clear that he had not begun his evening here. 'No sign of Mr Winkie.'

'Winkle,' I corrected him. He made a peculiar noise half-way between a snort and a giggle, then frowned at his glass accusingly. I picked it up, and mine, and led him to a minuscule table in a corner of the near-deserted establishment. We nursed those drinks, then two more, but before I was driven to a choice between permanent liver damage and being forced to leave, a man in a dress came into the bar.

His appearance answered a question: Other than the clothing, Merry Winkle had made no attempt to disguise himself as a female. A customer would have had to be blind, deaf, and dead drunk before making a mistake of gender. When I stood beside him at the bar, I could see that he had even neglected to shave that day.

'I'd like to buy the lady a drink,' I told the man behind the counter. The 'lady' turned to look at me, turned farther to stare in open disbelief, and only then remembered to assume a coquettish simper. I cut him off before he could launch into his spiel.

'Would you by chance be known as Merry Winkle?'

'I might, honey, if you're interested in a little company.'

'I am very interested in a little conversation, if that can be arranged? I shall of course pay you for your time.'

'Don't care what you call it, honey, I've got the time. Oh, and you've got a pretty friend, too.'

'Er,' Ledbetter said from my shoulder.

'Actually, it is mere conversation I require,' I told Winkle. 'Perhaps we might sit down with our drinks?'

It took some time to convince the man that in this case, 'conversation' was not synonymous with some variation on his usual professional activities, and he was still looking more than a little uncertain when Ledbetter went to fetch him another drink. I placed a dollar coin on the table, which he slipped into his flat bodice, then began.

'Mr, er, Winkle.'

'Look, I haven't used that name in a long time. Why don't you just call me Winfield?'

'Mr Winfield, then. Nine days ago, on a Tuesday night, you were seen with a client, walking along Market Street.'

He shrugged. 'You can see me most evenings, walking along Market with a client. Except Sundays,' he corrected himself, adding piously, ' "Remember the Sabbath and keep it holy." '

Young Ledbetter narrowly avoided choking on his beer, and I opened my mouth, then decided this was not the place for a lecture on the difference between Sabbath and Sunday. 'Most commendable of you, Mr Winfield. However, you had a client that night, a man somewhat shorter than you, who was probably a soldier.'

Winfield laughed, revealing a mouthful of teeth that explained the state of his breath. 'They're all soldiers and sailors, honey. Anyway, who is it says he saw me?'

I hesitated, loath to bring my client into this. 'Just a singer, who was going home late from the cabaret.'

'Well I--Wait a minute. You don't mean Billy Birdsong?'

'Do you know her?' I answered non-committally.

'Sure I know her, I used to sing in a revue when she was first hired. I had an accident, broke my foot. If I hadn't, I'd be on the stage like she is now. I'd've been the one to go off to France and get famous. I sing, too, you know.'

'I can tell from the timbre of your voice,' I replied. 'So you noticed Miss Birdsong one evening two weeks ago?'

'Her and a fancy man. She pretended she didn't see me, but she did, and she ran away down an alley before she had to talk to me.'

'Do you remember who you were with that evening?'

'Oh yeah. He calls himself "Smith", like I'd believe that. I call him Smitty. He's a regular, shows up about once a week. Although, come to think of it, he hasn't been by in a while.'

'Since that night, perhaps?'

'Damn! Excuse my French, but you're right. Wonder if it scared him off? If it did, it's mixed blessings. The man's a real bastard.'

'In what way?'

Winfield played with his drink, then fortified himself with a deep swallow. 'My regulars are what you might call a "specialised clientele." Not quite honest enough with themselves to walk up to a boy on the street, or even in a place like this. Smitty likes to make a kind of game out of it, that he thinks I'm a girl until . . . Well, I don't think I have to spell it out for you.'

'Quite.'

'He's not the only one, looks nice and talks all polite and then when the door's shut you're something stuck to the bottom of his boot. I mean to say, I know I'm just a . . . a . . . vessel, but don't know why that makes me any more scum than the men who use me.'

Ledbetter, who had just returned from another trip to the bar, stopped dead to stare at Winfield. The man in the dress saw the glass hovering above the sticky table, took it from Ledbetter's hand, and threw half of it down his throat.

However, it was a sentiment I had heard before, in other parts of the globe; I smiled in sympathy. 'Can you describe "Smitty" for me?'

'Little bit shorter'n me. Black hair, greeny-brown eyes, soldier's tan--face and hands, that is, pale under his clothes. Like a hundred others I've seen this year.'

'What about what they call identifying marks? A tattoo or scar, perhaps? An accent, a ring, an unusual pocket watch, the manner in which he combed his hair? Anything that stands out in your mind from a hundred others?'

'Smitty's not exactly what you'd call well endowed. Maybe explains something about his short temper,' Winfield added with a brief flare of bitterness.

I kept my face straight, not only at the unintended humour of this psychological revelation but at the thought of checking a line of suspects for that particular trait. I nodded encouragement; he played with his glass, thinking.

'His finger!' Winfield raised his eyes to mine. 'The little finger of his, let's see, his left hand. It stuck out a little when he moved the other fingers, all stiff, like he'd broke it. And it had dark spots in it, like . . .'

'Like he'd crushed it, embedding bits of gravel under the skin,' I finished ungrammatically.

'Exactly. Why, you know him?'

'Not yet,' I said with satisfaction. A few minutes later, sure I had received all that Winfield knew, I gave the man enough money to allow him the rest of the evening off, if not the week.

I was smiling as we left the speakeasy, holding to myself the vision of a misshapen finger with gravel beneath the skin, draped across the front of a slim book, as Jack Raynor's neighbour, Lieutenant Gregory Halston, came into the corridor to see who was moving about next door.

I did not smile for long. Always, the proof of villainy is far more tedious than merely identifying the villain.

My young assistant--who, I reflected, might be one of the more unlikely Irregulars I had employed, but also one of the more effective--was in favour of rushing to board the last Sausalito ferry of the night and storming the fort then and there.

Instead, I was leading him in the opposite direction, while he positively hopped about with frustration.

'But we know who it is!' he

protested, his voice ringing loudly through the silent canyons of the financial district. 'We need to go and catch him.'

We, I reflected, the smile returning briefly to my lips: We from a boy who had introduced himself by picking my pocket three nights before.

'And when we have caught him, what do we do with him?' I asked.

'Well, turn him over to the authorities,' he replied indignantly.

Such innocence and trust was, in its way, an encouraging sign. I stopped to look at Ledbetter's face in the light of the street-lamp, and found him looking at me with the enthusiasm and urging of a dog whose master held the ball. I had intended merely to take myself to my rooms and grimly contemplate the walls, but instead I found myself thinking, Why not? I placed my hand on his shoulder, and said, 'Mr Ledbetter, perhaps you might be of assistance by allowing me to review the case aloud.'

We adjourned to my rooms, ignoring the raised eyebrows of the doorman, the night desk clerk, and the elevator boy along the way. Inside, I turned up the lights and told him to help himself to a drink. When I came back from washing my hands, having exchanged my outer coats for a dressing-gown, he was sitting in a chair far from the desk.

'You really must learn to return drawers to their original state,' I advised him as I poured my own glass. I pulled open the offending drawer, saw with interest that he had merely looked, not taken, then closed it again and went to sit in the chair across from the furiously blushing, possibly reformed young thief.

'The man's name is Gregory Halston,' I began without preamble. 'He, too, is a junior officer stationed on Fort Barry, and as he has been there longer than Raynor, he is technically in a superior position.

'Either happenstance, or some unconscious awareness of a degree of similarity on the part of their commanding officer, brought these two young men together. And once they were assigned to the same post, they of necessity lived together, the only two officers in their half-deserted fort.

'Both men had a secret, the same secret, unbeknown to the other. I do not know if sodomy is a hanging offence in the United States Army, or merely cause for corporal punishment and dishonourable discharge, but once they had seen each other on the street, in similar circumstances, neither was in doubt.

'The two might have cast their eyes in opposite directions and agreed that the evening had never happened, uneasy but content that their black-mail was mutual, except for one thing: The following day a letter arrived, and Raynor determined to leave the Army altogether.'

'What letter?'

'From a legal gentleman in the southern part of the state. I believe Lieutenant Raynor made the fatal mis-take of telling his neighbour and fellow officer his plans, possibly under the assumption that Halston would feel reassured at his future absence. Instead, it had the opposite effect: Halston panicked, believing that once Raynor was safely out, their mutual hold over each other would fail. Guilt,' I mused, 'has an interesting way of twisting one's thoughts.'

'So, Halston bashed him and hid him in the gun room. We need to go tell his commanding officer.'

'How do you propose that we approach that revelation? None of us on this side of the Gate would make the most solid of witnesses on the stand. I, after all, presented myself as a Raynor family lawyer, which I am not. Or perhaps you would like to go in my stead?' I allowed him to consider that distasteful turn of affairs, then added, 'Or perhaps Miss Birdsong?'

'So we can't pin the bastard down because none of us could testify?'

'There is little proof other than our word.'

'But, his hand!'

'Ah, so you wish to place Mr Winfield on the stand?'

'Yeah, he'd be just great,' Ledbetter admitted, and took a hefty swallow from his glass. 'Come on, now, there's got to be some kind of evidence. Detectives always find evidence.'

'A foot-print that matches the shoe of a man who spends many hours down on his knee before a target with a rifle. As do half the men on the base. The cryptic note of a meeting-place, which again could have come from any side. Letters leading to inescapable conclusions that would mortify a family and turn their wrath against your friend the singer? I believe Jack Raynor would prefer to go unavenged, than have that path of destruction.'

Ledbetter slapped his glass down on the table, sending the contents flying, although fortunately the glass was nearly empty. 'So he's got away with it?'

'I did not say that.'

He looked at me askance. 'You're going to sneak up on him and shoot him in the back?'

'Mr Ledbetter, what sort of fiction do you read?' I asked, more than a little shocked. 'Certainly not. We simply need a better grade of wit-ness.'

'Do we have one?'

'Not yet.'

'Damn it, you sound awfully complacent about all this.'

'Perhaps,' I said, 'because I have done this before.'

I waited, to see if he could work it out on his own. His eyes narrowed in thought, and after a minute, began to take on a twinkle of excitement. 'You want to set a trap for him.'

'Something of the sort.'

'A secret meeting at night,' he said, his words tumbling in excitement, 'like the one he and Raynor had! Say, this is as good as a Sherlock Holmes story!'

Indeed, the unnecessarily melodramatic twist he proposed was just the sort of thing Conan Doyle would have enjoyed, and my immediate impulse was to dismiss it out of hand. However, I held myself and considered, and on thinking it over, I decided that it was true: a parallel meeting by night could be, as Ledbetter might put it, just the ticket. I found myself smiling.

'Mr Ledbetter,' I told him, 'you are a man after my own heart.'

Now it was just a matter of suborning a major of the United States Army.

THIRTEEN

It was a curious sensation, to find myself the conservative and hesitant half of a pair, but young Ledbetter had the bit in his teeth now, and nothing would do but that we compose a deliberately mysterious note and arrange to deliver it to Lieutenant Halston before morning. I sat at the desk with a piece of anonymous white paper and, after a moment's thought, wrote the following:

Gregory Halston, you were seen that night, but 50 dollars in cash will purchase my continued silence. Tonight, at the same hour and place he died.

'Hey,' my novice accomplice exclaimed, 'you're pretty good at this.'

'I ought to be,' I told him, which served to remind him that, in truth, he had little idea who I was or on which side of the law I walked. I retrieved the note, and placed it in a plain envelope, writing Halston's name on the outside. 'I shall take this over to Fort Baker in the morning, and have it delivered to him.'

'Oh no, you can't just give it to him.'

'I could, actually, simply telling him that some person unknown to me had handed it to me as I approached the grounds. However, I did not intend to do so. I shall merely leave it anonymously with the fort post-master.'

'Let me do it.'

'Your presence in the fort would take explanation, where I already have reason to be there. Don't worry, Ledbetter, I shall call on you for the evening's efforts.'

'You won't try to take this guy on all on your own?'

'By no means. It is a long-time habit of mine to depend on others when it comes to open warfare. And now, young man, you need to take yourself home and sleep through as much of the day as you can manage. I shall expect you at Fisherman's Wharf at ten-thirty tonight. Dress warmly, in dark clothing, and be sure nothing you wear rustles or rattles.'

He left me, reluctantly. I waited at the window until I had seen him pass down the street and round a corner, then resumed my outer garments and let myself out. By good fortune, a taxi driver was sleeping at the kerb, and interrupted his slumber to take me to Fisherman's Wharf. I arranged with him to continue his sleep there, as paid employment, and I was standing at the oddly-rigged fishing boat when the Chinese crew came up two hours later.

They were not pleased to see me at first, but the bills in my hand softened them considerably, and the promise of more bought me their services for all of Friday night.

Well pleased, I woke my snoring driver a second time and had him deliver me to the ferry terminus. At Fort Baker, I arranged for the letter to be given to Lieutenant Halston, concluded business with his commanding officer, and again crossed over to the city on the Bay.

Upon returning to the hotel, I tacked a note onto my door threatening violence to anyone who disturbed me, and slept through what remained of the daylight hours.

I woke, persuaded the hotel kitchen that I did require a meal at that hour, and dressed in the sort of clothing I had recommended to Ledbetter.

When the sun was well down on the horizon, the Chinese crew and I set out from the fishing boats and made north across the fierce currents. A small pier serving the emplacements at Fort Barry was tucked into a cove laid about with jagged rocks, with the Bonita lighthouse sitting at its outer edge and a single track of tramway leading straight up the cliff behind. As I rode the deck, in the fading light I noted the curious difference of colour in the ground on the right and left of the pier, brought together at a sharp fold of earth. I speculated about the presence of a fault here, what it meant for the future of the city behind me. And then the light winked out, and all was darkening outline.

The crew negotiated the dangerous rocks of the small bay, the captain directing them with terse commands as the rush of waters attempted to drive us onto one set of rocks or another. When we reached the pier, it was nearly dark. I stepped off the boat onto the boards, turning back to accept two lanterns from one of the crew. The first I placed at the west-ernmost corner of the pier's end. The other I set fifty feet up its ramp. Then I went back to call across the intervening water at the captain.

'Do you want me to light them for a few minutes?'

'No, is fine,' he answered; the concentrated expertise with which he studied his surroundings assured me that he had a chance of making it in with nothing but those two lamps to mark his way. After all, smuggling, which required night-time markers such as my two lanterns, was a common occupation along this coast. I nodded.

'Eleven o'clock, then.'

'Yes.' And his engines reversed him into the cove and back to the ship-ping channel. When he had gone, I settled my rucksack onto my shoulders and set out up the steep slope of the track leading away from the pier.

The hours passed slowly, aided by a flask of tea (coffee being too liable to give one away by its stronger aroma). The night's blackness was complete, three days short of the new moon, and the wind dropped by the time I made my way back down to the pier at half past ten.

Ledbetter arrived at the arranged time, and the lamps I had lit brought the Chinese boat in with neat competence. I led my young friend up the hill and settled him into his position, adjuring him to absolute silence. Or more accurately, I told him that if he lit a cigarette or fiddled with the change in his pocket, I would throw him off the cliff.

We waited.

Waves pounded on the cliffs below, leaving faint stirs of white in the darkness as their crests broke. The lighthouse flared at its set pattern, silent for once with the absence of coastal fog. The occasional night bird rasped overhead, a fox yipped in the distance.

And at two o'clock in the morning, as the mists began to creep up over the hills, a voice spoke out of the darkness.

'Anybody there?'

'Lieutenant Halston,' I replied.

The sudden beam of a torch pinned me down, blinding me and, to a lesser but necessary degree, the man wielding it.

'You're that lawyer,' the young man said after a minute. 'You were searching Jack's rooms.'

'I was in Raynor's rooms, yes, although I am not a lawyer. It was necessary for me to tell your major something of the sort in order to gain access.'

'Why did you need to gain access?'

'When he died, Raynor had something of mine. In fact, I was following him that night, trying to figure out how to get it out of him, when I saw you and him, right here.' The story was thin to the point of breaking--how would I, a civilian, have skulked about the headlands unnoticed?--but I have found that a man's guilt often stands in the way of rational thought, and so it proved with Halston.

'That wasn't me.'

I squinted against the light. 'There's another man of your build, rank, and voice living on the base?'

'Probably lots.'

'Is that what you told Jack, when you were trying to convince him that he hadn't seen you on the street in San Francisco with your friend Merry?'

Silence, with the waves beating at the shore. 'What do you want?' the lieutenant demanded.

'Merely the fifty dollars. Jack Raynor's death left me short of travelling money, and I need enough to get me home. Fifty should do it nicely.'

I thought for an awful moment that he would simply give me the money and walk away, but a man of Halston's sort understands that when fear and greed jostle for the upper hand, fear will never win out. When he spoke again, his voice was scornful.

'What did Jack have of yours?'

'The same thing he had that belonged to you.'

'He didn't have anything of mine.'

'He had your reputation in his hands.'

Silence answered the charge.

'Lieutenant Raynor saw you with the person who calls himself Merry Winfield. An unfortunate fellow, who might have made something of a success on the stage had it not been for too great a thirst for drink and drug. Any superior officer would take one look at the fellow and condemn you out of hand. Raynor could have led your superiors to you, and that would have been the end.'

'I didn't--'

'But the tragedy of this situation is, your friend Jack had no intention of turning you in.'

'He was leaving. Resigning his commission.'

'And he wished only for you to be happy for him.'

The torch-beam wavered, the waves and continuous breeze made the night seem alive, as we waited for Halston to decide what to do.

Then the beam held firm, and I prepared to throw myself to the side, for I knew what was to come: If Halston could not trust his friend, he would not trust me. He took a step back from me and his

363

hand thrust inside the open front of his greatcoat. His arm went in, then drew out, and the speed with which he moved told me all I needed to know.

I gave a great shout and threw myself to the ground, and the hillside came alive.

With a click the lights we had strung from three hefty batteries came to life, centred on the man with the torch. They confused him, and he held up the gun, not to aim at me, but to shield his eyes. As it rose into full view, the United States Army moved onto the field of battle.

'ATTEN-<u>HUT</u>!' the major's voice bellowed out, the one command to which even an officer reacted with immediate and unthinking response. The lieutenant's back snapped up and his hand jerked down several inches. He caught himself in an instant and made to stretch out his arm again, but it was too late. Ledbetter tackled him from behind, and while they were struggling, Major Morris strode up and brought one large boot down on the scarred hand that was stretching out for the gun.

It was over.

No doubt in the end, the major altered the scenario somewhat to explain the actions of his black-haired lieutenant. A flimsy tale of rivalry over the affections of a young lady would provide a more satisfactory tale than one of fear, guilt, and the twisted secret lives of two young officers. It mattered not to me how the major constructed his case against Halston, so long as punishment was dealt. And as the major had personally witnessed his officer's guilt, as he had required of me when I went to him that morning, punishment would indeed be meted.

He sent us home on the launch, and with the eastern sky going light, our knock brought Billy Birdsong from her bed.

'Tell me again how it happened,' she implored half an hour later. Curbing my impatience, I reviewed in précis the lengthy tale I had recounted once already.

'Merry recognised you, and you him;

Raynor saw Halston, and Halston him. Merry, who thinks you stole his deserved success, complained about you to Halston. And Halston believed you would do the same with Raynor, telling him who, and what, Halston had been walking down the street with. Which would leave Gregory Halston vulnerable.'

Billy Birdsong looked up sharply. 'Greg? You say his name is Greg?'

'Is that the name you were trying to recall?' I asked, but her face, crumpling in despair, had already told me the answer.

'Greg, yes, that was the name of Jack's friend! The only friend he ever mentioned to me. Jack said Greg was one of the blessings that made life possible, with long talks about books and music and life. How could he imagine that Jack would betray him?'

'One sees what one is, and Halston saw someone with the potential to do him harm. His fears preyed on him, but did not come to a head until last Friday, when Raynor told him that he had decided to quit the Army and get married. With Raynor still in uniform, Halston was safe. But from the outside, anything Raynor said could put Halston behind bars, or worse.'

'Married?' she cried. 'Jack?'

I put up a hand to quiet her, and continued, for from here on, we were covering new ground.

'It was no surprise to me that Raynor had matrimonial aspirations. The jeweller who made your necklace told me that Raynor had been looking at wedding rings at the same time. And his commanding officer said that he thought Raynor had recently begun to contemplate leaving the Army. Then in Raynor's desk, I found two family letters referring to his previous mention of marriage.'

'No,' the singer moaned, tears gathering along her lashes. 'Oh, no. It was all a . . . a farce? Oh, God, I thought Jack wasn't like the others. Do you know who she was?'

'She was you.'

The green eyes snapped up, the tears drying on the instant with astonishment. '<u>What</u>?' I smiled: The voice had been that of a man, not the singer's controlled contralto.

I took from my pocket the two letters from the lawyer in Los Angeles.
The first, couched in necessarily
enigmatic terms lest other eyes see
it, brought a small frown line into
being between her eyes. The second,
however, had arrived at my hotel as
I slept that very afternoon, hand
carried by special messenger from Los
Angeles.

Dear Mr. Sigerson,
    I received your wire, and as you
suggested telephoned the police to
confirm its facts. Thank you for
telling me of my client's unfortunate
death.
    I am sorry never to have met the
man, who struck me even in his letter
as a creative and forceful individual. As you suggest, his letter to
me concerned the potential repercus-
sions of an unconventional form of
marriage. At first blush, I laughed
it off as ridiculous, but when I had
looked more closely at the actual
wording on the books, I thought it
might be open to a certain degree of
interpretation. It is generally
assumed that the legal contract we

know as 'marriage' is drawn between a man and a woman. However, as with the case of the innkeeper you mentioned, there is no clear law against it.

Essentially, however, the simplest way ahead for the young man would have been simply to allow the world to assume that his wife was indeed a woman. He assured me that no casual acquaintance would know it to be otherwise, which is when I wrote to urge him to choose his servants, and especially doctor with great care, for any illness could bring disaster down on their heads.

The elements of the marriage contract that involves inheritance would have to be handled somewhat differently, for fear that after his death, the true nature of his spouse be brought to light, leaving her penniless and liable for prosecution to boot.

I hope this has helped to clarify the matter on which Mr. Raynor consulted me, and again, I thank you for your information. Please convey my condolences to Raynor's would-be fiancée, and assure her that the young man had every intention of caring for her as a wife.

Yours sincerely,
Samuel Kapinsky

The singer read the letter again, running her thumb over the lawyer's signature. 'Fiancée?' she breathed in wonderment, 'Me?' and read it again. When she had done so, she looked up.

'Who is this innkeeper he mentions?'

'You yourself provided that clue, when you said that Raynor had an interest in local history, specifically in its eccentric characters. Including the stage-coach driver who ran an inn south of Santa Cruz.'

'Mountain Charley?'

'Charley Pankhurst, who died in 1879, at which time it was discovered that he was a she. It causes one to wonder how many other women have worn trousers, cut their hair, and quietly placed themselves on the voting registry.'

'But I don't understand--what that has to do with me?'

'You told me that one of Raynor's

discussion questions was, What one thing would make you give up your life as it was? You told him, love. I should say he was about to take, as they say, the plunge, gambling that you would consider life with him as an alternative to the stage. After all, if Charley Pankhurst could sign a voting registry, why should Billy Birdsong not sign a marriage contract?'

'But that's not possible! Is it?'

'I have no idea. I think it likely Raynor himself did not know if Mr Kapinsky would have succeeded in identifying a legal loophole that would permit it. However, the letter suggests that Raynor intended to try. In either case, his sister's letter makes very clear that he was determined to proceed without benefit of law, were you willing to undertake the performance of a lifetime.'

When she and Ledbetter put their arms around each other's shoulders and began to weep copious bittersweet tears over the lawyer's letter, I took up my hat and left them to their romantic phantasies.

It was my opinion that, had Jack Raynor lived, it would have all ended in tears, mostly bitter, few sweet. Birdsong would have agreed to Raynor's proposal, telling herself that she was happy to trade her gay, free life for one of true love. But how long would it have been before the constraints of deceit ate into their bond? Even in the free air of California, the pair would have been constantly on guard, against doctors, servants, friends, family. Granted, everyone in California is from somewhere else, which means everyone in the state has had to re-invent themselves. But habits die hard, and a new identity that lies too far from the old can become an intolerable burden. Every man's death diminishes me, but some deaths create their own rightness.

As I strolled through the streets of San Francisco on that pleasant spring dawn, I grew aware that my spirits were more elevated than they had been before I set out on this case. I was, in fact, conscious of a veritable bounce in my step, and found that my throat was humming a little tune.

Yes, I would admit it freely: San Francisco had proved a most educational place, in the end.

FOURTEEN

Later that morning, at her desk in the homicide room, Kate let the manuscript fall shut against its clip, her eyes running across the opening line. *The mind is a machine ill suited to long periods of desuetude.* What a peculiar voice, the haughty yet humane narrator of this bittersweet story, a story based on a legal conundrum that eight decades later had yet to be solved. *Everyone in California is from somewhere else, which means everyone in the state has had to re-invent themselves.* What would young Lieutenant Raynor make of San Francisco today, where Jon, Sione, and Lalu made for an accepted definition of family? The motivation for Raynor's murder had been dark and twisted, like anything that grew in hidden places. That his brother officer—a gay man like Raynor himself—should have exterminated him just as he was on the verge of finding happiness was the most poisonous betrayal of all. She found herself hoping that Jack Raynor hadn't known who it was that moonlit night on the cliffs, assaulting him with the bat.

Then Kate shook herself: Don't be ridiculous, this wasn't real, it was a fable, it was fiction. She hadn't intended to read it in any depth, just skim for content, but read it she had, every word, and for those hours, it

373

had been real. As she drew back from what she'd once heard described as the fictional dream, she had to admit that it was, in the end, just a story: Sherlock Holmes in San Francisco. And maybe not even that: Philip Gilbert may have adopted the tale with open arms, but so far as she could see, the only references to her victim's favorite detective were jokes, and as a piece of writing, it sure didn't have the old-fashioned feel of those stories as she remembered them, all fog and gaslights and horse-drawn cabs and the incident of the dog in the nighttime. This story was as outrageous and colorful as . . . well, as a revue of drag queens.

She picked up the phone. When the English voice came on the line, she said, "All right, Mr. Nicholson, I've finished the thing."

"Glorious, isn't it?"

"Er . . ."

"I spent this morning rereading it myself, and all the while I could just hear old Sir Arthur in the background, sputtering his protests as the spirit of San Francisco took over his character."

"So you'd say that Arthur Conan Doyle actually wrote it?"

"Couldn't say, certainly not without seeing the original. But this will put a fox in the henhouse, that's for sure. The Holmesian world will be up in arms over this."

Irate Sherlockians were not Kate Martinelli's primary concern, not unless one of them had become so infuriated he'd bashed Gilbert over the head. "Aside from the coincidence of Mr. Gilbert's body also being found in a Point Bonita gun emplacement, why have I spent all these hours on it?"

"But . . . I should think it would be obvious."

"Not to me. It's amusing, and not badly written, but hardly a work so earthshaking someone would kill for it."

"Of course you're right. I tend to forget that most of the world looks at this stuff with a rather jaundiced eye. And the key questions here are, one, was this story originally written in the early 1920s, and thus is not a modern forgery, and, two, if it is from the Twenties, was it actually written by Arthur Conan Doyle?

"The thing is, we Sherlockians will start with those questions, but we'll rapidly shoot off in a thousand related tangents. In no time at all the question will move on from the prosaic, Did Conan Doyle write it? to the much more interesting, If Sir Arthur Conan Doyle took the time out from his hectic Spiritualism tour of America to create this story, only to abandon it unpublished, why? It would open an enormous window of speculation as to his experiences here. He liked San Francisco well enough when he got here, but by the time he left, he said that he found San Francisco unsympathetic and unspiritual compared to Los Angeles. It is generally assumed that the reporters here proved less gullible and awestruck than their Southern California brothers, but it could as easily be that this story seized him here, and colored his entire feeling about the city."

There was a pause and a rustle on the line, as if Nicholson had shifted in his chair and the phone had changed from one hand to the other. Settling in to his argument.

"You have to remember, this was a man who believed passionately in such things as channeling and spirit possession: He dedicated his life and his fortune to the cause. He would have allowed the story to come to light, despite the elements he would certainly have found extremely distasteful, even shocking, *if* he believed that the spirits were behind it. However, I don't know that he would then have felt obligated to put his name on the thing and submit it for publication. He could as easily have abandoned it unacknowledged. Sitting wherever it's been for eighty years."

"You're saying that Arthur Conan Doyle wrote about Sherlock Holmes and the drag queen because spirits told him to?" Kate tried to keep the disbelief from her voice, not entirely succeeding.

Nicholson laughed. "Personally, I wouldn't doubt that the old man had some kind of midlife crisis during the tour, which manifested itself not in fast cars or young women, but an offensive story. Don't forget, Doyle had already killed Holmes off once, only to be forced to resurrect him by popular demand. Here he'd have been nailing the coffin shut on the man's reputation—it was one thing to bring in some nice exotic drug addicts and blackmailers to add color to the stories, but transvestite singers and male prostitutes? People would never have looked at Holmes the same way again. Of course, they'd never have looked at Doyle the same way again, either, which would further explain why he thought the better of publication. However, no matter what you might say was the psychological basis for this story, Doyle himself would have seen it as something else entirely. Doyle might have been irritated with the popularity of Holmes, but he did bear his creation some grudging affection; he would only have put Holmes in such a hugely embarrassing situation if he felt positively driven to do so."

"If the spirits made him."

"Precisely. Something along the lines of automatic writing."

Kate pinched the bridge of her nose and sat quietly for a long time. Then she drew a deep breath, and said, "Look, let's assume for the moment that, if nothing else, an unpublished Conan Doyle story would be worth a lot of money."

"It would be worth a shitload of money, if you'll pardon the vernacular." He said the obscenity with a primness that made Kate grin in spite of herself.

"He didn't pay a lot for it," she told him, an understatement if ever there was one.

"All the better. If he'd paid a substantial amount, it opens the door to speculation that the manuscript was either a very expensively created hoax, or was stolen from the Conan Doyle papers—there've been rumors of that for years. In fact, I've heard that a set of Doyle papers is going up for auction in London very soon; a file from that might conceivably have been spirited away before the contents were catalogued. I haven't seen any evidence of the provenance, but Philip wouldn't have knowingly gotten involved in a shady deal, not if it could blow up in his face."

"What I've seen of the thing's history is pretty solid looking," Kate admitted.

"Then as I say, a shitload of money."

"When you say 'shitload'—"

"Half a million, three quarters, a million? It is unprecedented, so there's just no knowing."

"A million dollars for a short story?" Her voice climbed to a near squeak.

"There is no knowing," Nicholson repeated in a precise voice, which somehow indicated that a million dollars might be on the low side. Kate cleared her throat.

"Okay. Is there any evidence that Conan Doyle actually wrote it?"

"That, of course, would have been the main question behind the evaluation Philip would have had me oversee. I'm working at a strong disadvantage here, since I've not held the thing in my hands—when you've worked as long as I have in the world of rare books and manuscripts, you develop a smell for fakes, but all I have is the photocopy of a typescript. Right away, the fact of its being typed creates a problem, since most of the stories were originally written by Sir Arthur in longhand, and it is unlikely that he ever used a typewriter. However, some would tell you that he did, on occasion, employ a secretary to take dictation, and in this country, a secretary would no doubt be skilled on a typewriter as well."

"In other words it's all, He said, she said?"

"Oh no. The manuscript would be thoroughly examined. I actually had an entire program laid out for Philip—physical tests, of course, on paper and ink, although I can already tell you it was written on an Underwood machine dating from before the Great War, with the accents punctiliously added by hand. Those are the only corrections, by the way, which I mention as a point against its authenticity—Conan Doyle tended to go over typescripts and make the odd correction or change. I'd have to see the paper itself, to see if it looked like something that had sat in an attic for eighty years, or if it had been stored somewhere and more recently typed on. I'd have a stylographic analysis, to compare the vocabulary and grammar, the idioms used—the general style of its author—with actual Conan Doyle stories of the same era. I would have suggested which archives to search, which biographers to ask whether or not Doyle might have had some peculiar experience while he was here. One of the oddities—one of several oddities—is that when you compare the dates given to the days of the week, it isn't actually set in the year Doyle was here. It would appear to take place a year later, in 1924. Although that could easily be explained by Doyle's chronic lack of interest in such details—he was forever giving Holmes some piece of key evidence that, under scrutiny, was nonsensical."

"You know, I couldn't even see that the thing was about Sherlock Holmes. Seems to me we should be calling it the Jack Raynor story, or the Tale of Billy Birdsong or something." Kate realized that she was sounding irritable about the ubiquitous presence of the mythic detective, but Nicholson did not notice.

"Oh, I think it's fairly clear that the narrator is meant to be Holmes, from the internal references—the emerald stickpin, his habits, his manner of thinking, the discussion of monographs. Speaking off the cuff, it is not too dissimilar stylistically from the pair of first-person Holmes stories Conan Doyle published in 1926. The fact that the main character calls himself Sigerson means nothing—Sigerson was an identity Holmes had used before, when he traveled to Tibet as a Norwegian explorer during the early 1890s."

Which explained Gilbert's use of the pseudonym as his computer password.

Kate had abruptly had enough of this airy-fairy stuff: time for some actual information. Mainly, who knew to leave Gilbert's body in Battery DuMaurier? "Can you tell me who has seen it?"

Nicholson was silent for a moment. "Before all this, I'd have thought Philip would tell me—tell all the Diners—about it all along the way, from the moment he got it. However, he seems to have been remarkably secretive. Frankly, I have no idea who he told. He may have given it to someone some time ago, and that person let rumors leak out."

"I know, I saw the *Chronicle*'s piece about it that Philip e-mailed all of you."

"Leah Garchik's column, yes. She may even have

got it originally from one of the Diners. We'd first heard the rumor around Christmas, and Tom—Tom Rutland—had been back at the birthday dinner in New York, where they'd mentioned it, but there was nothing more substantial than whispers. We went around and around the topic during our own January meeting. We even hunted down the passage in Sir Arthur's memoirs, to be sure of what he had said. It's in the second volume of his *American Adventures*, if you're interested."

So that's where the Strand Diners had gone when they all left the sitting room, before coming back to don coats and say their goodbyes. Dinner and a reference book: what a fun group.

"We went upstairs to—good heavens," Nicholson interrupted himself. "It was on the third floor."

"What was on the third floor?"

"Doyle's *Adventures*. I just realized, we all missed it, entirely. You see, by Philip's rules, anything published during Sir Arthur's lifetime should have been on the ground floor, but Philip had it upstairs. That's because he was researching this very story. Call me a Sherlockian," he chided himself.

"Gilbert was trying to research it himself? But then he gave it to you for authentication."

"Oh, he would have done his own background reading, but with something this important, he wouldn't even have left it entirely to me. I might have coordinated the research, but I wouldn't have done all the actual work. I don't have access to a laboratory, for one thing. For another, he'd have wanted someone who didn't mind flying to visit the archives."

"That's right, you don't like airplanes."

"I'd have chosen the labs and the experts, coordinated their efforts. Do you have any idea who else he consulted? Philip generally made careful note of when he gave something to me. Even if he only gave out copies, it might be in his records."

"I only looked at the last couple of weeks. I'll check earlier. Any idea of which Diner might have given Leah Garchik the item?"

"You know, I wondered at the time how she'd come to hear of it, but when I phoned around, no one seemed to know any more than what she'd written. The woman may even have overheard a conversation about another thing entirely, and simply put it together with the local angle. For example, there's been a lot of talk lately about the Doyle papers, and not so long ago someone ran a piece about an unpublished story 'discovered' among Sir Arthur's papers, except that it wasn't by him at all, it was another writer who'd sent it to him, hoping for help finding a publisher. When I talked to Tom about the Garchik piece, he said he'd asked Philip, who didn't know anything. It wasn't until I'd read the story that I realized it was what the rumor had been about, which meant that Philip had known about it at the dinner, just kept mum."

"Why would he do that? I'd have thought, if he wanted to sell it, he'd have told everyone. The more publicity, the better."

382

"Sure, but he'd have needed to control it. Wild and unsubstantiated rumor is never as good as a formal announcement."

"He was intending to make an announcement, you think?"

"Yes, and I'd think fairly soon. He told me he'd made several copies, I think he was planning on sending them out within days. That's probably why he gave me the thing in such a rush. Something may even have been forcing his hand. I haven't picked up any talk about it, but if I do, I'll let you know."

"Thank you. And if you can think of anyone Mr. Gilbert might have shown the story to, could you let me know?"

"I can ask around, if you like."

"It would be better if you left the actual inquiries to me, if you don't mind," Kate said firmly.

"Fine, I'll make you a list of likely candidates," he said, seemingly unaware that his *candidates* would be Kate's *suspects*. She gave him the Detail's fax number, thanked him, and put the phone down, scrubbing her face with her hands for a while.

"Give me a nice drug-related shooting," she said aloud into the room.

"I've got half a dozen, you could take your pick," one of the other detectives offered generously.

"Thanks, I'll stick to my fictional drag queens," Kate told him, and looked up another number.

"Tessie's Antiques," said the familiar voice. Kate identified herself, allowed the talkative antiques seller to spill a few dozen words in her direction, then stepped into the flow.

"I had a question about that typewriter," she said. "It's going to take us a few days to take possession of it"—(particularly considering she hadn't even written up a warrant application yet)—"but you could save me some time."

"Yes, what can I tell you about it? Not much, I fear, I scarcely laid hands—"

"I just want to know what kind of machine it was. What make?"

"Oh, that's an easy one. I never did get around to cleaning it, but I did shift it from one place to another a few times, and then again, the name was still bright and bold across the front of it. An Underwood," she added, before Kate was driven to shouting at her. "Probably circa 1910. In quite good condition, beneath the dust. Probably not used a whole lot before it went into its attic, though one of its keys was slightly wonky. The lowercase *a,* I think it was."

"Thank you," Kate said, and hung up on the woman's voice.

Her next call was to the source of Lee's article, the *Chronicle* columnist. Leah Garchik was out, so Kate left a message asking her to phone back. No sooner had she hung up when the phone rang to tell her that the two World War Two vets who'd found Gilbert's body were there to give a statement.

They were a little confused about why they'd needed to give it twice, since they'd talked to the Park Police on Monday, but it was easier to tell them the tale of a bureaucratic mix-up than to go into the precise jurisdictional requirements of a case, and both accepted the story with cheerful resignation: One thing an Army vet knew was bureaucracy. By the time they signed their statements and left, arguing happily all the time, Kate was satisfied that they had nothing to do with Gilbert's death or the disposal of his body.

She spent some time online, cruising through the references that came up at the phrase "Sherlock Holmes manuscript," and found a lot of nonsense and a few very peculiar things. She was sitting back in her chair to read the printout of a London newspaper article concerning a dispute within the Conan Doyle family when the phone rang.

It was the English accent again, which started without a preliminary. "About that list of potential evaluators?"

"Yes, Mr. Nicholson?"

"I've got some names and numbers for you, but my fax machine seems to have a gremlin in it, and the repair guy isn't coming until next week. It's rather laborious to read this sort of thing over the phone, particularly the e-mail addresses—I don't know about you, but I'm forever getting letters wrong when I have to write them down. Shall I pop it into the post tomorrow?"

"How 'bout I drop by and pick it up this afternoon?"

"Okay, but I may be in and out. Can we set a firm time, so I'm certain to be here for you?"

"What about one o'clock?"

"The stroke of one it is."

She went back to her reading, made a dozen more phone calls, and at 12:58 rounded the corner of Nicholson's apartment building, finding him not only at home, but on the street across from the entrance. He was talking to a young blond woman—the same young blue-eyed blonde whose photographs were on display inside—as the latter rested her shapely backside against a bright yellow Volkswagen convertible. He spotted Kate's car and reached past the girl to pull open the Volkswagen's door. She laughed at something he said and got in; he leaned own to take the hand that she had left on the bottom edge of the opened window, pulled it to his lips and kissed it with an air of playfulness, then returned it inside to the wheel. The girl laughed again, started the car, and drove away, trailing her fingers out the window in a wave.

Nicholson watched the yellow car until it had disappeared around the corner; in turn, Kate watched him. Some portion of that final scene had to have been staged for her benefit, but then, men in their fifties were apt to show off a trophy like that one. Hell, a lesbian in her thirties would want to show off a trophy like that, and really, she had to give him credit, another man would have climbed down the girl's throat with his tongue to demonstrate right of possession. Nicholson turned, still smiling, to join Kate. "I am impressed with your punctuality, Inspector."

"To serve and protect," she quoted, and put her hand out for the folded sheet he pulled from his shirt pocket.

The page contained twenty-three names, seventeen of

which had e-mail addresses, and phone numbers with area codes ranging from Los Angeles to New York.

"These are people I know whom Philip has consulted in the past. I've worked with all but two of them, they're highly reliable and utterly trustworthy."

"This is very helpful, Mr. Nicholson. Thank you."

"And how is the investigation into his death going?"

Kate glanced at him curiously, realizing that, in Nicholson's mind, the investigation into the story was a separate, and probably more urgent, matter than the investigation into Gilbert's death. Like academics, she thought, collectors were a race apart.

"It's going ahead, Mr. Nicholson."

"Well, if there's anything else I can do for you, please let me know. And I know you can't promise me anything, but if I could have a look at that manuscript sometime, I would be most grateful."

"I will keep it in mind, Mr. Nicholson."

"I happen to know that Tom is Philip's executor, although I don't think the other Diners do—anyway, I had a word with him, and told him that I'll need a few minutes to make an announcement at the Diners' meeting tonight. I thought I should tell them about the story. I wish I could actually give them each a copy, but Philip hadn't made his intentions clear. I suppose Tom will have to sort that out.

"The point is, I meant to say that if you'd like to join us this evening, you'd be more than welcome. You'd have to put up with our questions, of course." He smiled, as if to apologize for the group's odd habits.

When Geraldine O'Malley had extended the same invitation two days before, Kate had put her off. Since then, however, she had read the story, and the need to know more about its background was pressing on her.

"You know, I might," she told Nicholson.

His friendly face lit up. "Great. We're meeting at Tony's Grill—you know where that is?—at six for drinks and business, dinner at seven, dessert and coffee around eight, nuts and Port by half past. You're welcome to join us for all or part."

"I'll see what I can do," she told him, thinking, *nuts and Port?*

KATE was on her seventh call to people who hadn't heard from Philip Gilbert in months, whose voices gave her no sense of avoidance or deceit, when Al Hawkin came in and pulled the preliminary autopsy results from the fax machine. He stood at his desk reading the pages, then sorted through his accumulated messages; when she hung up, Kate growled at him, "I hope you're not going to tell me Philip Gilbert was killed by a poison unknown to science."

He peered at her over the top of his reading glasses. "Had a bit too much of the detective story business, have we?"

"Bunch of loonies, all of them."

He nodded thoughtfully. "An attitude I always find productive. Did you skip lunch today?"

"Christ, Al, what are you, my mother?"

"Did you?" he pressed.

"I don't know. Yeah, I guess I did, I've been busy."

"Martinelli, step away from the phone. Let's go get a sandwich. And put on your coat, it's beginning to rain."

"I'm nearly done here, Al—"

"Well, I'm not, and low blood sugar makes you too irritable to talk to. Either we eat or I head home."

"All right, I'm coming. Jeez, you're bossier than Nora."

"I'll take that as a compliment."

In fact, Kate was ravenous, and tore into the first half of her ham on ciabatta like an unfed wolf. She slowed long enough to drink half the iced tea in her glass, folded a couple of French fries into her mouth, and felt her body relax.

"Okay," she said. "You want to go first, or shall I?"

"Philip Gilbert died of a heart attack."

"Damn," she said with feeling. Improper disposal of a body was nowhere near as serious a charge as murder, even manslaughter.

"However, in the coroner's opinion, it would have been directly related to the blow on the head."

"That's in the report?"

"It will be. There's a lot of technical language, but what it boils down to is, the shock of the blow killed him. Which, by the way, was from a blunt instrument that left no traces behind. And because whoever did it might have saved him by sticking one of his pills under his tongue, it's probably good for a murder charge, not just manslaughter."

Somewhat mollified that their efforts since Saturday

hadn't been entirely wasted, Kate ate another French fry and waited for Al to go on. When he had swallowed a bite of his hamburger, he did so.

"He was healthy enough, other than the weak ticker—that skinniness wasn't AIDS or anything. Time of death confirmed as approximately six to seven days before he was found."

"He was on his feet on Saturday morning, the twenty-fourth, phoning Ian Nicholson and then giving him the manuscript."

"And the ranger thought the body would have been discovered if it had been there on Saturday."

"He wasn't absolutely certain. However, Sunday it was definitely raining and nobody went hiking around the headlands. So Gilbert could have been there as early as Saturday night."

"Stomach contents indicated a heavy meal, something with meat and white beans in it, several hours before. And he might have had sex not long before he died, although the ME thinks he'd bathed afterwards. He took swabs, but there doesn't seem to be much."

Kate continued eating, long immune to any squeamishness at the contents of a dead man's stomach or anus. "We haven't found who he had dinner with. There was nothing of that sort in his refrigerator—either of his refrigerators—and it doesn't sound like the kind of meal he'd cook for one."

"Probably a restaurant, then?"

"I'd guess."

"Sherlock Holmes would say that guessing was a

habit shockingly bad to the rational facilities," Al said placidly.

Kate dropped her sandwich and stared at him. "Oh Christ, Al, please tell me you haven't become one of the loonies."

He grinned at her. "Nope. I read the stories a very long time ago. Don't worry, I'll leave my deerstalker at home."

"You wear a deerstalker, I'll shoot it off your old gray head. What else did the autopsy come up with? Signs of that broken statue?"

"Oddly enough, no."

Kate sat up sharply. "No?"

"Not in his scalp, not even in his clothing. Nothing."

"How can that be? It was all over the floor."

"Maybe it just broke into a few pieces, then got smashed further underfoot. You haven't heard anything from the lab?"

"I'll call and harass them some."

"The ME did find some foreign matter in the scalp wound. Coarse fibers, like—"

Her head came up sharply. "Like from a towel?"

"How'd you guess? Er, know?"

She sighed, and at his raised eyebrow, explained how towel fibers in a scalp wound came into the story she had read.

"Maybe I'd better take a look at the thing, too," Al said.

"I'll make you a copy."

"There were also indications that he was wrapped in

something else for a while, either a sheet or a tarpaulin. Their lab will take a closer look at his clothes, see if they give anything, but I think it's safe to say that he was well bundled before he was transported, so we're not going to find any trunk fibers on him."

That was too bad. Fibers from a car's trunk carpeting could be both revealing and incriminating, first pointing them at a specific make of car, later nailing down a conviction. Trouble was, even the amateurs knew that, and worse, were firmly convinced that every lab did every conceivable test for any case under investigation, and did them all within twenty-four hours. The victims were even more troublesome, complaining when the lab didn't vacuum and do DNA testing on hairs found at a burglary. "TV has a lot to answer for," she grumbled.

"So, where are we?" Hawkin asked rhetorically. "We've got the autopsy results and the labs will process what they found at the two sites when they can."

"Do we even know the blood on the chair was Gilbert's?"

"Something else for you to harass them about. What about the vic's history and contacts?"

"That's what I've been working on. I got a list of the people he might have asked to look at this story of his, in addition to a list of known acquaintances the lawyer sent on Sunday. I've reached about half of them. Nobody so far says they talked to him in the days before he was killed—I think the latest anyone admitted to, other than Ian Nicholson, was Thursday."

"And Nicholson saw him on Saturday. What about family?"

"Nada. The wife hasn't talked with him in maybe ten years, his nieces said they got Christmas cards from him every year so they knew he was still alive, but that's about it."

"No known enemies, no greedy relations. What about his love life?" Hawkin knew a lot of this, he was merely conducting a review.

"His lawyer seemed to think he didn't have any close relationships, period. Gilbert's friends-of-Sherlock dining club to a man said he was a nice guy who knew a lot and kept to himself. Hardly an indicator of extreme passion."

"And not burglary? He was sitting watching the television with his back to the door, someone could have snuck up the stairs, tried to just knock him out a little, and accidentally killed him."

"Someone who then immediately thought of the gun emplacement as an appropriate hiding place for his corpse."

"Pinning down who knew the story would be very helpful, true."

Kate snorted. "Understatement of the week."

"That doesn't entirely rule out burglary, since there could have been copies of the story lying around, or Gilbert could have told someone about it. You say the only thing missing seems to be the statue of the Maltese Falcon?"

"And his cell phone, and his pocket watch. I hope

you're not going to suggest that Gilbert's missing trophy is really a golden, jewel-encrusted Crusader statue. *The* Maltese Falcon."

"I think that was later than the Crusades."

"Whatever. Al, I absolutely refuse to let Sam Spade walk into this case as well."

"It would seem a surfeit of detectives, I agree. But we're basing that on the lawyer's statement that the statue's the only thing missing."

"You think the lawyer bashed him and robbed the place?"

"I haven't met him; is he strong enough to carry a body down the stairs and up that hill?"

"He looks it. Hell. Do we need to do a complete inventory of the place? It's an absolute museum."

"I haven't even been out there yet, and yes, I think we should at least take a closer look at its contents. Maybe not a complete inventory; if it's going to be donated to an institution, maybe the lawyer could be talked into stepping the process up, and we could have the inventory checked that way."

"Good idea."

"I'd also like to go out to the dump site again. I was too busy with the interviews yesterday to look at the emplacement."

"Today?"

"We'd hit too much bridge traffic. And maybe it'll be dry by morning. Let's take a run at the rest of those phone calls today, and go off on a little field trip tomorrow." He picked up the bill from the table. "I think this one's my turn?"

"Yep." She put on her coat while he sorted out some bills and tucked them under the edge of his coffee cup. It had begun to drizzle, that halfway phase between heavy fog and actual rain, and they turned up their collars as they walked back to the Hall of Justice.

"You know, I think it might be a better idea for you to take a look at that story before tomorrow," she said after a while. "Why don't you get on that, I'll do the phone calls?"

"I can take it home and read it tonight."

"It's more than a hundred pages. I know you read faster than I do, but you'll be up late with it."

"You just really want all those phone calls to yourself," he said.

"Oh yeah."

"How about if I start it now, and then check with you after dinner and see if you have any left you want me to do?"

"Actually, I thought I might go to the Sherlock dinner club meeting—not for the whole time, but they have coffee at the end, and I'd like to get a take on what Lee would call the group dynamics. Two of them invited me."

"You want me to come?"

"Only if you're interested. I don't know that it's worth coming back into the city for it."

"Would I have to wear a tux?"

"They're not going to get ankle-length velvet from me. No, I think they only wear costumes when they're meeting in someone's house, and this is at Tony's. Coffee's at eight, if you want, followed by the ever exciting 'nuts and Port,' but you should expect to have your brain picked about being a cop. At least one of them writes mysteries."

He gave an exaggerated shudder, and said, "You really should have armed backup before you go in."

She laughed. "Give me a buzz if you're coming."

"Will do."

While Kate glued the phone back onto her ear, Hawkin ran the manuscript through the photocopier. Two of the other detectives came in with a suspect to interview, a big guy who really wasn't happy about the whole thing; his voice reverberated through the homicide room even from behind the closed door of the interrogation room. Hawkin dropped Kate's copy of the story on her desk and retreated to the empty interrogation room, but it didn't take long before he was standing by her desk again.

Kate recited her usual message into yet another voice mail and looked up.

"You really don't mind if I go home with this?" he asked.

"I would if I were you. You'll go nuts trying to read in here." Al had prodigious powers of concentration, but even he had his limits, and all three men behind the doors were now shouting.

"Okay. I'll call you one way or another around seven, to see if you have any calls you want me to make."

"Have fun," she replied, then, "You know, I think I'd

do better at home myself. Hold on a sec and I'll walk down with you."

Lee was home, but the door to the consulting rooms was shut, so Kate left a note on the kitchen blackboard, to say that she was home but would be going out again at eight. There was a bit of cold and fairly stale coffee in the machine, so she poured it into a cup, nuked it hot, and took it and her armful of work upstairs.

The unrelenting glamour of police work.

FIFTEEN

Kate turned on the computer and logged on to the HolmesCam website, keeping her eyes on it while she was making the rest of her calls. As she had suspected, the archived recordings were heavily edited down, no more than six or eight hours a month of Gilbert reading, drinking tea, playing the violin, and occasionally of Gilbert and someone else playing chess or talking. Without sound, it had all the thrill of a silent movie without the flash of words on the screen, but it did not interfere much with the phone conversations.

Those, too, were fairly rote. Because of the time differences, she began with the East Coast and worked her way west. One antiques dealer in Boston had talked to Gilbert on the Monday before his death, concerning an estate sale that included a collection of old British magazines from the early 1900s. He'd expected to hear from Gilbert about a bid, and hadn't. Another of Nicholson's names was a very young-sounding collector with whom Gilbert had done a fair amount of business. The collector seemed more interested in a Japanese Sherlock Holmes comic book Gilbert had promised him than in the fact of Gilbert's death. He turned out to be thirteen years old; Kate put a line through his name.

On a roll now—even in these days of cell phones, it was often easier to reach people at night—Kate reached her third actual human in a row. This one was a document restorer and bookbinder whom Gilbert used from time to time, an elderly-sounding man named Israel who lived in Oak Park, near Chicago. On hearing his specialty, her ears pricked.

"Mr. Israel, have you been in touch with Philip Gilbert recently?"

"Not very recently," he answered, his English faultless but with a clear German accent. "Perhaps six weeks? I could look it up in my records, if you like."

"What did he contact you about?" Kate asked, hoping to hear him say, *A typescript short story.*

"He had several volumes that required restoration. All Conan Doyle stories—three Sherlock Holmes stories, two historical novels."

"Nothing to do with an unbound typescript?"

"No. Why, did he have such a thing?"

Kate was by now good at deflecting that question. "If he did have one, would he have consulted you about it?"

"Only if he wished to have it bound. And a typescript is not always a good candidate for binding. The paper, for one thing, is generally not archival quality, and the narrow left-hand margins limit what one can do with it."

"So he didn't mention—" Kate began, then stopped, her attention caught by unexpected motion on the monitor in front of her. She sat forward, hitting keys to freeze the action, but Israel was going ahead as if she had finished her question.

"He said nothing about a typescript, no. Although he did seem remarkably . . . playful perhaps is the word. For Philip, that is."

Kate took her hand off the keys, keeping one eye on the frozen screen. "When was this?"

"As I say, I would have to look up the precise date, but it would have been in early December. I asked him if he'd seen anything interesting lately, as one does, you know? And he gave an odd little laugh, high-pitched, which was unlike him, and said that one never knew."

"That's what he said? 'One never knew'?"

"It might have been 'You never know.'"

"I see. But that was all?"

"Yes."

"It would be helpful to know the date of this conversation, Mr. Israel."

"Do you wish to hold on while I look?"

"If you don't mind."

Despite its being evening already in Oak Park, Israel's records were close at hand: Either he worked late, or his office was at home. The sound of feet scuffling across floors and down some stairs was followed by pages turning, and then the old man came back on the line.

"December the fifteenth. A Monday, in the early afternoon, as I recall."

"Thank you very much, Mr. Israel."

She finished the conversation, wrote down the date, and turned at last to the computer screen.

She had set the recording to play the nonedited recent material, zooming forward from Gilbert's exit on the morning of Friday, January 23. The only change on the monitor had been the gradual ebb and flow of light in the room as the clock registered the hours of the afternoon passing. And then at seven o'clock a quick blur of feet at the very top of the screen, at which point Kate had hit Pause.

Now she watched the feet more slowly: a man coming in the front door and passing through into the house, either upstairs or to the kitchen. She noted the time, then went back to eleven that morning, seeing, indeed, those same shoes and gray trouser legs passing through, left to right, as Gilbert left the house.

She set the clock moving again, and at 7:38, legs traveled from left to right, heading to the front door: a man, and with the same stride as the earlier legs, but now in black pants and shiny black shoes.

Going out to dinner? Heading for the white beans that were found in his stomach?

Nothing more happened. Kate pushed the speed up, her eyes now glued to the upper inch of the screen, but long minutes passed. Gilbert had died with undigested food in his stomach. If that was Friday dinner, it began to look as if he had not returned home afterward. He'd changed into a dark suit and good shoes, left the house at twenty to eight, and by one, one-fifteen, one-thirty, had not returned.

The screen gave a brief flicker and continued showing a dim room with light spilling from the stairs, but Kate's fingers shot out to stop it, then reverse it.

The flicker had not been an electronic hiccup: In the blink of an eye, the clock in the corner jumped from 2:11 to 2:23. Nothing had changed, but time had passed.

Someone who knew the system had come in, turned off the camera, spent twelve minutes in the house, then turned it on again, most likely on his—or her—way out the door.

Kate stared with unfocused eyes at the monitor, trying to see the unseen.

Perhaps Gilbert came home at 2:11, accompanied by a person he did not wish to appear on the HolmesCam. Of course, she could think of any number of reasons for him to close the watchful electronic eye—prostitutes, drugs, an orgy of bestiality with small furry creatures, or just the desire for a little privacy. And for all she knew, there had been a hundred more such gaps over the months, which disappeared when Gilbert edited the recordings.

But say he came in with a friend, and turned off the camera himself. They went upstairs, Gilbert changing into his pajamas and dressing gown. He sat down in his study with a drink in his hand, and his companion bashed him, and left.

Turning the HolmesCam back on as he, or she, left.

All in the space of twelve minutes.

Another possibility was that someone else who knew Gilbert's system had come in while he was away at dinner, searching for—what? The manuscript? A valuable nineteenth-century Sherlock Holmes tea cosy? And while the camera was off, Gilbert just happened to come home and surprise his burglar. Who bashed him, changed him, carried him out, and reset the camera.

Even less satisfactory.

Which left the idea that Gilbert had died elsewhere, following his white-beans dinner, and the person who killed him had come to the house either to steal the manuscript or to remove evidence. He would have had the key from Gilbert's body, and either seen that Gilbert had not set the door alarm, or knew the code, or simply trusted to luck. All he really needed was to know where the switch for the camera was, which surely would include most, if not all, of the Diners. After all, the only evidence that Gilbert had died in his home was the blood on the chair, which could as easily have come from some other mishap.

As Kate stared unseeing at the stubbornly uninformative interior of number 927, the back of her mind began to clear its throat and draw her attention to a room nearer to hand. She drew her gaze from the monitor and turned it to the door, where a small person stood, lips pursed in impatience, arms planted on narrow hips.

"Did you want something, Nora?" Kate asked.

"I *said*, Mamalee says to tell you that if you want your dinner warm, you have to come now."

"Sorry, love. Two minutes."

With a shake of her head worthy of Lee at her most put-upon, Nora turned on her heel and stalked off. Kate moved to shut off the machine, but left it paused where it was. She'd meant to watch this last stretch of recording before this, and hadn't gotten to it—she was going to feel a real idiot if the camera showed Tom Rutland marching through the house with his client slung across his shoulders.

She put the screen to sleep, and went down toward the odors and noises of family.

After dinner and dishes but before bedtime stories, Kate fit in another hour at the computer. While the thing was speeding through time, registering no motion but the slow wax and wane of the sun outside, she phoned Lo-Tec Freeman at home.

She identified herself, and heard his voice go instantly defensive. "I'm not on call tonight," he said.

"This isn't about tonight. It's about that webcam hookup on Gilbert's computer. Did you guys find any kind of switch for it?"

"We haven't been to the house since Sunday," Lo-Tec pointed out. "We would have told you."

"Yeah, I figured you'd have said something. But there's a switch downstairs somewhere, and it might have a print on it."

She stopped talking then, knowing that he would be

pulled between professional pride, that he might have missed something, and affront, that she might be accusing him of missing something. In the end, pride won.

"You want me to go look?"

"Not tonight. But Hawkin and I will be there in the morning, if you can give us five minutes."

"What time?"

"Nine-thirty? Ten?"

"I'll be there," he said, and hung up.

She put down the phone and it rang, with Al's voice. "I'm not going to show up tonight, unless you need me," he said.

"That's fine."

"Interesting story."

"I kind of liked it, although I haven't a clue what it has to do with Gilbert's death. I managed to reach most of those names, left messages for the others, so I wouldn't bother with them if I were you."

"Anything?"

"Not really. They all liked him a little, were somewhat intimidated by him, sorry he was dead, but he hadn't said anything about a typescript or a new Sherlock Holmes story."

"Okay. Well, enjoy your nuts and Port."

Just after seven-thirty, the HolmesCam recording reached its end. On the Saturday, Kate had appeared, sitting in Gilbert's chair while talking on her painfully anachronistic cell phone. Chris Williams came through, then all was still for a while, until on Sunday Lo-Tec

404

had pulled the plug, and the screen blinked into emptiness. She turned off the computer, read Nora a quick
story, and went off to meet the Sherlockians.

Kate left the house just before eight. She lucked out
with parking, when an SUV the size of a small motor
home pulled out just ahead of her, down the street from
Tony's. The greeter (the place was not grand enough for
the man to be called a maître d') led her through the
tables to a back room. The door stood wide open and
voices came from within; when she stepped inside and
the greeter closed the door after her, nine faces looked
up, wearing varying degrees of surprise. Tom Rutland
and, a beat later, Ian Nicholson stood to welcome her,
but Ian, seeing Tom rise, sat back and let the lawyer do
the honors.

Rutland was the only one wearing evening dress; he
resembled a maître d' himself, among the ordinary suits
and dresses. Of course, the tux Rutland wore would
have eaten up a solid month's salary for a maître d', and
a restaurant employee would not have worn the small
"221B" pin on his lapel.

Kate now knew 221B was the London house number
of Sherlock Holmes.

"Hope I'm not too late," she told the room, and
added, "Bedtime stories to read."

As she'd expected, evoking a child instantly disarmed
any mistrust of the cop in their midst—although the
number of wine bottles on the table might have had
something to do with the ease of their welcome.
Nicholson introduced her by name rather than rank, and

she shook hands all around, receiving introductions to those she had not met before. Alex Climpson, winery supervisor, was the pudgy young man who had failed at a number of the quizzes the night of the party, with Wendell Bauer the even younger, rather shy-looking man, at Climpson's side tonight as he had been in the photo of the party she had printed out. Soong Li, as Chinese in looks as his name was, sat across from Bauer between Pandi and Venkatarama. Finally, at the far end of the table next to Thomas Rutland, the tall, dignified woman who had helped Gilbert the night of the party. Tonight she was wearing a soft wool dress instead of the severe white blouse and black skirt, and the hair on her head was still gathered up, although in a style less reminiscent of a stiff wig.

"Jeannine Cartfield," she said to Kate; her hand was hard: Did she lift weights?

"So you're all here," Kate said, sinking into the chair Rutland pulled up for her at the end of the table, her back to the door. He started to sit in his chair at the end facing her—had that been Gilbert's customary position?—but interrupted the motion to walk around the table behind Kate and open the door again. As he came back around, he said to Kate in explanation, "Gets stuffy in here." When he sat down again, Nicholson shot him a grateful glance, making Kate wonder if stuffiness was the problem, or an enclosed surrounding for one of the members. Yes, Rutland seemed to be stepping into the position of leader here, to the extent of providing for the members' comfort.

Jeannine Cartfield spoke up first.

"We decided that the dinner should go on. If nothing else, we needed to have a toast to Philip."

The woman's voice was even, her eyes did not look as if they had shed tears, and Kate wondered at her relationship with the dead man. "You've been in Sacramento, I understand?" she asked Cartfield.

Ian Nicholson murmured in low but ringing tones, "You have been in Sacramento, I perceive," and a gust of laughter ran around the table, sounding heavily fueled by alcohol.

"Sorry?" Kate asked.

"Sherlockian humor, Inspector," Cartfield said with a fond glance at Nicholson. "Yes, I just got back from Sacramento. One day turned into three—our state legislators can be remarkably difficult to pin down. I'm trying to arrange funding for some special programs through the Ferry Building."

"Maybe we could make a time to talk? If nothing else, I need to get a statement from you."

"Sure, any time."

Kate sat back slightly in her chair, to take in the whole group, and said, "Thank you for inviting me here. As you all know, my partner and I have been assigned to Philip Gilbert's murder." The room stirred at the word, and she said, "Yes, it has officially been classified as homicide. Most of you have already given us your statements, but I wanted to come here to see if I could get a sense of Mr. Gilbert himself. You nine seem to have been among his closest friends, although I'm told that Philip didn't really have close friendships, so I'd like to ask you to tell me about him."

No need to point out that telling Kate about Gilbert would invariably mean telling her about themselves as well: She wanted to be their bright-eyed friend, not an interrogating cop. Coming here alone, mentioning her family life, and shifting immediately to the victim's first name all helped nudge them into thinking of her as just another member of Philip Gilbert's circle.

"What do you wish to know?" Rutland asked.

"Big things, small things. Let's see—ah. Why would Philip have kept his keys on the top floor?"

Kate had chosen the seemingly trivial question with care: Whoever had entered the house for twelve minutes at two o'clock Saturday morning had almost certainly used Gilbert's keys, since even the cleaning woman didn't have a set. He—or she—had not used them to leave the house, since the deadbolt had not been turned, and might well have simply forgotten to return them to the ground floor in the haste of a surreptitious exit. Kate watched them, alert for any twitch or flush of guilt, but nine faces sat as before, until Pandi spoke up.

"That is a very interesting question, sounding positively Holmesian. His mysteries often turn on a small and obscure fact. I fear, however, in this case the obscure fact will remain obscure. I have seen Philip put the keys on the stand inside the door, it is true, but I have also noticed him carry the keys upstairs with him and leave them on the desk. I believe Philip found it unpleasant to have reminders of the present century lying out in the open in the ground-floor apartments."

"That's why he hid the alarm pad behind the picture?"

"Behind the Paget drawing, yes. Certain things were necessary, but jarring."

"Philip hated to break character," Nicholson volunteered.

"Exactly," Pandi agreed with a decisive nod.

"That's why he left the lights over the stairs burning, and the fake coal fire going?" Kate asked. "So he wouldn't have to turn them on and off?"

"I suppose," Pandi said.

"What about the dead bolt?" she asked. "When we entered the house, we found just the lock in the knob was set."

But again, if she had been hoping for a start of guilty memory, she was disappointed.

"He may not have intended to be gone long," Venkatarama answered. "He did not always secure his door as he should have. That, too, may have reminded him that he was not in the nineteenth century."

"If he didn't like going through the motions of modern life, how did he handle the webcam business? He switched that off from time to time."

Climpson spoke, for the first time since the introductions. "I helped Philip set that up, last fall. He needed an override, for privacy and whenever someone inappropriately dressed for the era was in sight of it, but he didn't want a visible switch. We disguised the device behind a framed photograph on the wall next to the stairs. It's hinged, like the Paget drawing, an early daguerreotype of Windsor Castle."

"So his . . ." Don't call it mania, she thought. ". . . his commitment to authenticity only extended so far?"

Geraldine O'Malley took this one. "Philip called himself a 'surface purist.' He would freely admit that his rooms abounded in borderline anachronisms and outright fakes, but it was a work in progress, and when he found something better, he used it."

Cartfield nodded. "Think of Philip's rooms as a kind of installation art, an ongoing experiment in living sculpture. He shaped it, he participated in it, he even loved it, but he wasn't limited by it. In fact, you could say that Philip's life was that same work of art. He lived and breathed Sherlock Holmes, imitated the man's values and ways of thinking, took on the dress, speech, and habits as a way of exploring the deeper issues of the man's righteousness and commitment. I hope you haven't got the idea that Philip was delusional, that he thought he actually *was* Sherlock Holmes? That couldn't be further from the truth. Philip was comfortable with modern life, lived most of the time in his apartment on the top floor. The bottom floor was his art, his discipline, his interest both aesthetically and emotionally, but it wasn't his entire life."

"It was like a religious discipline with Philip," said a new voice: Wendell Bauer, grad student. "Eastern monks seek enlightenment in the contemplation of an object or a painting. Philip sought it in a focused concentration on Sherlock Holmes."

Kate put on an unconvinced face, not difficult to do.

410

"Have to say, though, the place looks more like a shrine than an object of contemplation."

"I know what you mean." Climpson spoke up. "When I first saw it, I thought it was, well, more than a little creepy. And when Philip was playing the part, you could be excused for thinking he was delusional—come on, Jeannine," he said when she tried to interrupt him, "he would be so into it, even his voice changed. It was kind of spooky."

Tom Rutland stepped in to agree. "It's true—no, Jeannine, you've got to admit a person doesn't become that immersed in a fantasy world just because it's an intellectual or aesthetic form for him. Philip loved Holmes and his world. And he loved becoming Holmes."

Cartfield finally got her voice in. "Philip didn't become Holmes any more than Anthony Hopkins became Hannibal Lecter when they filmed the movie. He explored the character fully but it's hardly fair to make him sound like some sicko. The inspector here's going to think of Philip as a nut."

Kate kept her face very straight.

"Holmes was an enormous part of Philip's life," Rutland admitted. "The rest of us dress up a few times a year and play the game, but Philip played it day in and day out."

Cartfield turned to the redheaded man. "Ian, wouldn't you agree that Philip was acting?"

"Certainly, although what Wendell says has some merit. But I'm afraid that Tom may be right, that Philip was dangerously close to forgetting that it was an act.

These last two coups of his, the *Beeton's* and this story, they changed him. Didn't you think he'd changed recently?"

"He was excited. And distracted," Jeannine insisted, although she seemed more willing to accept criticism of Philip when it came from Nicholson than when one of the others said it.

Pandi agreed with Nicholson. "I know what you mean, Ian. At the last two meetings, he seemed excited, yes, which we now know was the story. But he was also apart, almost cold."

"Philip always was above mere friendship," Venkatarama observed.

"But how long has it been since you saw him laugh?" his cousin asked. "Philip had developed that habit of looking down his nose and giving a sort of condescending smile. It was really quite annoying."

"It's true," Rutland said. "The last few months he could be a real pain in the ass. It was like he'd decided to take on all the most abrasive Holmesian characteristics—superiority, brusqueness—"

"He was smoking a lot, did you notice?" O'Malley contributed.

"And not eating much," Climpson added.

"Another imitation of Holmes—feeding the brain and not the body," Venkatarama said in agreement.

"He stood by himself a lot at that party," said Soong Li.

"Like we were clients instead of friends." O'Malley again.

412

"I felt snubbed," said Pandi in his melodious accent. "As if he had decided that the proper pattern of behavior was that of Holmes to Watson."

"A casual abuse of friends," said Nicholson, unable to hide a trace of bitterness.

O'Malley turned to Kate. "This whole Holmes thing. To most of us it's a game; to others it is a passion. I'd have said Philip was in that second category, until the past few weeks, when it looked like he was getting into the third level: obsession."

"A friend described Sherlock Holmes as a self-medicating bipolar with obsessive tendencies," Kate told them. After a startled moment, everyone in the room began to laugh excessively, as if relieved to break the personal direction the talk had been taking. Ian Nicholson picked up the nearest bottle—which was indeed labeled Port—and filled all the glasses within reach. One of those, larger than the others, had been left over from the meal, but he now half-filled it and set it down in front of Kate. She looked apprehensively at the dark liquid but dutifully took a sip, feeling more than a little relieved herself: She'd blurted out Lee's analysis of Holmes without thinking, but rather than turn them defensive about their hero, the criticism had been taken as an affectionate joke, relaxing the room further. In a minute, they'd be calling her Kate.

"That's really true," Venkatarama said. "There are clear indications in the stories that he alternated between manic states and depressive ones."

"To the extent of suicide," Pandi said.

413

"Suicide?" This was Soong Li, looking confused, as if he wasn't sure he understood the English word.

"Oh come on, Raji," Cartfield said. "Holmes didn't make any suicide attempts."

"Reichenbach Falls was suicide. Even Conan Doyle understood that."

The room erupted with argument, and Kate sat back, watching the participants: Jeannine Cartfield, protective of Philip's memory, although she did not appear particularly devastated by his absence; Tom Rutland, assuming an authority in the group that several of the others did not want to give him; Ian Nicholson, warmly regarded by all and probably able to assume the mantle of leadership if he was interested; Pandi and Venkatarama, relishing the debate, contributing to it by the citation of one passage after another—and, going by how the others took the passages, the words were correct. Unlike Wendell Bauer, who offered a passage in support of something—what *were* they talking about, anyway?—only to get shot down instantaneously and corrected by three of the others. Even Soong Li caught up with the flow and tossed a reference to Conan Doyle into the fray, which was acknowledged by Rutland and incorporated into the discussion. Geraldine O'Malley appeared to belong to the more liberal wing of the group, quite happy to criticize Holmes as if she were talking about Gilbert; Alex Climpson wavered, unwilling to commit himself to either side.

Suddenly a voice cut through the room, saying, "I

have to say, I really could understand it if Philip had committed suicide." The gleeful tumult faded away, replaced by an uncomfortable silence. Several people glanced at Kate, but no one took the floor from Geraldine O'Malley.

She asked Kate directly. "It couldn't have actually been suicide, could it?"

Kate considered her answer, before saying, "Death itself was caused by a blow to the head, although there was no such object where he was found."

"I believe what we are wondering, Inspector," Cartfield said, putting a deliberate emphasis on Kate's title, "is if Philip could have rigged things somehow to look like murder."

Rutland interrupted angrily. "Why the hell would he do that?"

"We all agreed that he wasn't himself lately," O'Malley told him. "And you've got to admit that it would be like him, to do a version of Thor Bridge on us."

"What's 'Thor Bridge'?" Kate asked.

Rutland explained, "It's one of the stories where a mentally unbalanced woman kills herself and makes it look as if another woman, a rival, has murdered her. The solution has to do with weighting a revolver so it falls into the water after she shoots herself."

"No," Kate replied. "I don't think that's a possible scenario here."

They seemed, if anything, relieved. A part of that, no doubt, was the relief in knowing that Gilbert had not been driven to take his life when friends might have intervened, but Kate thought it was also gratitude that Gilbert hadn't been vindictive enough to have pointed a dead finger at one of them.

Which indicated the possibility, in their minds, that Gilbert might have been capable of such a thing.

"I have another question," Kate told them. "I gather Ian has told you about the story that had come into Mr. Gilbert's possession?"

Their faces lit up and a murmur of agreement rose up. Before one of them could question her about it, she said, "Not that it matters, but do any of you know how Leah Garchik might have heard about it?"

"I *knew* it wasn't about the Doyle archives," Climpson blurted out, sotto voce, but that was the only reaction. None of the nine, it would appear, had made the phone call to the newspaper columnist.

But now that the story itself had been brought up, talk turned to it: namely, when could they see it?

Without looking in Tom Rutland's direction, Kate said, "That's not up to the police. That's a decision to be made by the executor of the Gilbert estate, who has the responsibility of deciding what is best for the estate as a whole, whether that's keeping it under wraps for a while longer or letting the contents out. I'd say it probably won't be too long now." She stood up. "Thank you all for your hospitality, and if I haven't said it before, I am sorry for your loss."

But before she could push back her chair, Ian Nicholson was on his feet. "Kate," he said—and his use

416

of her first name sent a small jolt of triumph through her, which she was careful to keep from her face—"I think I speak for the rest of the Diners when I say thank you for coming and talking to us. And I hope I'm not being forward when I add that if you'd ever like to join us in a more permanent manner, you need only submit your name for membership."

A quick survey of faces made it clear that the other Diners were not quite as eager as Nicholson—most were noncommittal, although Jeannine Cartfield looked frankly apprehensive, and Thomas Rutland verged on the appalled.

"Thank you, Ian," Kate replied, "I'll keep it in mind."

She finished with her usual line of calling her if they thought of anything further that might have a bearing on Philip Gilbert's death, and escaped before they could recall the topic of the Holmes manuscript and gang up to demand her copy of the story.

The pause lasted just seconds; as she went out of the door, she could hear their voices rise, aimed at Nicholson: "Ian, there's really no reason—" and "For God's sake, Ian, you're not going to—" The last thing that reached her ears was the imperious voice of Tom Rutland, declaring, "All right, yes, I'm the executor, and as such I don't see why you shouldn't—"

The street outside seemed very quiet and normal.

SIXTEEN

Kate woke to fog on Thursday morning. She trotted downstairs to liberate a cup of coffee from the machine, and took it back up to shower and dress—choosing clothes designed for hiking rather than for interviewing witnesses. She carried her boots and her empty cup back down to the kitchen, where she found Lee making French toast, Nora making a drawing of the family, and the radio making music.

Beautiful, charming, normal family.

(She found herself wondering, *Could Jack Raynor have envisioned anything remotely like this, when he was looking at wedding rings?*)

Hawkin arrived, wearing his normal clothes and carrying his leather work binder, and sat down to a cup of the coffee Lee made freshly for him. Kate left them in conversation while she walked Nora down the street to her preschool, and when she got back they were talking about his daughter's boyfriend.

"I really wouldn't worry, Al," Lee said, standing up to clear the table. "Jules is very level-headed, and she still talks to both you and Jani. This boy may be older, but that doesn't mean he's going to dominate her. Not Jules."

"Yeah, you're right. And actually if he wasn't hanging around my girl, I'd probably like him. You ready to go?" he asked Kate.

"Let me just make one call."

To her amazement, Kate reached Leah Garchik at the *Chronicle* offices. She explained what she needed, details about the Conan Doyle piece that had appeared on January 16.

The woman scratched her metaphorical head for a minute before telling Kate that she'd have to look through her log to be sure, but she thought the paragraph about the manuscript was based on a phone call that had come in a few days before she went off on her two-week vacation. "I would have saved it for when I got back, since I'd already laid out my final column, except there was a paragraph I had to pull at the last minute. I was practically out the door, so I just grabbed whatever looked the right size and stuck it in instead."

"What was the original paragraph about?" Kate asked, automatically wary of any faint odor of coincidence.

"I don't remember," the reporter said, an equally automatic response: She did remember, Kate thought, but she was leery about revealing the contents of a pulled item. After silence had laid there a while, the columnist relented a bit. "It concerned an incident involving a local society figure's marriage. I was all set to leave when someone came running in with a news release saying that the woman had just been diagnosed with cancer, and it would've looked really tacky to bad-mouth her just at that point. So I replaced it."

"Who was the phone call from?"

"I don't know. Really, I didn't know him."

"You talked to him? Personally, I mean?"

"Sure. He sounded fine, not like he was trying to be Deep Throat or anything. You wouldn't believe people."

Kate, a cop, probably would. "Do you generally publish unsubstantiated rumors like that?" She tried not to sound disapproving, but Garchik didn't sound offended.

"Depends. If there was any meat to it, I might—like the piece I pulled, I'd checked with three people who'd been at the party where the incident had taken place. But a general rumor, especially if I make clear it's just a rumor, that's a different matter."

"The caller, did he have any kind of an accent?"

"Not really. He might have been English, but it wasn't strong. More like he'd lived there for a while, you know?"

Or like he was using the inflection as a disguise. "Okay, thanks."

"Do you mind if I put something into the column about this?"

That was a poser. "I'd appreciate it if you'd wait for a few days, Ms. Garchik. In fact, if you hold off, I should have something more solid to add to your story."

It was a red herring, but the newspaperwoman allowed herself to be distracted, and promised not to publish anything about Kate's call, at least for a few days. Kate thanked her and trotted downstairs.

THEY took Kate's car this time. Kate pulled into traffic and said, "So, what did you think of that story?" No need even to ask if he'd finished it: Al Hawkin would not have fallen asleep with pages unread.

He thought for a minute, then replied, "As investigations go, it was fairly solid. Given a complete lack of modern techniques."

She shot him a sideways glance; no, he was not making a joke. Although now that she thought of it, if you approached the tale as a piece of investigation rather than a story about people, his comment was valid. She chuckled, and said, "Of course, considering how backed up the labs are these days, we're not really much ahead of the Twenties in terms of using forensics to solve a case."

Parking outside the Gilbert house was simple on this weekday morning. Kate stood on the sidewalk for a moment, looking up and down the street: a gardening crew, a cyclist crossing three streets up, a woman rushing out the door and diving into her car. Once the woman had accelerated around the corner, not a soul moved for blocks; even the balding busybody across the street was absent.

"Not many families here," she said to Hawkin.

He looked around and nodded. "Quiet."

They let themselves in and Kate stepped forward to flip the pen-and-ink drawing to one side and hit the sequence, disarming the security system. She pulled on a pair of gloves and followed the line of framed sepia-colored photographs that marched along the right-hand wall to the stairs. One of those showed a large stone manor that might well have been Windsor Castle: On closer examination, she could see the hinge that held it to the wall. Using the tip of a pen, she lifted the picture and saw a neat silver switch, currently up in what was generally the on position. She let the picture fall shut, and went to see what Hawkin was doing.

He was standing in the sitting room, taking in his surroundings, a quizzical smile on his face. The room was utterly silent, and the mixed fragrances of the other day had faded to a memory—even the pipe tobacco was gone, with a rising mustiness in its place. All those horsehair sofas, Kate thought.

"My grandmother used to have this kind of furniture," Al said. "She had this chair that used to prick little holes in the backs of your legs, we always had to sit in it to take tea with her. Her whole place smelled like mildewing books."

"When we got here the other day, it smelled like lavender and furniture wax." She moved past Gilbert's chair and the now-cold fireplace to the far wall, then turned to look back at the hallway. She took a step to one side, then another, and when the angle was about what she remembered, she craned her neck at the wall behind her.

"There it is," she said. Knowing it was there, a person could easily see the small hole just above the picture rail. She thumbed her flashlight on and shone it up; sure enough, a tiny glimmer of glass betrayed the camera's minuscule lens.

Hawkin grunted, but was more interested in the wall over the fireplace.

"What do you suppose happened here?"

"It's a Holmes thing," she told him. "V. R.: Victoria . . . something. In one of the stories Holmes shoots the queen's initials into the wall. Apparently Gilbert thought it was too cute to pass up."

"Dangerous lunatic."

"Chris thought Gilbert hammered the marks instead of shooting them."

"Well, since Gilbert wasn't missing any fingers, I take it he didn't pound actual bullets into the wall."

"I imagine he hated having to fake it."

"I think you're right," he mused, picking up the wire net–covered bottle from among the nest of cut-glass decanters.

"That's a soda spritzer, I think," Kate told him.

"A gasogene, if memory serves. They tend to blow up on a hot day." He put the thing down gingerly, examined the bone-handled jackknife sticking up from the mantelpiece, then touched the small embroidered shoe that had been nailed up to one side.

"He had a pouch of tobacco in that," Kate said. "Only tobacco, as far as I could tell."

"No hypodermic needles with cocaine in them?"

"Hey, I forgot about that." *A self-medicating bipolar.* "No, we didn't find any needles."

He passed into the kitchen, running his eyes over the archaic fittings. "An odd thing to overlook. I'd have expected absolute verisimilitude."

"Right. Well, maybe he had his drugs hidden in the cut-out pages of one of the books. We didn't take them all off the shelves."

She'd meant it as a joke, but to her alarm, Hawkin eyed the laden shelves speculatively. However, in the end he turned away to climb the stairs.

The bell in the hallway began to clatter and dance furiously in the silence, and Kate went to let Lo-Tec Freeman in. The crime-scene inspector held out a piece of paper. She took it, and he shouldered his way past her without a word, leaving Kate to puzzle over the sheet.

It was the DNA results of the blood found on the chair upstairs, a match to Gilbert's blood.

"Thank you, Lo," she said fervently.

He shrugged, his print kit already in his hand, no classic rock tunes being sung today: Humiliation deadened the songs. Not only had Lo-Tec missed the scrap of porcelain, but she had scooped him in the webcam business, and moreover, he had missed this hidden button. Which was fine with her, if it brought her results, but she didn't want him permanently disgruntled.

"There was no reason to suspect this was here," she told the back of his neck. He said nothing. "I didn't even know about the webcam until late on Monday."

He peered at the job. "I saw the hookup on the computer, I should've known."

"Well, when you develop clairvoyance, Lo, you might put in for a raise."

He grunted, but from the angle of his shoulders, Kate thought he was somewhat mollified.

His next grunt was one of disappointment. He brushed the rest of the frame to be sure, and lifted a number of prints, but said, "These'll be the vic's. The print on the button itself is nothing but smear, most likely from a glove. I'll check these others and see, but don't hold your breath."

She thanked him and let him out, then worked the deadbolt handle a couple of times, thoughtful. If you had this kind of self-locking door, you probably would get in the habit of not bothering with the deadbolt unless you were going away for the weekend. Probably why builders stopped using them, to force people to attend to their security by the actual turn of a key.

On the top floor, she found Al in the doorway to the study, holding the photographs Kate and Williams had taken when they first arrived. The dried liquid in the bottom of the glass on the table had smelled like brandy, the contents of the marble ashtray all appeared to be pipe scrapings, the DVD in the machine had been the reproduction of a 1927 movie about, inevitably, Sherlock Holmes.

A name Kate was getting pretty sick of, by this point.

"It looks like he was sitting with a glass of brandy and a pipe," she told her partner, "getting ready to watch this old movie, maybe to make notes about it—there's a file in the cabinet full of notes about old movies, and his prints were on the glass, the pen, and the TV remote—when someone walked up behind him and knocked him out with this missing statue. He must have heard them because his head was turned slightly toward the door—the blow hit on his right temple instead of the side of his head. He bled onto the chair, but just a little—the perp probably grabbed a towel to wrap his head in. The killer cleaned up the pieces of the statue, except for one that ended up under the filing cabinet near the door. And as soon as it was dark, he put him in the car and drove him across the bridge."

Hawkin dropped the photos onto the low table and sat down in the tufted leather chair. He reached back with his right hand to feel the chair behind his head. "Gilbert was six feet?"

"Just a little over."

"I guess it's possible. Anyone shorter, I'd wonder."

Kate eyeballed the distance from Al's skull to the chair, and nodded. "Anyone under about five eight couldn't have bled on that spot, even if the perp managed to hit his head above the back of the chair. But I'd say Gilbert was just tall enough."

Al put his shoes onto the edge of the table, then said, "Where are his slippers?"

"What?"

"He was found with bare feet. Was he the sort to sit around in a silk dressing gown, pajamas, and nothing on his feet?"

"There's a pair under his bed on the second floor," she remembered. "And maybe one in the closet. I'll go see."

The modern bedroom had no slippers. She trotted down the stairs to its old-time equivalent, and saw the down-at-heels pair she remembered on the floral carpet beneath the bed. In the armoire was a pair of more ornate Moroccan foot coverings, which she thought might go well with the dressing gown Gilbert had been found in. She touched neither pair, but went back up to Al, who was still in Gilbert's chair, reading the reports of Gilbert's death.

"There are two pairs in the bedroom downstairs. I'll take them to the lab for prints. I should have caught that."

"I have the advantage of looking at the scene with ninety-nine percent of the work already done," he said, dismissing her self-criticism. "What about prints in here?"

"Mostly Gilbert's, the others belong to the lawyer Rutland and some of the dinner group. Gilbert had them up here after the party in early January—the house-cleaner wiped down all the woodwork once a month, and she'd done it the previous Thursday."

"Any sign of disturbance from carrying him down the stairs? If he'd been wearing shoes, he might have scraped the wallpaper, but he wasn't. You know, I wouldn't think it easy to sling a dead weight of, what, one hundred sixty pounds across your shoulders and walk down two flights of stairs, but there were no signs of dragging, either here or on the body."

"Which means we're most likely looking at a strong, fit male. Probably a man," she corrected, remembering Jeannine Cartfield's build and grip. "I could do a fireman's carry of one hundred sixty pounds if I had to, but not for long and definitely not down those stairs."

"And there's no blood here except for the chair back."

"The fibers the ME found in the head wound might turn out to match Gilbert's bath towels," Kate mused.

"That would support an unpremeditated bashing. If so, the perp might have found sheets to wrap the body in so it didn't pick up fibers from his car, but what about the wheelbarrow?"

"*If* he used one—those prints in the emplacement were not exactly definitive."

Hawkin didn't answer, since there wasn't much to say on the matter. He flipped through a few pages. "What about the fragments of statue?"

"What about them?"

"You'd expect to find signs of them along the trajectory of the blow, but it looks like most of the pieces were between the chair and the door."

"Except for the one behind the filing cabinet; the pieces were teeny, like sawdust. He could have transferred them to the carpet from his shoe, after cleaning up."

"Any signs of cleaning up? In the broom or dustpan, the vacuum, the mop?"

He knew there were not. "He used rags or paper towels, like I do when I drop a glass on the kitchen floor."

"And took the rags with him?"

"Since they're not in the garbage can."

Hawkin scowled at the crime-scene sketch, folded his reading glasses away into his pocket, and said, "Let's go back to where he was found."

• • •

THURSDAY traffic across the bridge was not as heavy as it had been the previous Saturday, and they drove underneath the northbound freeway and wound their way into the park. Kate turned in the direction of the one-way tunnel, no more keen on launching a car down the precipitous cliffside as a driver than she had been as a passenger. The signal light at the tunnel's entrance showed red; they waited for the green, Kate thinking of the story's narrator and his dashboard-denting trip through this same tunnel. The thing might be fiction, but the writer's terror had been heartfelt.

Cars emerged from the tunnel's end, and a couple minutes later, the light went green. This route wound among the park housing, artists' studios, information center, and other buildings without signs; Kate's thoughts again wandered to the story at the center of this case, and she shook her head ruefully.

"What's wrong?" Al asked.

"Oh, I just keep catching myself thinking about that story as if it was an actual case. I was looking at those buildings and wondering which one Jack Raynor and his killer lived in."

"Yes, I know what you mean."

They kept to the left at the Y, passing the Nike missile site, then circled around the conference center and the path leading to the lighthouse, finally pulling in across from the entrance to the DuMaurier battery, at the top of the hill they had been required to hike up the week before.

The entrance to the gun emplacement was still roped off with yellow police tape, but from its sagging appearance and the fresh footprints within, more than one visitor had ignored its message and pulled it up to pass beneath. Fortunately, the padlock had been replaced on the door to the room where Gilbert had been found; Kate paused at the entrance to the open-ended concrete tunnel and shone her flashlight at the ground.

"They found the tread marks along here, but after a week there was no telling if they came from a wheel-barrow or a bicycle. It could even have been a jogging stroller—God knows there's plenty of those in Marin."

Hawkin walked to the other end of the tunnel, to the amphitheater-like circle where the gun itself had once stood. The hillside spilled down toward the sea; two men strolled along the cliff top going north, while a woman with one child on her back and a toddler in a stroller—a thick-wheeled jogging stroller—passed them headed south. The wind was unrelenting; off to the right, two bright kites strained hard against their strings.

Kate tucked her hands under her arms, wishing she'd brought a warm hat. After a while, Hawkin had absorbed everything the view had to tell him, and retreated down the tunnel. Kate followed, digging the padlock key from her pocket. The hasp sprang open with the ease of unweathered metal; the two detectives drew out their flashlights and stepped inside.

The smell of death was nearly gone, faded beneath

the musk of damp. The floor had been vacuumed for evidence by the crime-scene team, but the old concrete walls were untouched, spalled and peeling. Kate's beam caught on a drop of water, trembling on the tip of one of the nascent stalactites.

"He came at night," Hawkin said. His voice echoed back at them from the hard surfaces.

"Most likely," Kate agreed. Nobody would risk unloading a body in pajamas in broad daylight. Fog might have made a reasonable substitute for dark, but if Gilbert had died as they thought, on or around the twenty-third of January, the fog had not cooperated. Rain, yes, but the risk would have been considerable.

"What are the travel restrictions in the park at night?"

"There aren't any restrictions," Kate said, with a brush of memory from the idea of midnight skate-boarders.

"So he could have driven up to the battery's front door, carried the body in, dumped him, been away again in, what, five minutes?"

"Longer if the lock was still attached. He would've had to come here, break the lock open, go back for Gilbert, either carry or wheel him inside, then pull the lock shut again."

"Let me have your car keys," Hawkin said, and they went back to the entrance. She watched him walk to the car, open the trunk, then walk to the driver's door and get in. When the door opened again, she noted the time on her watch. He walked briskly up the hill, ducking under the yellow tape and past Kate into the tunnel. At the door, he paused to work his flashlight back and forth as if using a pry bar, and after a reasonable expanse of time, pushed the door open.

He half-trotted back out the tunnel and through the trees to the car. Its trunk went up; Hawkin disappeared behind the raised trunk lid; the car bounced around a few times; and after a minute he reappeared, staggering out from behind the car with its spare tire balanced precariously across his back. Bent double beneath the awkward object, he plodded slowly up the hill.

Kate watched, suddenly apprehensive: A man who'd had a heart scare probably shouldn't be hauling spare tires around. However, when he went past her he was not breathing with any particular difficulty, and when he came out into the tunnel again sans tire, he appeared neither winded nor in any discomfort. He pulled the door shut, hung the lock back in place and pretended to thumb the screws back into the wood, then trotted back to the car and jumped behind the wheel. Kate marked the time and walked down to join him.

"Just short of five and a half minutes," she told him.

He got out of the car with a thermos in his hand, and led her over to the picnic table where the Coroner's men had gathered that first day. The two detectives sat on the table part with their feet on the bench and their backs to the battery, looking across the hills that were the Golden Gate and the rich orange bridge that spanned it. Al unscrewed the thermos, poured the coffee into its two cups, and set the larger one next to Kate while he rummaged in his pocket for a packet of sweetener. A large bird rode the wind, tipping and turning to maintain itself over a spot on the ground far below.

Al leaned forward and cupped his hands around the steaming cup, blowing gently across its top. "Would you have noticed that the soil here is different from the rest of the headlands?"

"No. Maybe if I'd first seen the two sides from a boat."

"When I was here on Tuesday, Dan Culpepper thought I should be educated about the headlands. So in between interviewing the residents, he lectured me on the history of the lighthouse, the difference between cannon and mortar, and the nature of Nike missiles. And he covered the ground. Two plates meet just off-shore, the North American and the Pacific. The San Andreas Fault defines the coast. And right here? We're sitting on top of a volcano."

Kate studied him out of the corner of her eye. "You're not talking about the investigation, are you?"

"Actually, no metaphor intended. I just thought it was interesting, that the reason the ground is different— green basalt, for your information, unlike the rocky sandstone you see on the opposite hill—is that over here is the remnant of a long-extinct underwater volcano."

All Kate could think of to say was, "Well, I guess we know something Sherlock Holmes didn't."

"Thank God for that. So: five and a half minutes, start to finish, assuming the perp knew exactly what to expect here."

"I agree. He'd have had to know the layout of the gun itself, and that there was just a simple padlock on this door. The padlock anyone could see, but surely there aren't that many people who know what's behind the door?"

"You'd say we're looking at someone from the headlands?"

"Or someone who's taken a tour of these installations."

"No, that's no good. It has to have been someone who knew the story itself. Unless Gilbert gave it to someone here, it's more likely that the perp assumed the story's description of the site was accurate. That once he'd pulled off the padlock, he'd find a room behind it that more or less corresponded with the given details."

Except that the body in the story was a young officer, not a middle-aged man in a silk dressing gown. Kate shook her head to dislodge the persistent, fictional Jack Raynor, then turned the gesture into a denial that fit their discussion.

"I'd say he at least came here and saw the outside of the emplacement. People don't tend to carry pry bars around in their cars."

"Unless you're a builder," Hawkin noted, but before Kate could recall if they had any carpenters in their pool of suspects, he went on. "Was the killer planning every step, do you suppose? Or making do as he went?"

"A bash on the head causing death by heart attack isn't exactly premeditated murder."

"I agree, the death itself may have been accidental, or

at least premature. But the disposing of the body was thought out."

"But why here?" Kate asked, making her contribution to the reasoning.

"Lieutenant Jack Raynor." Al's eyes were following the bird that sailed far above their heads, but Kate thought his mind was focused elsewhere.

"Which brings us back to the story," she said.

"I wonder why the author didn't put his name on it? Or her name. Seems to me that would be an automatic thing for a writer."

"Unless the writer was pretending to be someone else. Like Arthur Conan Doyle. Or unless it had a title page that got lost."

"If so, it wasn't numbered. The thing starts on page one."

"You think it might be a forgery after all? Elaborate, but everyone seems to agree that the stakes are pretty high."

"Is that a hawk or a turkey buzzard?" he asked suddenly.

Kate craned to look at the dark outline. "I don't know. Can you see if the tail is brown?"

"Too far away."

"Then it could be either. Does it matter?"

"No. Although it might have contributed to the decision to put the body inside the battery. If Gilbert was killed by a friend, that is, someone who didn't care for the idea of wildlife treating Philip Gilbert as dinner. It would also explain why, although he couldn't do much to rearrange the body, what with rigor, the clothing had been tidied around it."

"But we know he was put here by someone who knew him. I refuse to believe that bringing him to this gun emplacement was accidental."

"Of course not, but I mean someone with an emotional attachment to Gilbert. Something that went beyond their mutual interest in Arthur Conan Doyle."

She thought about that for a minute, then said, "We assumed he was in his dressing gown because he was getting ready for bed, but he could have been getting up. Either in the morning, or after a, what, romantic interlude?"

"Sex," Al said bluntly. "What did the autopsy say?"

"Swab was negative, but if he wasn't penetrated, and if he'd had a shower afterwards, it would be hard to tell. There was nothing on the sheets."

"On *his* sheets, no."

"You think he could have been killed elsewhere?"

"The urge to get a body out of one's house is considerable. If he'd died at home, the killer might have been more tempted just to arrange the body at the foot of the stairs or something and sneak away."

"But we found Gilbert's blood on the back of the chair, and the statue is broken and missing."

"The placement of the blood doesn't make me happy."

"What do you mean? The vic was plenty tall enough to clear the top of that chair."

"But if somebody hits you hard enough on the right

side of the head to knock you out, will your torso remain sitting upright in your chair? And will your head lean neatly back against the rest, in the direction the blow came from, and bleed gently into the leather?"

Kate's eyes narrowed as she visualized the room, the chair, the television set, the stain. "You would if your basher grabbed you and dragged you back."

Hawkin nodded, but said, "That would take some doing, to swing the statue and step forward in time to catch your vic before he fell out of the chair. Plus, there was no trace of blood on the carpet from a dropped statue."

Kate squinted in thought. "What if he used the statue to bash Gilbert, but it didn't break? And then he saw that Gilbert was falling, so he stepped forward and let go of it."

"It would have hit the carpet."

"Or he could have sort of tossed it behind him. It would break against the floor in back of the chair, explaining the piece we found and the tiny shards in the carpet."

"Yes," he said dubiously.

"So, would you rather have two doers here, one to whack and one to catch?"

"That doesn't feel right, either. It's nothing," he said and stood up from the bench, shaking out the dregs from his cup. "I just like to be able to feel how a thing happened, and I can't here."

Kate drained her own cup and dropped it onto the thermos. "So, what next?"

"No motive, no suspects. We need to reconstruct his last days."

"Bank statements and credit card records should be in any time."

"Those'll be a good place to start," he agreed. "You make an appointment with Jeannine Cartfield?"

"I threatened to arrive with uniforms and take her away in a black and white if she didn't set up a time. I'm going to see her tomorrow afternoon."

"While you're doing that, maybe I'll take a swing at the neighbors. You had a couple twinges there, didn't you?"

"The helpful guy across the street and the night nurse who lives next door," Kate recalled.

"I'll see what I can get out of them."

"When we finish, that's pretty much the entire run of contacts and records, and as far as I can see we've got nothing. Until Crime Scene coughs up a report, what else do you want to do?"

Far too early to consider the case cold. Still, it was one of those times Kate was grateful that at least the victim didn't have a family to answer to.

"You've got something this weekend, don't you?"

"Just a trip to Point Reyes."

"The whole weekend in Point Reyes, according to Lee. She made it very clear that I was not to expect you to show up for anything short of a hostage situation, with me as hostage."

Kate gave him a wry grin. "She's even rescheduled her Saturday client so we can have all day there. But honest, it's just Point Reyes, I can get away for part of the time."

"Well, let's see what we come up with tomorrow. It might be helpful to take just an hour or two and go over the high points, set things up for Monday."

"Say the word. I won't even tell Lee it's your fault."

"My vulnerable organs thank you," he said.

They climbed off the table and went to lock up, but instead of turning to the room, Hawkin continued on to the far end where the tunnel opened up for the gun, long gone from where they were. He stood, looking out over the gray-green Pacific, then shifted to study the ridge at the top of the cliffs.

A trail ran the cliff top between DuMaurier and Battery Mendel to the north, but to the south the ground was rough and overgrown. Hawkin set off in that direction, picking his way in inadequate shoes, with Kate behind him. A tongue of rock (gray, Kate noted) protruded into the ocean, creating a miniature bay far below, with refrigerator-sized rocks in the place of a beach. The swell of waves beat and retreated, beat and retreated, the white foam broken here and there by the heads of jagged black boulders.

In any number of places around their feet, the thin covering of soil gave way before a protruding knob of the substratum. Most were considerably smoother than their brothers in the sea below; some might have been chosen by a man looking for a place to sit and smoke a small cigar while he looked over the moonlit sea.

Hawkin murmured under his breath. " 'I am a young

artillery officer, fully dressed, anticipating a difficult interview.' "

Kate picked it up, and said, " 'It is two o'clock in the morning, at thirty-something degrees north, with a moon that is five nights after full.' "

"Lot of changes in eighty years, huh?"

"You think? 'Don't ask, don't tell?' Matthew Shepard and Gwen Araujo?"

"Christ, cheer me up why don't you, Martinelli? Come on, we got a case to solve."

They fastened the padlock back on the door, restored the crime-scene tape, and wrestled the spare tire between them down to the car's trunk. The winter green of the hills glowed in the sun as they passed through the headlands. A family with a small child in a backpack waited to cross the road, the infant staring seriously at them. Traffic was picking up on the bridge, and Al dodged through side streets to miss the worst city congestion.

They got back to the Hall of Justice shortly before four o'clock, to find the last month's bank statement and records from two of Gilbert's three credit cards waiting for them—an unusually fast response from the paper bureaucracies. Kate dug into those, Al laid out his interviews from Monday and Tuesday, and they worked in relative silence until it was time to go home.

It was just as well they chose the virtue of procrastination; if they had buckled down and built up Gilbert's final hours then and there, they'd have had to throw out all their calculations come morning.

SEVENTEEN

Hawkin picked up Kate at nine o'clock Friday morning, and drove to the Gilbert house. He had gone past the Hall of Justice to retrieve the Gilbert hard drive from the crime lab, and she connected it to the monitor and various cords, and turned it on. Al sorted the papers onto the low table, and as she waited for the computer to hum to life, Kate noticed the light on the answering machine, which had not been blinking the day before. She stretched out an arm to hit the play button, and the mechanical voice informed her that a message had been left at one-twelve the previous afternoon, a couple of hours after they had been there.

"Mr. Gilbert," said a chipper soprano voice, "this is Angie from Goode's Porcelain Repair. We have your bird ready for you, it looks just like new. You can pick it up Tuesday to Saturday from ten to six. Bye."

They stared at each other for a moment, jaws dropped, before Kate whirled and tugged open drawers in search of the phone book. However, the machine's surprises were not over yet. Message two, left about half an hour before they had arrived that morning, was another woman. By contrast, hers was a voice haughty with authority, although she sounded to be trying for a more friendly, even folksy, air.

"Hello Philip, this is Louisa Brancusi. You told me to give you a couple of weeks, and since it's two weeks today, I thought I'd give you a ring. You can reach me today in the office or on my cell, or any day, really. I'm going to be back in the Bay Area next week, I'd love to talk further. I know you have my numbers."

The machine added, *End of messages.*

There was no point in speculating while there was information to be had. Kate found the Yellow Pages and discovered, rather to her surprise, that there was such a category as Porcelain Repair. And Goode's was top of the list.

The chipper Angie answered. Kate identified herself, briefly explained that she was investigating the death of the man who had left an item for repair, and asked what Angie could tell her about it. Angie hesitated, and Kate resigned herself to having to go down in person—some people had no trust, particularly for things that mattered little. But Angie surprised her.

"Oh, that's too bad. Mr. Gilbert seemed really nice, and he was so upset about breaking his bird. It was a prize of some sort, for a book he'd written. When you say you're investigating his death, do you mean he was . . . murdered?"

"It's possible," Kate told her. "I'm going to put you on the speakerphone now, Angie. My partner is here, too, and it'll save me from having to repeat what you say. Okay?"

"Sure."

"It's Lieutenant Al Hawkin," she said, and hit the speaker button.

"Hello, Angie," Al said.

"Hi."

"Okay," Kate resumed. "You say Mr. Gilbert broke the statue by accident?"

"Yes, he said he bumped against it on a shelf and it fell onto the floor. Broke in about a dozen pieces. Like I said, he was terribly upset, because although the thing isn't very attractive in itself, and it probably cost a fraction of what I'd had to charge for repairing it, the value's in what it means to the owner, you know?"

"I understand. Can you tell me what day this was?"

"Sure, just a minute." There was a sound of paper rustling, then Angie's voice. "The tag says January twentieth. That was a, let's see, a Tuesday. And it was the afternoon, if it matters. Not too long before closing. That's not on the tag, but I remember."

"Great. Now, Angie, can you tell us anything more about what he said, how he acted? Just anything that made an impression on you."

"He was tall and he had a big nose, I remember that. A little snooty but kind of embarrassed too about his clumsiness. Polite. And he made a face over the estimate but he didn't try to argue me down. People do."

"Can you tell me about the statue?"

"Well, like I told you, it sat on a high shelf and he knocked it onto a hardwood floor, so it was pretty smashed up. He may not have realized how fragile it was, it looks very solid, although of course it's hollow. He brought it in a cardboard box, like they give you at a print shop, you know? The kind that store flat and they pop up to put your print job in? His was open and he carried it carefully, but he'd still lost a small piece

443

somewhere along the line. We had to fill it in, but it's at the back and the color's good, he'll never know. Or he would never have known," she amended sadly.

"We found that missing piece. It fell behind a filing cabinet."

"Did you? Well, too late now. He probably stopped looking after he'd sliced open his finger."

Kate looked at Al; Al looked at Kate. "He cut himself, you say?" Al asked.

"He sure did. People don't realize how sharp porcelain can be. I had to clean blood off a couple of the pieces before I could cement them together."

"And which hand would that have been, do you remember?"

"Um, let's see. His . . . his left hand. The middle finger of his left hand. He had a Band-Aid on it."

"Thank you very much, Miss . . . ?"

"Goode. Angie Goode. My father started the business, but it's mine now."

"Thank you. One of us will be down in the next day or two to take a statement, but you have been a great help."

"I hope you find out what happened. He seemed like a really nice man. Um, I don't suppose you know if anyone will want the statue now, do you?"

"We may need it as evidence, but if it isn't pertinent to the case, we'll turn it over to the executor of Mr. Gilbert's estate."

Kate hung up and found the number of Gilbert's housecleaner, Nika Kilanovitch. She reached the recorded voice of a young girl with an American accent, repeating the number and inviting her to leave a message. She did so, asking Kilanovitch to call her cell number.

She looked at Al; while she was on the phone, he had been paging back through the autopsy report. Now he pushed the document toward her on the table, tapping one paragraph before he stood up. Kate bent her head to read it, and indeed, the pathologist had been thorough, for under marks and scars was included: recent scar on middle finger of left hand.

The phone rang, and a heavily accented voice said, "This Nika Kilanovitch. I see message from you?"

"Thank you for calling me back, Ms. Kilanovitch. May I ask, you cleaned Mr. Gilbert's house on Thursday the twenty-second of January, is that right?"

"Is last time, yes."

"Had he broken something up on the top floor?"

"Yes, black bird. Not real bird, it—"

"A statue, I know. I wish I'd thought to ask."

"Sorry?"

"Never mind. You vacuumed up the pieces?"

"No pieces, or small, small pieces. Use paper towel on floor, I not want pieces, how you say . . . ?"

"You didn't want him to get splinters of glass in his feet."

"Splinters, yes."

"And you emptied the vacuum bag?"

"Always empty bag, take to can."

"And you took the paper towels to the can as well."

"Of course."

"Thank you," Kate said, and flipped her phone off.

She looked up to see Al lowering himself to the floor between the chair and the door, in the place where a statue on the shelf would have hit the ground. His left hand came up to rest on the back of the chair, precisely where the Luminol had revealed a smear of blood; he wagged his middle finger, which rested half an inch from where Crime Scene had scraped a trace of Gilbert's blood.

Gilbert had broken the Maltese Falcon himself; Gilbert's hand, not his head, had bled on the chair. Their entire theory of his death collapsed before their eyes.

But that was what an investigation did, promising pathways ended in washed-out dead ends.

Hawkin pulled himself up on the chair back, and brushed off his hands both literally and metaphorically. "Louisa Brancusi," he said.

"I don't remember the name from his address book." Kate went back to Gilbert's computer. She typed the first name into his e-mail finder without result, but the last name came up with three from LBrancusi, all in the past five weeks.

Brancusi was one of three partners in (as Kate found, making a detour to the website of the firm name given on the signature of the e-mail) a small but prestigious auction house based in New York. Profiles had been written about her in half a dozen important magazines, including a piece in the *New Yorker* that compared Brancusi's techniques with those of two men in other houses. The phrases "sweet-tongued tigress" and "walking the edge of ethics" made it clear that Louisa Brancusi met the boys on their ground, and then some.

For some reason, Gilbert had chosen to approach Brancusi, sending her an e-mail on January sixth (Wasn't that Sherlock Holmes's birthday? Kate thought) that said:

Dear Ms. Brancusi,

We met at the Victoriana auction your house held in November; you may remember me as the person who bought the two Kipling letters.

I have come into an item of what I believe to be considerable importance to the world of Sherlock-iana, and would like to talk about the possibility of putting it up for auction through your house. If you are coming to the West Coast at any time soon, I would like to get together with you and talk it over face-to-face.

I realize this may not be convenient, but I would prefer not to describe it prematurely in any great detail, particularly via the Internet. If you know who I am, you may consider the weight of my judgment when I say this is the sort of thing for which a reserve price in the mid six figures would not be at all unreasonable.

Yours, Philip Gilbert

Brancusi's response was immediate and positive,

although she tried hard to convince him that an actual meeting was unnecessary, and asked him for further information about the item in question. Gilbert flatly refused, and her third letter, dated the eleventh of January, gave in to his demands, telling him that something had come up to require her presence in San Francisco at the end of that very week, and suggesting that he might like to join her for dinner at a restaurant she'd heard was good. Gilbert had written back confirming the place and time.

Kate went back to the phone book, called the restaurant, played the privacy game with the woman with the French accent, and for the second time that morning managed to get the information she needed without driving across town for it: Yes, an L. Brancusi and guest had dined at the restaurant on Friday the twenty-third of January.

"Can I ask," Kate said, "do you serve a dish that has white beans and meats in it?"

"But of course," said the French accent, sounding offended. "Chef Martin's cassoulet is our signature dish."

"And I'm sure our dead man enjoyed every bite," Kate told her, and hung up.

Brancusi's auction house was shut, although it was not yet one o'clock in New York, and offered a voice message service. Instead, Kate hung up and tried the cell number Brancusi had given Gilbert in case he needed to reach her while she was on the road. There, too, a woman's voice suggested that she leave a message for Louisa Brancusi, and this time Kate did.

"Ms. Brancusi, this is Inspector Kate Martinelli of the San Francisco Police Department. I need to speak with you about a dinner you had last month with Philip Gilbert. Would you please call me on my cell phone, or if you prefer, you can leave me a message at the San Francisco Hall of Justice." She gave the general number for the Hall, as proof that she was indeed a cop and not some competing house's sneak.

With a sigh, she looked at the notes she had begun to make for the reconstruction of Philip Gilbert's final days. She drew a line across the entire thing, and started again.

It took several hours, hunting down phone numbers, following the sequence of e-mails in his virtual out-box, referring to witness statements, and comparing charges on his credit cards with receipts in his physical in-box, before they had the following time line:

Friday, January 23:

7:02–7:30: E-mails to eleven potential buyers for three different items (a pipe owned by Arthur Conan Doyle; a Sherlock Holmes cookie jar dating to 1924; and a first American edition of *The Hound of the Baskervilles* from 1902).

7:46–8:11: Online searches of two auction houses and various items on eBay, where he registered half a dozen bids.

8:16–8:38: Phone calls to Ian Nicholson, Thomas

Rutland, and Jeannine Cartfield of the Holmes dinner club. Looking back at the interviews, they found that Rutland had said Gilbert phoned about an appointment for late the following week—an appointment not actually made, he'd just been checking on Rutland's schedule. Nicholson had last spoken to Gilbert on the Saturday morning, so hadn't mentioned this Friday call; Kate phoned him and asked. He had a hard time remembering the subject of the call, but then decided that Gilbert had wanted to know if he was going to be around that weekend, and when told of the Seattle memorial, said that he might have something for Nicholson before he left, and asked when Nicholson planned to leave.

9:52: Credit card charge of $25.34 at the local dry cleaner's. There was no receipt for this in the in-box.

10:03: Credit card charge of $87.56 at a nearby stationer's, with a corresponding receipt in the in-box giving the details of a double-pack of black printer cartridges, a package of twelve ballpoint pens, and two reams of some rather pricey paper. They found the pens, still unopened, in the desk drawer; the packaging of one cartridge, the box from one ream of paper, and a used black cartridge, in the wastebasket under the desk; and the other box of buff-colored, high-cotton paper, open and partially used, on the shelf beneath Gilbert's printer.

11:44: Credit card charge for sixteen and a half gallons of gas at a station one mile south of the Gilbert house; the Lexus's gauge showed the needle all the way at the top.

8:00: Gilbert met Louisa Brancusi for dinner.

Saturday, January 24:

8:38: Gilbert made a call on his cell phone to Ian Nicholson's number, talked for three minutes, then went silent, forever. He was next heard from when his body was found on Point Bonita, precisely one week later.

Kate started to return the phone records to the file, then had a sudden thought. She looked back through them for the middle of January, and there she found the familiar number.

"It was Gilbert himself who phoned the tip to Leah Garchik," she told Hawkin with satisfaction. "He must have decided that fanning the flames of the rumor mill was the best way of promoting it."

Louisa Brancusi phoned Kate back a short time later, admitting that she had checked the other number first, just to be sure.

"That's fine, Ms. Brancusi. I need to know about your dinner with Philip Gilbert."

"Has something happened to Philip?"

This was tricky, since the woman was apparently the last person to see Gilbert alive, but there was no helping it: The SFPD was not about to fly Kate to New York for an interview. "I'm sorry to have to tell you, but yes, Mr. Gilbert died a couple of days after you met with him." She waited while the woman made noises of distress, which sounded almost genuine, then resumed. "First of all, Ms. Brancusi, can you tell me what Mr. Gilbert had for dinner?"

"He ordered the cassoulet," she said without hesitation. "Apparently it's the specialty, but it's too heavy a dish for my taste. I had soup and a salad."

"And what did you talk about?"

"Philip wanted to explore the possibility of giving us an item for auction. He wanted to make an event of it, the central lot in the auction, and wanted us to time it in May, to get in before the Christie's and Sotheby's London auctions. He wanted a dozen pages in the catalogue and a commitment to a certain level of advertising. I can't go into the details, in part because he hadn't yet told me what he had—he'd promised to talk to me in two weeks. I assumed he was shopping around the other houses in the meantime, although *nobody* was going to agree to what he wanted sight unseen.

"It was a frustrating meeting, to tell you the truth. I'd flown all the way from New York just to talk with him, and came away with nothing but vague promises. He just kept saying that it would be worth my while, and nothing else. If it had been anyone else, I'd have thought he was playing me, but I've had some dealings with him before, and he has a good reputation, although he can be a bit of a drama queen, thinking his stuff was

452

like a Fabergé egg or something. But I didn't really have a whole lot of choice, so I bit my tongue and told him I'd wait until I heard from him. I assume you got my name from the message I left on his phone yesterday?"

"Yes, and e-mails on his computer. Mr. Gilbert didn't tell you anything at all about the item?"

"Philip used the term 'definitive.' I took it he meant that in a technical sense, meaning an item that will change how people judge, write about, and analyze an artist's work in the future. You could say that an early and unknown draft of a Hemingway novel would be 'definitive.' "

Kate wondered if the woman's choice of examples was accidental. Brancusi might have picked up the rumor about a missing Conan Doyle story and be subtly inviting Kate to confirm it, or it might be simply that she handled so many manuscripts, it was her first thought. In any case, Kate would not be caught by the feeler.

"I understand. And he asked you to give him two weeks to think about it?"

"I need to know by next week if I'm setting up something for May. You can't put together a catalogue like that overnight. You wouldn't know what this was, would you?" she probed.

"I couldn't say," Kate equivocated.

"Because if his estate is going to sell it, I'd be extremely interested in handling it."

"I'll pass the word on to his executors."

"Thank you. Was there anything else?"

"Did he say anything during dinner about his plans for the . . . item?"

"Just that he would be selling it. I got the impression that he badly wanted to keep the thing for himself, but that it simply was too valuable to stay in his personal collection. Not every collector has the facilities to care for an item of world importance, or to deal with the publicity it would generate."

"Did anything else come out of the dinner conversation?"

"Yes. I told him that I had heard that Christie's was planning an auction of a large number of Conan Doyle papers. It hasn't been announced yet, but I have my contacts."

"Why did you tell him? I'd have thought this would tempt him to take his . . . item to them."

"I considered that, but I knew that Philip would hear about it sooner or later, and I thought that it was better to control the information myself. I told him that his item would be a welcome addition to their sale, but if he expected it to get much attention, he would be sadly disappointed. If, however, we could make it the crown jewel of our own sale of literary-related items, which would not be limited to Conan Doyle papers, he might attract a very different and considerably more diverse group of bidders. He could see the advantage in having his item in with such things as a first-edition Hemingway inscribed to Gertrude Stein and one of Faulkner's pens. Along with a number of lesser items, of course."

"Of course. But he didn't commit himself?"

"No, as I told you, he said he would need a couple weeks to decide. And that was pretty much that."

"What did Mr. Gilbert do when you finished dinner?"

"What did he do? He thanked me and we waited for the valet to retrieve my car."

"So you last saw him standing outside the restaurant?"

"Well, he was giving one of the other valets a tip and walking toward his own car. His had arrived first, but he waited with me until mine came. He was a man with old-fashioned manners."

"Would his car have been a black Lexus?"

"I think so. A black car, anyway."

"What time would that have been?"

"Gee, let's see. Perhaps a little before eleven. Of course, I was on East Coast time, so it felt like two."

"And you met at what time?"

"Eight o'clock."

"Thank you, Ms. Brancusi. If you think of anything else, could you give me a call?"

"Sure. And I'm sorry. About Philip. I liked him." She sounded surprised, either at the fact or that she was giving it voice: Gilbert had gotten under the skin of the honey-tongued tigress.

"A number of people have said the same," Kate told her.

Kate gave Al the gist of the conversation, and they both looked at the reconstruction. Where had Gilbert been between his 11:44 purchase of gasoline and his

8:00 dinner meeting with Louisa Brancusi? And even more urgent, where had he gone afterwards?

And one niggling question: Why had this techno-phobe, who rarely even carried his cell phone and whose records indicated that he had used it an average of twice a week, used his cell phone on the Saturday morning? Company records showed that the call was relayed through the tower nearest Gilbert's home. So why hadn't he used his home phone to place the call to Ian Nicholson, his last act before disappearing?

AT one o'clock they broke for lunch, walking down to the nearby center of shops, bank, and cafes. On their way back, Kate proposed that they begin their second run at the neighbors.

"I was thinking the lawyer," Al said, "but let's start here, sure. Together, or you want to divide and con-quer?"

"I'm meeting Jeannine Cartfield at four, but let's start here and see how it goes."

She found her notes on the Sunday interviews, and tried not to think about how slow progress was in an investigation: all week, and they were still sifting for threads that led somewhere.

"The woman on the left—as you look at this house, I mean—is a dancer. She gave me the name of Gilbert's cleaning woman, she works at a desk overlooking the street and saw Gilbert's comings and goings, noticed his car here and gone on the Friday. I think she'd have phoned if she remembered anything new."

"What about houses you didn't reach anyone at?" Hawkin asked.

"Just two of those—one is empty and has a For Sale sign up, the other the people spend the winters in Mexico. However, I had questions about a couple of places. One was the guy across the street who gave us the information about Gilbert's security company. He didn't know much when I interviewed him, but he kept hanging around outside while we were here, walking his dog, checking to see if we needed anything—did everything short of offering us donuts, and probably would have done that if we'd been here the next morning. Could just be a cop wannabe, but still . . . The other is the house next door—not the dancer, the night nurse. The more I think about it, the more it seems the woman was hiding something. And before you say it, yes, I know everyone's hiding something, but she was clearly not happy about having a cop at her door."

"Let's start with those two, then, and work our way around. You did interview the people on the next street, backing on Gilbert's yard?"

"Yes, O boss, I did. They heard nothing, saw less."

The Murray household was even less helpful that day than it had been on Sunday. A different elderly woman answered this time, after they'd rung the bell twice and nearly walked away. She identified herself as Miss Flanders, and informed them in a very shaky voice, hiding behind the crack in the door, that her sister Mrs. Murray was not at home.

Al stepped in for this interview—he was an expert with little old ladies. "That's right, she works, doesn't she?" he said, making a show of fumbling through the papers in his hand. "What was it, noon to midnight? Long hours."

"Tuesday through Friday," she agreed, not falling for the sympathy routine.

"Well, ma'am, we're going around the neighborhood asking about the evening of January twenty-third, to see if anyone noticed anything unusual with the house next door to you. Mr. Gilbert?"

"Next door?"

"That's right, 927."

"I didn't see anything."

"You recalled that after very little thinking," he said amiably.

"I wasn't here the twenty-third. I was in Texas."

"Houston, is that right?"

"Yes. My brother just got—got in. From South America. I needed to meet him and help him get settled."

"Where is your brother now, Miss Flanders?"

"I told you, he's in Houston."

"And you didn't see or hear anything around the twenty-third of January that concerned your neighbor?"

"I did not."

"Okay. Well, thanks for your help. We'll drop by maybe tomorrow and have a chat with your sister."

"Don't come early. She needs her sleep," she said, and closed the door.

"Tomorrow, then," Hawkin said to the wooden surface.

As they went down the steps, Kate told him, "Interesting to note that 'getting my brother settled' is pretty much the same words her sister used."

"Personally, I was taken by that hesitation before saying that her brother just got 'in, from South America.' Have to wonder if maybe it was 'out' that he got."

"We can check to see if they've just paroled any prisoners in Houston by the name of Flanders. Otherwise, I'm afraid your charming aw-shucks manner just struck out."

"I'm not the boy I was."

"Let's try the guy across the street."

The man across the street greeted them as long-lost colleagues, told his yappy white puffball of a dog to be quiet, offered them coffee, nodded at their refusal as if it referred to a trade secret, pressed them for details, put up both palms in a gesture of secret knowledge when Al reminded him that they could not tell him any, pulled his dog off Al's legs, nodded with great sympathy at Kate's admission that they hadn't progressed very far, offered them lemonade, accepted their refusal with another knowing nod, and finally permitted them to get to the point.

"Mr. Wallace, have you remembered anything else about Friday the twenty-third of January? I know you were sick, but maybe when you had to get up to go to the bathroom or something, you might recall seeing Mr.

Gilbert come and go? At any time during the day?"

"Please, it's Simon. And here, why don't we go upstairs?"

They protested that it was not necessary, but he was already moving toward the stairway, and insisted that they needed to see it.

So they followed him, trying not to step on the pile of fluff that scurried around their feet, and turned to the second-floor room at the front of the house. Simon Wallace walked to a wooden desk with a highly polished surface the approximate square footage of a marriage bed; Kate couldn't imagine how he'd gotten it up the stairs. He stood at the desk and pulled open a ring binder, turning it sideways and thumbing the pages until he came to a calendar page labeled JANUARY. But by the time he had it, both Kate and Al were looking beyond the desk to the setup at the window.

In the window stood a camera on a tripod, its lens something a paparazzo would drool over. On the room side of the three legs stood a chair; to the right was a small table with an open spiral notebook and pencil.

"Mr. Wallace," Al asked in a mild voice, "are you spying on your neighbors?"

"Conducting surveillance," Wallace retorted, stung.

"Why?"

"Well . . . Because . . . In case something comes up you need to see."

"So you don't always have this equipment set up?"

"It's my bird-watching kit. No, it's just been here since you came on the first."

Which meant that he would have nothing for the days they were actually interested in. However, rather than showing disappointment, Al maintained the disapproving attitude as he said, "Then you have no information for the twenty-third or twenty-fourth of January."

"Here," Wallace nearly shouted in his eagerness to prove his worth, "I've got photos of people coming and going. They say criminals often revisit the scene of the crime."

He thrust a stack of photos at each of them; Kate felt a bit sorry for the fellow, and looked at a few on the top, but as far as she could see, all the people were either criminologists or people who lived in the house. She flipped through a dozen more—there was one of her, sitting on the front steps of the Gilbert house talking on her phone and looking positively frumpy—then piled them together and handed them back to him.

"Mr. Wallace—"

"Simon, please."

"—I think it might be best if you were to stop taking pictures now and went back to bird-watching. Your neighbors might not be happy about it if they found out, and nothing's likely to happen now."

He looked sadly at the stack of snapshots showing the street outside. "I was just trying to help. . . ."

Al, however, had removed one picture from his pile. "Does Mrs. Murray in 929 have someone living with her?"

Wallace glanced at the picture, which showed a slim

young woman in athletic shoes walking a pair of slim young dogs past the Murray house. A window in the second story held a dark shape that looked like a man, although it could have been merely a shadow. But Wallace was nodding quickly. "Yeah, he's only been there for a few days. Big guy. Doesn't come out much."

"May we have this?" Al asked.

"Of course," Wallace said, all but wriggling in excitement. "Just tell me the number on the back."

Al turned it over curiously and read, "F19."

Wallace moved to his binder, flipped pages, and bent to make a note. Kate moved close enough to see what he had printed: *Surveillance photo F19; turned over to Inspector A. Hawkin, 2/6/04; 15:22 hours.*

She felt as if he expected them to salute him as they left.

EIGHTEEN

I've got to run if I'm going to catch Jeannine Cartfield," she said to Hawkin.

"I think I'll head back to the Detail," he said, "see if I can track down this guy next door. I'll drop you by the Ferry Building on the way. Or would you rather get your car?"

"No, I'm fine getting back. But how can you fit a neighbor into this?"

"Can't, yet. But it's a hole that needs filling, and you never know. He might be a paroled forger who did work for Gilbert—"

"Yeah, right," she said dryly.

"Or a home invasion."

She didn't take his suggestion at all seriously. As they drove, she chewed on the problem. After a while, she said, "It's all about the dump site."

"Yep."

"There's no gaping alibis, just the usual problems, and so far we've caught no one out in a lie. Nobody admits to knowing about the story, but somebody used it for the disposal."

"Nicholson knew."

"Nicholson was two hundred fifty miles away the night the body had to have been left, reading the damned story in his motel room. I checked. Even if he had a Ferrari and collected speeding tickets all the way, the return trip back to San Francisco would have taken him eight or nine hours. I think Gilbert gave someone else a copy."

"Rutland?"

"Either him, or Jeannine Cartfield. And I know I said it wasn't likely to be a woman, but she's a strong woman, and she has an air of . . . determination about her."

"Determination."

"You know what I mean. But look: Gilbert made three phone calls on Friday morning, to Rutland, Nicholson, and Cartfield. And the next day, Gilbert was in a rush to get the story to Nicholson before Nicholson took off for Seattle."

"That's right."

"What if someone else got ahold of the manuscript? What if Gilbert discovered that a copy was missing, or that someone had broken in and read the thing? If he wanted to control the publicity, he'd be in a panic because the news was about to break without him."

"But it hasn't broken," Al pointed out.

"Because when he confronted the person who stole the story, he—"

"—then killed Gilbert, and can't let it out without giving himself away. But he wouldn't have left Gilbert where he did, pointing directly at the story, if he wanted to be associated with it later. He'd have dumped the body on the beach, or tried to make it look like an accident."

"He might have done it in a snit of temper. Or maybe he's just stupid."

"A stupid Sherlockian? I think there's rules against that."

"Yeah, I know," she admitted. "I'm going in circles. But the dump site has got to be key."

JEANNINE Cartfield's instructions had been to phone when Kate arrived and she'd say where she was. So when Al had dropped her among the raw-looking forest of palm trees at the end of Market Street, Kate opened her phone as she moved through the plaza toward the newly restored Ferry Building, San Francisco's newest shrine to the art of living well.

"Cartfield," the voice said.

"This is Inspector Kate Martinelli."

"Ah good. Where are you?"

"Waiting at the signal to walk across the Embarcadero."

"Go ahead and cross, make your way down to the right, I'll be there in two minutes."

Cartfield swept out of the doors and greeted Kate with her powerful handshake, then said, "I do have an office, but I don't spend any more time there than I have to. You want to sit outside, or in?"

"Outside is good."

She led Kate to the patio of tables at the nearby restaurant, where the waiter appeared before the enclosure's gate had swung shut and greeted Cartfield by name. They chose a table with sun on it, and when they were settled, she asked Kate, "Do you want anything to eat, or just a drink?"

"A latte would be good."

"And I'll have a glass of the pinot grigio, thanks, Hal. It's been one of those weeks."

"Latte and a grigio," the waiter agreed. Cartfield's eyes lingered on his retreating backside, then she turned to Kate.

"Have you been to the Ferry Building before?"

Before, Kate figured, meant since its rebirth as a food Mecca, all the hallways and corners of the terminus filled with artisanal cheeses and breads, local wines and produce, restaurants and chocolatiers. She said, "I'm married to a foodie. We're down here at least twice a week."

"The Farmer's Market?"

"Wouldn't miss it."

Cartfield laughed with pleasure, and while they waited for their drinks, they talked about the process of the renovations, the enormous liberation of the water-front following the 1989 quake and its attendant removal of the elevated freeway, and the plans for the entire perimeter of the city.

With drinks in front of them, talk turned from Cartfield's business to Kate's. She took her notebook from her pocket, setting it out of view on her lap.

"As you know, I'm interviewing Philip Gilbert's friends and associates about what was going on in his life before he died. Primarily, this manuscript that Ian Nicholson was talking about the other night seems to have played a large part in Philip's life, toward the end."

"I can imagine."

"Did he give you a copy?"

"Who, Ian? Or Philip? Oh, it doesn't matter," she said with a shake of the head. "Nobody's given me the story."

Kate glanced down, as if consulting the blank page of her notebook. "You acted as co-host at Philip's party in January."

"I helped him cook," she corrected, adding by way of explanation, "I am a very good cook."

"He didn't talk to you about the story?"

"No."

"And we noticed that he phoned you on the morning

of January the twenty-third. What was that call concerning?"

Cartfield's eyes went out of focus for a moment while she conducted an internal search, then they came back to Kate's. "You're right, he called about the next meeting. I'm the secretary this year, he wanted to schedule ten minutes during the February meeting for an announcement. I guess we know what that was about, don't we?" she said, her mouth quirked in a painful smile.

"You went to college with Philip, is that right?"

"University, yes. We were both at the University of London in the early seventies, Philip reading lit and I was in economics. I hadn't seen him in nearly ten years when one day out of the blue he phoned to say that he'd just moved to town and did I want to help put together a Sherlockian dinner group? There was a Sherlockian group, of course, but he wanted to concentrate on the food more than they did. And I think he liked being in charge. No, correct that: I know he liked being in charge."

"A benevolent autocrat," Kate suggested.

"Always," Cartfield said, which Kate gathered meant she agreed with both elements of the description.

"Can you tell me what you were doing on the twenty-third and twenty-fourth of January?"

Cartfield reached into her pocket and drew out her PDA. She glanced up and said, "Electronic life preserver," then tapped at the keys and screen for a minute. "Oh, right. I was here on the Friday. Saturday I was up in Calistoga with a couple of friends, we had a weekend baking out the poisons in the mud baths during the day and restoring the poisons at night."

Kate took the details of the friends' names and numbers, although she did not imagine she would find any conflicts in the information. This was not a woman who would casually mislead the police. She set her closed notebook on the table, as if indicating that she was now off duty, and spooned some foam from her cup.

"I've been told that you and Philip Gilbert were close."

"We were friends, although I don't know about close. Philip lived in his own world, and allowed the rest of us to visit sometimes."

"You were lovers?"

Cartfield's head came up sharply, not in defense but in surprise. "Lovers? Where on earth did you hear that? No, we weren't lovers."

"Did he have any lovers?"

"I told you, Inspector, we weren't exactly close. His love life wasn't something Philip would talk about."

"Oh come on now, you've known the man for thirty years and you don't know who he shared his bed with?"

"I always thought Philip regarded sex as a mildly distasteful and rather messy pastime, best avoided by civilized people. Somewhat like Holmes in that regard, I'd say."

"So he was a virgin?"

"No, oh no. In London days he was a party boy, but that was a very long time ago."

"Did he party with girls or boys?" Kate pressed.

"Oh, both, for sure."

"He was bisexual?"

"A little ahead of his time, you know—the Seventies were conservative when it came to anything but number of partners. But yes, he, as the saying goes, swung both ways."

"Would you say he was the same now?"

"I wouldn't say anything about how he was since he moved here, he was a very different person. However," she said thoughtfully, "I have noticed since then that Philip's kind of experimental bisexuality is often the sign of a young person on the road away from being hetero." She looked surprised at what she had said, and eyed her empty glass accusingly.

"So you'd say Philip was gay?"

"I'd say there was a good chance. Although whether he practiced or whether it was as theoretical as a priest's, that I couldn't tell you."

And that was all Jeannine Cartfield had to say on the matter.

KATE caught a streetcar down Market for a few blocks, enjoying the feel of being a tourist in her own town, then walked over to the Hall of Justice. Al was still there, his ear glued to a phone, and she waved and picked up a phone of her own. She located the number in the Gilbert case file; luckily, the woman was home.

Corina Ferguson had been married to Philip Gilbert

for just under two years in the mid-1970s, when the young man came back from London and enrolled in a master's program at Harvard. Ferguson's own degree was from the University of Massachusetts, so they had probably not met in one of his lit classes, but her family lived in Boston, and she did still.

She came on the line with irritation clear in her New England accents. The irritation did not fade when Kate had identified herself.

"Couldn't you call at a more reasonable hour?" she demanded. "I have guests here."

"Just a brief question, Ms. Ferguson."

"Oh, well, go ahead."

"Can you tell me why you and Philip divorced?"

"*What*—my good woman, that takes some nerve—"

Kate broke into the protests with the practiced intonation of a cop who has heard it all and been impressed by none of it. "Ma'am, please, if you could just answer the question. It has to do with a lead I'm following up regarding his murder."

The harsh final word silenced the Boston voice for a moment; then, " 'A lead.' Was Philip . . . You hear about these things, and in San Francisco . . . Was it . . . I hope it wasn't one of those horrible gay bashings?"

Bingo. "Why do you ask that, Ms. Ferguson? Was Philip gay when you knew him?"

"No! I mean, why would I have married him if . . . But when you ask that question and he's dead, you said he was murdered, I thought . . . And it's San Francisco . . ." Kate continued to say nothing to rescue the

470

woman, just kept quiet. "No, he wasn't gay." Kate still said nothing; reluctantly, the woman went on. "Although, I have to say, since then, I have occasionally wondered. I mean, he was sweet, but the marriage, it wasn't really much in the bed department." She tried out a laugh, which fell flat, and then she sighed. "So I wondered, you know? You do, after all, even after all those years. And then six or seven years ago a friend mentioned they'd seen him in a restaurant somewhere, with an actor. Which made me think that maybe . . . Anyway, I never knew, but I hope he was happy. Happier than he was with me, anyway."

Mentally, Kate reviewed the epitaphs she had been collecting for Philip Gilbert, and found that of the long-estranged ex-wife surprisingly touching.

When Hawkin got off the phone, she told him about the conversations she'd had with two of the women in Gilbert's life. He sat back with his hands locked over his stomach, and shook his head in wonder. "A closeted gay in San Francisco? Who'd have thunk it?"

"Well, Louisa Brancusi did say he was old-fashioned. What about your shadowy brother?"

"We were right, he's an ex-con name of Wayne Flanders. Not on parole, he served his whole time. Seventeen and a half years. Grand theft auto, felony drunk driving, felony manslaughter."

"Got drunk, stole a car, killed someone," Kate translated.

"More borrowed than stole, it belonged to a friend of his. And the driver of the other car was drunk, too, so it wasn't like old Wayne killed some family of six on their way to a church picnic."

"But still."

"And no parole because he refused to apply. Found Jesus in prison and thought he ought to serve his full time."

"Think we need to roust him?"

"I don't know. I'm tempted to let it go for now."

"I agree. Okay, so what have we got over the weekend?"

"You've got a trip to Point Reyes with your family. All weekend. You're going to relax and have fun and freeze to death on the beach."

"Look, I can run back for a few hours on Saturday afternoon if you think—"

"If I drag you away, Lee will flay me alive."

"Yeah, probably," she admitted. "But only when she's finished with me."

"I think it's not a bad thing to let everyone settle down for a couple of days. Let 'em begin to relax and we can hit them again Monday. And some of the lab results should start to come in, too. That should give us a new set of questions to work with."

"I hate weekends," she grumbled.

"No you don't. Weekends are our friends. Weekends keep us from going up in flames. Weekends keep our marriages from going up in flames. Weekends keep—"

"Right, okay, say no more, I'm off, and the world can just deal with its own problems. See you Monday."

"Have a great time. Bring me a seashell. And do not

think about the case. That's an order."

"Yes, boss," she said. She slapped her things together, looked around as if she'd forgotten something, and strode out the door. In ten seconds, her head was back in the room.

"Um, Al? Lee will probably insist that I leave my cell phone home. But we'll have hers with us. You do know that number, don't you?"

NINETEEN

At a quite ridiculously early hour on Saturday morning, Kate came awake, thinking of buff paper.

After staring up at the darkness for the better part of half an hour, she gave up on sleep, grabbing whatever clothes she could lay hands on without opening drawers and tiptoeing downstairs with them. She put on yesterday's garments in the living room, lit only by the streetlight down the block, let herself silently out of the house, and drove away. She stopped to buy a takeaway latte and a large bag of pastries from an early-hours bakery, and in the absence of legal parking, pulled across a driveway down the street from the Gilbert house, leaving a note with her cell phone number displayed under the wiper blade.

The house was still, the air dead and damp after two weeks of emptiness. She went upstairs to the third floor, set her cup on Gilbert's desk, and pulled the used ream of buff paper from the shelf under the printer. She sat in

the chair across from Gilbert's—she was now convinced that he had not died there, but still—and began
to count.

Her cup was empty and her fingers weary by the time
she reached 274. She made a note of the number,
opened the drawer of the printer and removed the buff
pages still in there, and counted them as well. She
added those 22 pages to the other, subtracted the resul-
tant 296 from the original 1,000 sheets making up two
reams of paper, came up with 704 sheets, printed off
between the purchase of the paper Friday morning and
Gilbert's death. She laboriously divided those sheets by
118, the number of pages of the short story. Four pages
short of six complete copies of the story, which, considering that a ream was not necessarily an exact count
and her fingers might have missed a page or two,
sounded pretty close to her.

So, if Gilbert had made six copies of the story, what
had he done with them?

She consulted the file she had brought with her, found
the combination to the safe, and looked inside: The
ledger in the bluish folder had been entered into evidence, but the rest of the safe's contents had been
checked and left where they were. And as she thought,
one upright folder held 118 pages of buff paper. In addition, three of the mailing envelopes lying flat on the
safe's floor held the story, addressed and ready for
sending. One would go to Jeannine Cartfield, which
Kate found interesting—why not Rutland? Or was the
loose file copy for him? The other two envelopes bore

names familiar to her from Nicholson's list of expert Sherlockians, Peter Blau in Maryland, and Les Klinger in Los Angeles. She'd spoken with both men: Blau had not been in touch with Gilbert since November, when they had spoken about a rather beaten-up copy of a Conan Doyle novel that might or might not have the author's signature, and Klinger had exchanged a series of e-mails with Gilbert in January regarding corrections to a book he was putting the final touches on, two volumes of annotations on the Sherlock Holmes stories. Both men had asked if she knew anything about a recently discovered short story.

Four copies here, one already given to Nicholson, although not noted on the ledger: Where was the last? Hawkin had proposed a scenario of theft and violent confrontation: Perhaps Gilbert had, after all, been killed right here. Not with the falcon statue, as it turned out, but with some other blunt object, his head bound up before it could bleed, the story snatched up by his murderer . . . for what purpose?

They had thought that the statue was missing, and based a scenario on that, only to have it crumble with a phone call from Goode's Porcelain Repair. But what was she to make of the other missing objects: a seldom-used cell phone and a copy of the manuscript? Oh yes, and his pocket watch on a chain.

But the dump site was the key. Someone knew where to leave Gilbert's body, someone who had seen the story. Nicholson was the obvious suspect for that, but Nicholson had left town on Saturday morning, and the Point Bonita Park ranger had considered it highly unlikely that the shattered padlock and the body behind it would have been simply overlooked on that sunny day. And Nicholson had indeed been on the road—a detailed receipt from his motel confirmed that he had checked in just before six o'clock (which was right, for having left San Francisco near noon and stopping for the meal he'd charged to his card in Red Bluff, along the way). Furthermore, he had logged on to the motel's high-speed Internet connection for an hour and twelve minutes beginning at eleven-forty that night, then checked out the following morning well before seven, having eaten breakfast at the motel's buffet. He had stopped briefly at his cousin's house in Eugene on the way north, midday on Sunday, before arriving at his friends' house in Seattle at the end of a long day.

There could have been a conspiracy, of course, among Gilbert's acquaintances—one to murder, one to dump—but evidence supporting that had yet to appear, and in Kate's experience, such organizational tendencies among amateurs were unlikely.

Which left her with a Mr. X. Someone who had been in the house when Gilbert was lounging in his pajamas, someone who had seen the story (either that night or previously) and grabbed at the chance of duplicating the body dump.

Too complicated. Much more likely to have been Mrs. Murray's parolee brother, losing his temper at the parking situation.

But how would he have known where to take the body?

Circular thinking led nowhere. Kate retrieved her empty cup, closed up the safe and the house, and took the bag of scones and muffins home for her family's breakfast. At a more reasonable hour, with the sounds of suitcase packing and calling voices all around her, she phoned Hawkin.

"Al, we really need to meet with Tom Rutland."

"Okay. Any particular reason?"

"Basically, I just don't trust helpful attorneys."

"Reason enough for me."

"No, I was thinking. I can't remember the exact details of Gilbert's will, and if I went to the Detail to check on them, Lee would divorce me, but as I recall, Rutland's authority as executor of the estate is pretty much absolute. He can set up a museum and hire a curator, or he can dispose of what there is and buy other things—in other words, he controls the entire Gilbert estate, manuscript, *Beeton's Annual*, Sherlock Holmes teapot, and the lot."

"Mm." The sound was noncommittal, but Kate took it as a sound of meditation, not disagreement.

"I was also thinking, Rutland is someone you might expect Gilbert to have shown the story to early on—not only his lawyer, but a fellow Sherlockian, a person who would immediately recognize the value of the manuscript, both in monetary terms and in the fame that would come with it. We know Gilbert talked to Rutland on Friday morning, although Rutland says it was to see if he would be free for a meeting the next week. Then Gilbert went out and bought the materials for making copies of the story. What if he gave Rutland a copy the following day, just didn't mention that he'd given one to Nicholson as well?"

"Are you suggesting that Rutland intended to steal the manuscript outright?"

"That's possible, I suppose." She hadn't thought the lawyer's motivation quite so blatant, but she tried to work her way into that potential scenario. "If he'd thought the original was in Gilbert's office safe, and if he believed Gilbert had told no one else about it, what was to stop him from claiming it as his own dis-covery?"

"But Gilbert had already been around, back in December, establishing the thing's provenance."

"Again, Rutland might not have known that. Or he could have intended to claim that Gilbert was doing it on his behalf. It would be Rutland's word against that of a dead man, concerning a million-dollar hunk of paper that nobody knew Gilbert had. It might have looked like a stack of cash just lying there waiting for him."

"But the original wasn't in the safe, it was in the bank," he pointed out, then asked, "When Nicholson revealed that he had the story at the dinner the other night, did Rutland show any reaction?"

"I wasn't there when Nicholson told them, although when reference was made to it, he seemed to handle that without discomfort. But then, Nicholson had told him earlier in the day that he needed a few minutes that night to make an announcement. Rutland might well have guessed what it was about, and been prepared."

"You have to wonder, if Rutland had the original in his hands and then Nicholson made that call, whether there might've been a second body in the battery."

"Third," Kate corrected without thinking.

"Martinelli—" Hawkin started, but Kate was already backtracking. "Yeah, yeah, I know, Jack Raynor was fictional. But if Rutland killed Nicholson to shut him up, he'd have to take care of the people who knew about Gilbert's purchase of the story as well, Magnolia Brook and Paul Kobata."

"Bodies right and left," he said, and Kate had to agree, it seemed unlikely. "But that brings up another point: Why leave Gilbert at the gun emplacement? If it was Rutland, you'd think the Berkeley hills would feel more natural."

"He and Gilbert might have been in Marin anyway."

"With Gilbert in his dressing gown? And Rutland a much-married man? Of course, with three sets of alimony, maybe he decided men would be cheaper," Hawkin grumbled, having had some experience with alimony himself.

"Or else his choice of location was directly tied to what I was saying earlier, that Rutland looked to become an eminent Holmes authority on the back of Gilbert's estate. Nothing would get that off to a bang like the publicity of Gilbert's body and the story. He'd launch straight into the morning shows."

"Sounds pretty calculating."

"It doesn't mean that he actually killed Gilbert. Maybe it was an accident after all—Gilbert hit his head and died, if not at home then somewhere else. The lawyer either found him, or someone called in a panic, and he had this brilliant idea of how to use Gilbert's death to his own benefit."

"Not premeditation, but very fast thinking?"

"He's not a criminal lawyer, but the man lives and breathes the most convoluted, far-fetched detective stories—some of it would surely have rubbed off on him."

"You could be right."

"So what do you think about an interview?"

"You want to know where I am?"

"Why? Where are you?"

"At my desk, in the Detail, with a copy of the Gilbert will in front of me."

"And . . . ?"

"And two minutes before you called, I left a message for Rutland, saying that we wanted to see him on Monday morning." When she did not respond, he continued, "My next phone calls are to double-check on that alibi he gave us."

"Al, sometimes I don't know whether to hate you or to love you."

"I am a force of nature, like Sherlock Holmes," he said placidly.

Kate made a rude noise into the receiver. "What time do you—hold on a second." Kate rested the phone against her thigh to muffle the sound and said to the small person in the doorway, "You guys ready?"

"Mamalee says two minutes and we're drivin' away without you, but I don't want to leave you here, I want you to come. You promised."

"I'll be there in one minute, sweetie. Have you used the potty?"

The green eyes rolled. "Of course. And Mamalee already asked me."

"Well, a girl can't pee too many times. Tell her just one minute. Sorry, Al," she said into the receiver, "I've got to go. Do you want me to call you tonight?"

"No, I want you to have a relaxing weekend. I'll make a date with Rutland for Monday, and see you Monday morning."

Implacable as Lee, Al Hawkin hung up on his partner, abandoning her to the affections of her family.

TWENTY

Kate parked at the Hall of Justice well before eight o'clock on Monday, invigorated not only by the chance of getting her teeth into Thomas Rutland, who had annoyed her since the moment she had laid eyes on him, but also (she had to admit) by two days spent in the salt air with her family, during which she'd had no more urgent puzzles on her hands than the species of the bird sitting at the other end of the binoculars from her and what kind of pancakes to order for breakfast. As if to underscore that a holiday from work was a necessary part of clear thinking, as she walked toward the building, she felt one of those small clicks of synthesis in the back of her mind, and stopped dead, allowing it to develop.

She had been mulling over the dinner party at Tony's, nine disparate individuals brought together by their interest in a fictional English detective, and idly holding that up beside the weekend she had just spent with Lee and Nora, where interests and commonalities seemed to spring from their very pores.

As her mind skimmed over that night, she thought of Ian Nicholson's charge against Gilbert, accusing him of *a casual abuse of friends*. Casual abuse happened all the time in a relationship; it might also be called *taking me for granted*. A weekend together, during which two people might rediscover themselves, was a necessary part of life, like air into the lungs.

It was then that another phrase floated into Kate's mind: *Philip hated to break character.*

And so she stopped walking, her head bent as she sought to trace that statement back to its source.

It had also been said at that dinner. And also by Nicholson.

Ian Nicholson had been making a passing comment on Gilbert's idiosyncrasies, more fond than critical. And although it was by no means technical language, it struck Kate now as slightly off, as a phrase not everyone would use. Lee, for example, might comment on the psychology of role playing; a cop's mind might chew on the similarity between Gilbert's act and that of a person hiding from the law, or at least from his past.

Break character was a thing an actor might say.

A friend mentioned they'd seen him in a restaurant somewhere, with an actor. . . .

Gilbert and an actor, six or seven years ago.

And at that same dinner, someone had asked Ian if he'd thought Philip was acting.

She trotted up the steps and through security, impatiently jabbing the elevator button. In the Detail, she shed her things on her desk and sat down in front of the computer without taking off her coat. Hawkin greeted her, and she nodded absently.

I should've thought about this on Friday, Kate berated herself. After I talked with Gilbert's ex-wife on Friday, the bells should have gone off. Of course, even if I'd known Friday, I couldn't have done anything, time zones and office hours being what they are. All I lost was being preoccupied for two days at Point Reyes, and driving Lee nuts.

Hawkin said something, but she copied down a phone number before looking up at him. "Sorry?"

"I said, we need to leave if we're going to catch Rutland today. He said he could give us half an hour, then he's in court all day."

"You go get the car, I'll meet you out in front."

He was waiting for her when she trotted down the front steps of the Hall, but he hadn't been there for long.

"What was that about?" he asked as he turned onto Mission.

"I had to hunt down Ian Nicholson's agent—ex-

483

agent, I guess, since Ian hasn't worked as an actor in years. The secretary said he might not be in until noon, New York time, but I gave her my cell number. If it rings, I'm going to leave you with Rutland and take it." She told him about the small leap her mind had taken, although as she described the link, it sounded considerably more tenuous than it had at the time. Almost apologetically, she ended by saying, "I just thought it was something we should look into."

"I agree," Hawkin said, and they left it at that.

THOMAS Rutland lived in Berkeley, but his office was a short walk from the Oakland courthouse, in the upper floors of one of the new downtown high-rises. Despite the location, his practice was predominantly financial, and the building and the office décor reflected the expectations of monied executives, particularly young ones. The receptionist was as sleek as the furniture, and ushered them into Rutland's office without delay. Probably, Rutland had not wished to advertise the presence of cops on the premises, and told her not to keep them waiting.

He got out from behind his desk to welcome them, shook hands, offered coffee, and at their refusal, settled them down and returned to his seat. He was wearing his lawyer's uniform today, brilliant white shirt, slightly daring necktie, and suspenders, his jacket, draped over the back of his chair, dead black with just the faintest hint of a pinstripe in the fabric. On the lapel was a tiny spot of blue: the 221B pin.

Kate and Al took their time sitting down, running their eyes over the view, the desk, the office. On the wall to the right of the desk were two framed pictures: one a lithograph that reminded Kate of those in Gilbert's house, this one showing a man seated at a desk, talking to another man standing in front of him; the other was a large color photograph of Rutland in a room that again reminded her of Gilbert's house. The lawyer was sitting in a chair, wearing a silk dressing gown, with a pipe in his hand and a violin held awkwardly across his lap: playing Holmes.

On the wall across from where he sat, next to the door, Rutland had hung a trio of photographs showing, in descending order: the lawyer in running shorts with a number on his chest, crossing the finish line with a pack of other runners of many colors; bent over the handlebars of a racing bicycle, spattered with mud; and emerging from the water in the midst of a crowd of other men, his eyes locked on some goal.

"You do triathlons?" she asked him.

He glanced at the photographs with just the right degree of modesty. "That's the Iron Man."

"Impressive," she said, and sat down.

"I don't have as much time to train as I used to," he answered. "Mostly now I just do half-marathons. So, what can I do for the San Francisco Police Department today?"

Hawkin said, "Can you tell us again what you were doing on the twenty-third and twenty-fourth of January?"

"The twentieth—wasn't that the weekend I went golfing in Palm Springs?"

"So you said."

"Well, I went down with some friends in their private plane. Wheels up out of Oakland at four, forty-eight hours in the sun, and we came back Sunday afternoon around five or six."

"And you didn't leave Palm Springs during that time?"

"Not at all. Inspector, it sounds to me like you're treating me like a suspect."

"A witness at this point, Mr. Rutland. But I will need the names of your friends and of the hotel where you stayed."

"We were in a private home." He began to bristle. "And I don't know that these are the kind of people I want bothered about this."

The kind of people, in other words, who wouldn't be pleased that their upstart friend was being investigated by the police.

"Still, we're going to need those names."

"I think I should consult with one of my colleagues before we go any further, Inspector."

"You really think that's necessary?" Hawkin asked. Without looking, Kate knew that he was raising one eyebrow, as if to say, Sir, I hadn't really considered you a suspect until just this moment.

"Before I give you those names, yes. Was there anything else you wanted?"

Kate's turn. She made a show out of opening the

notebook in her hand, flipping the pages, comparing two sheets of completely unrelated scrawl, and finally looking up. "Mr. Rutland, in October of the year 2000, complaint was filed with the California Bar Association by the family of Mrs. Eugenia Baxter, accusing you of having manipulated your client Mrs. Baxter into writing you a remarkably generous settlement in her last will and testament. Similarly, in April of 2002, the family of Rosemarie Upfield—"

"Those charges were dropped!" he snapped.

"True, although I could find no record of an actual investigation by—"

At that he slapped his hand on the desk and stood, so forcibly his chair crashed back into the wall behind him. "I think that's enough for today, Inspectors."

As if he had neither moved nor spoken, Kate said, "In regards to the Gilbert estate, I would like to know if your role as executor was Mr. Gilbert's idea, or something you suggested?"

"I want you to leave." His face was dark beneath the tan, his voice harsh.

"It just seems so convenient, you being there and ready to step into the position."

He snatched up the phone, knuckles so white he might have been about to use the receiver as a weapon rather than a means of summoning help. "Yvonne, call building security."

Hawkin turned to Kate and said, "I don't think Mr. Rutland wants to talk to us today."

"I get that impression, too," she agreed, and stood up.

They left the office riding on a wave of steam.

In the elevator on the way down, Hawkin said, "That was the most fun I've had all week."

Kate had to agree. "It also showed that not only does Mr. Rutland have a quick temper, but that he's almost as obsessed with the Sherlock Holmes thing as Gilbert was."

"And," Hawkin added complacently, "our triathlete has plenty of muscles to be hauling unconscious bodies around."

BACK in the office, Hawkin got on the phone to see what his many and varied contacts could tell him about Thomas Rutland, while Kate searched for the missing details on the life of Ian Nicholson and waited for the agent to call her back.

Ian Nicholson had been born in a western suburb of London in 1956. He came to the United States two weeks after his graduation from some English university Kate had never heard of, taking up residence with his deceased father's younger brother in New York.

Like so many before (and after) him, young Nicholson wanted to act. His degree had been in art history, but his heart lay on the stage. Very fortunately, his uncle proved not only a responsible caretaker, but an intelligent one, and although young Ian did indeed land the occasional acting job, his uncle also helped steer him into a job cataloguing old books and letters for a large antiques dealer. After a few years he was working full-time at one of the bigger auction houses; it appeared that he was set on his road.

However, the English lad with the interesting face did not want an auction house, he wanted the stage. After two years of full-time employment, in 1983 he quit the big-name house and joined another, smaller establishment that was pleased to employ him part-time, saving themselves the cost of insurance benefits while it allowed the young man to chase down acting jobs.

Unfortunately, the jobs didn't do much chasing back. At the time he packed up and moved to San Francisco, in 1999, he had not used his Equity card in nine and a half months.

Nicholson's ex-agent was a well-established figure, Saul Adler, who seemed to work with a younger partner and the secretary whose voice came on the phone at a quarter to noon, asking Kate to hold for Mr. Adler. Adler's voice evoked a vivid image of well-chewed cigars, a straining waistband, and the Bowery. Kate figured that he was probably a svelte vegetarian born in the Midwest, but in any case, he knew Ian Nicholson.

"Ian? Sure, he was with me for years. Far as I know, he's not working anymore."

"That's what I understand. Can you tell me why he quit?"

"Came into a little money, inheritance or insurance, don't remember exactly. Not that money would have made any difference if he'd really wanted to stay, but Ian was, what, forty-two, -three? Hadn't worked in months—my kinda work, I mean, he had another job somewhere, selling antiques or something—and the money just let him admit it wasn't gonna happen for him."

"Not much of an actor, then?"

"Actually, the kid wasn't bad, and he could play British or American, but Casting had a real problem with his face. He was made for supporting roles in a romantic comedy, and I could've built him a solid career, but he wanted drama, and he wanted the lead. I just couldn't sell his face, especially after he hit forty—not handsome, not ugly enough to be a type, too distinctive to fade into the crowd. Add to that the problem with flying—you know about that?"

"He told me, yes."

"Something to do with being locked up when he was a kid, I think. In an icebox or something, his wife talked about it once, just a little, to shut me up grousing about having to turn down a part. Anyway, it pretty much left out every job more than a couple hundred miles away. That was the capper. Ian thought about moving to LA and taking up television, but even then he'd have had to turn down anything on location."

"Was he badly disappointed?"

"Nah, he'd heard it coming. Bright guy, you know?"

"A lot of changes all at once, though."

"Changes? You mean the move?"

"I was thinking about the divorce."

The noise that came down the phone line sounded as if the agent had swallowed his cigar stub, but when he kept talking, Kate figured it had been a laugh. "The divorce wouldn't have troubled Ian. Wasn't really a marriage in the first place. They were friends, sure, but she needed a man to show her nice Catholic family, he needed insurance—health insurance, you know? Her job gave him Blue Cross, and in exchange he showed up at Christmas and stuff."

"A show marriage, then?" Kate's spine began to tingle, as it did when a suspect's eyes suddenly dodged to one side during questioning.

"I don't know if that's fair," Adler replied. "It was at first, but he and Christy, they were fond of each other, you know? They never lived together, but he moved to the same building, right next door, so he saw a lot of the kid."

"The kid?" The tingle grew.

"Daughter, what was her name? Cute little thing, I could've found her a ton of kid roles if they'd let me, but Ian put his foot down. Monica, that's it. Monica the Moneymaker, I called her once. Those blond curls—man."

"Blond. And blue eyes?"

"Like the Caribbean."

Or like the water at Cabo San Lucas?

"Where does she live, do you know?"

"Probably LA. I saw her not too long ago, a small part on a daytime soap. She'll get more, I'd be willing to bet—twenty-two or -three now, and God, she's a stunner."

"So she's an actor, too?"

"She was then. You want to talk to her mother about it? I've got a number for her somewhere."

"That would be great."

He was of the generation that might have dropped the phone on the desk to flip through a Rolodex, but it being 2004, he was talking into a headset and retrieving information from a PDA. However, habits die hard, and he muttered and cursed under his breath as if the receiver were lying on the desk instead of hovering two inches from his mouth. "Where'd I put the damn thing? Christy, Christy, what the hell's her last name—ah, gotcha, baby." Then, in full voice, he said, "You still there?"

"Still here."

"Here you go then, she's Christy Bennington now, used to be LaValle." He read out a number; Kate wrote it down.

"Her daughter, Monica. Is her last name Bennington, too, or Nicholson?"

"Not Bennington, that's the guy Christy married after Ian. Accountant? Stockbroker? He's in money, anyway. I think the girl kept LaValle. Sounds better than Monica Nicholson."

And in the acting world, sound and looks were all. "Thank you, Mr. Adler."

"You see Ian, tell him Saul said he shouldn't be a stranger."

"I'll do so."

Next up was Christy Bennington, formerly Nicholson, née LaValle. She answered the phone full-voiced with a chorus of dogs in the not-too-distant background.

"I told you I can't come out, I wish to hell you wouldn't do this, Lizzie."

"Um, Mrs. Bennington?"

Silence, but for yips and howls.

"I'm looking for Christy Bennington?"

The phone gave a rustling noise, but even with being muffled against the woman's body, Kate jerked away from the earpiece at the bellowed "SHUT UP!"

The command took effect instantly, and the woman's voice said, considerably lower in both tone and volume, "Sorry. Who is this?"

Kate identified herself, explained that she was attempting to get some background information on a witness, one Ian Nicholson.

"Ian? What's he got himself involved in now?"

"Is he often 'involved' in things?" Kate asked.

"Oh, you know Ian," the woman said with a laugh.

"No, I don't, actually. I've barely met him."

"Oh, of course. Well, I didn't mean anything. Just that, when I knew him, he was forever coming up with The Great Scheme."

"Illegal?"

"No," she said sharply, but then modified it to, "Well, one or two of them I sort of wondered about, they might have been in grayish areas. But I used to tell him that he'd find himself in a jam one day, when he sank all his money into a one-of-a-kind letter that turned out to be a forgery or something."

"His 'great schemes' generally had to do with manuscripts, his job in the auction house?"

"I suppose it was his way of keeping up his interest in what could be a pretty boring sort of job," she said, which Kate took as a yes. "He'd probably have made a fortune in it if he hadn't been so scrupulously honest. You can't believe what he'd get offered to slant his appraisals."

"But he wasn't willing to do that?"

"I used to tease him about being a coward, that he could retire if he was willing to risk a little jail. But he wasn't."

Nice to know the threat of incarceration worked some of the time.

"Mrs. Bennington, I need to ask you about the nature of your marriage to Ian Nicholson."

" 'Nature,' " she repeated, although Kate could hear that she knew quite well what Kate was asking.

"I've been told that your marriage was essentially one of convenience."

"Yeah, I guess you could say that. At one time, I had my hopes, but as it turned out, Ian just wasn't wired that way. I was young enough to take it personally for a while, but fortunately I grew up. And as it turned out, it was really for the best: I don't think he and Monica would have been as close as they became if we'd been your basic nuclear family."

"So Ian is gay?"

"He practically invented the word. He keeps it under wraps, or did when I knew him, so he didn't get type-cast when it came to acting jobs, but yes, he's definitely gay."

"Monica isn't his daughter?"

"Hardly. She wasn't yet one when they met, though, and Ian's the only father she's known."

"Do they see a lot of each other?"

"From time to time. She's very busy—she's an actress, she's just read for a role in a CBS movie—and he doesn't fly, but when she has the weekend off or something, sometimes they'll meet halfway. He and I bought her a car together last year."

"A yellow Volkswagen bug?"

"Yes, that's the one. Isn't it adorable?"

"Very. Mrs. Bennington, could I have your daughter's phone number, please?"

"You need to talk to her, too? This thing that Ian's . . . that you think Ian may be caught up in, is it serious?" She sounded nearly as apprehensive about her ex-husband's involvement as she did her daughter's.

"I really can't talk about it, Mrs. Bennington. He's just a witness, but you know how things are these days, we have to dot every i and cross every t."

"Sure," she said dubiously, and recited her daughter's number.

"And Mrs. Bennington? I'd appreciate it if you wouldn't call either Ian or Monica about this for a day or two. It's mostly a matter of checking testimony, but it might really confuse matters if you talk to them about it first. Okay?"

"I guess."

"Just for a day or so," Kate repeated, thanked her, and hung up. She looked at the daughter's phone number, but instead of dialing it, she stood up and went to find some coffee. When she got back, she ignored the piece of paper and logged on to the Internet, hunting down the website for an aspiring young actress.

The studio portrait on Monica LaValle's web page showed the same lively blond woman on Ian Nicholson's wall. Kate stared at the photo until it went out of focus.

She had seen him kiss the young woman's fingers: Nicholson had taken Monica LaValle's hand, kissed it, let it go.

Kate had read the gesture as a lover's farewell, and built her perception of Nicholson to include a girlfriend half his age. Running the memory through her mind's eye, she had to say, if she hadn't just been told by two people that he was gay, she'd have been inclined to think that Nicholson and his stepdaughter had made a radical and decidedly creepy change to their relationship once Monica hit maturity and the West Coast. A Woody Allen thing.

However. Could that kiss have been the considerably more casual gesture of, say, a loving dad? Could that pressing of lips to fingers have been a salute of self-mocking formality, an affectionate farewell to a loved adult daughter? One who, moreover, shared the older man's profession of actor?

Yes: Don't forget that. Nicholson had been an actor before his unsaleably distinctive romantic-comedy face condemned him to obscurity. And although Kate had not known too many actors, she had met enough to doubt that any person once consumed by the life would ever fully give up the habits.

Ian Nicholson had once been an actor: "not a bad actor," according to his jaded agent.

Which brought up the question, Was he one still? Did that gesture encompass both things at once, both real and affectation?

Remember, too: Kate's presence on that street at that precise time had been expected, might one even say *orchestrated?* She had come around the corner in time to see Nicholson and the young blond woman standing outside the girl's car. He had casually reached across her to open the door; she had gotten in; he had picked up the hand resting on the open window and . . .

A performance, for Kate's benefit? She'd felt something of that at the time, only she had thought the intent of Nicholson's act was that of a middle-aged man demonstrating his virility behind a gesture of surface innocence—kissing the girl's fingers as if to say that he had no need for a more blatant display of manhood.

What if what Kate had been shown was meticulously choreographed to demonstrate the precise reverse: innocence concealed behind a gesture of middle-aged wolfishness?

No—not innocence. Because *if* Nicholson actually had been putting on an act that afternoon, *if* he had deliberately presented the approaching cop with the image of Monica-as-girlfriend, then there was a reason for the deception.

She knew now that he was gay, a fact she had not possessed at the time.

And for the past five years, Nicholson had lived in close proximity—physically, professionally, and socially—to a man whose death Kate was investigating. A man, furthermore, whose own sexuality had been called into question by his friends.

Her hand hovered over the telephone, stayed by another consideration.

Question: Had Monica been an innocent player in that deftly acted scene, or had she been in on it?

Kate thought about it: the mild surprise on the girl's face when Nicholson had turned and opened the Volkswagen's door; a playful trill of the fingertips as she accelerated away.

Either Monica LaValle was a twenty-three-year-old Judi Dench, or it had been no act.

Kate glanced at her watch, wondered if one in the afternoon was a good or a bad time to reach a young actress, and decided there was only one way to find out.

It was a cell number, and the young woman answered with the professional tones of a person who might be talking to a casting director unawares: half breezy, half throaty. "You've reached Monica."

Kate identified herself in the dullest possible terms— as a cop, yes, but in bored tones and with a flat recitation that she was confirming the statement of a Mr. Ian Nichols that his daughter Monica Lavel was in San Francisco in the middle portion of January 2004 and could she confirm that statement?

"Er, no," the girl said. "I mean, if you've, like, got our names right. He's Nicholson, not Nichols, and my name's LaValle, but I wasn't in San Francisco the middle of last month, just last week. What's this about?"

"I am not at liberty to say," Kate rattled off. "Questions should be addressed to the investigating officer, Inspector Alex Hawkin." Al's name was Alonzo, but using a slightly wrong name was the way they alerted each other to the need for extra care. Kate's name in such instances was Kayla. She stepped away from the bored-clerk voice and asked, "Um, wait a minute. Could I have the dates you were here? Some of these guys couldn't type numbers if their lives depended on it."

"I drove up Monday night, had a filming Tuesday morning, and came back to LA on Wednesday afternoon. I don't think I was up there at all in January."

"Tuesday the third and Wednesday the fourth of February," Kate repeated.

"That's right."

"That explains it. It says here 'Tuesday and Wednesday, three and fourteen,' with just the numbers, you know? January three and four were a weekend, and thirteen and fourteen February isn't until next week, so I thought it might be thirteen and fourteen January. The typist just screwed up. Hope the weather was decent for you."

"It was awesome. I even got a little sunburn, driving back with the top down."

"Better here now than it is in July," Kate commented. "So Ian Nichols—sorry, Ian Nicholson—is your father?"

"That's right. Well, originally my stepfather, if you want to get technical, but he's my dad now."

"Okay, well, if we need anything else we'll call, thanks." Kate broke the connection before the young woman could turn any questions on her.

When Al Hawkin walked into the homicide room five minutes later, he stopped dead at the look on Kate's face.

"Either you ate something that really didn't agree with you or you don't like where this is going."

She did, she realized, feel more than a little queasy, but the problem was with the information she was working to digest, not the lunch she had eaten. "Al," she said grimly, "we have to talk with Ian Nicholson."

TWENTY-ONE

The first hitch to a clean interrogation of Nicholson as a suspect came at his door. Kate stared through the reinforced glass of the entrance foyer, then bent her head to the speaker again, putting on a voice of one Sherlockian to another. "Ian, please. We need to talk with you."

"You don't want to talk with me, you want to arrest me," his voice said from the speaker. "I can see the uniformed people you've brought with you."

"Ian, remember, I knew the security cameras would

show you the uniforms. I came here openly, to talk to you."

The speaker was silent. Kate looked at Al, then at Chris Williams, who had asked to be in on the arrest; by the looks of him, he'd been up all night reading their reports. "Ian?" she repeated.

The two uniforms shifted uneasily, eyeing the glass as if measuring it for resistance to their rams. "Please, Ian, you're an intelligent man, you can see we're not going to just go away. Let us in and we'll talk."

"Okay," said the speaker, and even through the tinny reception they could hear the grim resignation in his voice. Five cops unclenched their hands—prematurely, as it turned out. "I'll talk to you, and you alone."

"I can't do that, Ian."

"Sure you can. You come in here alone, we'll talk about what you have against me and what we can do about it, or else I get on the phone to my lawyer and you get nothing from me, absolutely nothing."

Kate let go of the speaker button and put her back to the eye of the security camera. She looked at Hawkin. "What do you think?"

"Bad idea."

"Hard to justify breaking the door down."

"He killed a man."

"This is not a violent offender, Al," she argued. "He bashed Gilbert on the head in what will probably turn out to be a lover's quarrel, and when Gilbert died he got rid of the body. He'll serve me coffee and talk and start crying and I'll politely cuff him. He's not about

501

to suddenly turn nasty in my face."

Williams volunteered his two cents' worth. "I haven't met the guy, of course, but from everything I read, he sounds pretty reasonable."

"I want to talk with him, Al, and if this is the format that makes him comfortable, let's take it as the first step."

He looked from her to the camera, and his hand came up to rub his mouth as if in thought. Through his fingers, he said, "If he tells you to leave your gun outside, you come out again. And you keep your phone on while you're in there."

"Will do," she said, and reached for the intercom button.

"Ian, my partners here don't much care for it, but they've agreed to let me come in and talk to you for just a little while. You want to buzz me in?"

"Have the others stand back."

Making the others stand back was no guarantee that they wouldn't rush the door before it closed, but Kate took the command as an encouraging sign of Nicholson's lack of criminal sophistication. She waited until the others had retreated, and when the buzzer sounded, she opened the door and stepped through.

The moment she was out of sight of the security cameras, Kate pulled out her phone, pushed the automatic dial for Al's number, muted the sound reception, and dropped it into her jacket pocket. It would be muffled, but loud voices would get through, and loud voices would be what Al would need to hear anyway.

The courtyard fountain was on, with no birds today, and dark with the slant of the afternoon sun. Somewhere in the complex music played. The door to Nicholson's apartment was standing open, but there was no sign of the man himself. Inside the door, Kate stopped and called, "Ian? You want me to shut the door?"

"Oh, just leave it open. If those brutes you have with you need to break it down, it'll cost me a fortune to replace the lock."

"Whatever you want. I'll come upstairs, shall I?"

"The coffee's on."

She walked up the stairs, conscious of cool air flowing all around her. The fire was going, she saw when she reached the sitting area—a real fireplace, with wood, a necessary counterpart to the wide-open windows that explained the breeze along the stairs. He was in the kitchen, wearing an oversized sweater with a lot of cables running up and down the front of it, and she moved in his direction, hands openly displayed but not formally up in the air: Keep it casual.

"Thanks for seeing me, Ian," she said easily. "I know you're concerned about out intents here, but this really is for the—"

The phrase strangled in her throat and the world shuddered into something slow and eerily focused: Nicholson's hand came up above the dividing wall with a gun in it. She'd had a gun pointed at her before, but it got no easier with repetition. The cool air went icy, and the sweat started under her arms and in her hair. "Ian," she said, in a voice that would have sounded loud even if she hadn't been trying to make it so, "you don't want to be holding a gun on me."

Small comfort, knowing that Al would have heard her words, that all the machinery of police support would begin to move in about five seconds. The gun was a .38, but it seemed the size of a cannon, and held steady. She thought of Nora, and Lee, and then she shoved away fear and love and everything but necessity, and became a cop again.

"I'm really sorry about this, Kate," he said; she would have sworn he meant it, too.

"Ian, put that down and we can talk."

"I'm going to have to ask you to lay your gun on the desk and go sit on the chair in front of the fireplace," he told her.

"I can't do that, Ian."

"Kate, please?"

For some reason, the plea brought her up in a way that threats would not have done. She made an effort to look past the rock-steady length of steel to his face, that interesting and unsaleable face of his. His expression, she finally noticed, was apologetic rather than aggressive, a touch nervous but very far from panic. Kate's anxiety retreated a fraction: Twitchy nerves were even worse than open rage when it came to pressure on a trigger.

Nicholson could be talked down, she decided. He'd used her name; he wasn't standing with the gun in her back gibbering about making a break for it; he wanted to talk. If she could remind him that he was a reasonable man, he would eventually put the gun down. If, on the other hand, she refused to disarm, or tried to leave without talking to him, his finger might well tighten on the trigger. She put her own note of apology into her voice, and held up her hands in a sort of shrug.

"Ian, I really can't just take off my gun. There are regulations, you know? The worst thing in the world is for a cop to lose her weapon and have it turned against her."

"I don't need your gun, I already have one," he pointed out.

"Still."

After a moment's thought he asked, "What if you tossed it out of the window?"

Kate was encouraged at his attempt at being reasonable. "And let some neighborhood kid find it?"

"Call your partner. You can drop it to him." When she hesitated still, he added, "I would like to talk, and I want to do it here. Honestly, I don't want to hurt you."

Not wanting to indicated that he *would* hurt her, if he believed it necessary. She would have to trust Hawkin, and her own instincts, to get her out of this. "Okay, Ian, I'm going to reach for my gun. I'll keep my fingers open so you don't have to worry that I'm about to use it. And I'll empty out the bullets and then drop the gun out the window. But I'm going to need to use your phone to call my partner—my little girl was playing with my cell phone the other day, and I think she decided it needed a bath." Use his name often; provide him with humanizing details about his hostage; remind him that she was a friend, and on his side; above all, stay calm.

He nodded at the portable phone on the desk. She dialed Al's number, and was kicked into his voice mail, since his line was still open to hers. She spoke as if he was on the line, careful to add the appropriate pauses, but loudly enough for him to hear through the phone in her pocket. "Al? Yeah, this is Kate. Look, I need you to walk around the apartment building and stand under Ian's window so I can drop something down to you. Well, it seems he's not happy about having my gun in the place, so I'm going to give it to you for safekeeping. Al, don't worry, it'll be fine, just come around to the window." She paused for a moment as if listening, pursed her mouth in impatience, and snapped, "Al, just do it." She punched the phone's off button, and then, facing Nicholson, pulled open her jacket to show him the gun in its shoulder holster.

"I'm going to pull it out with two fingers. Now, I have to use both hands to take out the clip, but I'm leaving the safety on, can you see? Okay, there's the clip, we'll set it right here, and I'll just ease out the loose round, and we'll set that right next to the clip. There: empty."

On either side of the big plate-glass windows were smaller louver windows, unscreened and cranked open full, the cold winter air pouring in. With the gun dangling from her left hand, she stood staring down at a remarkably empty street (the police barricades having been set up out of sight from the Nicholson apartment) until Al came around the corner. He stopped on the sidewalk ten feet below her feet, his face unreadable—as if she'd need to see his face to know what he was thinking. She threaded the gun between the tilted glass panes, let Al position himself underneath it, and let it go. They held each other's eyes, an entire conversation in a moment, then Al turned and walked away. Kate looked at Nicholson.

"You can sit down now," he said. When she was in the chair, he came around the divider from the kitchen, his eyes and the weapon off Kate for perhaps half a second. She did not move, just waited until he was sitting in the sofa twelve feet away.

"I'm afraid with this gun business you're going to be in trouble now, Ian," she told him.

"And I wasn't in trouble before?" he countered, summoning a wry grin.

"Not as much, no."

"You're telling me you didn't come here with all those others to arrest me for Philip's murder?"

"Ian, your friend Philip died of a heart attack. It's not going to come to a murder charge."

"Do you honestly expect me to believe that you regard his death as from natural causes?"

"It's not quite that simple, of course it isn't. But it's a far cry from first-degree murder."

"What would be the charge?"

"Manslaughter, maybe. The Parks Service may charge you with illegal disposal of a body. Admittedly, that's a step up from littering."

He was not distracted by her attempt at humor. "Those still sound like felonies and jail time."

Obviously it's jail time, you idiot, she thought—for Christ's sake, you've pulled a gun on a cop. But she didn't say that, just continued to treat the whole thing like an unfortunate misunderstanding that might go away if they demurely cast their eyes in the other direction. For some reason he was thinking of her as a friend: Play on that.

"I really don't know, Ian, the charges would be up to the DA. Look, why don't you just tell me what happened, we'll see how we can spin it for you."

Nicholson stared at the gun in his hand as if wondering how it had gotten there, and Kate braced herself. But in the end, he drew a slow breath, then suddenly seemed to relax, as if letting go—unfortunately, not of the weapon itself. He allowed it to rest on his knee, where at least it was pointing to one side, and for the first time Kate noticed that it was an old, rather beautiful wood-handled revolver. He studied the gun as if it held his past and his future in the grain of its handle, and gave a small noise that sounded remarkably like a chuckle. "'Spin it,'" he repeated. "As my daughter says, 'Sure, *that's* going to happen.' But look, Kate, before we open the doors and let in the tides of bureaucracy, I want you to know what happened. You, personally. It may be the last choice I have in this life. And I feel as though I owe it to Philip, poor bastard, to tell the story to a pair of sympathetic ears, before the notebooks and tape recorders take over."

"That's fine," Kate said, hating to interrupt but knowing that she had no choice, "but before we get started, do you mind if we just take care of reading you your rights?"

However, Nicholson had no objection, seemed rather to find the process of recitation and agreement amusing. Normally she would have had him sign a rights statement, but she decided not to push her luck. She hoped at least Al was listening in, if it came to witnessing this highly irregular interview in court. At the end, she sat back in the chair, settling with her hands crossed easily, erasing any trace of officialdom from her expression or her position.

"First off, you want to know if I killed Philip," Nicholson began. "Yes. Yes, I did."

"Where was he when he died?"

"Right here. I mean, almost exactly right here. He was sitting in that chair across from you, and I threw a bottle of champagne at him. It hit his head and knocked him out of the chair, and I went downstairs to get myself under control. When I came back into the room, he was still on the floor. He wasn't breathing."

"This was on the Friday night? January the twenty-third?"

"Yes, although by that time it would have been Saturday. I suppose you've figured out that we were lovers?"

"We put that together, yes."

"Philip was so . . . It was just bizarre, in this day and age, to be so absolutely paranoid about anyone 'finding out,' but that was Philip for you. It was . . . Well, to tell you the honest truth, I think he felt a responsibility not to be gay. Because his business, his life it seemed, lay in evoking Holmes. It was as if by publicly admitting that he was gay, it would be tantamount to saying that Holmes was gay as well. I know, it's nuts, but he used to get so irate at the suggestion that Holmes and Watson might be more than friends—" He broke off, and shrugged apologetically. "I'm sorry, Kate, you're not interested in any of that. Suffice it to say, Philip was adamant. So I never told anyone about us. We'd been together on and off for six years."

"Since you moved out here from New York."

"It started in New York, and he was one of the reasons I moved out here. Although I don't know if I should use the word 'together,' since we barely were. Maybe five or six times a month he'd come over here, spend the night, leave early the next morning. A few times we went away, that was lovely, but generally it was here, and short."

"You didn't go to his house?"

"Not for sex. And even when I went there for business reasons, he was uncomfortable with it, would push me out as soon as we were through."

"So what happened on Friday the twenty-third?"

"It was that . . . that *fucking* manuscript," he burst out in despair. "God, I wish he'd never found the thing."

"The Sherlock Holmes story." "*The Tale of Billy Birdsong*," a voice in the back of her mind suggested, but she did not let the stray thought register on her face.

"Yes. It was going to change his life. That's what he said: *'change my life.'* A thing like that, you can't imagine what it would do to a scholar: You present it, you offer analysis, you make a good pile of money off it, and then you spend every second of the rest of your life defending it. Defending *yourself,* against charges of fraud and hoax, rolled eyes and patronizing words and claims of fanaticism and mental imbalance. Madness, to even contemplate it. You know that Conan Doyle ended up hating Holmes for taking over his life? Well, Holmes would have taken over Philip's life every bit as completely. And of course it was the end of us, that was already clear to him."

"Because of the dinner he had that night."

"Louisa Brancusi." He spat out the name.

"You sound like you know her."

"I worked with her, briefly, in New York. God, she'd have ripped him apart, taken credit for the discovery or at least shifted it closer to home, set up one of her pet scholars as the expert. I can just see the catalogue copy now: 'Unprecedented Literary Discovery!' 'Conan Doyle's Lost Masterpiece!' The press would have been out for blood. Philip imagined he could handle Louisa. He didn't even understand that to her, an accusation that the thing was a hoax would be just another way of driving up the price."

"He was going to offer her auction house the manuscript to sell?"

"He might as well have delivered his balls on a platter."

"But surely he understood what the publicity would do?"

"To some degree. That's why he told me we'd have to stop. For a while, he said, while the spotlight was on."

"And you were angry when he told you that."

"I was furious. Partly that he'd even think of handing it to Louisa instead of me. You see, when he gave me the story to read, I thought he was telling me that this was a project we could work on together. A partnership, with me taking care of the commercial and analytical side. But his attitude was, Louisa has all the machinery for publicity already at her disposal—that was his phrase, 'the machinery for publicity.' Probably her phrase, come to think of it. He said that we'd have to break off 'for a little while,' because he'd be under public scrutiny and needed to keep everything simple and aboveboard. Jesus. As if anything of Philip's life would remain his own once the story came out.

"But I think what really tipped me over the edge was the way he did it. He had the dinner with Louisa, he came here with a bottle of champagne—Taittinger, no less. We drank a couple of glasses and went to bed, and afterward he said he wanted to talk. So while he was showering, I made up a fire, he came up in the dressing gown I gave him for Christmas and a towel around his neck. He poured out the last of the champagne, and then he announced that would be our last night. *For a little while.* It was just such an absolutely, barefaced . . . *shitty* way to do it. Bring the bubbly, bang the boy, and then oh by the way, it's been real, ta. Fuck him. I was so pissed I picked up the bottle and just threw it at him, marched downstairs and stuffed his slippers and pipe and hairbrushes and crap into a pillowcase. When I came back to give it to him, there he was on the floor, going cold." The shock of the discovery was still vivid in his voice.

"How long were you downstairs?"

"Maybe half an hour, forty-five minutes. I get weepy with champagne," he admitted. "Always have. And I didn't want to come back upstairs with my eyes all red."

"So what did you do then, when you found him?"

"I was going to call 911, of course. Had my hand on the phone and the first two numbers dialed when it occurred to me that I'd killed him. I had, myself. Maybe if I'd known it was actually a heart attack I'd have dialed the third number, but I looked at him oozing into the rug and I knew how it would look. Lovers' quarrel, heavy bottle—the damned thing didn't even break."

"So you put him in your car?"

"Not right away. I sat looking at him and my brain just seemed to take over. It was like, all those years of reading the Holmes stories, that gear was right there, waiting for me to shift into. I knew I had to get him away, and it came to me that I could make it look like something from that damn story. I don't know— Looking back I see it was crazy, but somehow that story was responsible for his death, and I wanted to rub its nose in it. And maybe . . . maybe it was that I wanted to do one last thing for Philip. To make him the centerpiece of his very own mystery." He shot Kate a glance and then looked away, saying in a low voice, "That probably makes no sense to you."

"No, it does," she lied. *Keep him talking.* "So, you'd read the story that day, Friday, and not Saturday night in your motel as you said before?"

"That's right. Philip came by around noon on Friday and gave it to me, said he hoped I could read it before he came back that night."

"But you wanted us to think he was alive on Saturday morning."

"Right."

"I understand. So anyway, there he was, lying on the floor. What did you do then?"

He frowned. "I think it started because of evidence. You know, hairs and DNA and all that. I remember thinking how convenient it was that he'd just picked up his dressing gown from the cleaner's and was wearing a pair of pajamas I'd just laundered. So when I got a couple of clean bedsheets and wrapped him in them, it was rational, or anyway as rational as I was just then. I stripped the bed and put the sheets into the washer, and stuck the glass he'd used into the dishwasher and turned it on, but by the time I got out the vacuum cleaner it sort of changed, as if I had found something sticky and disgusting on my hands and couldn't get it off fast enough. It was like a panic of revulsion, this mad need to erase every trace of Philip from my life and my house. I wanted him gone, all memory, all traces."

"But Philip himself was still here?" Kate asked,

thinking: *Vacuum cleaner; maybe he forgot the bag: have to tell Crime Scene.*

"Bundled into a pair of clean white sheets. But not in here—I'd carried him to the downstairs hallway. Come to think of it, it was the same place I stick a sack of garbage on its way out to the bin."

It looked as if he was about to weep, so Kate broke in with a distracting piece of practicality. Which incidentally might explain some evidence. "You must have wrapped his head in something, so it didn't bleed through to the floor. A towel, maybe?"

"Only the one he'd had around his neck. It was already sort of bunched up under his head when he fell, so I just tucked it in a little, more to hide the blood in his hair than anything else. He didn't bleed very much at all. Then I wrapped him in the sheets and carried him downstairs."

"Wasn't he heavy?"

"Sure. But no heavier than what I dead-lift at the gym."

"What time did you finish cleaning?"

"I don't know, it was such a frenzy. At least one o'clock, maybe closer to two. I just stopped, utterly exhausted, with the disinfectant spray in my hand."

"And then you took him out to the car?"

"No. I was afraid one of my neighbors might have been coming home late and would see me staggering around under a body, or catch sight of me on their security monitor—there's no recording made of that, in case you're wondering—so I left him downstairs and took

515

his car back to his house. I wore gloves. And a ski hat, which felt dumb but I didn't want anyone to recognize me. I parked his car in a spot down the street from his house, and let myself in. I knew his alarm code, since I'd been standing right behind him a couple of times when he opened his door."

"You also know where the switch to the webcam is."

"The—? Oh right, the HolmesCam. I remembered it just before I stepped out of the foyer. I didn't know if anyone would be able to see my legs in the dark, or if they could identify me by my shoes or something, but I thought it was better not to take the chance."

"You spent twelve minutes inside."

"Was that all? It seemed like forever. I needed to remove anything I could find that might be connected to me, although in the end, there was almost nothing of mine there. And then I saw his cell phone in his desk, and I thought maybe I could use that to lay a false trail, so I took it, along with a copy of the story he had in his desk. The gun is his, too," he added, looking down at where it lay on his knee. "He kept it in his bedside table."

"So you left the car there and walked back across town?"

"Took me forever, and I was scared to death the whole time that I'd get stopped and they'd find the gun. I took off the ski cap so I'd look all white and innocent, but I must have sweated a gallon of water. Anyway, I made it back without any problems, and found the place dark and silent, all my neighbors safe in bed. I rolled up my garage door and let up the boot—the trunk—and propped open the entrance door. Then I just carried Philip straight out through the courtyard and across the street and put him in the trunk. I did use some more towels then, in case the blood leaked through the sheets and stained the carpet in the boot, but there wasn't much by that time."

"So you drove across the bridge in the early hours of Saturday morning?"

"Oh, no. I left him in the car and went to bed. Well, not to bed; first I bundled everything up in plastic bags—his clothes, the rug he'd fallen on, the cleaning rags, his toothbrush—and put them in the backseat of the car. Then I sort of curled up for a while on the sofa. I may even have slept.

"At eight the next morning I got in my car and drove to Philip's neighborhood. I kept thinking of him, lying there behind me in the boot. I kept wanting to check on him, as if to see if he was comfortable or something. Anyway, I pulled into a fifteen-minute space in the next block from his house, and I made a call with his cell phone to my home machine, letting it run for a few minutes. As if we'd had a conversation, you see? I know there are records of what tower a call goes through, but I wasn't sure how accurate the positioning is, so I thought I'd better make it as near his house as I could. Then I came back here, slept for a couple more hours, and then sat just behind my curtains and watched the neighbors. They came and went a lot, since Saturday's the big shopping day, but about eleven there was a gap of nearly forty-five minutes when they were all either away or inside with their doors shut. As soon as I had my window when I could say, That's when Philip came to give me the story, with nobody able to contradict me, I left."

"With him still in the trunk."

"Unfortunately."

"But you didn't drop him then, either?"

"A sunny Saturday in Point Bonita? Never. I drove north, stopped at a motel at the far side of Lake Shasta, the Something Lodge"—Lakefront, Kate silently provided—"and checked in with a credit card, then turned around and drove back to Point Bonita."

"You had dinner first."

"I did, didn't I? I had to leave signs that I was there, too late to fit in a drive back to the Bay Area. Did you talk to the waitress?"

"Not yet."

"If so, ask her what I was doing. I did a very nice impression of a man wrapped up in the typescript he was reading. I'd hate to think my performance was wasted." He added it with a touch of his old spirit.

Not a bad actor, his agent had said.

"And as soon as you signed for the meal, you left."

"It was dark by then, and no one would notice my car gone from the car park."

"Interestingly enough, someone used your room's Internet connection while you were away." Kate watched him closely, since there existed still the possibility of conspiracy here, but instead, his face went boyish with a smile of delight.

"It actually worked, didn't it? Astonishing, considering my lack of skill on the computer, but a friend used to set hers to send an e-mail at a given time, and I figured that if it could do e-mail, it could do other things as well. I found the scheduler function and set it to download some enormous files, and, amazingly, it did. I take it you didn't look at how much actual web surfing the machine was doing?"

"Not yet," she admitted. "We would have eventually."

"And I could have told you I fell asleep for an hour and a quarter."

"But instead, you drove five hours south to Point Bonita."

"That's right."

"Did you go the ocean road, or through the tunnel?"

"I was afraid someone would hear me, so I went down the cliffs, and Christ, what I would have given for a full moon. It was absolutely black and I was scared shitless, certain I'd go over those cliffs. I'd been out there a couple of weeks earlier with Philip—no doubt he was looking into that story, although he didn't tell me that—and I knew all too well how high those cliffs are. It was starting to rain and I had to use the parking lights a few times when my nerves got too bad. But I made it, and broke open the lock—oh, I forgot to mention, I stopped at one of those enormous hardware stores off Highway Five and bought a pry bar, a pair of bolt cutters, and some other things, paying cash of course—and left him where the story said he should be left."

"It couldn't have been easy, moving him out of the car."

"It was a fucking nightmare. I opened the trunk and thought I was going to pass out. He smelled. Like a meat shop. And he'd gone all stiff, inside the trunk, so it took me forever just to haul him out without scraping him on the car and leaving behind evidence. I left the sheets and towels in the car, sort of peeled them back so they wouldn't drop anything from their outer surface onto him, and I put on gloves and a giant shirt and a knit hat that I'd bought earlier, so as not to leave my hairs or fingerprints on him. And then I pulled and yanked at him until I finally could get myself underneath him. I nearly dropped him then and there.

"I'd backed the car up to the emplacement, so I only had to move him about thirty feet, but I thought I'd rupture something by the time I finished. The only good part of it was that by the time I'd wrestled with him I was angry at him again, which helped.

"When I'd left him there, still all curled up like he'd been in the car, I put the padlock back on the door and hoped nobody would notice it for a while. I couldn't face going back up the cliffs, so I drove very, very slowly out past the houses and through the tunnel, with my lights off until I was on the main road. I made it back to Lake Shasta at about five in the morning. I tell you, a motel bed never felt so good. But I only allowed myself to sleep for an hour, so I could sign for breakfast and check out early. Sunday was an absolute hell of exhaustion. By the time I reached Seattle I was a wreck—I only got there by drinking gallons of coffee and driving with the windows wide open, singing loudly all the while. A truly macabre journey."

"What did you do with Philip's clothes, the sheets, all that?"

"The clothes I dropped in a Goodwill box. And one of the places I stopped for coffee on Sunday, in southern Oregon, had a Laundromat a few doors down. I dumped a whole bottle of stain remover and some bleach into the wash cycle, ran it on cold, then put the stuff in the dryer and fed in a lot of quarters and drove away. They were good sheets, and as far as I could see the stains were nearly gone—someone will have quietly helped themselves to the lot."

"What about the cell phone?"

"I smashed it underfoot, then fed its pieces into Puget Sound, along with the bolt cutters and the pry bar. And I even remembered to phone Philip a couple of times and send him an e-mail, as an innocent man would have done. It was eerie, hearing his voice on the answering machine."

"Which leaves you with the gun."

"Yes," he said with a sigh. "I know. Have I told you everything you want to know?"

"Philip's pocket watch?"

His face shifted, and all the sorrow that had been kept at bay by telling the story swept in. He swallowed, blinking to keep his gray-blue eyes from filling. "I . . .

Philip loved that watch. It had once belonged to one of Conan Doyle's sons, or so he was told. Anyway, I couldn't bear to smash it. It's in my top drawer, downstairs."

Which about covered it all. Except for one thing.

"You haven't told me about Monica."

The sorrow fled instantly from his face, replaced with raw fear; for the first time, the man with the gun looked as if, friendship or no, he might use it. "You leave her out of this. She had nothing to do with any of it."

"I didn't think she did. You did, however, make use of her visit to lead me astray. You wanted us to think she was a girlfriend."

After a minute, his body grew less taut, his hand allowed the gun to lower again. "I hesitated to do that. I didn't want to bring Monica into it in any fashion at all, but she happened to be in town filming a two-second bit on a television drama, and so she was convenient." He added modestly, "Improvisation was one of my stronger points in my days as an actor. But I promise you, she did not know anything."

"I believe you."

He studied Kate's face, and decided that she meant it. "So, was there anything else?" He was beginning to look cold, despite the sweater, but Kate did not want to distract him by suggesting that they close windows.

She cast her mind back, and came up with small and insignificant details. "You didn't use a wheelbarrow to move Gilbert to the emplacement?"

"A wheelbarrow? Good heavens no, how would I

have got it in the car? I slung him across my shoulders. It wasn't far, and as I said, I can dead-lift more than he weighed."

"So," she said, trying hard to conceal her apprehension behind a matter-of-fact question. "What now?"

"Now we go and meet your friends outside."

"Really?" she said, her voice coming far too near to a squeak of surprise for an eighteen-year police veteran.

"Sure. I think we're finished here, and I'm sure they're itching to take a look at my floorboards."

"They'll give you the warrant as soon as you're outside."

"No need for a warrant. You're welcome to look anywhere. Just please don't leave too much of a mess."

He stood up, and looked around as if to make sure he wasn't forgetting anything. "Shall we go? You first."

"Ian, leave the gun here. Please."

"I'll carry it with me to the door, thank you very much. Once we're out in the open, with witnesses, then I'll let you have it. I promise."

"You must give it to me then, Ian," she told him. "Cops really don't like it when a suspect walks out with a gun in his hand."

"I'll keep that in mind," he said. "Go on now."

Her spine crawled with tension, walking with a gun at her back, but he stayed too far behind her to give her an opening to seize it, and there were no distractions as they crossed the courtyard. The place was utterly still, even the earlier music now fallen silent; Kate knew that there would be a sniper and other officers out of sight throughout the apartments overlooking the courtyard. However, Nicholson took no notice, because the apartment complex was always still.

They reached the front door, the broad expanse of glass. Outside, silent as the courtyard, was an expanse of humanity: uniforms and plainclothes arrayed behind a sea of marked and unmarked departmental vehicles. In the distance, behind police tape, the inevitable pack of press. Al Hawkin stood in front of it all, out in the open next to Chris Williams. He was holding the phone to his ear with one hand, while the other rested on his gun. His weight was forward on his toes, ready for the approach he had heard coming.

Ian hesitated, stared out at the crowd. Kate measured the distance to his gun, but as if he had heard her, he shifted it. "God bless me," he said. "Where did they all come from?"

"I told you, cops really don't like it when you draw a gun on one of them. Al has been listening to us this whole time."

"You're wearing a mike?"

"It seemed a good idea," she said, not exactly a lie. "Now, Ian, give me the gun."

She thought he was going to argue, or maybe just turn back to the building. But he moved his hand an inch in her direction, then stopped.

"Can I ask one favor?"

"Your favors are about used up, Ian."

"I'll give you the gun, but can I walk behind you until we get to the car? I'm sorry, but having all those angry cops standing there, I'd really be happier if you were between me and them."

"Ian, they're not going to open fire with me standing there."

"I know. Intellectually, I know, but going out there first, I'm afraid I would just piss myself. And if I'm behind you, Monica isn't going to see my face a hundred times on the evening news."

A little late to think about that, Kate thought. She put out her hand, unwilling to negotiate further. His hand wavered, then the gun tipped and came out to her. She took what felt like her first unconstricted breath in many hours.

She snapped the gun open and knocked the five bullets it held into her palm, pouring them into the front pocket of her pants. The gun itself she tossed backhanded toward the courtyard; it flew across the polished marble of the foyer floor and vanished.

Now she could afford to grant Nicholson his wish.

"You might want to put your hand on my shoulder, so you don't trip on me if I have to stop."

"Thank you," he said. "For everything."

She pushed the door open and stepped out; Nicholson moved with her, his left hand resting lightly on her shoulder. She halted, spread her arms, and opened her mouth to shout, "Hold your fire, he's surrendering, he's not armed."

But only the first two words left her mouth. As Kate began to speak, Ian's fingers tightened on her, pulling her body back. At the touch of his face against her right

525

ear, at the murmur of his voice in her hair, she broke off to turn in his direction. But his hand was already in motion, sliding down and center as if to pat her on the back. When it reached a spot directly between her shoulder blades, he paused for an instant, gathering all the strength in his rugby player's muscles, then shoved hard. Kate shot forward, staggering open-armed into the street before she fell. She rolled, recovered, and pushed her weight up on one arm in time to see Nicholson snatch a long, dark, gunlike object from the waistband of his jeans and lower it at the nearest cop, who happened to be Al Hawkin.

"NO!" she screamed, feeling his hand sliding down her shoulder, hearing the echoes of that English voice murmuring into her ear: *"Can't do planes, can't do jail, I'm very sorry,"* a moment before he propelled her out of harm's way.

As the fingers of her free hand stretched out to him, the street exploded.

TWENTY-TWO

Wednesday evening, little more than forty-eight hours after she had watched Ian Nicholson die, Kate lowered herself onto the armchair in her living room and decided that yes, her lungs had decided to go on breathing. She was shaky and fragile and there was still a high-pitched ringing in her ears; she hadn't managed to choke down an entire meal since Monday; a long, dreary process of departmental hearings lay before her; she was regularly overwhelmed with the self-loathing of having allowed herself to play into Nicholson's hands; and she knew without a doubt that if Ian Nicholson were to miraculously appear before her, healthy and grinning, she would strangle him with her bare hands for dumping her back into the shit. But she kept reciting platitudes, telling herself that this too would pass, that she would one day feel as if she belonged here once more, that he'd have managed his suicide one way or another without her.

In a minute, Lee came in with a full wineglass in her hand and set it near Kate's right hand. Kate cocked an eyebrow at it. "I shouldn't," she said.

"Days like this are why God invented wine."

"I like your therapeutic method better than the department counselor's," she replied, and swallowed deep. Lee went away. A few minutes later Nora came in and stood with her feet between Kate's, her two hands braced on Kate's knees, studying Kate's face. Kate was struck by an overpowering urge to sweep the child up and wrap her arms hard around that warm little body for an hour or so, but comforting a mother in that way was a burden no child should bear. So instead she ruffled the mop of curls and allowed Nora to climb up into her lap unaided, and after one firm hug, forced her arms to draw back and drape loosely around the child leaning against her chest.

"Are you sad, Mamakay?"

"I'm not sad, exactly. But sometimes you see someone else who's really sad, and it makes you a little less happy, you know?" The unnecessary tragedy of it all, Gilbert and Nicholson, Raynor and Billy Birdsong, all the lives ruined, for nothing. She pulled herself away from the maudlin reflections of society's failings.

"So what did my little monkey do today?" she asked into the warm hair.

"I played and I worked."

"I hope you did both really hard."

"I did. We looked at paintings in school and I helped Jon and Lalu make cookies and, and Bet'ny's having a birt'day party and Mamalee says I can go, we're going to ride ponies down at the beach and have a cake and eat hot dogs!"

At this last revelation, the blond curls came off Kate's shoulder so Nora could witness her mother's astonishment, and Kate obediently raised her eyebrows and put her mouth into an O. Satisfied, Nora lay back against her, and Kate smiled: For the daughter of a cook like Lee, hot dogs were every bit as thrilling as ponies.

"When is this magical affair?"

"Sattiday."

The funeral was scheduled for Saturday, the fall of the curtain on Ian Nicholson's final performance, a play scripted, directed, and acted by him. The black gunlike object had been a long-barreled butane lighter, all its deadliness in the stance and attitude of the man wielding it. She'd watched the film clip, and even knowing what it was, she would have sworn he had a gun. Not a bad actor, indeed.

From where she lay on the ground, her hand outstretched as if to snatch him back to safety, she had seen five rounds hit him. As the sheets of glass behind him shattered and exploded into the calm marble foyer, she had seen five bullets reach their mark, each impact tugging him this way and that before his muscles gave way.

She had scrambled to her feet and run toward him, careless of the possibility of further shots; knelt beside him; taken his hand—his right hand, the left one being a bloody mess—and held it, looking directly into his eyes. Gray-blue eyes, holding hers as he felt the end come for him; a look of mild surprise, a glimpse of something resembling humor, and the brief pressure of his fingers on hers. Then, nothing.

She blinked, looked into Nora's green eyes, the child frowning as she shook Kate by the shoulder. "You're not listening to me," she accused, and Kate shivered.

"I'm sorry, sweetie, what did you want?"

"I said, can you come to Bet'ny's party with me and Mamalee?"

"I'll have to see if I can. I have something I really have to do that afternoon, but if I can come, I absolutely will."

A moment's pout, and then Nora was back against her shoulder. A cop's daughter, she had already begun to learn that sometimes life came first, and sometimes death did.

When the wine was gone, Kate could feel its warmth but did not lust for more, which was a relief. Nora stayed with her, on her lap, although usually she would

529

be off and racing about. Kate was grateful for the child's willingness to be hugged, but when Lee came through a while later, she gave her partner an expression very like a grin.

"Your daughter is a born therapist," she said.

Lee knew in an instant what Kate was talking about, and she compounded the therapy session by scooping up Nora, then sitting down herself on Kate's lap with a now-squealing child on top of both her mothers. Kate said, "Oof," then did her best to wrap her entire family in her inadequate arms until all three were giggling and they ended up in a heap of arms and legs on the floor in front of the chair.

The phone rang. Lee's hand was closest, so she picked it up, then had to extricate herself from the pile in order to hear.

"Sorry, what was that? Oh, I don't know that this is a really good time."

"Time for what?" Kate spoke from the floor.

Lee told the receiver, "Just a minute," and cupped her hand across the mouthpiece. "It's Maj. She wants to come over, says she can bring a pot of white beans and homemade sausages she's been working on for days."

Kate felt a twinge at the phrase "white beans" but repressed it firmly. "I don't mind. Tell her to come ahead."

"You sure? I thought you'd want a quiet night."

"I do, and I don't."

Again, Lee knew precisely what she meant. She

530

uncovered the phone. "Maj? Come on over. I was going to grill some things, we can have your beans with them. About an hour?"

The grill was sizzling, the beans were warming, the kids were transforming the living room into a sheet-and-cushion fortress, when Roz descended on the house like a psychic whirlwind. Kate took one look at the invader, formally suited, her priest's collar in place, and wearing an expression of almost incandescent happiness, and she raised the barbecue tongs in an unconscious but heartfelt gesture of defense.

"Roz, what the hell are you up to now?"

Roz swept across the patio and pounced on Kate, wrapping her arms around the smaller woman and picking her up off the ground to whirl her in a circle. That she had already done the same to the other two women was clear by their bemused expressions as they looked out from the door to the kitchen.

When Roz stood away from Kate, she stooped a bit to look straight into Kate's face, then turned to the other two women with the same intensity. "You haven't heard any news today?"

"Roz, I've been pretty tied up," Kate said. Some political prisoner had been freed from a long and oppressive incarceration, she thought, or a closely fought piece of legislation had squeaked past. Three women stood there with identical fond smiles on their faces, waiting for Roz's effervescence to boil over as she told them all about it, but to their surprise, she did not. With a spark of anticipation, she appeared to shove a cap on her excitement, and instead of spilling all, she said, "Promise me you won't listen to the news tonight. Promise me? And if someone calls and asks if you've heard, you'll hang up on them—promise?"

"Heard what?" Kate asked.

"Doesn't matter. Just promise me, please?"

She sounded so like Nora—please please PLEEEASE?—that Kate had to smile through the inner darkness. "Sure, if somebody calls to tell me any good news, I'll hang up. For how long?"

"Just tonight. Honest, you'll be so glad you did, I promise."

And that was all she would say about it that night.

But the next morning, Kate sat up in bed at some ungodly hour, the chimes of the doorbell fading in her ears. She glanced at the bedside clock, realized that it was not all that early, and then the bell went again.

She grabbed her robe and scurried down the stairs, but the bell was going again before she reached the door. "For Christ's sake," she sputtered as her bare feet slapped on the wood of the stairs, and "Shit," when the fourth ring came as her right hand made contact with the doorknob and her left the deadbolt lock.

"What the fuck—Maj? What's wrong?"

But as soon as she focused on Maj's face she could tell that nothing was wrong. In fact, it was just the opposite: Maj looked as if she had caught whatever happy bug had infected her partner the night before. She bore a large white bag in her hand. Behind her stood Mina with a carrier tray from Peet's Coffee;

behind Mina came Satch with another white bakery bag. The fragrant procession pushed past Kate; as they went by, she noticed that Maj was wearing a skirt, Mina was dressed for church (looking considerably older than her sixteen years), and nine-year-old Satch had a necktie on.

"What the hell is going on?" Kate said, closing the door and following them through to the kitchen.

"You need to get up and get dressed," Maj said. "And get Lee and Nora up, too—oh, there you are. We need to go in ten minutes."

"Go where?" Kate demanded. Hearing the simultaneous echo of the words coming from the bottom of the stairs, she looked and saw the two sleep-rumpled Leonoras. One of them had a thumb in her mouth and red pillow-wrinkles on her face; the other just had the pillow-wrinkles.

"You'll see. Come on, have a latte and a muffin, and get some clothes on."

"Not until you tell me what is going on."

"I will tell you when we get there. Oh, please, Kate, trust me. It's not one of Roz's schemes, I promise you'll love it. But it's best if you don't know until you see it. I swear."

"Yeah," Satch chimed in, "there's all these—"

Mina whirled on him with a loud "Shhh!" as Maj said, "Satch! You promised."

The boy clapped one hand over his mouth, but his eyes were dancing. Kate knew she could get it out of him in two seconds flat, but instead she stepped forward without a word, took two of the cups, handed one to Lee in passing, and started up the stairs.

Behind her, Maj called, "You might want to wear something nice."

A minute later, the elevator rumbled and Lee came into the bedroom.

"Do you know what this is about?" Kate asked her.

Lee stood still with her shirt half-unbuttoned. "I think so," she said at last. "Can I *not* tell you?"

"You want to go along with Roz on this?"

"If you don't mind."

"Just so long as it's not going to get me fired," Kate said, and pulled a departmental T-shirt out of the drawer. Then she noticed Lee, surveying the closet with a frown on her face. Kate looked at the T-shirt, put it back into the drawer, and carried a clean, ironed white shirt and black jeans to the shower instead.

It wasn't any ten minutes, but soon they were assembled again downstairs, awake now and beginning to take on something of the inexplicable excitement of the others. They all climbed into the minivan that Maj had bought the year Satch entered preschool.

They had, in fact, slept later than usual that morning, and the streets were already thick with the morning commute, both in and out of the city. Maj headed downtown, then shifted up Van Ness toward the Civic Center.

When they got to City Hall, Kate spotted a *Chronicle* photographer trotting up the steps, and her eyes narrowed.

"Maj, what *is* going on?"

In answer, Maj pulled over to the curb, although she made no move to open the door. They sat and looked at the gilded entrance of City Hall. Another reporter scurried inside, following close on the heels of two women, one dressed in a tuxedo, the other in long white silk.

"Is this some kind of a party?" Kate asked.

"You could say that," Maj answered. Mina grinned at her mother, Satch giggled merrily, and Nora piped up from the child seat.

"Is there a birthday party?"

"Better than that, sweetie," Maj told her, and Satch bounced around as if his skin were too small.

There appeared to be very little business as usual around City Hall that morning. The standard contingent of homeless gazed in astonishment at the activity, which would have made an upturned ant's nest look calm by comparison: Two men, hand in hand, ran up the steps, both wearing tuxedos; a minivan pulled into a red zone out in front of the Hall, a uniformed patrol looking on benevolently as the van's driver and two passengers unloaded armloads of flowers.

"Why the hell is the entire gay commun—" Kate started to ask, but then she saw the bakery van and the decorated cake, and it hit her.

"Oh my God," she said. "Maj?"

By way of answer, Maj popped open her door, and a kid in a red jacket pulled himself off the low wall and trotted forward. He opened the driver's door with the gesture of a valet, and Maj turned around to look into Kate's face.

"Roz thought that you and Lee might like to be among the first legally married lesbians in San Francisco."

Kate could say nothing, just sit with her mouth open.

"Absolutely legal," Maj replied, reading the sense behind the silence. "Thanks to his advisors, our new mayor has decided that discrimination is unconstitutional. If you want a marriage license, it's here for you."

Lee had twisted around in the front seat to watch Kate. Kate stared at her, and slowly found herself beginning to grin. "I'm not even going to ask if you will marry me," she told Lee, "because I've already done that and you said yes. So I guess now's the time to make good on your promise."

"We're going to get married?" squealed Nora's voice from the back. "Really *married?*"

This, Nora seemed to think, was even better than a birthday party with hot dogs and ponies combined.

And Kate couldn't argue with that. She seized Lee's hand, stuck her other one back for Nora, and said, "Yes, my sweetheart. We're going to get married."

Some time later, standing at the door to the County Clerk's office with Lee and Nora, Roz and Maj, Jon and Sione, clutching the hastily photocopied form that read "first applicant/second applicant" where "bride/groom" had once stood, Kate glanced back down the growing line of men and women waiting their turn. Their faces were young and old, dark and light, male and female;

they wore bow ties and T-shirts, white silk and blue denim, velvet and battered leather, tiaras and hand-knit hats; they carried backpacks and flowers, folded news-papers and small jeweler's boxes; they had kids of all sizes or were little more than kids themselves. But all the people in the line, every one of them, wore just the same expression: stunned with joy, incredulous and expectant, and absolutely certain of what they were doing.

And for an instant, Kate caught a glimpse of someone she knew, or thought she knew. Down where the hallway turned, a tall young man with close-cropped blond hair and eyes the color of lapis lazuli stood gazing down at his brown-skinned, green-eyed beloved.

For an instant, the blue eyes came up and touched Kate's, and then the crowd shifted, and they were gone.

POSTSCRIPT

After the ceremony, the joyous celebrants piled into various cars and drove across the City to Fort Mason, where they took over a large portion of the veg-etarian restaurant on the water and ate organic salads and festive-looking entrees while looking out over the boats, the sea lions, and the Golden Gate Bridge; the north side, where the bridge came back to earth at the joining place of Forts Baker and Barry, was draped in grass so green it hurt the eyes. The room was loud with the lunch crowd: Roz was on her feet half the meal, making the rounds of the restaurant's other patrons; Nora and young Satch spent two hours giggling together; and Kate and Lee sat with their hands joined most of the time.

Married.

Somewhere between the champagne toast, made to the health of wise politicians, and the candle-strewn dessert, created hastily at Roz's request just for the occasion, a fax machine on the other side of town wheezed into life. The machine was in the Hall of Justice, occupying a precarious niche of the crowded Homicide Detail. It grumbled and hesitated, as if disapproving of the effort, but in the end, it generated a single page.

The sheet bore the heading of the Golden Gate National Recreational Area, and read as follows:

Kate—

I know we're finished with the Gilbert case, but just for your files, I meant to tell you that I finally got a chance to search the records for Fort Barry, and going back thirty years, I could find no report of a body discovered or an assault committed anywhere in the vicinity of Battery DuMaurier.

Funnily enough, I did find a short mention of something close, though it's way too early for our purposes. I was glancing through the journal of one of Fort Baker's early base commanders, and he mentions that the body of one of his officers was found in a gun emplacement—no names, no details, just that. Odd coincidence, but like I say, it's too early to have anything to do with the Gilbert case. I think the date was 1924.

Chris Williams

AUTHOR'S NOTE

It is hardly fair to blame America for the state of San Francisco, for its population is cosmopolitan and its seaport attracts the floating vice of the Pacific; but be the cause what it may, there is much room for spiritual betterment.

—Arthur Conan Doyle,
Our Second American Adventure

I have, I fear, tinkered with the headlands landscape just a little and added one gun battery, surplus to requirement, to the already considerable maintenance tasks of the Golden Gate National Recreational Area. Battery DuMaurier is located along the cliffs to the south of Battery Mendell, and looks, as Ranger Culpepper says, very similar to Battery Wallace. Those interested in the history of the guns and Fort Barry as a whole will find information and links on my website, www.LaurieRKing.com.

One of the joys of being a writer is the opportunity to meet new and enthusiastic residents of the various worlds one temporarily occupies. In the GGNRA—the Marin Headlands National Park—thanks go particularly to a trio of rangers: Roxi Farwell, whose unflappable response, upon being informed that a mystery writer wished to stash a dead body in her park, was that said writer would require a Special Use Permit; John Porter, who showed me where the bats live and the soldiers slept; and John Martini, who knows where the bodies are buried.

In the world of the real-life SFPD, I am grateful for the time and expertise given me by Inspector Holly Pera and Inspector Joseph Toomey of the department's Homicide Detail. Why busy people like that put up with the questions of writers, I'll never know.

Thanks, too, to Marybeth McFarland, Law Enforcement Specialist with the GGNRA, for leading me through the convolutions of the Park Police. If I have nudged the question of jurisdiction beyond the realm of likelihood, it's not her fault.

In the world of Sherlockians, particular thanks to the ever-patient, always forgiving, eminently well-balanced, and yes, quite real Leslie S. Klinger, Peter E. Blau, and Richard Sveum.

Stuart Bennett, antiquarian bookseller, helped with the arcane details of the collector's world.

Abby Bridge again permitted me to pepper her with questions about historical San Francisco.

Leah Garchik kindly allowed me to drop a Sherlockian mention into her excellent column in the *San Francisco Chronicle*.

John A. T. Tiley again aided in introducing me to the subtleties of things military.

The real Chris Williams, whose generosity to the Youth Literacy Program of Chicago's Centro Romero ended *her* up here, in an alternate existence.

And as always, the patient and supportive staff of the McHenry Library, University of California, Santa Cruz, helped with a thousand and ten details. Particular thanks are due to Margaret Gordon and Paul Machlis.

To everyone who lent a hand, named or not: Thank you. And I'm sorry if I listened with a deaf ear and mangled all your tidy facts; we writers are such a contrarian lot.

Finally, lest the reader imagine the legal inquiries made by Lieutenant Raynor to be a convenient fiction, I mention the excellent *Colonel Barker's Monstrous Regiment* by Rose Collis, subtitled *A Tale of Female Husbandry*. In it, Ms. Collis describes the life of Colonel Victor Barker, born Valerie, and includes a photograph of the official marriage certificate issued in Brighton, England, to "Victor" and his wife Elfrida in November 1923.

Center Point Publishing
600 Brooks Road • PO Box 1
Thorndike ME 04986-0001 USA

(207) 568-3717

US & Canada:
1 800 929-9108